Shake off the Ghosts

MIRANDA NEWFIELD

Previously published as SHAKE OFF THE GHOSTS by Michaela Wright.

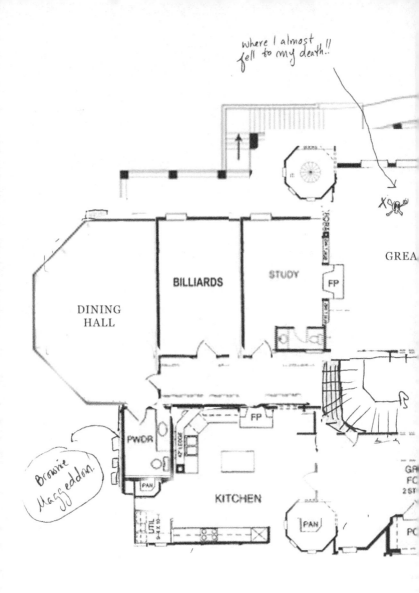

CAVENDISH HOUSE

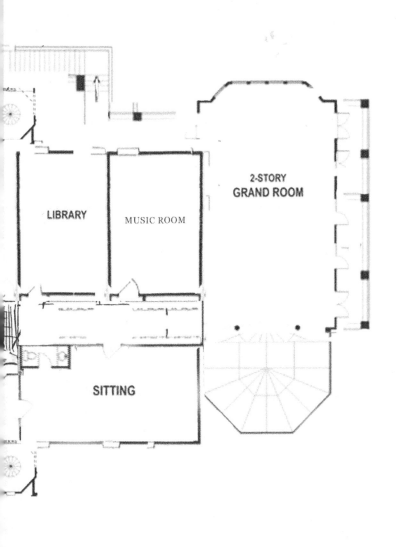

One

S WEET MOTHER OF GOD, *what have I gotten myself into?*
"Cor? You there? Are you there, yet? Come on, lady. Don't keep me in suspense."

I stood with the phone in my hand, listening to the concerned voice on the other end, and couldn't for the life of me find words to respond. All hell was breaking loose in my mind.

"You're there, aren't you? God, I am so jealous! I haven't been back to Scotland in so long."

Jealous, Patti? You're jealous? If only you could see what I see.

"Ye gonna be alright, lass?"

I stood in the dark driveway, the gravel grinding under my sneakers as I stared into the dark, the massive shape of Cavendish House looming all around me.

"Hang on, Patti. Give me a minute."

I turned back to the cab driver and gave a sheepish smile. "I think I'll be alright. Is there any chance you might just stay right there – just keep your headlights shining on the house until I get inside?"

The cab driver was an older gentleman, a sharp nose holding up clear-rimmed glasses as he peered out the window at me, then up at the dark estate. "Ye sure this is where you're stayin? Sure they're expectin ye?"

I swallowed. "I am."

"Well, bless," he said, leaning back in his seat as he straightened the scally cap atop his head. "I'll stay put, then. Ye wave when you're alright for me to go, aye?"

"Thank you so much," I said, hefting my duffle bag up onto my shoulder. I turned toward my fate and swallowed hard.

The phrase *'You bit off more than you can chew'* was flitting through my mind - naturally in my mother's voice. I shut my eyes and took a deep breath before making my way up the last few yards of the driveway. The cab driver turned the volume back up on his radio, casting the smooth jams of Foreigner's *I Want to Know What Love Is* across the highland countryside.

Nothing had ever felt so surreal – and fitting.

The headlights shone bright across this creeping monolith of stone, history, and rampant neglect – the place I would call home for the next two months – but it couldn't cut through the solid black of being in the middle of east overshoes nowhere Scotland.

Yes, I said East Overshoes. Don't you say that? Is that a New England thing? Whatever, so is the phrase 'I'm wicked fucked,' which I was beginning to worry would also apply to my current predicament.

"You there?"

I brought the phone back up to my ear. "I am, yes. Sorry about that."

"Are you listening to Foreigner right now?"

I couldn't help but laugh. "Oddly, yes."

Of course, I was. Of course, the universe would play Foreigner right now. And that song in particular.

That's what would happen to me in the middle of Podunk nowhere Scotland.

Because despite traveling the world over, I'd never been more truly alone in my life than I was at that moment. And in another couple of minutes, even the cabby would be gone.

I say again, "What have I gotten myself into?"

Patti sighed, softly. "Well, if it's really so bad, you know you can always come home."

I grunted in disagreement. "Yeah, no. Not if I can absolutely avoid it."

"Is she really that bad?"

I paused. "Yes."

She was referring to my father's fiancé, Diane. She'd come into my life years before with a forced smile, but she'd never liked that I was back living with Kenny at the time, and once she moved into Kenny's house – she made it as clear as possible that I was no longer welcome.

Truth was, I'd rather chew glass than live under the same roof as Diane Meyer, and I'd been traveling the world for two years to prove it.

"What's that?"

"Nothing, Patti. Sorry, hang on. I'm trying to find the key to get in."

I made my way up to the steps and stopped, staring at the doors.

Patti was on the other side of the Atlantic, and the closest 'friend' I had was an hour's drive south in Perth, Scotland – and he wasn't answering his phone anymore.

Not answering his phone in the kind of way that makes a girl think he might not be interested anymore.

Good thing he waited until I got to Scotland to evaporate. Awfully kind of him. Especially since he's the guy who got me this stupid housesitting job.

"Well? How does it look? Is it magnificent?"

"Uh, you could say that, I suppose."

Ivy overtook the façade of the massive structure long ago, and the once neatly kept garden slithered around the corners of the mansion with thorny derision. In the light of headlights, I couldn't even see the whole of the house. I silently prayed that I'd find the house with electricity once inside. Otherwise, I'd be rocking a dead battery on my phone in less than an hour, with no way to charge it, and the closest shop was a miles-long trek down a dirt road Scotland wanted to forget.

I'm going to be eaten by wolves, aren't I? I thought.

Do they have wolves in Scotland?

And I had no car.

Peachy.

"Are you going to have to break in?" Patti said on the other end of the line, her voice taking on that familiar concerned tone she'd favored since we were little kids.

Patricia Hannity was my cousin and the kind of woman that grows up to be a Park Ranger.

Literally, she's a Park Ranger.

Normally, her hyper-concerned nature would get on my nerves, but at that moment, it was the one thing keeping me from a panic attack.

I shook my head. "I don't have to break in. She told me where the key is."

"You know, I really think you should file a complaint with the service. She should've never left you high and dry like that. It's not like she didn't have three months to plan to pick you up at the train station or anything."

Despite Patti being unable to see, I shrugged. "There's not much I can do about it, now. I didn't get this job through the service – this was through Christopher. Just hoping I can get in, maybe find something to eat."

The woman Patti referred to was Jocelyn Read – executor of the Cavendish estate.

"Ah, yes. Christopher," she said, and I could practically hear her nose crinkle. "I mean, I haven't been there in a long while, but they must have Uber or something like that?"

I laughed. "It's fine. I managed."

"Managed. The pound is currently worth almost twice the dollar. Her negligence cost you a hundred-dollar cab ride!"

"I know -"

The phone buzzed against my ear, startling the shit out of me. I stopped to read the screen – Joceyln Read.

"Oh, thank Christ! Ok, she's calling me back."

"It's about time! Alright, let me know as soon as you're settled and can tell me about the house, ok. I'm dying to hear how haunted it is."

My stomach turned. "Shut up. That's the last thing I need to think about right now. Call you later."

I quickly switched calls, desperate to hear my *employer's* voice. "Hello!"

"Ms. Turner?"

"Corinne's fine," I said, glancing back to the lights of the cabby with a sheepish shrug. I had half a mind to propose to him for being so patient.

"Corinne, I'm so sorry I missed you at the station today. Something came up. Completely unforeseen over here. Have you managed to get to the estate on your own?"

"I have, yes. Had to take a cab from the train in Keith. Wasn't cheap by any means – I think about one hundred and -"

"That's wonderful to hear. Have you settled in then? Did you find the key alright?"

I rushed up the cracked stone steps to the looming wooden door, one of the few surfaces not covered in plant growth. Along one of the railings was a sorry-looking flowerpot, a long-dead something now brown and soggy drooping over its sides. I lifted it up and found my prize – a tarnished old key that left a perfect silhouette in the dried dirt beneath the pot when I picked it up.

"Actually, I'm just arriving now, but I have the key."

"Oh, wonderful. Alright, once you're inside - I know it's late, you'll be wanting to get to bed, I'm sure - head on up to the top floor. There are rooms made up for guests in the south wing."

The south wing? Good lord.

I unlocked the heavy wooden door and pushed the massive thing open, feeling it catch on something just inside.

"Is there electricity running, here?" I asked, staring into the dark.

"Of course. I wouldn't leave you out there stranded," Jocelyn said, her tone betraying a half-distracted level of interest.

I let the wooden door swing as far open as it would go, then fought to take a breath. I wasn't sure what wonders I might find inside – or horrors, as I was quickly realizing.

"The light switch is just along the front wall – to the right of the door. Or left, if you're coming into the house."

I leaned inside, half afraid some Lovecraftian creature was in the dark, waiting to grab me by the face and eat my scalp. I ran my hand over the dusty wallpaper until my fingers caught on an old-fashioned switch.

With a soft click, the grand entryway was alight, glowing amber from a chandelier hanging high overhead.

"Wow," I said, at a loss for any other word.

The foyer betrayed all manner of its once and former glory. There was a split grand staircase at the far end of the entryway, leading up to a second-floor landing with stairs to a third curving out of sight. The walls were covered in dusty old paintings and the ceiling high above betrayed ancient wooden beams. Even the banister of the staircase looked hand-carved, a unicorn rearing up with flared nostrils.

Speaking of flared nostrils, what the fuck was that smell?

I glanced across the room, scanning the scattered leaves and branches that somehow found their way inside. Among the dried leaves was a tiny brown shape.

A dead something - whatever it was.

I let my eyes go wide as I stared down at it. "That's a great omen."

"What's that?" Jocelyn said.

"Nothing, sorry. Just muttering to myself."

High doorways lead out of the room in every direction, two or three doors per wall, and a crisp gust of wind was creeping in through a busted window by the front door. It looked as though that window had been letting in the elements for some time.

I took a deep breath. "It needs a lot of work."

Jocelyn called to someone on the other end, seemingly delegating to some minion, if the tone was to be trusted. Then, she returned her attention to me. "Well, of course. That was rather the point, wasn't it?"

Oh, lady... you undersold this shit so hard.

"Right. Of course. I just – I didn't realize it was so -"

"Mr. Douglas had his peculiarities. Now, we simply need to keep an eye on the place until the estate is settled."

I dropped my duffle bag by the front door, making a point to avoid the mouse corpse as I pushed the door shut. It left a perfect arc of clean floor through the dust in its wake.

"Well, I mean – the front hallway should be a quick fix. Just need to find a broom and patch up the window. I didn't see the car. Is there a garage somewhere? I could head into town, maybe pick up new panes of glass tomorrow?"

"No, no. There's no need for that. You're not there to fix the place up. Throw a piece of paper over it or some such. It'll be quite enough to clear out the rubbish and make sure it doesn't -"

Ms. Read trailed off a moment.

I stared at the dusty, neglected room, vowing to ignore my 'employer.' There was no way I was living in a squirrel's nest for two months. The window was getting fixed.

Jesus Christ, put a piece of paper over it? You've got to be kidding me.

"Keep an eye on the place. Make it seem lived in so area hooligans don't get any ideas, that's all we need from you."

"Ok," I said, stooping to pick up a rather large branch that was partially jammed through the window. "Are there a lot of hooligans in this area of Scotland?"

"Well, no."

"Ok - and I know you said Mr. Douglas lived here until last month, so do you think there might be some food I can eat? I haven't eaten since yesterday. Or if you let me know where the car is -"

"Oh, sorry Corinne. I've gotta dash, but please keep me posted on how you get on. You can always email me if you have any questions."

"Email you? Wait? Is there wi-fi?"

The phone went dead, and I was alone in the dilapidated space. If Quasimodo himself had sauntered out from a back room to lead me to my chambers, it wouldn't have surprised me.

A moment passed before the honk of a car startled my attention back to the door. I spun around, darting back out onto the steps to wave at the still waiting cabby. I caught a glimpse of his hand waving back, then watched as the headlights pulled around and headed down the dirt road and out of sight, the echo of *All the Young Dudes* by Mott the Hoople whispering through the air behind him.

I stood there for a long moment, letting the full weight of the dark set in.

My life was seconds from turning into a horror movie, and I knew it.

Well, at least I die with a sense of humor, I thought.

What had Christopher gotten me into?

I turned back to the grand hall and fought to breathe.

My months-long adventure spent in a Jane Austen-caliber estate was looking far more like a Bronte novel, now. Somebody was going to end up blind or dead at the end of this story.

"If there's a crazy lady living in the attic, I'm out," I said aloud, as though the house itself was listening and capable of laughing at my jokes.

I kicked the duffle further into the hall, watching the patch of dusted floor appear behind it, and heard a strange noise from somewhere in the house – high-pitched and almost alive.

I waited a moment for it to return. Nothing came.

Well, fuck. That's a good sign.

The air wasn't heavy like some houses – as though the rooms are alive and watching you. That was the way I'd describe a haunted house – heavy. Thick with intention.

This house felt thick with something, alright, but that something was dust.

I ducked my head into the kitchen – an ancient, high-ceilinged hall of a room with a fireplace I could easily pitch a tent and camp in if needed. I flipped the light switch to find only two of the dozen light fixtures worked.

Awesome. We're roughing this shit so hard.

I stood there a long moment, imagining the tasty things I'd find congealing and rotting in the massive fridge across the room. I snatched a paper towel from the counter, surprised to find such a thing waiting in the otherwise miserable space, then turned on my heel. The hunt for unrotten food was an adventure for another damn day. I was too exhausted now.

I hustled into the hall, snatched the dead mouse up off the floor with the paper towel, and tossed it out through the broken window. I didn't dare open the door again. That felt like inviting an escaped convict to be waiting on the steps with a grin.

No to that, I thought, locking the front doors with a loud, malicious click.

That sure showed that roving band of murderers what's what!

I thought better of trying to hunt down a window-worthy sheet of paper and resigned myself to worry about it tomorrow. I'd spent all day on a train, my feet were killing me, and I wanted to curl up and reevaluate my whole life. I hoisted the duffle bag onto my shoulder and headed up the massive stairs and reigned myself to hunting for my room in the far reaches of the upstairs. I moved through the house like some timid thing as I scanned every wall for the next light switch. Some offered no response as the long-forgotten bulbs had blown before I arrived, but enough still offered light to get me up to the third floor. I reached the top of the grand stairs to find a breeze blowing in from one side of the house, leaving me sure there were more broken windows and fresh horrors lying in wait in the 'east wing.'

I followed the better-lit hallway, dragging my heavy duffle bag along the corridors, trying not to bump the side tables or wall sconces as I hobbled along, glancing into rooms for a sign of my 'accommodations.'

There was an unspeakable eeriness to the place at that late hour. I had no doubt the house maintained its eerie complexion even in the light of day, but with the howl of the wind through broken windows greeting me in the distance, I was sure a little daylight couldn't hurt the sheen. I wanted nothing more than to sleep, to find my bed, and forget the long and tiresome day. I had some trail mix in my bag. I could find the car in the morning.

I could survive one night in complete isolation, right?

The last room on the left offered windows on two walls, a made bed, a pair of dressers, and a hint of blueish light casting in from the crescent moon outside.

I gave my duffle bag a swing and let it loose into the dark room. A flash of movement caught my eye down the hallway.

Oh, fuck no, I thought.

I stopped dead, staring in the direction I'd come. I didn't hear any movement – there were no footsteps or voices to betray company, and I'd certainly locked the front door. Not that the house was exactly air-tight.

Still, the air was heavier now – heavy in the way I knew all too well.

"Hello?" I called, keeping my voice quiet.

I cringed. Isn't that always the way murder victims act in horror movies? Call out to the psycho so he knows exactly where you are to skin you and eat your scalp.

Why am I so obsessed with scalp eating?

Ah, the things we contemplate right before our deaths.

I stared for a long moment, then exhaled through my nose. "Quit being a jackass, Turner. It's an old house, and Patti's probably right – it's haunted as hell."

Still, I stood there watching the landing at the top of the stairs. Though I wanted desperately to pretend it was a trick of the eye, I could've sworn I'd seen skirts swoop around the corner and out of sight.

After a long, quiet moment, I slipped into my bedroom and shut the door tight behind me.

As though on cue, the high-pitched sound returned. It was closer this time, an undeniably living sound.

I pressed my forehead to the door. "Please stop being creepy, thing," I said.

The 'thing' responded with another high-pitched cry in the distance.

I stepped back out into the hallway and called again, "Hello?"

I made a point to speak in the most high-pitched, happy-sounding tone I could.

It inspired a response.

The cry was muffled, but clear enough to betray direction. I moved back down the hallway, faster than I'd come, turning my ear toward the sound as I called again. "I hear you! Where are you?" Still in that same sing-song tone.

The cries grew louder, coming faster now in agitation. I stopped at the top of the stairs and listened. The cries were coming from the dark side of the house - the east wing.

Well, shit. It was nice knowing you, life.

I swallowed and trudged into the dark, my phone steadied in my hand to light the way.

"I'm right here. Tell me where you are," I said, only to have the cries double, now coupled with a pathetic scratching sound. I stopped just outside a closed door, feeling the cool air from broken windows in the neighboring rooms. Beneath the door, a line of blue betrayed moonlight through a window beyond, and in that beam of light, a tiny shadow was moving from side to side beyond the door.

I turned the doorknob and opened the door a crack. The room within was cold and damp, and I quickly caught sight of the disarray within. A massive pile of old soiled mattresses lay gathered at the center of the room, at least a dozen deep, and just above them, a brown and black stain of water damage across the ceiling. The roof here was clearly letting all manner of weather in.

And there, in the middle of this miserable, forgotten place, a tiny, fuzz-covered little kitten stood on the floor, creeping toward my ankles with that same pathetic mewling sound.

"Oh, sweet pea!" I exclaimed, and all fear of the house evaporated. I knelt beside the tiny gray kitten, holding out my hand in wait. The little beast rushed over to me, bypassing my hand to rub his face across my knee. He set his paws up on my thigh and dug in his claws, fighting to climb up me.

My heart melted in an instant, and I scooped him up. He slammed his forehead under my chin as I rose to my full height and turned back toward my bedroom.

I wasted no time calling Patti back.

"You named him what?"

I sat on my bed dangling a tassel from my sweater onto the covers as the tiny grey kitten lunged and chased after it. "Mr. Darcy."

Patti laughed on the other end of the line. "Of course you did."

"Why not? It's a wonderful name!" Even I couldn't keep a straight face as I said these words. "How can you not love it? I'm staying in this massive estate, a regal little gentleman crossed my path – it's clearly fate."

"You are such a nerd."

I smiled. "I know, but you should see his little face! He's so handsome."

"I think it's a wonderful choice. You deserve a Mr. Darcy in your life."

I caught her tone. It made me frown. "Hey, he could still reappear, couldn't he?"

"I suppose," she said, but it wasn't the least bit convincing.

We were talking about Christopher Menzies, a handsome, rakish Scot who I'd met in London just a few months before. We'd hit it off really well.

Or so I thought. As much as two people can hit it off with months of texting, face-timing, and inappropriate flirtation.

Hell, he was the reason I was there, getting me this job when I was fleeing an awful housesitting experience in Birmingham.

And yes, I'd taken the job to escape the god-awful situation, but there was something else luring me up to Scotland. The promise of finally getting to see Christopher, again.

After I housesit for two months in this Podunk estate.

Where he had threatened to come shag me, repeatedly.

Then he stopped responding to messages five days before my train to Edinburgh.

Patti sighed on the other end of the line. "I'm glad you're not buying that 'something came up' line he was pulling before."

'Something came up' was Christopher's go-to excuse for disappearing. Sure, he worked well over sixty hours a week in a lab studying candida or some other thing, but he also promised to make the trip worth my while.

Then something came up.

Or more aptly, nothing came up, because he wasn't here.

I stopped flitting the tassel in front of the kitten for a moment.

Chris was supposed to be my gallant Scottish lover, the man every woman like me dreams of meeting on a trip to London.

"Nothing. You haven't done anything. I'm just very busy."

That was the last thing he'd said to me when I asked what might've inspired his disappearance. Almost a week ago.

Bastard.

If only I hadn't become so utterly and completely smitten with him – and the sound of him whispering naughty things in that perfect Scottish brogue of his.

Damn it.

Now, I was curled up in a dilapidated castle with a kitten named Mr. Darcy, all because he'd convinced me to come north, and now I was in hell house, fighting tooth and nail to hang on to hope rather than wallow in broken-hearted disappointment.

Mr. Darcy did a barrel roll across the comforter and startled me with the sheer magnitude of his cuteness. I laughed, grateful for the distraction.

"Is it so wrong to want to just travel to Scotland, find my own Scottish soul mate, and live happily ever after?"

Patti laughed. "You know how I feel about that."

I sighed. "Yeah, how is that going? The divorce moving along?"

Patti had found her own Scottish lover while in college, married him, and moved back to America with him, only to have him leave her high and dry after five years of marriage.

"Not as fast as I'd like, but it's moving."

"Oh, good. I'm glad."

I flitted the string in front of the kitten, but his eyes were growing droopy. It was time for bed.

"Just remember, alright. Scots don't – the guys over there, they don't work like guys here. You might think a guy really likes you, but the second you mention dating or commitment – anything more than a quick shag, he'll evaporate."

I took a deep breath. "Awesome. That's just awesome."

"There are exceptions, but – sadly, it's true. Dating is just a different animal over there."

"Good to know."

We both remained on the phone for a long moment in silence. I didn't want to hang up. Hanging up the phone meant I was alone again. Alone in the middle of Scotland, in the middle of a neglected estate, surrounded in all directions by trees, fields, dirt roads, and the unfamiliar.

And now I had a kitten to contend with, and though I'd found an old can of chicken in the kitchen pantry, I had no litter box to speak of and no way to go buy one.

And if Patti wasn't on the phone, I'd go back to hearing phantom phone vibrations where there were none, constantly disappointed that Chris still hadn't gotten in touch.

Talking to Patti was one of the few worthy distractions.

"You should get some sleep," Patti said.

I groaned. I was tired in many ways – just not the kind that inspires sound sleep.

I said my goodbyes and did as Patti advised. I pulled my headphones out of my bag, set my passport and cash on the bedside table, then clicked off the bedside lamp before curling up under the covers, a tiny ball of fur slithering down to sleep in the crook of my knee.

I startled awake. There hadn't been a sound as far as I could tell, nor a sudden movement from the tiny kitten still serenely asleep beneath the blanket. Still, I'd woken up as though thunder split the sky just over my head.

I fought to adjust my eyes to the dark, watching the wall and the light from the window as I fought to steady my racing heart.

The weight of the air didn't dissipate. There was something strange about it, something unearthly and oppressive – as though I was being watched.

I swallowed, pulling the blanket up to my chin as I stared at the open door of my bedroom.

Open door.

I shut that door before going to bed, didn't I? Hadn't I made sure to shut it so Mr. Darcy wouldn't sneak out in the night and get himself stuck somewhere in the far reaches of the house?

I turned my eyes toward the window, then reached to the bedside table for my phone.

How long had I been out?

A shadow crossed the open doorway and startled me upright, my phone skittering across the floor. I watched the door, the phone's light casting an eerie glow on the Persian rug. I stared at the hallway outside, my eyes wide, as though I might adjust to the dark by force.

I was regretting those haunted house jokes from earlier.

"Hello!" I called for the third time that night. Like an asshole.

There was no response. Still, I was sure I'd just seen someone walk by.

Someone in a floor-length blue dress.

I felt Mr. Darcy stretch across the blankets, barely inconvenienced by my sudden thrashing. I slipped my legs out from under the covers and set my socked feet on the floor. I turned on the bedside lamp, finding my passport absent from the table. I made a mental note to find where it'd fallen when I wasn't being hunted by a homicidal maniac.

Never taking eyes off the doorway, I hustled across the room to the fireplace and snatched up the first hard object I could lay hands on – a fireplace poker. I gripped it in my right hand and scrambled to straighten my phone, pulling up the keypad to call for help.

Corinne, you're an idiot. What are you going to do? Cry "Don't worry, Mr. Darcy. I'll protect you!" right before you run into certain doom?

"Who's there?!" I called.

God. If *Murder Victim 101* was a class, I'd be a tenured professor. "I have a weapon! If you leave now, you can beat the cops. Who I just called! Just now! They're already on their way!"

They weren't on their way. 911 had done absolutely nothing when I smashed my thumbs into the screen of my phone.

You sound like a complete idiot, Corinne.

I curled my fingers tight around the fireplace poker and slipped out into the hallway. I glanced back in to find Mr. Darcy sitting on the bed watching me, his fluffy ears framing his still sleepy face. Before I took another step, the kitten curled back around himself and started cleaning his front paws.

I froze. A muffled sound echoed from somewhere downstairs. Somewhere.

Jesus, there could've been a murderer living in this massive house when you walked in today – could've lived with you for months and you'd never know! Until you were dead, Corinne! Dead in a closet somewhere – with no scalp!

I padded down the hallway on the ancient carpet runner, feeling the tassels slip beneath my toes as I rounded the corner toward the staircase.

"I mean it! I will hurt you!"

I listened to the sound of my own voice echoing off the high walls of the house, the stairs curving down below toward the first floor, and the muffled clang and clatter of movement below.

Whoever they were, they were clearly unaffected by my threats. It sounded almost as though they were settling in to cook a meal in the massive kitchen.

The nerve of some murderers!

"Hello!" I called again.

No response.

It was like I was inviting him to come and kill me, and he didn't even have the good graces to RSVP.

I tip-toed down the stairs, keeping my back to the wall as I rounded not one or two, but three bends in the massive staircase.

It was a freaking castle, after all.

And in that massive space, this lunatic had made a point to come all the way up to my room, walk by, then go make a sandwich?

The nerve!

Had my waking up startled him away? Was he now searching for some god-awful torture device in the kitchen cupboards?

Of course, this is how my life ends. Of course, it is.

I leaned over the railing, fixing my eyes on the kitchen door. The room was dark with no sound coming from within.

I tightened my grip and stepped down onto the hardwood floor, knees bent in a ready stance.

A voice crooned from a side door, and a figure appeared in the dark, coming toward me. "*And loooove, love will tear us apart, aga* – Fuck me!"

I swung out blindly toward the voice with everything I had. The vibration rocked up the length of my arms, a metal twang echoing off the high walls as the poker made contact with something solid in the dark. Every muscle in me spasmed and revolted, my elbows jamming with the impact. I hissed in pain as something massive clattered to the ground with a hard thud.

"Christ! What are ye doin!?"

I turned toward the voice again, but the poker wouldn't budge. It was lodged in the now split banister head, its sharp edge shivved between grains of wood.

"Get out! I've called 911!" I screamed.

"Ye know that bloody thing is almost five hundred years old, ye mad cow?!"

"The police are on their way!"

The figure shifted in the dark, moving toward me before I could pry the poker free. His hand loomed over my head a moment and I braced for impact, closing my eyes.

This is it. It was nice knowing you, scalp.

The loud clang of the poker being pried free from the banister shattered my brave stance. I stumbled back, my backside hitting the bottom step hard as I fell.

"It doesn't matter what you do to me! The police will be here soon, and you'll go to jail and some bigger dude will find you in the shower and do it to you -"

"Will ye shut up?" He said.

The man still remained half in the dark, but as he moved closer, I could see a half-unbuttoned flannel shirt and dusty jeans. He seemed rather laid back for a hardened criminal on the prowl for murder and mayhem.

"No, I won't! Get out before the -"

"The polis come?"

His tone was so blasé, it was almost infuriating. "Yes! Before the po*lice* come!"

"Rang up 911? Bringin the full fury of the law down upon me?"

I glared into the dark at the man, my whole body shaking with fear and now a rising rage. "I did!"

"Bloody good that'll do ye!" He hollered. "This is Scotland! It's 999, here!"

The man marched across the large hallway and an instant later, the chandelier burst with light overhead.

He was lean and dark-haired, a thick mane growing past his ears in wild curls. His sleeves were folded up his forearms, and the flannel was open enough to betray a band t-shirt beneath. The Cure, I thought.

He shot me a glare, his nostrils flaring.

Dear God, those eyes. Blue and piercing.

This was a surprisingly good-looking murderer.

Before I could move, he was surging across the room toward the stairway banister, mumbling, 'for fuck's sake' under his breath.

"Ye've practically destroyed it, ye have."

I swallowed, turning my attention to the half chunk of a unicorn head that now lay on the hardwood floor. I frowned, watching him turn it over and inspect it. Before I could make sense of what I was seeing, I found him glaring at me.

"Christ, I'm home one night, and already the place is worse than I found it. And there's a fuckin American destroying it! How appropriate! What the hell are ye doing here, anyway!? Ye bloody squatter!" I opened my mouth to return the assault, but he continued. "I've half a mind to call the polis myself!"

"I'm not a squatter!" I screamed, and my hands began to tremble violently. If I wasn't careful, I'd start crying.

Because that's just how I roll.

And there was nothing more unpredictable than adrenaline.

"Well, I certainly didn't invite ye. Explain yourself!"

I flailed for words, trying to still my panicked mind long enough to explain my – and his - presence. I found my courage and glared right back at him.

"I don't have to explain myself to you! You've no right to be here, either! At least I'm hired to be here!"

"Hired? Oh, well. That changes everything. I wonder how your employer will react when they hear ye've destroyed a five-hundred-year-old, hand-carved banister! Who hired ye?"

I stifled. I couldn't begin to imagine what it would cost to replace.

Wait – how does one replace something priceless and one of a kind?

They don't. They probably go to prison.

"It's not my fault! I was defending myself!"

"I said who hired ye?!"

"Jocelyn Read!" I screamed, trying to drown the realization of his words.

I could see the rage in his face waver to confusion.

"Executor of Cavendish House and Estate! I *work* for the Douglas family! What claim do you have to be here?!"

The man leaned down to me, bringing his nose so close to mine that we almost touched. The proximity forced me back into the hard ledge of the steps. "I'm Bran Douglas. I'm the bloody owner," he whispered. Then, he tossed the fireplace poker onto the floor at my feet with a clang and marched toward the kitchen, the smell of something burning drifting out from the dark room within.

Two

*H*OUSESITTER NEEDED FOR PALATIAL *Estate in Highland Scotland.*

That's what the ad said when Christopher sent it to me.

I'd done this before – traveled to exotic locales to take care of people's houses, cats, horses – whatever - while they were away. I'd lived in Ireland, Southern France, even the tropical land of Wisconsin, all in exchange for simply making sure someone's house didn't burn down and their animals didn't starve. It'd been an amazing experience thus far, so when the opportunity to be the caretaker of a fourteenth-century Scottish castle came across my path, I jumped at it.

Not just because it would bring me closer to Christopher.

No one told me it would come with a pompous Scot storming around the place.

"It's in need of some tending," Jocelyn said in her first email. "We're looking for someone who might have some handyman skills. If you were married and had a husband who might know his way around -"

I stopped her there. Little did Ms. Jocelyn Read know I was not only raised by a contractor, but I *was* one, myself. 'If there is anyone better suited to the job, I'll eat my hat,' I'd said.

It looked like my hat might be all I was eating. The Housesitters' site rules normally stated Ms. Jocelyn would need to provide my first night's meal, but this wasn't through the site. This was through Christopher, and he wasn't responding to messages.

And I was trapped here with pompous ass extraordinaire.

I didn't dare slip down to the kitchen and start raiding the place for fear Mr. Snooty would tear me a new asshole.

That and the last I'd checked the pantry, all there was to speak of was dusty cans of Oxtail soup. I could take a cab to visit the shop closer to the village, but I didn't exactly have the petty cash to be hiring another cab.

I'd have to find the car.

Or grow a hankering for Oxtail.

If I couldn't find the car, I was sure I'd be chewing on the wallpaper soon enough.

The house was brighter in the daylight. There were skylights in the floors of the third story I'd completely missed the night before, and they let light in from the third floor into the lower levels. I stopped halfway down the hallway to adjust a couple of the bedroom doors that had fallen off their hinges. Then, I marched through the house with feigned confidence, bringing little Mr. Darcy down to the kitchen for some water and another round of that canned chicken from the night before.

He growled and grumbled to himself as he ate, splaying his paws on either side like a convict fresh out of prison.

"You must have friends, somewhere, hm? Maybe a Mr. Knightley hiding somewhere?" I said, turning my attention to the stove. Despite the massive fireplace in the kitchen, there was a modern Aga stove toward the outer wall, a dusty red kettle set atop it. I made quick work to clean it off and fill it with fresh water before plopping it atop the hot burner and waiting to hear it hiss.

Mr. Darcy was done with his chicken breakfast before I had even dropped my tea bag in the cup.

I took the first couple of sips, cringing at the unfortunate taste of the tea, then pulled my phone from my pocket and brought up Ms. Read's contact - again.

"Hello?"

I stiffened. Jocelyn Read was finally answering her phone after a frantic morning of missed calls.

Finally, I thought.

"Oh, thank god you're there! Hey, uh – so I need to square a couple of things up with you."

"Hey, Corinne. Now isn't the best time, actually."

I ignored the brush-off. I wasn't about to go the rest of the day – or any length of days for that matter, without getting answers from this woman.

"This can't wait, is someone - else supposed to be here. Because there was an incident last night, and I think the banister is busted. I didn't mean to, but I thought there was an intruder -"

"You broke a banister?"

I paused, swallowing as I searched for words. "It was an accident. You didn't tell me there was going to be -"

"Look, I really can't talk right now, Corinne."

I straightened, panic creeping into my voice. "Wait! Before you go, I need to know what I'm supposed to do -"

"Oh, sorry, Corinne. It's getting a bit too loud here. I'll ring you when it calms down in the office. Ta ta."

And the line went dead, leaving me standing in the middle of the kitchen feeling like an ass with a cooling cup of rancid tea in my hand.

I sighed, slumping back into the kitchen counter with such defeat, I nearly spilled my tea down my front. Mr. Darcy sat at my ankle, licking his paws with the satisfied look of a well-fed cat.

My stomach responded by growling, angrily.

A subtle movement in the kitchen doorway caught my eye. The man from the night before was standing there, leaning into the doorjamb and wiping his dusty hands on a rag. "You're still here?" He said.

I took a breath, the steam of my tea drifting up into my face. I straightened, newly empowered despite the helplessness I felt in my conversation with Jocelyn. "I am, yeah."

He sighed, sauntering into the kitchen before tossing the rag into the fireplace as though some roaring fire waited to catch it and burn it to ash.

"Is the kettle fresh?"

I startled, stepping aside as he barreled up to the counter beside me. "Yeah. It's still hot."

"Lovely," he said under his breath. "Ye didn't drink that, did ye?"

I turned just as he gestured to the box of tea on the counter. I frowned. "Yes. Why?"

"Christ, woman. It's probably older than me. Here."

He pulled a fresh box of tea from a shopping bag on the counter, still wrapped in plastic.

I frowned down at my foul-tasting tea and cringed, pouring it out in the sink.

Despite the animosity he threw my way, he took the cup and poured new water into it, then set the steaming cup on the counter before me.

A second later, he dropped a new tea bag in the cup.

Surprisingly civil for a man who thinks I'm squatting in his house. How British.

The man who claimed to be Branson Douglas, heir to Cavendish House, was taller than me by several inches. He had sideburns framing the sides of his face, a perfectly straight nose, and the sternest brow I'd ever seen.

It made for some exaggerated eyebrow-raising, I soon noticed.

He shot me a sideways glance. "Can I help ye?"

I shook my head, turning away. I'd been staring at him like an idiot. I couldn't help it. Some part of me wanted to decipher whether this man was likely to murder me in my sleep. I was sizing him up.

Can you blame me? What proof did I have that he really was the owner? Because if he was, why on earth would I be hired to live here for two months?

I was also – maybe, sort of checking him out. Whatever, don't judge me.

He was handsome, and I'd noticed.

I wondered how Jocelyn would feel knowing I was in the middle of sharing tea with this blue-eyed charlatan.

I slipped back along the counter to give him space as he poured milk and sugar into his tea.

"And where did this little vermin come from?" He said, jutting his chin toward Mr. Darcy.

I glanced down at my doting little friend, who was now curled up in a ball with his back end firmly planted against my foot. "Vermin? He's not vermin!"

"He might as well be. There's got to be at least half a dozen of the bloody things out in the stables."

"There are stables?" My tone startled me. Despite the panic of his arrival the night before and the discomfort of my resulting circumstances, (I'd locked and relocked my bedroom door three times the night before) I'd forgotten the very thing I'd most looked forward to when I arrived – exploring.

"There are, aye. No horses, of course. Right, what the hell are ye doin here?"

My mouth fell open. In the light of day, and in a far calmer mood, Bran Douglas carried himself with an air of regal propriety I'd only experienced in early Nineteenth Century romance novels. His stern brow was set as he watched me, waiting for a response, and his accent gave every word he said an air of importance.

The night before, I'd been armed with a sense of entitlement. I belonged there. That phone call had deflated me, severely.

"I could ask you the same thing," I said.

He glared, impatiently.

"What proof do I have that you are who you say you are?"

He stared at me for a long moment, a look of bored irritation on his handsome face. Finally, he reached for his back pocket. I jumped back at the sudden movement.

He laughed, pulling out a wallet. A moment later, he handed me his license.

Branson T. Douglas.

He wasn't lying.

"Well, so what? How do I know you're related to *The* Douglas family? You could be anyone off the street."

He made a sound that was somewhere between a sigh and a groan, setting his tea on the counter before marching out of the kitchen.

I took a deep breath, the room feeling much larger with him gone.

"Are ye waiting for a written invitation?"

I startled, finding him waiting in the kitchen doorway, still glaring.

I hustled to follow, leaving my own tea on the island. He was several steps ahead of me, and I doubled pace to keep up.

He disappeared through the grand doorway beneath the stairs, and I found myself standing in a room like nothing else I'd ever seen.

The hall was clearly of another time, medieval in architecture and décor. This room was a full three stories tall, and its open-beamed ceiling was clearly original to the house.

"There ye have it," he said and gestured toward the fireplace, or the massive object hanging over it.

Only then did I realize I'd been standing there, gobsmacked.

I looked up to find an antique genealogy chart, calligraphy listing Douglas names all the way back to the year the home was built – 1393.

Holy shit, I thought.

He crossed his arms over his chest, the lapels of his shirt pulling open just so, baring a small hint of dark chest hair beneath. "Satisfied?" He said.

I shook my head, confused.

Branson pointed a finger to the names at the near bottom of the chart.

There was a black squiggle over one of the two names, but the unmarked line was in perfect calligraphy – Branson T. Douglas.

He was the heir.

That fact alone took the wind clean out of any sails I may have been packing beforehand. I was dead on the water.

And I was unpacked in one of his many bedrooms, and one of the few that wasn't fallen into disrepair to boot.

I swallowed. "Then who is Jocelyn Read?"

He sighed. "Executor to my father's estate."

I shot him a sideways look, confused, but fighting to find my footing. "Well, she hired me to be here. I'm housesitting -"

"Squatting."

"House. Sitting," I said, taking on a firm, obstinate tone.

"What does that even mean?"

I gave an exasperated sigh. "It means the estate paid me to live here and keep an eye on the place. So, I'm here, keeping eye on the place."

"Right, because I can't do that myself?"

I shook my head. "Apparently not! I don't get the impression she knew you were going to be here."

"Well, I am. So, you can go."

We both stood there in silence for a long moment. I was searching for the courage to fight him. I had nowhere else to go in the whole of Scotland; Christopher certainly wasn't inviting me to his place, and I'd spent the first installment of my wages on necessities and the train ticket to get there.

"What kind of person travels across the world to stay in some dilapidated castle, anyway?"

I glared at him. "A brave one."

His eyebrows shot up, and he gave me an appraising look. He didn't disagree. "Yes, well. I suppose vagrants can be brave."

I inhaled through my nose. "You're a dick."

The words were out before I even knew they wanted to be said. My stomach shot into my throat.

Surprisingly, he chuckled. "Ye're not the first to say so. How long are ye meant to be here?"

"The end of next month."

He snorted. "Bloody hell. Course ye are. And ye're supposed to interfere with my working on the house, then?"

"What?"

"I see ye're learnin what an abhorrent cow our Ms. Read is."

I couldn't deny it was the exact way to describe the woman I was dealing with. "She is making my life a bit difficult, yes. I haven't been paid since I arrived."

"How much does she owe ye?"

I stifled but thought better of being secretive. Perhaps knowing my salary, he'd take my claim more seriously. "Forty-five hundred – for the two months."

"And has she paid ye already?"

"I got the first installment before I arrived. The second installment is supposed to come now that I'm here, and the last when I'm done."

"Well, I wouldn't hold your breath. Ye're not getting any of it, now."

I scoffed, but his words swept the rug from under me. "What?! That's nonsense. She is going to pay me, or I'm going ballistic on that woman."

Bran laughed. "If ye were hopin to get paid, ye probably shouldn't have broken the banister."

I froze. "Oh god. She wouldn't -"

"She absolutely would. That woman is a fuckin gorgon. And the banister ye broke is easily worth seventeen thousand pound. Easily."

My mouth fell open. I was both devastated at the notion of having harmed such a magnificent treasure and horrified to think that I was stranded in east bum Scotland without a dime to my name – and now possibly seventeen thousand pounds in debt.

Fuck a duck.

"And let me guess, ye've no other accommodations for two months, aye?"

I shook my head. "I wasn't supposed to need any."

"How the hell were ye gonna feed yourself? Get around? There's literally nothing for miles. The nearest pub is a two-hour walk."

"She said I'd have everything I'd need. Wi-fi, cell service - there was even an estate car that I would have access to."

Bran doubled over, his eyes wide in an astonished smile. "Ye're joking?"

"No, I'm not!"

Bran tugged at the sleeve of my shirt as he headed toward the door. His voice rose in volume, the sound of it echoing off the high walls. "Come on, then. I'll show ye to your car."

I exhaled in a relieved sigh. If only one thing went right, I could survive. I had a few pounds left. Enough to get a few things at the shop to eat. Enough to survive and maybe feed and get a litter box for little Mr. Darcy, whom I snatched up in my arms before following Bran out into the front hall.

"Ye're bringing that little pest with ye?"

"Mr. Darcy is not a pest," I said as the kitten rubbed his jowl along my cheek.

Bran stopped in the open doorway, the cool air breezing in from outside. "Ye named the cat Mr. Darcy?"

I rolled my eyes. "Seriously, does everyone have to have an opinion about the name of my cat? It's a good name!"

"Aye, of course, it is. Alright, follow me."

Bran stopped by a bench in the hallway, throwing something on over his shirt. Then, he headed out the door.

I took a moment as I laid eyes on the gray sky outside. Then, I stepped out into the cool morning air and hurried down the steps to keep up with Bran's long stride. He was wearing jeans and a cable knit, cream-colored sweater with a high collar around his jawline. The flannel button-down peeked out at the sleeves, making Bran Douglas look as quintessentially British as any man I'd ever seen.

That man could fill out a sweater, folks.

Mr. Darcy burrowed under my chin, seemingly content to go for a walk in the cool air.

Bran marched down the gravel drive past the corner of the south wing. I glanced up at my bedroom windows, and for the first time since my arrival, took in the estate with clear eyes.

It was as beautiful as it was neglected, and its sad, dingy state made it all the more heartbreaking. There was history and craftsmanship hidden beneath every crack and broken piece. There were even stone gargoyles on the corners of the roof, all with gaping mouths that would vomit rainwater away from the house with suitable looks of displeasure on their faces.

Bran's pace was quicker than mine, and I hustled to keep up, still excited at the prospect of a car and a means to get around – to be self-sustaining. He turned the corner to head toward one of the several outbuildings toward the back of the house. I saw the stables, but also other buildings for purposes I couldn't imagine.

What do rich people build extra houses for?

"Should be right back here," he said, sauntering around the corner of the stables and out of sight.

I doubled my pace, jogging around the corner after him with Mr. Darcy purring in my arms. I rounded the overgrown corner, taking high steps to make it through the rising brush and brambles. Mr. Darcy squirmed and I held him tight as he tensed in my arms. Clearly, he was a little nervous to be heading into the wilds.

"Aye, indeed. Here she is," Bran said, waving his arm out in a grand gesture toward something still out of sight. He flashed me a wide grin betraying a startlingly beautiful and infuriating smile, then he moved out of sight.

I followed, rounding the second corner, and found Bran standing by a massive pile of junk, rusted fragments of old scaffolding and cross beams having crumbled atop it over time. Beneath the chaos, an old battered tarp was strewn over what looked to be the hood of an ancient vehicle.

"Keys are right here," he said, grabbing a small bundle hanging from the outside wall and tossing it in my direction. I caught them, startling Mr. Darcy enough to dig his claws into my collarbone. "Good luck getting it started. Though, if ye're capable of such a thing, I'd wager your skills would be better suited healing the sick, or turning water into wine."

Bran shot me another grin, just as beautiful and just as infuriating as the last. Then, he turned back toward the corner of the stables, striding through the tall grass like a gazelle.

"Wait!" I called, fuming as the keys ground together in my tightened fist. "Do you think this is funny?"

"Aye. I do, actually."

"Well, it's not! How am I supposed to get around?"

Bran stopped at the edge of the driveway and spun on me, flailing his arms up in exasperation. "That isn't my bloody problem!"

I faltered a moment.

He wasn't wrong.

He turned down the drive and walked away.

I scurried to follow after him. "Is that really the only car?"

"It is, aye. My father didn't leave the house in the last two years he was alive."

I frowned. I was frustrated and panicked, but this notion gave me pause. It was a sad thought to think of a man burrowed away in such a place, even if by choice.

"That car doesn't look like it's moved in far longer than that! There has to be another car."

Bran's determined stride caused a harsh grinding sound as the gravel moved beneath his boot heels. "Or your *employer* played ye for a fool. Believe me, it wouldn't be the first time she's done that to someone."

I stopped at the bottom of the steps leading back up to the house. Bran strode through the front door with an air of entitlement I no longer felt. If the house was his, what right did I have to come and go as I pleased? Even if Jocelyn Read claimed to be the executor of the estate, I couldn't help but feel like my presence was an imposition.

Still, no matter how uncomfortable I might feel, I'd taken the first payment and I didn't have the money to return it if I left early. Hell, I didn't have enough for a fucking cab ride out of here!

I was fucked.

I stood there for a long moment, the ancient car keys growing damp in my hand.

"Wait, Mr. Douglas?" I said, following him inside. He was back in the kitchen now, checking the kettle for another cup of tea.

"Call me Bran, please."

I paused, startled by the request. "Bran. I know this isn't your problem, but -"

"Are ye quite sure? Do ye really know that?"

"Yes! But I don't have anywhere else to go, and I don't have any way to go there if I did! The only money I have while I'm here I'll have to pay back if I leave -"

"So, she has already paid ye?" He said after swallowing his first sip of tea.

"No. Yes. I said that! She is - did. I haven't gotten my second payment yet, but she's paying me in installments. Was supposed to come through upon arrival."

"What about the first installment?"

"I spent the first. If I leave, I don't have anything to give her."

Bran leaned back on the counter. "Is that why ye ate canned chicken for dinner last night? Because ye're strapped?"

I glanced toward the recycling bin in the corner. "I actually didn't eat that. That was for Mr. Darcy."

Bran stifled a laugh. "Of course. Then, what did ye eat?"

"Nothing."

And my insides would be eating themselves if it wasn't for this constant thrum of anxiety.

Bran stopped, staring at my feet with his free hand firmly planted on the edge of the counter behind him. He stood quite still for a long moment, then took another sip of his tea. "Do ye have any money, at all?"

Mr. Darcy began to squirm, so I crouched down to let him loose on the kitchen floor, taking the opportunity to hide from my answer. His tone was softening, despite the righteous indignation he'd shown before.

"I have a little left."

"Enough to eat, but not enough to stay somewhere else, aye? Christ," he said, under his breath. He drank down the last of his tea and turned for the sink, rinsing the cup as he spoke. "And how long are ye meant to stay?"

"I already said, until the end of next month."

Bran set the cup down beside the sink with a little more force than was needed. I was surprised it didn't break.

"Fine," he said, then went quiet for a long moment. "Fine. If ye stay out of my way, I'll take ye to the shops tomorrow to grab a few things, aye?"

I swallowed. "Really? Ok -"

"I'm not doin it today. I've plans, and I don't like changin my plans."

I nodded. "No, that's fine -"

"I just need ye to stay out of my way."

"Yes, of course – I mean, I was hired to work on it myself -"

"And don't pester me," he said, swinging open the door to the fridge as he snatched up a pair of work gloves sitting on the kitchen island. The contents of the fridge clattered and sang with the sudden jostling. "There's eggs. And you'll find rashers are in the fridge. A loaf of bread in the freezer. I'm sure ye can find the toaster."

"Oh, I don't want to take your food."

He exhaled out his nose, barely glancing my way. "Fine. Then starve. I'll be upstairs. Don't need me."

Bran marched by me into the hallway, then disappeared up the stairs, half muttering under his breath as he went.

"Wait, does that mean I'm staying?"

Bran stopped at the foot of the stairs, shot me a sideways glance, but didn't speak.

The answer was a begrudging 'yes.'

"Feel free to explore the house. Just don't set fire to anything," he called from upstairs.

I stood in the front hall, staring up at the high ceiling and grand staircase above, the light teeming in through the skylights and high windows.

I still had a place to stay. One source of anxiety was gone.

And I would have access to a shop. A second source of anxiety was gone.

Now if I could just make Jocelyn pay me, and if Christopher would stop ignoring my god damn messages, I might not feel this awful knot in my –

"Oh – and the wi-fi password is *Falstaff*," Bran said, calling down from the upper landing. "Capital F. You know, in case you wondered. We're not entirely uncivilized in Cavendish."

I stood there a long moment, my stomach in my throat as Bran glared down at me from above. He'd given me permission to exist, but I still felt so out of place and unwanted. I almost preferred the idea of being stuck there alone with no wi-fi. Stuck there with a landlord who didn't want me felt worse.

Much worse.

A landlord who would be sneaking about the house at night while I slept, I thought. I remembered the figure that passed my bedroom door the night before, ignoring the fact that I was sure I'd seen the sway of skirts as they passed. I made a mental note to lock my bedroom door again that night.

Bran held my gaze a moment longer, then he disappeared down the hall into the east wing, leaving me to wallow in my thoughts.

Despite the anxiety I felt, my thoughts were *eggs and bacon*.

I took a deep breath, watching little Mr. Darcy curl figure eights around my ankles before returning to a small piece of hay we'd brought in from our trek into the brush. I watched him for a long minute, then I set my jaw and marched back into the kitchen to procure a couple of eggs for breakfast.

Three

THE HOUSE TOOK ON a strange life with Bran working in the distance. Everything from hammering to the violent thrum of singing pipes in the walls. I could guess what manner of work he was doing but didn't dare draw closer for fear of enraging him.

I decided to play it safe and keep my explorations to the downstairs.

"Do you feel safe?"

I held the phone to my ear and spoke softly. Despite Bran being two floors away, I was whispering like an idiot. Like the house itself was going to take notes and give a presentation to him later.

"I am a little concerned that I still can't find my passport but other than that -"

"Oh, where'd you last see it? Do you think he took it?"

"No. I think it's just tucked away in a bag I don't remember or something. He doesn't strike me as a homicidal murderer or anything."

"They never do," Patti said, forebodingly. I laughed.

Patti sighed on the other end of the phone. "Well, I guess that's good. See, I told you not all Scots are dreamy and charming."

I ducked my head into the rooms off the kitchen, finding a tiled storage room with glass cases and wood cupboards. It was similar to one of the mansions I'd visited in Newport, Rhode Island – a built-in safe room where they stored the silver and china at night so the servants couldn't steal it. I stepped inside, feeling the crunch of god knows what underfoot.

"I can vouch for that. Nothing charming about him."

I opened one of the cupboards and found them filled, but not with china and silver. It looked as though some breed of creature had taken up residence in the empty space. Whatever silver and china may have once existed, it was long gone.

I dodged backward, slamming the cupboard door before I caught some airborne monkey spawn virus and wiped my hands on my jeans.

"How about the house? Is it gorgeous?"

I made my walk across the hall and found a gorgeous dining room, at its center was a long table to seat dozens, and two chandeliers hovering above it.

"It is and it isn't. Kinda hard to really explain what I'm seeing."

Patti knew it was in shambles, but I hadn't had the heart to tell her just how bad. I knew she'd be concerned, and a concerned Patti would tell my dad.

I didn't want anyone to worry any more than I was.

"Is it haunted?"

I stopped in the dining room, my fingers running through the dust on the table. "Do I have to answer that?"

"It is, isn't it? Come on, Cor. I know you have a theory."

She wasn't wrong. We'd spent much of our childhood exploring creepy places or having slumber parties where we tried to creep each other out. And I'd stayed in a few creepy places in my travels, but admitting out loud that I thought – no, I was sure I'd seen something the night before...

Well, let's just say, it made my skin crawl.

I sighed. I hated the thought of some spooky thing listening to my conversation as much as Branson. "Yeah, I think there's something around."

She squealed on the other end of the line. "Oooh, details! Details."

I closed my eyes and fought not to sound impatient. I didn't blame her. We both loved ghost stories and spooky places. What she didn't seem to understand was that hearing ghost stories and living with them were two very different things. I'd discovered that in a couple housesits over the years.

"You can just feel it in the air – that heaviness of something around. And I think I saw a woman outside my bedroom last night."

Patti squealed again in a mix of delight and fear.

"I'm glad *you're* enjoying this."

"I am, I am! So, are you still staying for the full two months?"

Good question, I thought. It was going to be a very different job with the owner of the house trudging through the place the whole time. My favorite pastime of lounging in my underwear was entirely out of the question.

I answered Patti's questions, chasing Mr. Darcy back into the foyer. He tip-toed into a small alcove under the far stairs, and I discovered a small door there. Thinking it was a closet, I opened it. The sudden rush of cold, dank air rushed up into my face as I stared down ancient stone steps to darkness below.

A cellar.

Or more aptly, the setting of a horror movie I didn't intend to star in.

Thankfully, Mr. Darcy didn't find the space inviting either, and he skittered off down the opposite hall. I followed, frustrated that my exploration was being dictated by the mad distractions of a kitten. I had cupboards to snoop, damn it! I chased him past what looked like a music room and into a billiard room, both in varying stages of disrepair. The kitten skittered into the second door, and I followed to find the billiard room looked to double as an office study, its shelves still offering hundreds of old books. The billiard table surface was scuffed and torn, and the billiard balls still tucked into the pockets. Mr. Darcy made me kneel down beside the table to snatch him out from beneath it. Once I had him properly contained, I let myself look around. The wallpaper was dusty, and I ran my hand over the textured surface, leaving the sheen of satin glinting in the light from the windows. It was a rich red, almost burgundy, and it made the room feel like it should be filled with pipe smoke and brandy in crystal decanters.

Instead, it was filled with forgotten junk on one side of the room – a collection of old newspapers that was at least a thousand deep, all piled atop each other and tied in bundles by twine. Besides the papers, a mountain of old coffee and baked bean cans, waist-deep and covered in rust and dust.

I made my way back toward the front hall. Letting Mr. Darcy loose to do his own exploring despite never letting me out of his sight. I made my way past the stairs and into that massive room beyond.

"God, you really should see this place," I said, the echo of my voice apparent even over the phone.

This was my favorite room, so far. Instantly, I was transported to another time. I'd heard Cavendish House was ancient, but the rest of the space seemed like an estate straight out of a Regency novel, not a Highland legend. Yet, as I walked into the Great Hall, it became clear that this part of the house was untouched, left to retain its ancient charm.

The walls were lined with tapestries, the windows framed in wood and every pane of glass showed the distortion of waves and ripples in its making. I shifted my weight from left to right a moment, watching the green shapes of trees outside warp and undulate through the changing glass. I smiled, turning my attention to a massive tapestry of a unicorn.

The smile died, instantly.

I cringed, remembering the banister that I destroyed.

That's gonna ruin my day for years to come, I thought.

Still, I fought to distract myself, listening to Patti describe her divorce proceedings as I walked around this seemingly well-kept treasure in the midst of squalor everywhere else.

The Great Hall was the height of the entire house, its beamed ceiling so high above me, my voice echoed even when I just whispered to Mr. Darcy. He was eyeing one of those tapestries with a little too much fervor in his eyes.

"We should facetime, then you can show me the place."

I froze with my fingers tracing over the stitching of a tapestry.

"Yeah, that's not gonna happen. The last thing I need is for Mr. Douglas himself to walk up while I'm taking selfies in his parlor."

"It's not selfies, it's facetime."

I shook my head. Somehow, sharing the state of the place didn't feel right.

Even in the Great Hall.

On one wall, there stood a massive fireplace, its mantel a massive slab of stone. Chairs that belonged in a museum lined the outer walls.

I let my fingers graze against every surface, feeling mischievous, like a kid who is fully capable of reading the 'Do Not Touch' signs in the museum, but happily waits until the guard isn't looking to pick the nose of a statue. The tapestries beside the fireplace were different than the rest, their colors long dimmed by neglect and sunlight pouring in from the high windows on the back wall. These tapestries showed men in fine clothes and fancy hats, all gathered with their hands squarely planted on their hips or in gesture to each other.

I glanced up at the genealogy chart again, straining to make out the calligraphied text across the parchment. The antique paper was shielded by glass and displayed in a gold frame. I moved closer to it, unable to read the words at the top of the chart, the names and dates so old, I could barely comprehend them.

John Douglas; b. 1309.

"No way," I said aloud, and my voice sounded far off.

I followed the lines downward, the words becoming easier to read. Finally, just near the bottom quarter of the parchment were the last two names. The first name had what looked like sharpie scribbled on the glass over it, but the scribble was faded enough to read.

Callum Montgomery Douglas; b. 1987

Branson Tennyson Douglas; b. 1989

I gave a half-laugh. "Branson Tennyson, huh?"

Somehow, I hadn't noticed that before. I was admittedly frazzled at the time.

"What's that?"

"His middle name – it's Tennyson."

I could hear Patti's smile in her tone. "Well, you know his parents are readers, at least."

"Were. I think he's inherited the house because his dad just died."

"Oh," she said. "I suppose I might forgive his mood a little, then."

I stood on the warped floorboards, inspecting every scuff and mark with curiosity, but this comment made me pause. Patti was called away then, making me promise to text with updates and pictures. I agreed, hanging up and turning my attention back to exploration. I spotted a divot in the ancient wooden floor, bending to run a finger over it.

How long ago did this dent happen? Was it by the heel of some soldier's boot? The chair of some regal lady being pulled out for her to sit at the table?

Or did some squirrel chew through the wood this past summer while hiding his nuts in the walls?

"No! Shit!! Shit!!"

I spun around, facing the rest of the house as though it had come charging in the room toward me.

Bran's panicked voice carried through the house, despite distance and the muffling of massive tapestries all around me. Despite ignoring his random swears that morning, this time sounded urgent. This time something was really wrong.

I turned, unable to stop myself from running toward the sound.

Ever the Girl Scout.

I hauled myself into the front hall, leaving Mr. Darcy in the Great Hall to fend for his tiny self.

I hadn't dared bother Bran since our last conversation. I didn't exactly feel entitled to the stay there anymore, that's for sure. Still, it sounded as though he needed help. Maybe, if I could be of use, I wouldn't feel so terrible just breathing the air in his vicinity.

"Christ on a bike!" He screamed again, and the walls thrummed with a sudden surge of ancient pipes.

I careened up the stairs to the third floor and down the hall toward his voice, hearing a telling sound of water spraying wildly.

I arrived at the door of a washroom and had to shield my eyes from the spray of water. Bran was there, no longer clad in his wool sweater, but instead pinned on his back under a porcelain sink with a wrench and a broken-off piece of ancient lead pipe in his hand, his black t-shirt soaked through to the skin.

"Well, shit," I said, turning back down the hall and taking off for the stairs. I barreled back down to the front hall and swung open the door to the cellar – the cellar that I'd discovered and been too afraid to explore that morning. I hadn't gone far enough to spot the pipes while exploring, but I knew quite well where most houses hid their plumbing. In my urgency, I forgot how terrifying those dark steps had been.

Like many houses I'd visited before, the air down there felt heavy, and not in a warm, fuzzy kind of way.

The pipes and valves were clearly lined up at the top of the cellar stairs. I turned the small handle by ninety degrees and heard the thunderous spray of water slowing, then silenced upstairs. Bran's voice remained loud as he continued to holler his frustrations.

I made my way back upstairs, taking them two at a time as I hurried to meet him.

I rounded the bathroom door to face him. "What kind of a jackass doesn't shut off the water main before they start pipe work?"

Bran was seated on the floor now, his Cure t-shirt clinging to every inch of him as he sat there in a two-inch-deep puddle of water. "What?"

"Seriously? It's common knowledge. Rookie move, guy. Rookie move."

Bran's eyebrows shot up in frustration, but instead of yell at me, his expression softened. "And how would ye know better?"

I rolled my eyes, then pointed at myself. "Raised by a contractor. I've been learning construction since I was seven years old, and even at seven years old, I knew to shut off the water main before working on pipes. Especially old ones."

"It had a cut-off valve up here -"

"Old pipes," I said again, letting each word drip with disappointment.

Bran glanced down at himself then back up at me. "Wait, you have construction experience?"

I raised my eyebrows.

Oh, taking the time to actually listen when I speak now, you snooty bastard?

"Uh, yeah. That's why I got the job of taking care of the house."

Bran gave an exasperated exhale. "Why would she hire a contractor if she didn't want you to do any work?"

I threw my hands up in feigned exasperation. "That's what *I* said!"

Meow.

I turned to find Mr. Darcy hovering just down the hall from me, staring up with his own piercing blue eyes. He sauntered closer to the door and glanced into the bathroom only to frantically shake his paw after touching it to the tiled floor.

"Is it coming through to the floor below?" Bran asked, rolling up onto his knees.

"I didn't check, though by the looks in here, probably."

"Fuck. Did ye shut off the water to everywhere?"

I nodded, stooping to pick up the kitten before he could try to venture into the bathroom further.

"Would ye check the linen closet there? See if there might be any towels."

I shot him a look. "I thought I was meant to leave you alone. What was it you said? *Don't need me?*"

Bran sighed. "I apologize. Would ye please, for the love of Christ, forgive my rudeness and check the closet for bloody towels?"

"Fine."

I opened the cupboard to find only dust. Then, I marched down the hall searching for the next bathroom or bedroom with an en suite attached. Each room I glanced into was in a sadder state than the one before – piles and piles of junk filling every inch of free space. The sight depressed me, making me grateful I was staying on the brighter side of the house.

Or one of the brighter *rooms* in the house. There weren't many.

I gave up the search in the East wing and ran to my own room, snatching up every towel I could find. I left Mr. Darcy there and piled all the towels into my arms, running back along the hallway to the gutted bathroom. I stopped in the doorway and stared a moment, slackjawed. Bran was standing in the middle of the disarray, shirtless, wringing his black t-shirt out into the sink.

I stood there for a long moment, forgetting how to speak.

"Oh, brilliant! What a star!" Bran said, lunging across the bathroom, his sneakers squeaking on the tiles as he took the bundle from me. He flung them down onto the floor, watching them instantly soaked through by the flood.

I watched as Bran sopped up as much as he could with the first towel, then tossed it the sink. He crouched down to do it over again with the second towel, his shoulders taut as he fought with the heavy thing. He was standing by the sink again before he shot me a wary look.

"Could I convince ye to try tidyin that corner, there?" He said, gesturing to my side of the bathroom.

"Oh! What?" I said, throwing down a towel. "Yes, of course." The room was huge for a bathroom, a large clawfoot tub in one corner, its finish chipped and discolored from years of abuse. I slopped the towel around in the slowly receding puddle, bringing my own dripping mess to the bathtub to wring out as Bran threw one of his towels at my feet. A moment later, he was crouched down behind me, soaking up water, his head less than two feet from my backside.

If I turned around, the bastard would be faceplanted into my hoohah.

Not that I was thinking about that – at all.

I stiffened, bending awkwardly at the waist to keep from twerking directly in his face as I worked.

Because face twerking didn't seem much better than faceplanting.

"I'm mad to even attempt this. Just say it." He said, suddenly, joining me at the side of the tub.

I startled, his bare arm brushing against mine as we wrung out the towels. I fought to keep my eyes straight. "Attempt what?"

Bran chuckled. "All of it," he said, gesturing to the room. I was quite sure he meant more than just that washroom.

I finished wringing the towel and turned back to the room, finding the last flooded corner before throwing my towel down. I glanced out into the hallway, remembering the line of doorways that led to massive junk hoards. "Well, if you're doing it alone, yes."

Oh, Corinne Turner, you are one smooth operator.

"Aye, I knew it would be, but had to give it a go. Clearly, I'm a bit stubborn."

"No," I said, feigning shock.

"Suppose that's the Douglas side."

I hoisted the towel back up and returned to the tub. "What is it you're trying to do, anyway?"

It was Bran's turn to sop up more water, and he dropped to his haunches behind me again, forcing me to straighten as the weight of the towel strained my lower back. I had half a mind to sit on his head out of spite.

Bran stopped what he was doing a moment, half glancing my way over his shoulder as though he meant to speak. He seemed to think better of it. "Trying not to lose the place."

"Oh," I said, giving the towel one last good wring. "I thought you said you were the heir."

"Oh, I am. Sadly, I've inherited a tower of shite."

Bran held a hand out to me, and I handed him the newly wrung towel. He dropped to all fours and pushed the two massive towels across the floor, sopping up the last of the water. A moment later, he was standing at the tub with me, dropping them into its depths before turning back to the sink. He knelt beside it, his bare back moving and rippling with the effort of his arms.

I admit it. It was super distracting.

Branson Douglas looked like a statue one would find in the Louvre, imagined by a randy Michelangelo, who not so secretly harbored an affection for beautiful men.

Naked, beautiful men.

Suddenly, I could understand Michelangelo's weakness.

And was feeling inspired to carve marble.

Too bad the beautiful man before me was such a dick.

He hissed, mumbling salty language as he inspected the fractured pipe. I moved forward by a few feet, catching sight of the damage. The pipe coming up through the floor was disintegrated - desperately in need of replacing.

"There's no way I'm gonna be able to fix this now," he said, and it was clear he was talking to himself.

I swallowed, searching for the most confident tone I could muster. "Well, if I were you, I'd go copper."

"Pardon?" Bran furrowed his brow as he turned toward me.

"Copper is pricier, but you won't need much for just this job. You could do PVC for cheap, but that whole input system needs replacing right there, and PVC won't handle a hot water intake. You can drain with PVC, though, so there's something -"

"Ok, stop right there," he said, rising to his full height. "Ye were serious – about the construction work, I mean, aye?"

I fought the urge to roll my eyes. "No, I'm just making up words as I go. Talking shite, as they say."

Bran smiled.

It startled me.

"Talking shite, aye? Ye've been in Scotland a while, I take it?"

The thought that I was adopting the lingo made me smile. "No, just been talking to a Scot quite a bit."

He gave a half shrug. "I see. Well, what other construction have ye done?"

I straightened. I suddenly felt like I was on a job interview – for a job I'd already been hired for.

My brain was beginning to hurt.

"Well, I – uh. I've done -" I took a moment. No one had ever asked me to compile my knowledge before. They'd simply heard I was Kenneth Pace's girl and stepped aside to let me work. "I've done everything from basic demo to full builds, from foundation to roof. I can frame, lay drywall, shingle a roof, install basic electrical components – once the wires are in place, of course. General plumbing installs, lay tile..."

I stopped, finally catching sight of Bran's expression. He was staring up at me, mouth open, eyes wide in rapt attention. If I'd had my phone on me at that moment, I'd have taken a picture.

I'd never felt so smug in my damn life.

I turned my head to look out the window, trying to hide my smile.

"Jocelyn knows ye can do all of this?"

I tilted my head, considering. "Not the particulars, no. She knows I have experience as a groundskeeper. And that I can drive a tractor. And I did tell her I've worked as a handyman – or woman, but given how little she actually listens to me when I speak -"

I stopped myself. I'd almost forgotten who I was talking to. For all I knew, this was the Schmeagal version of Bran, and soon he'd turn back into Gollum and try to bite my finger off or something.

"Go on. I was listening," he said.

"Yeah, why are you so curious all of a sudden? Thought I was a squatter you were barely tolerating."

"Ye are, but I'm beginning to think of ways ye could earn your keep."

I scoffed. "Oh yeah? Plumbing skills do it for ya?"

Bran grinned, and I swear, there was a hint of flirtation to it. "Oh, ye have no idea."

It threw me completely off guard.

Be cool, Cor. Remember what Kenny taught you. Use your contractor voice or half the men you work with will try to talk over you, question your judgment, talk down to you. Don't give them the chance to even try.

Confident. No nonsense. Brass balls.

I stared at him, feeling my chest tighten. "I don't know. I kinda signed a contract saying I'd -"

"Stop me from fixing my own house?"

"No! There was nothing like that. Just that I wouldn't – I don't know. I'm just worried she's going to turn around and demand the money she gave me back if I don't follow my end of the bargain."

Bran nodded. "What if I cover it?"

My eyes went wide. "What?"

"If she demands your wages back, I'll cover ye. Hell, I'll fucking pay ye what she promised ye if ye can really do everything ye say."

I took a step back, my hands splaying out in front of me. "Are you serious?"

He moved toward me, coming to stand just inches away, his blue eyes staring down at me with a new intensity. "I've got less than two months to make this place somewhat livable, or they're gonna take it from me. Until then, I'm in fucking limbo, and though I haven't the funds to hire a crew, I'm sure I can pay the fee of a housesitter who earned the job with her promises of fine craftsmanship."

"Hold on," I said, my stomach turning. "How the hell do I drop that bomb on Jocelyn? If the house isn't technically yours, and I tell the lady that hired me to go screw – I'm going to end up homeless and stranded in the middle of east bum Scotland."

"Not technically mine? What fucking rubbish! Look, Corinne. This is my house. It's mine and my sister's, and there is no court in the country that would proclaim otherwise. And if I have *your* help, I might actually get to keep it at the end of next month. If no, my dad will have gotten what he always wanted, and they'll auction the fucking place off, and we'll lose our birthright. So - please," he said, and his voice dropped to a near hush. "Please, please, please. I'll stock the fridge, I'll move ye to a nicer room once we clean it out – anything ye need."

"I thought my room was nice -"

"Come on. What do ye say? Will ye help me? Even with just smaller tasks. I assure ye, it will add up."

I stood there in the weathered bathroom, my eyes averted from his pleading expression – and his naked chest. It was impossible to deny that if Bran Douglas wanted to, he could use those blue eyes for evil.

I stared out the window at the gray light of the world, hearing the strange sounds of Scottish birds as they flitted by.

"Who is going to protect me if she comes after me?"

Bran lunged forward, his hands together in an almost prayer as he beamed at me. "I will!"

I went to roll my eyes, but he stopped me.

"Yes! I'll make her rue the day she was born if she so much as threatens a penny in your bank account or a hair on your lovely head."

I swallowed and took a deep breath. "Will you let me think about it?"

His face fell, but he nodded. "Of course. Of course, take your time."

I continued to stand there, staring past him at the window. "Ok. I'll think about it."

Bran reached for me, touching his hand to my shoulder in an awkward pat of camaraderie. I pursed my lips together and forced a sheepish grin.

"Alright, well. Given I've destroyed the pipes on this project, I'm gonna head off to work on something else for now," he said, moving past me and out the door, his wet t-shirt wadded up in his hand. He disappeared out into the corridor just as a tiny mewing thing appeared in the doorway. Bran reappeared, his wet hair beginning to bend and flick up as the curls dried atop his head. He bent down to the kitten and snatched him up to have a look at him. Then he stepped back into the bathroom and handed Mr. Darcy to me. "Please. Ye'll let me know as soon as ye've decided, aye?"

I nodded, and he was gone, leaving me in the wake of his plumbing catastrophe with Mr. Darcy purring in my arms.

I took in the room with new eyes now – the eyes of a contractor preparing to give an estimate for the cost of work. My Dad brought me onto hundreds of jobs as a single father, and I'd watched him assess everything from full remodels to simple wall patches. I'd learned to predict his judgments until he started sending me to potential jobs to do the assessing for him.

This room, had Dad been hired to fix the place, wasn't the worst I'd seen. There were a few broken tiles behind the toilet, the pipes under the sink and to the bathtub were in dire need of updating, and the tub needed a refinish, but other than that and a fresh coat of paint, the ceiling was intact, there was no apparent water damage like other parts of the house, and the fixtures were showing only the minimum wear of time. A good shine would turn the whole room around.

"Also, anything special ye might like for tea -?"

I screamed. Mr. Darcy panicked in my arms, digging his claws in as he fought to get away. I let him loose, moaning as I pressed my hand over the scratches. I turned to find Bran standing in the doorway, again. "You son of a bitch," I hissed, softly.

He gave a sheepish shrug. "Sorry. I just wanted to – sorry. Thought I'd maybe butter ye up a bit?" He said, giving me an eyebrow wiggle. Then he winked and turned to dart off again. Yet he stopped in the doorway, leaning back in to point at the scratches. "Sorry about that."

I glared at him. He held my gaze, taking the full brunt of my chagrin like a gentleman. Then off he went, leaving me to clean the blood off my collar without a working sink.

I ran my hand over my face, feeling more out of place than I ever had in my life. Somewhere in the house was a man working as best he could to restore his home to its former glory while I took up space like some entitled – American. I couldn't imagine him defeating such an undertaking alone, but still – I'd signed a contract, hadn't I? Ms. Read was still my boss, technically. Even if she wasn't paying me.

My inattentive, ungrateful boss who'd tucked me away in the servants' quarters of the massive place like some fucking scullery maid, only to live with the intolerable Douglas heir – and not tell me I'd have a roommate.

That bitch.

Meow.

Mr. Darcy hopped up onto the windowsill and was looking out the window at the bright but dreary day. I rounded the massive tub to see what drew the tiny kitten's attention. Outside, Bran was marching across the drive, a large chunk of wood over his shoulder. He was back in his sweater now, his broad chest softened by the high collar and warm snuggly shape of it. I watched him from my window and took a deep breath.

Then, I turned back to the room, pulling my phone from my pocket.

I dialed up Jocelyn's number and crossed my fingers that the woman wouldn't answer. I wasn't sure I was up to being brushed off again.

"Hello," Jocelyn said in that same distracted tone.

"Hi, Ms. Read. Hey, this is Corinne Turner. I know you said you'd call me back, but something has come -"

"Corinne, again. I said I would call you back when I am free to speak to you. I don't know how I could be more clear."

The sudden shift of tone triggered something deep in my chest. I could be a docile and gentle creature to be sure, but I did not take kindly to rude people.

I felt my heart begin to race, a side effect of my rising temper. I was close to giving this woman a piece of my mind. "Yes, I realize that, but this can't wait. It couldn't wait yesterday, eith -"

Jocelyn sighed on the other end of the line. "Ms. Turner, you lost all right to complain when you destroyed priceless property. You should feel blessed I'm not involving a barrister to contend with what I'm sure will be several thousand pounds worth of damage. I will get back to you when I am available. If you don't want to wait, you may feel free to pack up your belongings and find another place to stay. Good day."

The phone went dead.

I stood there with the phone still pressed to my ear, my heart pounding in my throat. I could feel my hand trembling. I let my arm relax, setting the phone on the sink as I glanced down at my little gray furball friend now forming a serpentine formation around my legs.

I turned on my heel, high stepping to escape the kitten's assertive devotion, and marched out into the hallway.

I flew down the stairs into the front entrance, glancing around each space as I made my way through.

Light fixtures in the hall need to be reaffixed. Chandelier bulbs and windowpanes in the entrance need to be replaced. Front door hinge needs new screws. Pottery on the steps needs to be thrown away. Hedges bordering stairs need to be trimmed. Fresh gravel on the drive wouldn't hurt. Potholes filled.

I kept a running tally of just how much work was needed as I stormed down the drive toward the barn. I grabbed the old door handle and flung the door aside just as a table saw burst to life within.

I stopped dead in the doorway, watching Bran lean over the saw, wood shavings flying up into his face, his eyes hidden behind protective goggles. He finished his cut and set the wood aside as the saw slowed, leaving me half deafened from the noise.

He lifted his goggles, his drying curls poking out around the band as he raised his eyebrows at me. "Welcome, Ms. Turner."

"There's no way the two of us are going to be able to get this house fixed up in two months," I said.

Bran tossed his goggles onto the saw table and took two hurried steps toward me. "We don't have to completely fix it up. We just have to make it livable."

"I counted thirteen small projects just on my way out the front door. And that was on the nice side of the house."

"I know. I know, it's huge. But if we can empty out all the old rubbish from upstairs, finish the roof, get the plumbin in order – I promise ye, it will be enough. Whatever we *can* do, it will be enough."

I took a deep breath and exhaled. "And you'll pay back whatever I owe Ms. Read if she comes calling for it?"

"Of course! I'm a man of my word!" Bran was beginning to shift on his heels as though dancing in celebration.

I tried to ignore how endearing it was. "And you will take me to the shops? Whenever I want? Because I'd like to get a cat box before Mr. Darcy becomes accustomed to shitting in the bathtub every night."

"Is the mongrel shitting in the -" He stopped, catching my glare. "Aye, done. Absolutely, I'd be delighted."

I inhaled through my nose, milking every second of this moment. "Ok. I'll do it. I'll help."

"Really?"

"Oh, hell yes," I said, letting my words drip with venom. "That's what she gets for hanging up on me. Hope this ruins her day."

"Brilliant!" He said, punching the air so hard he spun in a circle. "Oh, I promise! It'll ruin more than just her day!"

Bran lunged toward me but caught himself before trying to embrace me. On some level, I think I was disappointed. He offered up his hand to shake mine. I took it, and his grip was as firm as mine, just as my father taught me. His eyebrows shot up as though he was surprised by it. He met my gaze and smiled. "I have a feeling ye're gonna be a godsend, Corinne Turner. I promise to make it worth your while."

He shook my hand again, as though for good measure, then turned back to the table saw. I watched as he bent down to something out of sight behind it and tossed a massive chunk of wood into the air.

"Alright, then. First thing's first. Let's go fix this bloody thing, shall we?"

Bran gave me an eyebrow wiggle and strolled past before I could see what was in his hands. I scurried to catch up, eyeing the wooden shape on his shoulder. He marched along as though carting a prized boar after a hunt.

I followed behind him into the house. Bran stopped at the stairs and dropped to his knees beside the broken banister, hoisting the missing head up to reposition it. He shot me a sideways glance, wordlessly waiting for help. I scrambled to his side, taking up a perch on the bottom steps, and helped align the ancient thing. My eyes widened at the sight of my once broken unicorn head. The regal beast was now held together by newly installed dowels and anchors hidden in the depths of the wood.

After a few salty outbursts and half a tube of wood glue, the antique carving was back in place, and to the untrained eye, right back to its former glory.

"There. The princess will be none the wiser," Bran said, winking at me. Then he hopped to his feet and bounded up the stairs like a schoolboy released for Christmas break. "Come on upstairs then, Turner. Let's get started, shall we?"

I stared up the grand staircase, holding my breath as the house echoed in every direction around me.

Dear god, what have you gotten yourself into? I thought. Again.

Then I slowly made my way upstairs.

Four

A STRANGE GRINDING SOUND slowly drew me from my sleep. I kept my eyes closed, listening to what sounded like wheels on the gravel driveway. I stretched, still half asleep. The braying of horses startled me awake. I rolled out of bed and moved to the window to see what had come up the driveway.

There was nothing there – no horse-drawn carriage and riders. It was just a dream.

I smiled, and for a moment, felt transported.

I also felt like going right back to sleep.

I was back under the covers before a new sound drew my attention to the bedside table.

I glanced across the bed to find Mr. Darcy curled up at my side, sound asleep just as the vibrating sound died away.

I rolled over in bed, feeling the crick and crack of joints I didn't know I had, and I straightened my legs in a full stretch. When I released, both my knees popped as they always did after a day of extensive use.

Branson Douglas was no slave driver by any means, but he came damn near close.

I'd spent the afternoon with him, rushing back and forth down the halls of the east wing as Bran explained every little detail that needed doing – roof rework, junk hauling, coats of paint, etc. He didn't have the proper piping to fix the bathroom sink, so a 'jerry rig' job with some pipe poached from a bathroom in the far reaches of the third floor would have to do, allowing for the water main to be turned back on without causing some biblical flood in the far reaches of the third floor. After that, we'd gone from room to room up there, jotting down a tally of all the jobs that needed immediate attention.

"It's going to be almost impossible to really assess the chaos until we clear out all this junk," I'd said, standing outside the door of the very room where I'd discovered Mr. Darcy on my first night.

Bran sighed. "I know. I'm just worried I'm going to uncover a corpse or some other awful thing up here."

I laughed there in my bed, remembering.

I turned to catch the time on my bedside clock – 8:27.

No wonder I still felt tired. I'd only gone to sleep six hours ago.

The humming sound returned, and I furrowed my brow. This time I was awake and could recognize the vibration of a phone going off. I launched an arm across the bed to snag my phone from the bedside table.

Facetime call from Chris.

My heart leapt into my chest.

Holy shit, he's calling. He's calling? Now? Answer the phone, you idiot!

I sat bolt upright, giving my hair a quick tussle before wiping the sleep from my eyes. What did he want to talk about? Did he have a message from Jocelyn? Was he calling of his own volition? Did he still want to see me?

And really - what was he doing calling this early in the morning?

It filled me with a strange amalgam of dread and excitement.

Not exactly the wakeup I'd expected that morning.

"Hello," I said.

The screen came to life, and there he was. My chest grew tight at the sight of him.

Christopher Menzies was the epitome of tall, dark, and handsome, but with an almost wily look about him, the way any woman imagines some rakish pirate from a romance novel would look. He had a perfectly trimmed mustache and goatee that framed his bright smile every time I made him laugh, and he'd let his hair grow out for months now. He was rocking a full mane of dark brown hair, its wildness curling in just at his shoulders. His dark brown eyes only added to the somewhat bohemian way about him. He was a modern, dapper,

Scottish brogue spewing pirate, and the sound of his voice was as soothing as Mr. Darcy's purr when he wanted it to be.

"Hey," he said, smiling into the phone camera.

He wanted it to be.

The sound of his voice brought every ounce of fondness I felt for him flooding right back.

My heart raced at the sight of him. It always had.

"Good morning!" I said, smiling as I checked the tiny image of my own face to make sure I didn't look like a duckbill platypus. "How are you not at work?"

Chris seemed a bit distracted, pulling a paper bag into view as he pulled his breakfast out to eat. "I've actually just got home. Had the night off last night and partied a wee bit too hard with the lads. Still pished."

I laughed. "I thought you said you had to work late every night this week?"

Chris shook his head. "No. Was free as a bird. Spent half the night with my bloody feet stuck to the floor of the Loft Nightclub. Awful. You look lovely this morning."

My face flushed, and I covered my face with my free hand.

"Aye, a man could get used to waking up to that. God, what I wouldn't give to be there with ye right now."

I smiled compulsively. The thought was the most pleasant thing I could imagine. If I remembered correctly, when he wrapped an arm around my waist the night we met, resting his head on the top of mine, making me feel small and sheltered and safe – something I'd never felt in the arms of a man before - he smelled nice, too.

I could imagine my bed smelling like him. It made me giddy.

"Sh!" I said, my eyes shut tight. I found it so hard to look at him when he talked like that. The roguish way he got when he'd had a couple of drinks was one of the many things that wooed and won me over in those months since I last saw him. The thought that this handsome, flirty thing was only an hour's drive away stirred me in a whole new way.

I could see him, finally.

I could actually get to feel his touch after all these months of him threatening to accost me with his sexual desires. In less than two hours, he could be here.

The thought made my lady bits all tingly, and I instantly forgot the disappointment of not hearing from him when I arrived.

"What are ye wearing, then?" He asked, his tone suddenly dropping an octave.

My face burned as I leaned back down into the pillows and sighed.

I knew that tone. He was in a mood.

God, I'd missed his moods.

"Why don't you show me?" He said.

My face burned with a smile.

I made my way out into the hallway with a light step. Morning orgasms will have that effect on you, so it seems.

Especially the kind you have on the phone with a handsome Scotsman.

My Austen-loving side was as sexually satisfied as the rest of me.

I hit the top of the stairs just as Mr. Darcy took off past me, flitting down the hall toward the east wing.

I cooed to him, hurrying to snatch him up before he could duck into his favorite room and disappear on me. I was beginning to think he liked those mattresses for unfortunate reasons.

He didn't squirm, but instead, tucked his head up under my chin and purred away as I carried him down the stairs.

"There ye are. Was beginning to wonder if I'd see ye this morning."

Bran stood at the kitchen counter in what looked like the same jeans and sweater as the day before.

"Do all Americans sleep until noon?"

I marched across the kitchen, fighting not to smile as I made my way to the kettle. "It's not noon," I said, calling him an *ass* under my breath. The last thing I wanted my new 'roommate' to know was that I'd spent the morning having facetime sex with a Scottish beau. I couldn't help but grin as I remembered Chris showing off his Pac-Man boxer shorts as though they were male lingerie.

"The skip arrived a bit ago, so we're good to start hauling all that god-awful nonsense out the door if you're up for it."

I nodded, pouring milk into my tea.

"I don't imagine it's going to be pleasant, but it really is the thing that will make the biggest difference when the inspectors come."

I stared into my teacup, listening to Bran hem and haw about the coming workload, but I was just too giddy to worry.

Chris wasn't ignoring me. He wasn't playing me or forgetting me - he was just busy.

And he'd made it clear that morning that he still wanted me.

No amount of unpleasant work could ruin my day.

It was only a matter of time before I'd be getting laid.

The mere notion of that made my knees weak.

It had been a while, that's all I'll say.

"I've got a gorilla's head mounted on the wall in there somewhere I'd like to uncover and hang over the mantle in the great hall."

"What? Really? That's awful!" I said, startled by Bran's flippant tone as scenes from *Gorillas in the Mist* came flooding to mind.

"No, not really. For Christ's sake, have ye been listening to a word I've said?"

I shook my head as though shooing a fly and turned to face him. "Sorry, I'm just a little distracted. What were you saying?"

"Clearly. I said I've rallied the courage to go after my biggest nightmare first."

I raised an eyebrow. I knew the room he meant – Mattress Mountain, as we'd coined it the day before.

"I imagine getting the worst out the way will make the rest feel like a pleasant holiday."

"Yeah? Is the second floor not as bad?"

He averted his eyes. He stared at me a moment, confused. "The second? Oh! Ye mean the first floor. *First*."

I stared at him as he made fun of me. Apparently, we were on the ground floor, and the first was up the stairs, the second above that.

I rolled my eyes. "Are you done? Because I'm willfully going to forget everything you just said."

He paused, fighting to hide a smile as he looked away, pensively. "I think I may be, aye."

"Good. So is the *second* floor any better?"

"Ehm, I wouldn't say that, no."

His tone made me wonder whether the larger bedrooms downstairs weren't just as god awful as the third story, just with more room for junk.

I wasn't looking forward to any of it.

I shrugged. "Then Mattress Mountain it is."

Bran hovered by the kitchen door as I buttered a slice of toast. "Indeed, and if we do find the corpses of my father's missing gardener and groundskeeper, we can be traumatized together."

I turned, the buttered piece of toast hovering at my lips. "Wait. Missing what? Did your father – are there actually people missing?"

Bran gave a half-smirk. "Honestly, I wouldn't put it past the old bastard. I'll be upstairs. Do come up as soon as ye can, please."

"On the third floor?" I called, giving a teasing glare.

He smirked at me and muttered something under his breath. Then, he disappeared, his footsteps betraying his quickened pace up the stairs. I munched away at my toast, deciding to add a smear of loganberry jam before leaving the plate in the sink and following the youngest member of the Douglas family into the chaos of his birthright.

The hallway was just as dark as the previous days when I reached the top floor and headed after Bran. The long corridor took on an eerie feel during the daylight hours. It was as though this side of the house swallowed light, many of the windows within the rooms along its length blocked by massive piles of long collected junk. I followed along the corridor, glancing into each open door as I passed. I reached halfway down the hallway and stopped at the only closed door, my brow furrowed as I scanned up and down the length of the corridor. Despite having explored the space thoroughly the day before, I couldn't quite be sure if this was the right one.

I took hold of the doorknob. "Bran?"

"Here."

I nearly jumped right out of my skin, screaming as Bran lunged back into the hallway from the opposite doorway.

"Sweet Jesus! Don't do that!" I hissed.

His eyes went wide, half-annoyed and half-amused. "Well, I do apologize, but the door seems to be jammed."

Bran hurried down the hall with a cream-colored box in his hands, then crouched down to an electrical outlet. A moment later, his Bose speaker was filling the space with familiar sounds – *Brown Sugar* by The Rolling Stones.

Bran stepped up to the door, nudging me aside as he stepped up to try the key. The ancient metal thing clanked and turned in the lock, but when Bran jammed his shoulder into the door, it didn't budge. He tried again, this time shaking the whole door in its frame. Still, no luck.

"It was wide open this morning," I said, glancing down the hallway toward the south wing and the middle stairs.

"Was it?" He asked, his voice strained with effort as he tried to shove the door open again.

"Yes, Mr. Darcy came scurrying down here this morning, and I had to snatch him up before he snuck inside. Didn't want him hiding on me, again."

Bran gave the door another shove, the high corner of the door moving in the frame enough to betray light from the window within the room, but the lower half stayed put. It was almost as though someone had placed a massive object in front of it on the other side.

"Fer fuck's sake?" Bran said, muttering to himself as he rubbed his shoulder.

"We can always start elsewhere, yeah?" I asked, gently shooing Mr. Darcy away as he approached the door.

Bran slumped against the doorjamb, catching his breath a moment. "Damn it, I literally downed a dram of whisky to take on this project. Rather disappointing."

"Wait, it's like – 9 am."

Bran turned to me, his eyebrows up just slightly in an impatient glare. "I am kidding, of course."

"Oh. Oh?" I shook my head, watching Bran sigh in resignation before heading down the length of the hallway.

Though it felt almost bizarre, I was becoming accustomed to the idea of Branson Douglas joking.

He did seem to be doing it more and more.

His energy seemed off, as though the obstacle of a jammed door was stealing the wind right from his sails.

I glanced down the corridor. "Alright, then why don't we start at the room furthest down, make our way back along the hall, yeah?"

He shrugged and took off, leaving me to hustle down the corridor to catch him. He gave the half-closed door a good heave and the grinding sound of objects dragging over the hardwood floor within betrayed just what was in store. Bran gave the door one final hip check and stepped inside.

I held my breath a moment, then followed.

The piles in this room, unlike many others, did not obscure the window completely. This room had piles of old newspapers lining the solid wall, and peppered among those piles were heaps of old cardboard boxes, a couple of lamps with dusty and torn lampshades, an ancient bicycle, a pram made out of brown wicker, and several broken picture frames leaning against the piles.

Yet, the most confusing sight within the room was piled along the left wall. In among the many cardboard boxes and water-stained newspapers were no less than a dozen old crockpots of every make, model, and size one could imagine. I moved to join Bran in the room and had to step over several more crockpots, a long-forgotten tower of them having clearly fallen across the threshold of the room.

The two of us stood there in silence for a long moment, taking in the scope of the project – the scope of just one of a dozen projects that sat stewing in grime and chaos along the third floor.

Well, fuck.

I pulled on one work glove, feeling the thumb slide on fully as Bran took a deep sigh and planted his hands on his hips.

"What?" I said, watching him. "We can handle this. This is nothing."

Bran scanned the room again, furrowing his brow. "I know, I know. It's just -" He paused. I was startled by the strangeness of his tone. It sounded as though he was going to share some deep-seated remorse or some troubling ache he was harboring. The sudden change in demeanor softened me to him, instantly.

"What is it?" I said.

He gave a regretful frown. "I just – I really thought I had a slow cooker up here somewhere."

I lost it.

Something about his delivery, his wary tone, the look of regret and disappointment – it all congealed into this glorious moment that caught me so off guard, I snorted. His eyes went wide and he beamed at me just as I slammed my gloved hands over my face, trying to stifle the noise. The snort just made me laugh twice as hard, and even Bran's expression grew uncharacteristically jovial.

I fought to stifle my laughter as *Good Times, Bad Times* by Led Zeppelin began to play from the speaker down the hall.

"Alright, woman. Let's dig in. It's gonna be a lot of stair climbing this morning," he said, crouching down to gather up some of the fallen crockpots. I fought not to break out in laughter again. "I hope ye stretched. Oh! And be mindful of the door. That's a fifty-thousand-pound painting just behind ye, there."

"What?!" I said, spinning around to find a gold frame peeking out from behind a pile of cardboard boxes. I turned back to him, glaring. I was sure he was pulling my leg, but when he met my gaze and shrugged, I stopped.

He wasn't kidding.

The two of us took to the project like demons, Bran demanding that I refrain from looking inside any of the boxes.

"But what if there's something valuable or meaningful - to your family maybe?"

"If it meant anything to me or my father for that matter, it wouldn't be in a water-logged cardboard box. It all goes. There's nothing that could be in any of these rooms that I want to keep."

"Says the man who pointed out a priceless painting just leaning against the wall there."

"Aye, it's not priceless. It's fifty grand. I had a feeling it might still be up here somewhere."

"What if there's more like that? You don't want to check, at least?"

He gave me an impatient look. "If ye wish to take on that task, go right ahead. There are only a few items up here that I might be concerned with, and those things wouldn't be in boxes. The boxes go in the bin."

"Alright," I said, watching him march out of the room with another armful of crap. I took another moment to pile junk into my arms to haul down the stairs. We worked on that one room for well over an hour. It was a cool day, but sweat was gathering on my upper lip before long. I made my way up and down the stairs, trying not to breathe too heavily between trips to the massive skip outside. Bran sloughed off his sweater by the third trip downstairs, the cream-colored garment turning gray and black from patches of old dust. He left it hanging over the banister in the front hall before marching back upstairs behind me, his hair growing curlier at his ears as he began to sweat as well.

Soon, I could feel the dust clinging to my wet skin, and though I attempted to wipe the sweat onto my bare arms, I could feel it congealing on my forehead and chin.

I was feeling sexy as hell.

That was sarcasm, in case you missed it.

I'm earning my shower today, I thought.

It took less than an hour and a half to completely empty the room of all junk, and on my last trip down, I returned from the skip to find Bran standing in the room alone, fighting with ancient drapes to let some light in.

When the drapes tore from the lightest tug, Bran tore them down from their rod and folded them up in his hands. The gray light of the outside world showed the room anew.

The crown molding was still intact around the ceiling and floorboards, and though the paint was peeling in the far corner from water leaking through a failing roof, the olive-brown color of the walls was now in clear view. I approached the second set of windows on the east side of the room and pulled down the old drapes there, flooding the room with light for the first time in what I was sure was a decade or more.

Bran tossed his bundle of drapes toward the door and whipped a rag out of the back pocket of his jeans, wiping it across the dusty paint.

The olive-brown sadness wasn't a symptom of time and neglect – it was the actual color of the walls.

Bran made a disinterested harrumphing sound. "Well, that's odd."

"What?" I said, moving across the room to stand beside him and stare at the wall. This felt familiar to me. Hearing Kenny grumble was a sign he'd discovered some unexpected project to add to the tally.

"Hmm," he'd say when he realized the back steps of a house had old termite damage, or *"Ah, shit,"* when he discovered black mold creeping across the drywall in some sad basement rumpus room.

"What is it?" I asked again, staring at the wall as though it might talk to me if I looked deep enough.

"Well, it seems this paint color was chosen by someone who hates the sound of laughter."

I swatted at him, trying not to snort again as I laughed.

This was almost startling.

Bran had somehow managed to make every effort, every trip down the stairs, every new discovery of yet another crock pot, one of the funniest things that had happened to me in weeks, and always – every single joke he made, he did so with a deadpan stoicism that I was convinced made it even funnier.

"Are ye quite alright?" He asked, giving me the side-eye as I doubled over again.

This wasn't just the paint that was making me laugh. This was me replaying the crockpot comment, the flagrant Monty Python voices, the raised eyebrows and side-eyes he'd given me all morning. Every time I'd laughed that morning, I'd relived every other moment of laughter, and they'd compounded now. I was helpless to it.

As a result, every time I laughed, it became harder and harder to stop.

I nodded, tears gathering in the corners of my eyes. "I think so."

"Good, then. Do ye still have your phone? That list we're keeping?"

I nodded, fighting to still my mirth.

"Good then. Would ye add white paint to the list?"

My eyebrows shot up, but I did as I was asked.

"What?" Bran said, eyeing me.

I typed the words 'boring white paint' into my phone. "What? I didn't say anything."

"No, ye didn't have to. Do ye no like white? Is there another color ye'd find better suited?"

I stopped, watching Bran for a sign. Was he kidding? Was he actually interested in my thoughts, or was he snidely waiting to snap at me again? With his deadpan humor, I honestly wasn't sure. "I think - whatever you think will be lovely."

"No," Bran said, wiping his dusty hands on his pant legs. "It was rather clear in your expression that ye had another notion. Please, share. Because if it is left up to me, every room will be white."

I cringed, involuntarily.

"See, ye did it again."

I grimaced, cursing my complete lack of poker face. "Sorry, it's not that it would be bad or anything, it's just -"

I took a moment to take in the room. It was now completely empty, its tired hardwood floors in desperate need of a sand and polish, but otherwise, a beautiful room. I shot a look at each of the four windows, the crown molding, and finally nodded. "You might consider a cream yellow. Could warm the space up in here quite a bit."

"Brilliant. Write that down," he said and marched right past me out into the hallway.

"Well, don't just agree with whatever. Do you want to try a few different -"

Bran stopped in the hallway, turning back to me with a look of forced patience. "Have I given ye the impression that I am likely to just agree with anything ye say?"

I pursed my lips. "Uh, that's a no."

"Exactly. It was a fine idea, and I agreed with your assessment. I'm not an interior designer, so if left to me, they'd all be white. Or I'd burn the whole fucking thing to the ground and be done with it, so please - feel free to make suggestions."

"Alright," I said, letting the word linger.

"And I sincerely mean that. Ye say ye've worked in contracting, if ye see a job that needs doing, please yell out so that all the cinema can hear ye."

I smirked at him.

"What?"

Yell out so that all the cinema can hear you.

I knew that quote. "Monty Python?"

It was Bran's turn to raise an eyebrow. "Ehm-" he said, furrowing his brow with an almost half-smile. "Aye, actually. Good catch."

He sauntered off to the next doorway and gave a few loud outbursts of feigned glee at the sight of yet another room filled with junk. I listened as he rummaged within the room, all while typing up *grab a metric butt load of paint swatches* into my phone. Then I marched into the miserable disarray to join him.

The afternoon went by surprisingly fast. The second room was toward the front of the house, and its windows offered far more light than the previous room. It was half empty of its many various trinkets and tired wicker baskets when Bran had the brilliant idea of opening the windows and fixing a makeshift chute to the skip below. Suddenly, we could toss armfuls of junk into the skip without having to climb up and down the stairs over and over. Once the chute was in place – a break that gave me enough time to sweep and mop the floor in the first of the rooms - we finished emptying two more rooms in the amount of time it took to clear the first.

Bran returned from a trip to the chute with dusty but empty arms and stood in the doorway as I finished sweeping up. I glanced his way just as he broke into a quick soft shoe dance move across the empty space. It was startlingly endearing.

"God, I had no idea how fucking liberating this would be."

I watched him. The stoic and almost abrasive nature had been fading away throughout the afternoon, but the smile and soft shoe dance moves were bordering on surreal.

"At this rate, we'll be done in a matter of days instead of weeks. What a miracle ye are!" He said, lunging toward me and grabbing my hand. Before I could protest, he wrapped an arm around my waist and spun me around as though the two of us were waltzing to Chopin.

I laughed as he spun me out across the dusty floor, the broom still clutched tight in my hand as a Fleetwood Mac song echoed down the hallway. I pulled out of reach before he could grab me and pull me back in. He didn't skip a beat, breaking out in a cha-cha with his arms positioned as though he still held me, and he began making up a song to go with the distant rhythm of the radio.

"*We're gonna get so much done. Jocelyn can suck my meaty bollocks.*"

I stifled a laugh, darting past him out into the hall. Bran continued his nonsensical song as I glanced down the corridor. The light on the floor had changed somehow, making it seem brighter despite the time of day.

I stood there for a moment, my brow furrowed as Bran continued crooning in the next room.

'*The ceiling in here is utterly fucked. Why dear dad were you such a cock?*'

I was too distracted to laugh at his song. Something about the hallway had changed, and it was giving me an uneasy feeling. I took a couple of steps down the hallway toward the new light, realizing as I went that another door was open – one that had been closed all morning.

One that had been jammed shut when we tried to open it.

"How'd you get it open?" I said, barely more than a whisper.

"What's that?" Bran called back.

I didn't respond. The air felt heavy all around me. I knew what that meant.

As I approached, a tiny gray shape sauntered out through the open door. My stomach lurched.

"Mr. Darcy, you little shit."

I dropped down to him, giving his cheek a rub before glancing into the open doorway.

I held my breath.

The light from the window beyond the massive pile of soiled mattresses was obscured by something new.

A figure.

There was a woman looking out the window at the gardens.

"Hello?" I said, my stomach shooting up into my throat. My mind was racing. Was this Jocelyn? A crazy homeless lady holed up in the mattress dungeon?

Or was it something else entirely – something impossible.

Oh, shit. Please god, don't be seeing what I think I'm seeing.

"Excuse me?" I said, the words felt clumsy in my mouth.

The woman didn't move.

She stood a little taller than me, slight shoulders and chestnut hair pulled up into a graceful knot atop her head. She stood with her hands held behind her back. The posture itself was unspeakably regal.

I felt small in her presence.

Shit. This has to be Jocelyn. And Bran's singing about her gargling testicles.

"Bran?" I called, glancing back down the hallway. "Hey, Bran!"

He popped his head out and seeing the expression on my face, hurried down the hall toward me, a dance rhythm still in his steps. I gestured frantically toward the open doorway, waiting for him to see her.

Bran went wide-eyed as he approached. "Well, look at ye! Ye got it open. Christ, this isn't one I'm looking forward to. God knows what sort of masochistic sex club shenanigans those foul things have seen."

I waited for him to notice the woman, but Bran simply took hold of the door, inspecting its mechanisms and knob for a reason why it was jammed that morning.

"Bran," I said, growing impatient with his sudden joyful and distracted mood.

He shot me a look, raising his eyebrows. I leaned into the doorway and pointed to the window.

The woman was gone.

Oh, god damn it. Nope. Nope, nope, nope, nope!

I hissed in shocked protest, lunging as far into the room as I could go, desperate to find the woman and make her explain herself – make her explain this feeling away.

I was halfway across mattress mountain before I realized what I was doing. I just had to prove myself wrong. I had to find an explanation for what I'd seen.

*Jesus, Cor. Chill out. Chill out. It's not what it looks like. It's not –
No, it totally is. Who am I fucking kidding? House is haunted. House
is definitely haunted. It's only a matter of time before I'm murdered in
my bed by creepy twins and a seven-foot-tall clown. I've seen this movie.
It doesn't end well!*

"Ye really want to do this one now? I was feelin rather peckish myself
-"

"There was a woman here!" I said, breaking the shelf of an old
bookcase as I tried to lean on it to get a better look at the window.
Dusty knick-knacks came crashing down onto the mattresses. I just
barely managed to catch my balance before I landed ass first on the pile
as well.

"What are ye on about?" Bran said, glowering at the mess that
tumbled onto the floor beneath my feet.

"A woman! She was right here! I swear to god -"

I stopped, staring toward the floor. The floor in front of the
window was completely covered, two mattresses jammed up against
the wall at the bottom of the pile.

Oh, come on!

The woman standing there had been taller than me, but not
monstrously so. Had she been balancing atop these mattresses, she
would've stood taller than the window frame.

I was doing what normal people do when they see the impossible –
try to disprove it.

But I wasn't a normal person. I knew damn well what I'd seen. I just
didn't want to admit I was living in a house with a ghost. Not a ghost
this brazen, anyway.

"What woman, Corinne?"

I didn't speak. I just stared at the window, fighting with my memory
to explain what I saw. There was no closet for the woman to hide in,
and the window was closed and latched. There was nowhere to escape
to except to burrow into the pile of mattresses, and that didn't look
like an easy endeavor to manage, especially in the three seconds that I
looked away. Unless she pulled a Scrooge McDuck, diving into it like
a sea of gold coins.

Why couldn't Bran have seen it, too?

I stood in the dingy red room, glancing up at the peeling satin wallpaper and the black stains across the ceiling overhead.

"Well, I'm definitely gonna need to patch the roof here, it seems. Just grand -"

He stopped mid-sentence as my foot slipped down between a mattress and something rough and metallic. I winced, feeling the textured edge slip under my jean leg and scrape across my ankle bone.

Oh, that drew blood, I thought.

Bran lunged forward, reaching out a hand to me as I fought to catch my balance.

"Careful, there. Careful. Liable to need a Tetanus shot if ye get too close to that old thing."

I gripped Bran's hand tight and lifted my wounded foot out from between the mattresses and a small wood stove. I stumbled back across the mattresses, Bran helping me onto solid ground.

I shot a side-eye toward the far wall, and the fireplace there, then I crouched to inspect my ankle.

There was blood, but nothing too troubling.

"Ye alright?" He said, crouching down to see for himself.

I pressed my pant leg over the scrapes. "*Tis but a scratch*," I said, averting my eyes from my fellow Monty Python enthusiast. When I finally stood up, he was smiling.

I felt strangely satisfied by that fact, but I was too hopped up on adrenaline and pain to comment. "Who the hell puts a wood stove in the same room as a fucking fireplace? I mean, Jesus."

Bran exhaled through his nose in a half-laugh. "Who collects a pile of mattresses eighteen deep?"

"It's not eighteen, is it?" I said, stopping to stare at the window again. The pile was something to behold, but I had other things on my damn mind. The fact that I was apparently living in a Stephen King novel was the most pressing issue.

"Did you really not see her?" I asked, finally.

Bran furrowed his brow again, splaying his arms toward me as I moved to lean on the mantle. I could feel blood running down to my shoes.

Fun times.

"See who? And are ye sure you're alright?" He said, his blue eyes wide with a mix of concern and frustration.

"Yes, yes. And I mean the woman! The lady who was standing in the window."

Bran gave me a strange look, and I half expected him to assault me with snark and snoot. Instead, he gave a pensive shrug. "No, I didn't see her."

He didn't see *her*.

Something about his tone made me certain that though Bran Douglas didn't see the woman in the window, he was wholly aware of whom I spoke.

The marrow in my bones went cold.

Patti was going to love this.

"You know that house is definitely gonna be haunted," she'd said.

That bitch.

I froze just as the room filled with a guttural burbling sound. I turned to find Bran smirking at me.

"Well, sounds like somebody's famished."

I pressed my hands to my stomach, still wary to take my eyes off the window.

"Come on, then. Let's get ye something to nosh. It is about tea time, I'd say."

I stood there a long moment, the hairs on my arms standing on end. If I left now, who knew if there'd be much light left to work by. I had so little desire to be in this wing in the dark that the thought of going hungry a while longer sounded just fine by me.

"No, no. I've got another round in me. Do you want to start another room - or this one, I guess?"

Bran stopped in the doorway, staring back at the massive pile of mattresses.

Please say no. Please say no. Please, for the love of god, say no!

"Nay, I think we've had a full day. I'm gonna have a wash and start something for tea. I have a feeling I'll need a stiff drink for this one. Perhaps we should save this one for last?"

I exhaled in relief.

Bran disappeared out into the hallway, and my whole body seized. It was less than a second, but I couldn't stand being alone in that room. I lunged out the door, scanning both directions for my partner. He was halfway down the hallway of the south wing and ducking into his room.

I followed suit, refusing to glance over my shoulder as the heaviness of the air seemed to walk with me down the hall.

Five

T HE NEXT MORNING, I found Branson already done with breakfast by the time I reached the kitchen. I popped the last can of chicken from the cupboard and spooned some onto a plate for Mr. Darcy before following Bran back upstairs.

I was feeling a little groggy.

Let's just say I didn't sleep all that well the night before.

I reached the landing of the third story and stopped. The once jammed door was still open.

I wasn't exactly looking forward to walking past that room, again. "Bran?" I called.

I know, for someone who loves ghost stories, I'm a massive chicken.

That's the thing – I don't mind a couple of footsteps or misplaced keys, but a full-blown apparition?

No, thank you.

Bran called for me to join him. He'd disappeared into another room on the brighter side of the house. I followed suit, keeping my eyes straight as I passed the mattress room - and from the woman that wasn't there.

This room wasn't half as bad as the previous two we'd worked on. It had a few piles of old newspapers, some crumbling cardboard boxes, their contents looking like deteriorating sweaters – or *jumpers*, as Bran quickly corrected me. There were a few pieces of trash and empty soup cans, but the main filler of the room was a set of dressers and a tall, splintering chifferobe that stood a foot taller than Bran.

I took a deep breath, almost regretting my decision to help Branson reclaim the third floor. "Well, if we toss all the junk out the chute, then get that freakin chifferobe out of here, it might be a pretty quick job."

"Pardon? Get what now?"

I stared at him. "The Chifferobe?"

He snorted. "I'm sorry, I didn't realize I was living in a Harper Lee novel."

My eyes went wide, and I pointed at him. "You just earned massive points for knowing that!"

"Did I?" He said, giving me a double eyebrow raise. Still, he was fighting a half-smile. Clearly, he appreciated being appreciated.

We made quick work of the small stuff, making repeat runs to the neighboring room where the chute was still clamped to the windowsill. The bundles of old clothes and dusty papers slid down into the skip with a satisfying *swoosh*, clamoring atop the mass of crock pots and forgotten whatnots. We made our way back and forth until the room was almost clear, me making a deliberate effort to never be in the hallway alone for fear the woman might peek out from Mattress Mountain and glare at me with bloody eyeballs or some other fresh horror. On our final trip, we both sighed at the sight of that massive, rickety old thing – the chifferobe.

I thought it might've been quite nice in its heyday.

"Alright, let's get this bastard out of here," he said.

I nodded, stepping up to the beast. "Sounds good."

Bran saddled up beside me, both of us reaching up to the upper sides of the chifferobe to pull it away from the wall. It made a terrible grinding noise as it moved across the hardwood, a distant skittering of dust and god knows what vibrating about within.

"I have a wicked craving for a kebab," he said, coming around to the front of the piece. I joined him there, holding my hands against the upper cupboard doors as Bran grabbed the top and leveraged it forward over us.

I felt a stretch of wood go soft under my palm and moved my hand further to the side. "Yeah? I don't think I've ever had one."

"What?! We must remedy this! Chicken kebab with garlic and chili sauce? That'll change your bloody life -"

The wood crumbled under my fingers and my hand went straight through the cupboard doors just as the side splintered in Bran's hand. It was crumbling to the touch. The chifferobe lurched forward over our heads, my hands disappearing through the doors as it poured dust and debris over us, raining down on us like an ash cloud on Pompeii. One door completely fell off the front as the other was held in place solely by my body being in the way. I closed my eyes tight against the rain of debris as Bran fought to heave the beast off of us. I pulled my arms from within, the wood thankfully too soft to scratch the skin. Still, I felt a prickling sensation across my arms. The chifferobe straightened, its hind legs slamming back down onto the floor with a thud as I ran a hand over my arm to brush off the dust.

The dust fought back.

I startled, Bran brushing his hands over his hair as I focused on the brown flecks across my forearms. They were moving.

"No – oooh my god!!" I screamed, the pitch high enough to shatter crystal. I was covered in tiny brown bugs. I flailed violently, feeling the tiny legs scurrying over my skin as I swatted and scraped them off.

"What the hell are you on – Oh fuck!" Bran began high-stepping across the floor. I almost didn't want to look down.

The floor was moving. Hundreds, if not thousands of these little beetle-like things were crawling about, freshly loosed from their chifferobe prison. They'd been eating the wood from the inside. I screamed again, lunging across the room for the bedroom door, still feeling the itch of movement on my skin. Bran joined me in the hallway, his hands wildly swatting at his hair. I shuddered and shook, shaking my own head to loose whatever beetles were still scurrying through my hair, prying the hair-tie free to let my hair hang loose. I could feel tiny things in the strands and I screamed anew.

"Oh god! I feel them fucking everywhere!" I cried, my tone coming through in a mad whine. I felt something prickling across my cleavage and instantly tore up the tank top, prying it over my head until I was standing there in my bra, throwing the shirt onto the floor then dancing around it like some tribal rite of exorcism. The pants came off right after.

"Come on!"

Bran grabbed my arm and pulled me down the hall. I couldn't see where we were going as I was now struggling with my hair and the sheer notion that there might be a million bugs crawling in it. An instant later, I could hear the water of the shower running.

"They're all over me!"

I lunged under the spray first, dragging my nails over my skin like some horror movie scene. Bran's large frame filled the small shower, gently pushing me aside as he set his head directly under the spray, digging his fingers through his hair. I could see tiny brown specks swirling in the water at our feet, and again I started whining with disgust.

"I hate you! I hate you so much," I cried, letting the words milk every ounce of childish protest I could muster.

"Hold still," Bran said, turning me toward the spray of water. I felt the warmth of it flatten my hair to the top of my head, then felt fingertips moving against me with deft precision.

"Oh god, they're in my hair. Are they in my hair?!"

"Hold still, woman! Hold still."

His fingers moved again, then he buried them in my hair, letting them run over my scalp. Had I not been utterly certain there were beetles crawling into my brain at that moment, it might've felt nice.

He gathered up the mass of my hair into a ponytail and ran his fingers down the length of it, careful not to pull. I joined the pursuit, running my own fingers up along my scalp. I didn't feel any more little flecks or bits in my hair, but I was no less sure that they were chewing their way into my skull.

Is *this* how I lose my scalp?

"You're alright. I don't see anything," he said. Then he moved me out of the shower stream and ducked his own head beneath. A moment later, he was crouching before me, demanding I return the favor.

"What are we, fucking gorillas? This is so awful!"

"I know, I know. Just do it. The sooner it's done, the sooner we can burn the fucking house to the ground!"

Despite the anguish and disgust I felt, I had to stifle a laugh.

I found his hair free of anything crawly, and I told him so. He stood up then to his full height, and I froze. His bare chest was inches from my nose, and his wet skin was grazing against my own.

Oh shit. How did I end up in my fucking underwear?

I pressed my arms across my chest, a new painful awareness of myself. Bran glanced down at me with a cocked eyebrow, then without a word, reached his hand down toward my chest.

I froze.

Sweet Jesus, was he about to put the moves on me? This posh asshole was going to use bugs as an excuse to cop a feel? I'll shank him!

Despite my racing thoughts, I didn't move to stop him.

Bran pinched a tiny brown fleck from the fabric of my bra and let it run off his fingers into the drain. I broke out in a whole new round of flailing.

It took no less than twenty minutes for us both to return to our rooms, dry off, convince ourselves we weren't now rocking thunder-scabies, and get redressed.

When I met Bran in the hallway again, he was standing just outside the chifferobe room, the door now firmly shut.

"So, that room is gonna need a bug bomb and an industrial-strength hoovering. And I haven't the tools. Ye up for a trip into town?"

I swallowed, still scratching at my arms at random intervals, but agreed. There was nothing more I wanted than to get out of that fucking house.

Bran sauntered back down the hall, cooing to Mr. Darcy softly as he passed. The good kitty had followed me from my room.

In the instant he was gone, I felt my solitude in that hallway like an anchor chained to my feet. I turned for the stairs, desperate to flee the heaviness. In the wake of the beetle assault, I'd almost forgotten to be spooked.

Almost. And I was quickly reminded the second Bran walked away.

Bran was already halfway down the stairs, and I power walked down the hallway after him, keeping my eyes straight for fear that if I turned back, the woman would be standing in the doorway, watching me.

I found Bran in the kitchen, the pantry doors flung wide open as he stared at the bare shelves within. I moved to join him, fighting the urge to glance back at the kitchen door.

Bran pulled down a dusty can of oxtail soup, an even dustier can of baked beans, and a sticky jar of strawberry jam that had cracked years prior.

"We ate the last of what's in the fridge, didn't we?" He said, his nose crinkling as he set the old cans aside.

I nodded, pulling down a box of cereal.

"Ye might not want to touch that. I'll bet the house there's bugs in it."

I tossed the box back onto the shelf and started scratching my arms anew. I touched a finger to the pantry shelf to see the gray layer of time wipe aside, leaving the dark sheen of the stained wood beneath.

Bran turned around, leaning against the pantry shelves as he crossed his arms in pensive disappointment.

"What?" I said, pulling down the last can on the shelf - another dusty Oxtail soup.

"If we had a slow cooker, we might not have this problem."

I swatted at him. "It's not funny. You said we were going to the shops! Don't toy with me. This has not been an easy morning, damn it."

He smiled and nodded, surging across the kitchen toward a sweatshirt that he'd left over the back of his chair from breakfast. "I'm just having a look to see what we need. Come on, then. We'll head down the shops for some nibbles and supplies. Might be able to start painting by week's end! Do you have any idea how amazing that is?"

He was already across the kitchen and out the front door before he'd finished his sentence, me scurrying to grab my own sweater and follow behind.

I had no desire to be in that house alone.

Not anymore.

The visit to the shops went, quickly. I grabbed cereal, milk, bread, jam, and peanut butter – as many essentials that could tide me over in a pinch – that I could afford, of course.

I admit I spent an embarrassing amount of money on Cadbury chocolates.

The rest was spent on Mr. Darcy.

Bran went culinary, buying steak, a chicken roaster, red potatoes, and parsnips. He even snagged a bottle of red wine and a six-pack of Newcastle, assuring me that he'd find an excuse to pop the cork.

He then grabbed a package of Jaffa Cakes, tossing them into the cart.

The building supply store consisted of Bran slamming a list down on the information counter while I perused paint swatches. With Bran's order placed and my first paint mixed, we marched out with little more than a gallon of paint, a stretch of copper pipe, a handful of paint swatches, and bug napalm.

The rest of Bran's order would be delivered the next day.

It was strange seeing him out in the world. The way he spoke to people - interacted with clerks and strangers in the parking lot – he was polite, soft-spoken, even respectful.

He was nothing like he'd been when I met him.

I wasn't sure whether to feel special or cursed.

With that. we were off again, Bran in a hurry to get back to the house and to work.

When he was behind the wheel of his car, he was focused and almost frantic, glancing at his phone for music in between each song, nearly clipping road signs and fence posts as we blew down old farming roads.

On the way to the shops, I yelled at him until my throat hurt, almost completely missing the handmade sign on the side of the road in my frantic efforts to not die. My protests only drew his laughter. On the way back home, I demanded he give me his phone before agreeing to get back in the car. I'd half expected him to drive off and leave me in the lot outside Tesco, but he relented, letting me take control of the music for the trip home.

We were fifteen minutes into our half-hour drive when I spotted the same sign on a rather overgrown stretch of road.

"What did that sign say?" I asked as we careened down the winding roads of the Highlands.

"Haven't the faintest. Some church thing or what not, I imagine? Hold on."

Bran leaned into a curve in the road, me lurching toward my door as I held on for dear life.

"Could you drive a bit less -"

"Come now, if ye want to get anywhere up here, ye have to learn to speed."

I'd witnessed this very theory when in the back seat of a cab upon first arriving, and I was *not* a fan. Even the cabby was happily barreling down sheep-lined single-lane roads and breezing through quaint little villages. Still, this was my first car ride in days and my stomach was empty. If I got nauseous, there was nothing to come up.

"Please! For the love of god. I get car sick very easily."

Bran shot me a sideways glare. "Ye survived the trip here, ye'll survive the trip back," he said, watching me. Apparently, my face spoke volumes. "Christ, ye're serious?" He huffed, slamming on the brakes as we came up to a small stone church on the left side. I leaned out of my window to get some air, and the beautiful structure caught my full attention as Bran slowed down to let an elderly couple mosey across the street.

"Ah, lovely. What are these codgers doin out? It's not Sunday."

I scanned the cars outside the ancient church, gaggles of happy faces heading in on a late Saturday morning. I turned back to the sign along the roadside, straining to read the somehow familiar words.

"Pull in here!"

Bran glared at me, then up at the church. "There's no place I'd rather avoid more."

"Oh man, we have to stop," I said, unbuckling my seatbelt.

"What? Feeling reborn then, are ye?"

I pointed to the parking lot with a stern glare. "I have to see this. Come on, it will only take a minute."

Bran furrowed his brow as the road ahead cleared of elderly meanderings, and surprisingly, he did as I asked.

I was nearly speechless.

He was halfway into a spot when he groaned his further disapproval. "This better be something spectacular."

"Oh, I'm pretty sure it's going to be awful!" I said, clamoring to get out of the car.

I marched around Bran's little roadster, stepping aside to let the same elderly couple go ahead of me toward the church. The man and woman were both hunched just so, the husband a few inches taller as he led his slow-moving wife, her hair neatly tucked under a handkerchief.

"Don't mind us, lass. Ye go on ahead," the older gentleman said, offering a tip of his hat.

I smiled. "No worries. I'm in no rush."

The church was stone-faced and ancient, surrounded by gnarled trees that looked nearly as old as the church, and there were crumbling graves tucked just beyond. There was a collection of ruins in the graveyard, signs of a former out-building that crumbled centuries earlier.

Centuries.

The notion of something that old stopped me in my tracks. This church was likely as old as Cavendish's oldest sections.

And people were still coming here to worship.

Or in the case of this Saturday debacle, gathering for a church potluck.

The smell was undeniable – fish. Fish and fry and spices I didn't quite recognize, but beneath it all, that steamy, heady, misty smell of boiling fish.

"New England Clam Bake?" Bran said, coming up to my shoulder to read the sign, raising his eyebrows at the elderly couple that hobbled along ahead. "What, pray tell, have ye gotten me into?"

I hopped in place a moment, unable to contain my excitement. Even I found it surprising how grateful I was for this little slice of home.

"I swear, I must control the universe with my mind or something because the fact this is in Scotland is absurd."

"That it is," he said, not even bothering to feign interest.

I was inching closer to the door and could just catch sight of a teenage boy taking tickets and pound notes and coins in exchange for entry to the soiree. I began rummaging into my pocket for what I knew to be one of the last pounds to my name.

And I was going to spend it on god-awful shellfish stew.

Living the god damn dream.

I was almost dancing in a strange giddy excitement. "Where I come from, these pop up every weekend during the warmer months."

Bran looked to be barely tolerating me. "Well, what is it, then?"

I waved Bran away as he pulled a few pounds from his pocket, grumbling the whole time.

"It's a big sorta barbecue thing, kinda. They bring in all sorts of seafood and lobster and clams and everything – then they boil it all in a big pot and serve it with everything you can think of. Potato salad, pasta salad, cornbread. God, I can't even fathom how such a thing is happening in -" I glanced up at the church as though I might find a sign declaring the name of the tiny town.

"Kinvale," Bran said, startling me by both his knowledge and the fact that he was actually listening. "So ye've brought me to eat boiled dinner. How novel."

"No! You don't have to eat anything. I just – I'm starving and – I'm kinda homesick."

Bran followed along behind, rummaging into his pocket to pull out a ten-pound note, handing it to the woman waiting at the table before I could pay for myself. He then marched past me toward the long, buffet-style table, grabbing up a paper plate and bundle of plastic cutlery.

"Oh, this is palatial and sad in equal measure," he said, poking tongs into a silver dish of beige gunge.

"It's a church pot luck, don't be a snob!" I hissed, taking a scoop of potato salad. The congealed mass made a 'splurching' sound as it splattered down on my plate.

I couldn't wait to eat it!

I fought the urge to laugh when Bran's eyebrows shot up in feigned excitement. I moved down the line, pretending to ignore him as he daintily took a scoop of pasta salad.

"Well, good morning to ye, lovely. I've no seen ye in the church before. Are ye new to the area, then?"

I startled around to find the older woman from the ticket table hovering by the deviled eggs, a nametag stuck to her generous bosom that read *Hilda*. "Oh, I am, yes."

"Have ye family in the church, then?"

"Oh, um – no. I'm -"

"Oh, are ye here with this lovely thing -" The woman trailed off, staring at Bran for a moment. The woman blanched. "Wee Branson? No, it can't be! My lord, ye've grown, haven't ye?"

Bran turned away, pretending to suddenly be enchanted by the potato salad.

"Look at ye, now!" Hilda went on, pushing me aside to get a bit closer to Bran. "Ye didn't go hungry, I see."

Bran was clearly not returning the excitement.

"Mary! Mary, will ye come here, love. I want ye to meet someone."

Another middle-aged woman made her way past a few gray-haired gentlemen in vests and dress shirts to join us by the table.

The air around Bran was almost electric.

"Ye'll never guess who this is!" Hilda said.

"Because that's not who I am," Bran said, his lips losing their color as he pursed them together.

Mary gave Bran an appraising look. "No, I don't imagine I would."

My eyebrows shot up at the woman's accent. She was American.

"Branson Douglas! Douglas? Of Cavendish House?"

"Oh, aye," Mary said, and the 'aye' brought a smile to my face. As American as Mary was, she clearly spent a good amount of time in Scotland. "Are you going to fix the place up, then?"

Bran quickly shook his head, shrugging his shoulders up as he tried, unsuccessfully to hide his face from the older woman. "I'm sorry, Madam. Ye must have me mistaken for someone -"

Hilda swatted at him. "Oh, what rubbish! I'd recognize one of the Douglas lads any day, given all the trouble the two of ye got into. Your poor father."

"Still not me," he said, growing increasingly terse. His body had stiffened at this comment, but he turned away like some shady character looking to rob a convenient store.

I watched Bran for a moment. He'd made comment about the church outside; he certainly knew the place, and Hilda certainly knew him.

Why was he trying to hide who he was?

"He's staying with me, actually," I said, shooting Bran a sideways glance. I quickly made a grand gesture of snagging up one of the deviled eggs. Hilda's face lit up, instantly. It was clear the deviled eggs were her offering to the affair.

"Is that so? And who might ye be then? I'm quite sure I'd remember your face," she said, giving me a meaningful look.

"I've only just arrived. I've been hired on to look after Cavendish House."

"Have ye now? Quite the undertaking, isn't it? For just a wee thing as yerself?"

I fought the urge to go off on a tirade about my qualifications and capabilities. I thought better of it. I'd learned to choose my battles when it came to people making sexist assumptions about my skillset.

And Bran had already worn me out in that department days earlier.

I swallowed the venom and smiled, gesturing to Bran. "Well, I have Floyd here to help, so I'm not alone."

"Floyd?"

The word came in stereo as Bran, Mary, and Hilda all repeated me.

I just gave Bran a gentle elbow nudge. "Yes, ma'am. He's been a life saver. I don't know what little old me would do without a big, strong man around to pick up heavy things and make decisions."

Damn it, Corinne. I thought you weren't going to start shit?

Hilda stared at me for a moment. "Well, that's good then, aye?"

Despite scolding myself, I noticed a smirk on Mary's face.

Bran offered a half shrug. "I'd hope so."

Hilda straightened as she redirected the conversation. "Och, I'm so glad. Was a right crime what your father – what the previous owner did to the place. We've all secretly prayed one of the Douglas sons might return and wrest the place from his clutches before it crumbled to the ground. There are those who've been trying to take the place from him for years, it was in such a state -"

Hilda spoke with wide eyes, leaning in to me as though she might share some conspiracy. I found that strange, given the only person in the room who might take issue with her gossip was the man to whom she was prattling.

Whether she called him Floyd or not, I was sure Hilda knew damn well who Bran was.

Bran leaned over the table to grab a napkin, making a point to move down the table just a step. "Aye, well, death wrested it from him before it came to that. Not for lack of trying though, I'm sure," Bran said.

Hilda stared at him again, as though waiting for him to meet her challenge and crack in its wake.

He didn't, and instead, Bran turned away from the woman, heading further down the buffet. I tried to free myself from the conversation as well, stuffing a bite of unfortunate pasta salad into my mouth. Hilda continued regaling me with disdain for the state of Cavendish House while also fawning over the poor, feeble old man, abandoned by his sons to live in squalor all those years.

I glanced down the table, watching Bran with a sudden heaviness as he poked a spoon into a massive crock pot of baked beans. The heaviness evaporated as he caught my eye and gestured to the crock pot with a look of wild wonder.

I choked with laughter, spewing potato salad across the front of Hilda's silk blouse. I clapped a hand over my mouth as Bran stifled his own laughter down the table.

"I'm so sorry!" I said, scrambling for paper napkins to offer the woman. I could feel Hilda's side-eye like a sunburn.

"That's fine. Just fine. I'll go clean this up. Ye enjoy yourself," Hilda said, turning away, her face red.

I shot a glare down the table at Bran as his face turned the same shade.

"Where are you from, then, Miss?"

I startled to find Mary still standing at my side, a half-smile on her own face. "Sorry, Corinne," I said, "And I'm from Acton. Massachusetts?"

Mary smiled, offering a handshake. "I'm from Newburyport."

My eyes went wide. I took note that Mary had a damn strong handshake. I decided I liked her, instantly. "Oh, no way! How did you end up here?"

Mary smiled, glancing over her shoulder at the gray-haired man in the brown vest. "My daughter came over to attend college in Aberdeen, and when I came to visit, I met her lovely history professor. That, as they say, was that."

My heart felt light, suddenly. "Oh wow. What a – that's such a nice story. Good for you."

The history professor gave a wave, then turned back to his conversation with another parishioner. He was about as dashing as a ham sandwich, but Mary's smile when she looked at him was enough to melt my heart.

"So, is this Clambake your doing, then?" I asked.

Mary nodded. "It is. It's such a small community, anything to get the older lot out of the house is worth it, these days. Not sure it's going over all that well, though."

I glanced back to the small reception room. There were two dozen round tables, each offering eight or so seats, but a good number of the tables were empty or had only a couple people at them. In the far corners of the room, a crowd of young children ran in and out of the door, and a couple older kids – in their teens, it looked – were leaning against an old stage. They all looked like they fashioned themselves from a James Dean flick.

I took a moment, imagining the lives that had seen the inside of this church – the weddings and christenings and clambakes. I imagined myself in that stone space, a man in full kilt and jacket standing at my side as some Scottish reverend officiated my wedding to a rakish Scotsman – maybe named Christopher.

Oh my god, Cor. Shut up. Stop it.

"Am I right to think you might not be leaving, either?" Mary said, smiling.

I shook my head, loosing the silly notion of Christopher from my mind as I followed her gaze over to Bran. He now stood towering over a plate of decadent-looking brownies, glancing around as though he planned to steal the whole thing.

I shook my head. "Oh, no. No. Nothing like that. He's just helping me with the house. I'm done at the end of next month."

Mary's eyebrows rose and fell in a subtle gesture before she gave my hand a pat. "Well, enjoy. It's as close to home as I could get it up here in the middle of nowhere."

I smiled at the woman. "Oh, it's amazing. This absolutely made my day."

Before I could regale my host with clambake commentary, Mary leaned in, glancing back at her husband as though afraid he might be spying on them. "If you're caretaker up at the old place, is there any chance you might let an old man come snoop around when you've got the place to sorts?"

"What's that?"

Mary gestured to her husband who was still fully ensconced in conversation and what looked like a tray of tiny hot dogs on toothpicks. "He's been absolutely in love with the history of the place since we met. He grew up in Kinvale, but never had the chance to see the house. Well, save for late-night drive-bys, if you can imagine."

I glanced toward Bran, then back at Mary. "I don't know, it's not really my place to -"

"Of course. Of course. It was a shot in the dark, really. Just looking for ways to cheer him up. Retirement hasn't been as blissful as he imagined."

"I mean – I don't know, but I could ask?" I shot a look toward Bran.

Mary spotted it and gave a half-smile as she feigned ignorance.

"I'll see what I can do," I said.

Mary reached for my hand and squeezed it. "You're a peach, if you can manage it. Bruce tells me there are banisters in the front hall that are older than any other structure in the whole of Kinvale."

I fought the urge to cringe. "Oh, he's not lying. I've encountered those banisters myself."

I was halfway through my sentence when a high-pitched wail drew our attention. Mary made her way to the kitchen to join a flustered Hilda, who was flitting her damp silk shirt as she waved from across the counter.

"Here. I've brought ye a brownie."

I turned to find Bran standing beside me, his plate devoid of food. He set the massive confection on my plate, then licked the crumbs from his fingertips.

"That was awkward as hell," I said, glaring up at him.

"Was it? I had no idea."

I shook my head, watching him nonchalantly dig into a piece of brownie. "Are you a fugitive or something? Seriously."

He rolled his eyes. "No, I just don't wanna be interrogated about my bloody father, thank ye very much."

I glanced around the room, catching the teenagers in a bout of laughter by the stage as I made eye contact with them. I turned back to Branson, watching his expression as he took a second bite.

I sighed. "Sure, whatever you say – and come on, you have to eat something other than freakin brownies. At least try the stew?"

Bran crinkled his nose as he looked down the table toward the massive pile of seafood and veggies. "Must I?"

"Yes. You paid to come in, you must eat."

"Can I just eat some of those lovely baked beans? I recognize those at the very least. I might be rather unfortunate company for the rest of the afternoon, but biological warfare seems a fair trade for making me take part in this rubbish."

How did he do that? He somehow managed to be both endearing and infuriating in the stretch of mere seconds.

I chuckled, shaking my head. "No, you're at least eating some manner of fish. Get over here, you snooty bastard."

"Snooty?" He said, trudging along behind me.

The two of us grabbed food and parked at an empty table together. Bran did little more than poke at his plate, though he did scarf down two massive brownies.

I was on my second helping of potato salad before Bran spoke again. "You know, it is rather soon to be homesick, is it not?"

I swallowed hard, startled by the question. "Excuse me?" I said, the words thick with potato salad.

"This *do*, here. Ye said ye wanted to come because ye were homesick, but ye've only just arrived, what - four days ago?"

I shook my head, searching for something to say. "Well, yes and no. I only just arrived here, but I've actually been away from home for six months, now."

Bran's eyebrows shot up, and he poked his fork at a piece of fish, lifting it to his crinkled nose before taking a bite. "Where have ye been if not home?"

I shrugged.

Anywhere that would have me.

I didn't say that out loud, though.

"All over the place. London for a long while. That's where I started. Then Bath. Did a quick nightmare stint in Birmingham, then I came here."

Bran glared at me. "Ye live quite the high life for someone trapped and penniless in my house."

I rolled my eyes. "I've been housesitting. That's what I do – how I get to go all these places. I go where the jobs are, I stay and take care of people's pets or watch over their house, and they pay me to live there."

"Really?"

"Yes. And before you say anything, I'll have you know it's a very economical way to travel. I can say I've lived all over the world -"

"In other people's houses."

"Yes."

He nodded, jamming a bite of cornbread into his mouth. "Ye're a *professional* squatter."

I wanted to kick him under the table.

I didn't speak, turning my attention back to my food as the gaggle of teen boys continued snickering by the stage.

"A professional squatter," he said again, letting the words drift off as he broke off a piece of my brownie and popped it in his mouth.

From endearing to douche - a matter of seconds.

"You're a dick."

He gave me an eyebrow wiggle, as though agreeing with my assessment. That was all the more infuriating.

I wasn't about to tell him why I was hiding out in other people's houses. My own sad life was none of his business.

87

We finished eating and Bran snatched up our plates to clear the table. I took a moment to look at the gathered crowd. The notion of a New England anything in the glens of Scotland was beyond strange, but enough of a novelty to bring people in it seemed.

All because the woman from the North Shore found a Scottish Professor and never left.

Lucky bitch.

I thought about a certain Scottish doctor friend and smiled. Maybe Mary was right; maybe I *would* never leave.

Good god, Cor. One morning masturbation session and you're picking out wedding songs. Shut the hell up!

I stood just outside the great hall, my belly full of 'Clambake,' and scanned the crowd of parishioners. Bran appeared at my left shoulder, blowing air through pursed lips after his trip to the loo.

"Bloody hell. Should call this do, 'Shit yerself for Jesus.'"

I convulsed in a strange amalgam of laughter and then sudden terror as the contents of my belly shifted and burbled. I'd been starving, but I'd clearly eaten too much.

That cornbread was expanding at Mach two.

Bran shot me a side-eye. "Better run to the toilet now, or ye'll never make it!"

I laughed, swatting at him, and marched out into the parking lot.

I'm allowed a little gas after such a feast, damn it.

Bran raised an eyebrow at me, clearly unwilling to let go of the joke yet. "Ye sure? This decision could lead to lifelong regret."

I slammed my car door, glaring at him through the windshield. "Yes, I'm fine. Let's go."

Bran gave a shrug and tossed his keys in the air, catching them behind his back to show off for the gathered teenagers, then he opened the driver's side door and climbed in.

The drive home was rather uneventful, Bran no longer careening with the same abandon as before.

I found myself watching him now. The way his knuckles lightened with every turn, or the way he shifted gears – a calm confidence that didn't need to be observed to be impressive. He shot me a sideways look, once, but didn't say anything.

He rolled his window down a crack as we drew closer to home, blowing out air through pursed lips as though frustrated by something.

We were coming up over the last hill before the turn to Cavendish House when a strange burbling sound filled the small car.

I turned toward Bran, eyebrows raised. He pressed a hand to his belly and closed his eyes.

Oh no, I thought.

"Regretting that 'Shit yerself for Jesus' comment?" I said.

"Don't remind me."

I grinned. "Serves you right! Professional squatter, my ass."

"Don't mention asses, right now."

I stifled a laugh but straightened in my seat. He was a massive pain in my ass, but I hated the thought of him feeling unwell.

All because I wanted something to remind me of home – without actually having to go home.

Bran groaned and shifted in his seat as the car picked up speed. He was growing fonder of the gas pedal with each passing second, but I didn't complain this time.

We careened around the last corner into the driveway of the house, Bran gassing it yet again as he barreled down the long windy drive of the estate. The trees grew sparse as we approached, and I caught view of the eaves of the house in the distance.

"Almost there," I said, as though reassuring a child.

Bran groaned. "Sweet Christ, I call use of all the plumbing when we –"

The car squealed to a stop, gravel kicking up under the wheels as the trees parted and betrayed view of the front of the house.

There was an unfamiliar car parked at the bottom of the front steps.

"Fer fuck's sake," Bran growled, unlatching his seatbelt and launching himself into the tiny backseat. I leaned hard to the left, dodging his flailing limbs as his feet sailed past me.

Six

M Y HEART SHOT INTO my throat. "What the hell are you doing, you lunatic!?"

He shimmied down into the backseat, shooting me a pleading look from the floor of the car. "Car's idle. Slide over to the driver's seat and pull the rest of the way up. If she asks anything about me, pretend I left the night ye arrived."

"What? Whose car is it?"

Bran smacked the back of the driver's seat to declare his urgency. I glared at him like I would a child mid-tantrum. Still, he padded the back of the seat again, his eyes growing wider with near desperation. I tried to make further query, but Bran simply shimmied further down between the seats, pulling an old box of books forward in the seat to cover his face from view. I had to haul my legs over my head, nearly breaking off the rearview mirror as I fan-kicked across the front seat.

Finally, I was in the driver's seat. I tried desperately to remain calm, but my stomach was lodged in my throat now.

Who the hell was in the house, and if Bran was afraid of them, shouldn't I be, too?

And all of that chaos aside, I'd never so much as sat in the driver's seat, let alone driven a car in the U.K. Still, I pressed a foot on the clutch, shifting into first as I gripped the steering wheel for dear life, hoping something steady to hold on to might still my nerves. The car lunged forward, then jerked and stopped, the engine going silent.

All hopes for calm were smashed, as Bran exploded in disdain behind me. "Good god, are ye tryin to kill me?"

I started up the car again and glanced back to find Bran clutching his stomach just as the car filled with that same rumbling sound of sickness.

"Christ, what did ye make me eat?" He said in a barely audible whine.

I gave the car the gas again, and it took off like a shot only to jerk to a halt just before reaching the other car.

He loosed a whirlwind of fury, smacking the back of the driver's seat. "What have I done in this life to slight ye? Seriously, woman!"

"I'm sorry!" I hissed, my eyes darting toward the front door. "I've never driven a standard left-handed like this! I'm doing my -"

I glanced back at him and he waved frantically at me just as his stomach burbled.

"Don't look at me! Pretend I'm no here – oh dear god, I think I'm gonna shit myself."

The car bucked forward one more time, and I could barely stifle my laughter as Bran moaned behind me. I apologized as I fought to nonchalantly take off my seat belt.

"Just go inside and get her out of here as fast as ye fucking can!"

"Who?!"

"JOCELYN!"

My stomach turned. Jocelyn was not someone I wanted to meet just now. "Jocelyn?!"

"Aye, get her out of here. If she asks after me, feign bloody ignorance!"

"Why don't you want to see her -?"

"Because she's bloody awful! For the love of god!"

"What am I supposed to say about the massive dumpster? She's going to know I didn't -"

"Just say it was here when ye arrived! Jesus, woman! Have ye no mercy in your fuckin heart? Go! Go now – oh god."

The burbling sound took on a sinister tone, and I lunged out of the driver's side door and took off up the stairs. I was happy to be away from whatever was about to happen in the backseat of Bran's Audi.

I stopped dead at the doors as a thought struck me.

Look natural, Cor. He wants you to look natural.

Natural wouldn't leave the groceries in the car to fester.

I turned back, rounding the car to the passenger's side.

"What the fuck are ye doin?" Bran hissed when I opened the door.

"Calm down, you ass! Let me get the freakin bags so I look normal."

"Good luck with that!" He said, the spite instantly punished with another growl of his belly. He exhaled through pursed lips and made a weeping sound. I wanted to unleash my frustration on him, but sympathy won. I snatched up the handles of the grocery bags and heaved them up before slamming the back door of the car with as little regalia as possible.

Come on, Cor. You're just coming home from the shops in your bitchin rental car. You're not a weirdo with a man hidden in your backseat, who may or may not be shitting himself as we speak. You have every right to be here. Chill out. Be cool. Be so cool.

I stopped in the front hall, listening. There were voices in the house somewhere upstairs.

I shifted the bags from one hand to another, letting the car keys jingle as I did. "Hello?"

Did that sound innocent? It sounded pretty innocent, right? God, why is this my life?

"Yes, is that you, Corinne?"

It was a woman's voice, but there was a second deeper voice speaking, though I couldn't make out the words.

"Uh, yes? Who's up there?"

A figure appeared on the landing above and set her hand on the railing, her bangle bracelets clinking against the old wood. "Oh good, there you are. So nice to finally meet you."

My eyebrows shot up. "Jocelyn?"

I fought every cell in my being not to say her name like I was being accosted by a bad smell. Not sure I succeeded.

"Of course, who else would it be?" She said, the deeper voice calling something to her from somewhere further into the house. For a split second, my heart shot into my throat. What if Chris was here with her? They were friends, weren't they? He is the one who got me this job – he could be here.

Couldn't he?

"Where is Branson?" She said.

I furrowed my brow, giving a head swivel of disdain. I was instantly embarrassed by my own ham acting.

Jesus, what are you, auditioning for a Broadway production of Clueless? Too much, Corinne! Rein that shit in!

"He's gone. He's been gone since that first night."

"Has he?" Jocelyn said, glancing back down the hall toward the male voice in the distance. She rounded the corner of the landing and came down the stairs. "Because there looks to be a lot of work going on here."

Jocelyn Read was a tall, statuesque creature, long, maple brown hair swaying over her bare arms as she sauntered down the stairs in a sleeveless blue dress, fitted to hug every curve of her figure. Her heels were a matching blue, and easily three inches high, making Jocelyn six feet tall as she walked up to meet me. I wasn't a short woman by any means, but I still found myself looking up to meet Jocelyn's hazel stare.

She seemed to be making a deliberate effort to show me the inside of her nostrils.

My father would hate her.

I swallowed. "Nothing too major. Just doing as you asked. Clearing out some of the junk, trying to make getting around a little easier."

Jocelyn crossed her arms, her bracelets clattering with every movement. "You expect me to believe you're doing this all by yourself?"

I tilted my head to the side just so, but I stopped before I could spew words. The vitriol I wanted to shower this woman with was intense. "Well, it's just junk removal at this point."

"What about the bedroom doors? There were several off the hinges, now they're back in place. Who did that?"

I pursed my lips. Those were all me, and she spoke of them like I'd invented cold fusion. "I did. Have I done something I wasn't supposed to? You did tell me to fix the place up enough to have the inspectors in."

"Yes, and you took it upon yourself to have a skip delivered?"

I turned for the kitchen door, suddenly fuming. I wanted to punch this broad. I marched off, tossing my response over my shoulder.

Two could play this game, bitch.

"I didn't. It was here when I arrived," I said, setting the bags of groceries onto the kitchen island with a thump. I wouldn't have Jocelyn Read lording over me – not today, not ever.

I opened the first bag to pull out a package of sliced turkey only to feel a sudden tightness in my bowels.

I froze.

Oh, shit. Literally.

"You know, if Bran has been around, I'm not going to hold you responsible. He's the one breaking the law, not you."

I exhaled through my nose, waiting for the cramp to pass. "I'm not concerned about breaking the – wait. What?"

"If Branson Douglas is on the property, he is breaking the law. Trespassing. Let alone if he's going around 'fixing the place up.'"

I stood there for a long moment, fuming. "Why is he trespassing if it's his house?"

"Did he tell you that?"

I shook my head, but she continued before I could answer.

"Arthur Douglas hasn't been in contact with either of his children for two decades. The courts will decide whether the house passes to them or sells. Until then, he's no more right to be on the premises than a stranger off the street."

I stood there silent, fighting the urge to glance toward the kitchen windows. Was Bran close by? Could he hear this conversation? Would he hear if I threw him under the bus for being the lying sack of shit he was?

Yet, I didn't say a word.

Jocelyn stared at me a long moment, then marched across the kitchen to look out the window. "Where'd you get the car?"

"It's a – phew," I paused, blowing air out through pursed lips. My stomach was churning, now. This was fast becoming dangerous. "– it's a rental."

I left the groceries on the counter and headed out into the hallway in search of the bathroom.

Jocelyn followed. "That's a rather nice rental."

I turned on my heel, feeling the familiar clammy sensation creep up the front of my throat. "It was all they had. Which reminds me – are you going to be able to deposit my second payment soon?"

Oh, I was feeling feisty now.

Hold on, Cor. Don't get crazy.

Jocelyn gave a half-laugh. "Given your comment about the railing, I'm afraid the fee will be for -"

"Railing seems fine, Joss. Is this the one you were talking about?"

Both of us turned toward the stairs to find a lanky, ginger-haired figure tapping his knuckles against the solid head of the carved unicorn.

Not Christopher.

I almost rolled my eyes at myself for hoping otherwise.

I turned back to smile at Jocelyn, but my body quickly distracted me. I pressed my hands to my stomach and wallowed in regret.

Dear god, what did we eat?

Jocelyn's eyebrows shot up. "I thought you said -"

"I'm sorry, I'll have to continue this conversation a bit later. I've got to find a restroom."

"No, no. Wait one minute," Jocelyn said, following on my heels.

I ignored her. I was about to have a very unfortunate experience, and if Jocelyn wanted to be involved, I wasn't in the position to fight her.

I was off, rushing up the stairs toward my bedroom. I didn't want this event to happen within earshot of anyone.

Jocelyn's heels clacked on the wooden stairs just behind me, but I did my best to pick up the pace, my belly clenching harder with each step.

I wanted to curse Bran's very existence – for the derision of my employer, for that banister, for every poor decision I'd ever made, but at that moment, this unfortunate turn of events was entirely my fault.

Just had to stop at that clambake, didn't you, Cor?

"I'm sorry, but I simply can't believe that you've been doing this work all on your own."

I doubled my pace. "I don't particularly care what you believe. Excuse me."

The words were out before I'd considered them.

The unmitigated panic of dysentery will do that to a person.

"Excuse *me*!" Jocelyn countered, picking up speed behind me. "You were hired to keep the place in order, not play interior designer with someone else's estate."

I turned down the hallway toward my bedroom door, limping now as I tried to keep my glutes clenched. I lunged into my bedroom, slamming the door behind me, and with a quick flick of the wrist, locked the door.

"Miss Turner!" Jocelyn said just outside, her voice growing shrill.

I ignored her, turning for the bathroom. The overwhelming sense of gratitude I felt at that moment was palpable. I was alone, I was inches from a toilet.

I was going to survive this day, damn it.

Mr. Darcy cooed from the bed as I hobbled to the bathroom door.

I flung the door open and instantly regretted it.

"Get out! For fuck's sake!"

Bran was doubled over on the toilet, his face going quite pale as he flailed at me to close the door.

You've got to be fucking kidding me!

"What the fuck are you doing in my bathroom, you asshole!?" I hissed, fighting to keep my voice quiet despite the sheer, unmitigated rage I felt.

It was a miracle I didn't shit my pants in rage.

Is that a thing?

It is now.

"Ms. Turner, I suggest you open this door, right now."

Bran gave me a sheepish, panicked look. "I'm so sorry!"

"My room? You prickless -" I said, my voice almost rising as I nearly doubled over with a new wave of cramping.

"I'm sorry!" He said, the sweat glistening on his brow. "I thought it was the safest bet."

"Why!?"

"Because of all places, I didn't think she'd come snooping in *your* room."

"Did you? Did you really? You son of a bitch!" I held my breath, clenching my ass tighter than an Italian speedo model.

"Don't blame me! Ye're the one who simply had to stop for some delightful church -"

"Fuck you! I hope you shit yourself to death!"

"Excuse me?!" Jocelyn called from behind the door.

"Nothing!"

I turned away from the bathroom, scanning all memory of where the nearest working toilet would be just as Jocelyn knocked on the door again.

Where was the nearest bathroom? Another bedroom in the hallway? But was I sure all the bathrooms had working plumbing? I'd seen just how unfortunate some of the bathrooms were in the house.

Bran was sleeping in a room about three doors down. He would have a bathroom.

He'd also have all his stuff lying about.

"God damn it!" I screamed, caring little who heard me. I was two seconds from dying of shame. I was allowed an outburst or two.

My belly growled from somewhere primordial and deep. Working plumbing or no, I was about to lose this battle.

Corinne! Find a toilet and desecrate the shit out of it!

Pun intended.

I flung the door to my bedroom open to find Jocelyn well down the hallway now.

Holy shit, there is a god!

I rushed down the hall, glancing into the rooms as I passed. "Corinne! Why is this door locked?"

Jocelyn was calling from off in the east wing. I was barreling ass down the stairs.

"No clue!"

Her companion responded to the question, his voice quieter. Still, I could hear him.

"It's not locked, it's jammed."

I knew exactly which door Jocelyn referred to and yelled back as I hit the bottom steps. "It does that!"

I didn't have time to consider what that door being not only shut, but jammed again meant.

Given we'd left it open when we drove to the shops.

"What's behind it?" Jocelyn called, her tone accusatory.

God damn it! "Junk!"

Jocelyn was mid-sentence when I rounded the hallway toward the dining room and shut myself into the small bathroom off the servant's hall there. The tiny space was little more than an old chain-pull style toilet and a pedestal sink, but as far as I was concerned, it was fucking Xanadu.

I dropped my jeans, sat my ass on the cold porcelain seat, and loosed the demon that was wreaking havoc on my insides, the miserable sound of it echoing off the high tiled walls. I exhaled, a sense of relief so palpable that I actually sighed.

"Ms. Turner?"

I startled. Jocelyn was directly outside the door.

Something inside me snapped.

"Jesus, lady! Can't you tell I'm literally dying here! Leave me alone for a few minutes for the *love of god*!"

My body spasmed in another wave, the sounds of colonic vengeance yet again filling the space. It was the most unladylike experience of my life, but I didn't care anymore. If Jocelyn wanted to listen to me blast ass from here to Timbuktu, she was welcome to it, there was nothing that would stop my bowels from their exorcism.

"Well – fine. I'll be waiting in the kitchen -"

I seized and another round of rockets firing filled the silence.

"I'll be upstairs with Thomas. Please let me know when we can have a conversation." With that, Jocelyn's heels tapped down the long hallway and out of earshot, and I sat there praying to whatever gods would listen.

The bout lasted a good ten minutes. I imagined poor Bran upstairs going through the same Asspocalypse, but having to desperately try to keep himself quiet.

What a way to be discovered – because your bowels give you away.

After a long lull, I ventured to my feet. I stood in front of the mirror for a long moment, gauging my insides for further revolt. When they didn't clutch in on themselves for a long moment, I found the courage to pull my pants up.

I stood there staring at my reflection. This was not, by any means, my most graceful moment. I was embarrassed to the point of wanting to lock the door and never leave that tiny water closet, but I knew I had to face her at some point.

And despite the seething hate that I felt for Branson T. Douglas at that moment, I *had* promised to make Jocelyn leave – and keep him a secret.

I'd committed to aiding and abetting, and I didn't even know why.

Now, if I didn't face this woman, who knew how long it would be before she stumbled on poor Bran in her efforts to harass me?

I splashed cold water on my face and headed out into the house.

I figured I'd survived birthing Beelzebub from the anus, I could handle whatever this woman threw at me.

"As I said, the door jams. I imagine it's moisture in the air or some such," I said as I rounded the upstairs landing. I knew that was a lie, but how do you tell two strangers that there's a ghost who doesn't want anyone messing with her mattress pile?

You don't. You don't say that.

I joined Jocelyn and Thomas in the hallway. The corridor was lighter than I remembered, each room Bran and I cleared now offering up a new source of light to the enclosed space.

Jocelyn turned to me as Thomas fixated his full attention on the stuck door. Clearly, he'd heard about my bout with bowel Satan and wasn't too keen on making eye contact.

Jocelyn was of sturdier stock, though her glare had softened when she turned to me. "Look, I'll forgive the tone downstairs, but as far as the house is concerned -"

I put a hand out, as though sternly denying a yipping Pomeranian. "I'm gonna stop you right there."

Jocelyn's eyebrows shot up. Clearly, my tone startled her as much as it did me.

"I was promised various accommodations for this job in return for my services as a housesitter and handyman. Not the least of which was transportation. I've done this for years, and there are protocols that you said you were quite aware of. I've upheld more than my fair share of the bargain as described in the contract we both signed. Going forward, I expect to not only receive the second installment of my payment, but also reimbursement for the cab ride I was forced to take from the train when you or your driver failed to collect me from the station. Shall I go on?"

"Excuse me?" Jocelyn started. She seemed to like this phrase.

I was happy to note it was losing its edge every time she said it.

I continued. "Given you pride yourself on professional conduct, I will give you another three days to deposit my wages into my account before I will contact the legal team representing the estate directly to further my claim. As far as Branson Douglas, he is not of my concern, and at no time during my stay here should I have ever been subjected to unexpected guests, nor made to act as bouncer for the property. You've fallen short of your end of the contract and I will not tolerate the blasé disregard for not only my compensation but my safety. Savvy?"

Savvy? What are you, a pirate? Too much! You ran with it too far, jackass.

Yet, Jocelyn stood there slack-jawed for a long moment, Thomas shooting me a sideways glance from his perch on the floor. Clearly, he didn't mind seeing his employer getting her ass handed to her verbally either.

"Now, do you have any particular work that you'd like me to refrain from doing?" I asked, taking advantage of her shock.

She began to shake her head, then regained her wits. "No. I mean, yes. Don't do any remodeling or massive work on the place. Just clear the junk so the inspectors can see that it's falling apart, alright?"

"That sounds fine. I can do that."

"And -" Jocelyn faltered, straightening up as though to recover. She paused, taking a deep breath. "Your payment will be deposited within the week."

"That's lovely, thank you. I'll send a bill to the estate for the rest of my expenses. Now, I'm going to go put my groceries away. Let me know if you need anything further."

I turned and marched back down the hallway, making a deliberate effort not to glance back. However pious and ferocious I'd become, my heart was pounding in my throat. I sauntered into the kitchen as though I lived there, my head held high enough to detach from the rest of me.

"Fake it til you make it," my Dad always said.

I emptied out the first grocery bag, moving carefully as I still didn't trust my insides. I was halfway through the second bag when I heard a soft hiss from the corner of the room. I turned to see a pair of blue eyes staring in from the dark hallway.

Bran.

I glared at him and mouthed the words, "You son of a bitch."

This guy. This guy right here – Mr. "You're a professional squatter." Mr. "This is my house!" This son of a bitch had no more right to be there than I did.

No, he was worse. He had *less* of a right than me. I was being paid to live in squalor.

I was going to give him the unholiest of reamings.

I wanted to sock him in the chops so bad, my hand was twitching.

His eyes were wide as he pressed a finger to his lips, pleading with me not to rat him out. I began to wonder if I murdered him somewhere in this house whether anyone would find him before he became an expected part of the dilapidated décor and I was already halfway around the world in a country without extradition.

And yet, what was I doing?

I was staring at the source of all my trouble - and I was silent. Glaring, but silent.

I slammed the package of Jaffa Cakes onto the counter with a little too much oomph and felt the wafers crack and crumble under my fingers.

Good, I thought. *They're not mine. They're this asshole's!*

There was a bustling from the foyer as the visitors made their way downstairs. I turned back to the hallway door, a sudden uncontrollable wave of concern.

Bran was gone.

Jocelyn and Thomas left fifteen minutes later without another word. I listened to the doors latch behind them. A moment later, the car engine purred to life outside, and the gravel spitting from beneath tires announced their departure. I moseyed over to the kitchen window and watched as their car pulled back down the drive and out of sight, two heads clearly visible in the front seats.

They were well and truly gone.

I spun around, marched across the kitchen, and flung open the hallway door. "Where are you, you motherfucker?!"

The hallway was dark, but I could feel him nearby. I stepped out into the dark space, my fists clenched at my sides. He ran past me, a partial grin on his face, like a naughty teenager trying to dodge an angry teacher while skipping school.

"You lying sack of shit!" I said, following him out into the front hall.

He was standing by the double doors, locking them as though such an act might protect him from felony charges.

Do they have felony charges in Scotland? Would breaking into your family home and fixing it up count as a felony?

Do I care?!

Bastard!

"Hey, I didn't lie to ye. It *is* my house!"

"Get bent! That lady made it very clear that you're not supposed to be here."

He was shifting in place, a strange, excited dance that one might expect after outrunning the cops as a hooligan. "Technically, no."

"Technically?!" I scanned the room frantically for something to throw at him, but with the hall freshly swept and the window patched, there was nothing on offer. I ran back into the kitchen, grabbed the package of Jaffa Cakes from the counter, and returned to the hallway, chucking the package directly at his head.

It nailed him right in the temple.

He flinched, caught the package of biscuits before it could hit the ground, and nonchalantly opened it, popping a broken cookie in his mouth.

I seethed. "I'm going to kill you in your sleep," I said, as deadpan as I could manage.

He laughed.

That made me twice as angry.

"Come on? What do ye expect me to do? She's tryin to take the place from me. What choice do I have?"

"What do you mean *take it* from you?"

He exhaled through his nose and took another bite of cookie. "She's trying to get something out of my father that isn't hers to take."

I furrowed my brow, irritated that I couldn't make sense of this. I was irritated that he was breathing, at that point. "Why would she be trying to get something out of your father?"

He pursed his lips and his eyes went wide in this almost boyish expression. He shrugged. "Because, technically, she's my stepmother."

If my jaw didn't drop, I'd be surprised. "No."

Jocelyn Read was barely older than me. How the hell did such a woman end up married to a hoarding hermit in a dilapidated mansion? Was she a Munster?

"Oh, aye. She married him 'bout two years ago from what I've heard. Never spent as much as a night in the bloody house, but thought she'd come in and snatch what little the old bastard had. Little did she know he had fuck all – and Progeniture is a lovely thing."

I stared at him a moment, confused.

He smirked. "House is heirship property. Doesn't go to the wife. It goes to the eldest son."

I stood there staring at Bran, watching him slam another Jaffa Cake into his mouth. After a moment, he realized I was staring and gestured to the package of cookies in offer.

I barely had the sense to shake my head no. "No one in their right mind likes chocolate orange."

I was being spiteful for spite's sake at that moment.

"So what, is she just trying to screw you out of your inheritance? Because you and your brother were such 'hellions?'"

"We weren't bloody hellions," he said, the words taking a bite that felt long instilled. He took a deep breath, brushing crumbs onto his jeans. "Sort of. I imagine she married him thinking he had a mad stash of cash somewhere, but by the time he died, all the income he had left was through the house's trust. That money transfers to the current owner when the last one dies – and that would be me."

I glanced around the place. "There's a trust for this place?"

"Oh, aye. Meant to pay for full-time groundskeeper, housekeeper, additional part-time staff, emergency repairs – all that nonsense. Anything left over is pocket money for the Laird."

"Laird?"

"And good ol' Dad just fired the staff, let the place fall apart, and bloody gambled his allowance away – like the bell-end he always was. All in an effort to take his children's only inheritance away."

I felt a knot forming across my brow. "If there's an income for the property, why don't you hire a crew?"

He shrugged. "Because it's not technically mine, yet. Given the state of the house, if it doesn't pass inspection next month, they can force us to 'sell' to the crown – for a pittance. Nowhere near what it's worth. If it's sold, then the funds become part of the estate. The estate she can claim part of."

"You can't be serious."

"Oh, but I can," he said, pulling another cookie from the package and taking a bite.

I replayed every interaction I'd had with Jocelyn thus far. She'd not once claimed a connection to Bran's father, never once called him 'my husband.' She'd made it sound like a business transaction, nothing more.

And to top it all off, Christopher hadn't said anything, either, and he'd assured me what close friends the two of them were.

I was careening toward conspiracy theorist at breakneck speed.

"So, she doesn't want you here, because then the house might pass inspection?"

"Exactly. Then it will be mine and my father's efforts to destroy the place and her efforts to marry an old codger for his money will have been for naught. God, I hope she actually shagged him. Serves her right."

I fought the urge to cringe. "Then why didn't you just tell me all of this?"

He set the biscuits on the sideboard and pressed a hand to his stomach. "She was paying ye to stop me. Ye'd have called the polis on me if ye knew I was trespassing."

"You don't know that."

He paused. "Can ye blame me for assuming, given ye tried to kill me upon our first meeting?"

I opened my mouth to respond, but no words came.

I had no money unless Jocelyn actually came through on her promise of funds. I had nowhere to go given Christopher wasn't responding to texts again.

And at this point, would I even want to if he did?

Yet, above all of those notions, I had this burning need to help. Not just Bran. Bran was a dick of epic proportions – a flagrant, unholy dick, and he'd lied to me. It wasn't him that I felt beholden to suddenly.

It was the house.

This house had been not just neglected, but abused out of spite. This house that had stood longer than anything I'd ever encountered. If the crown reclaimed the property, it might be fixed up, yes, but then what? Sold to someone with no blood claim to the place? Opened to the public as a tourist attraction with offices and fax machines filling the upstairs bedrooms where once Jacobites met in secret to discuss rebellion?

Could I walk away from this?

Or more importantly, could I face the consequences of staying and doing the exact opposite of what I was hired to do?

And then, of course – could I tolerate the lying bastard I'd be working with in order to do it?

The two of us stood in the grand space for a long moment, silent.

Finally, Bran took a step toward me, his hand out as though reaching for mine. "Please, Corinne. If she gets what she wants, then my father will have succeeded. I don't know if I could live with myself if that happens."

The sincerity stopped me in my tracks, as did the sudden warble of my insides. Clearly, whatever I'd eaten wasn't done with me, yet.

Bran stood before me, a pleading look on his face. "I need your help. There's just no way I can do this alone." His expression changed and he listed hard, leaning into a nearby doorjamb. "Oh god, I shouldn't have eaten those."

With that, Bran took off back down the kitchen hallway to the tiny bathroom beyond.

Bran wasn't there to hear my response, but I'd known my answer before he'd even asked.

I stood in the front hall, the high ceilings giving the silence an echoing feel, and stared after him, the same question I'd asked myself a hundred times that week creeping to mind.

What have I gotten myself into?

Seven

"LET ME SEE THE place, Cricket. Show me around!"

I stood in the middle of my bedroom, Mr. Darcy meowing at the bedroom door to be allowed out into the house, and more importantly fed his breakfast.

"It's in a freakin state, Dad. I almost don't want to show you."

"You have to!" He said, his eyes getting wide on the other end of the world. He'd demanded I Facetime with him for this very reason. If there was another person in the world who would geek out over fixing up a fourteenth-century castle, it was my stepdad, Kenneth Pace.

Or Dad, as I always thought of him.

"There's no way to truly appreciate the work if I don't see the before, girl. Come on, now. Let's have a tour!"

I sighed. I'd shown him my palatial quarters, the tiled bathroom with tiny square porcelain tiles lining the floor and walls, all the way up to the wainscoting and tin ceiling.

A tin ceiling. In a bathroom.

My god, what this house must've once been.

And will be again, damn it. I thought.

"Alright, but don't judge, ok?"

"Don't judge? Seriously, you hit the jackpot as far as I'm concerned. Let's see the worst of it. Come on."

The worst of it?

No one would question that this man raised me.

I opened my bedroom door and headed out into the hallway, Mr. Darcy scampering off up ahead.

"And where'd you get the cat?"

I snorted. "It was here when I arrived. It was kitty fate."

"Kitty fate, indeed. Careful, you might end up with raccoons and rats for pets if you're lucky."

I rolled my eyes. "I already ended up with a hundred wood chomping beetle friends the other day."

I shuddered. I could still feel them on my skin if I let myself think about it.

"Oh, that must've been fun. Did you bug bomb the place?" Dad asked.

I nodded but refused to speak on it further. I was feeling itchy just at the mention of those tiny little bastards.

It didn't help that I had to take part in hauling the chifferobe from hell down to the skip with Bran after the bug bombing. I could hear the dead things skittering around inside with every shift of its weight. Bran assured me the bug bomb and the shop vac attack would be enough to get rid of them. I told him he couldn't vacuum my soul, and that was where I still felt them crawling.

So, he'd poked me with the shop vac hose, naturally.

What a dick.

"Oh, look at that crown molding," Dad said, stopping me halfway down the hall.

I turned the phone to show him around, offering up a panorama of the corridor. "No, Dad. You don't even know. Check this out."

I hauled down the rest of the hallway and shot down the stairs, turning the phone around to show him the unicorn-head banister. "This bad boy is over five hundred years old."

He went on to regale me with 'Wows' and 'Damns' as I took him from room to room, showing him the good and the bad. We were eyeing the massive pile of old bean and coffee cans in the billiard room when Bran's footsteps startled me around.

"Hey, Dad. Can I call you back? I think we're about to get back to work."

"Of course, sweetheart! Of course. Hey, don't forget to take before pics, alright? We could use those on the website when you come home. Show people what kind of work we can do, yeah?"

"Mhmm," I said, forcing the sound out. I couldn't exactly tell him that every ounce of work I was doing was technically illegal. I also couldn't tell him why I didn't want my work on his website.

Would be false advertising, given I wasn't planning to work for him again.

That was a massive conversation that simply wasn't going to take place with me across an ocean.

I mean, how do you tell the man who took care of you your whole life that you can't work with him anymore because his new girlfriend makes you regret your very birth whenever you're near her?

"Alright, kiddo. Call me back when you get the chance."

And then he was gone, my phone screen going back to the sexy kilted model I liked to ogle from time to time when I glanced at my phone.

I found Bran in the kitchen, cramming a piece of toast into his mouth, a steaming cup of tea in his left hand.

A multitasker to the letter.

"Good morning. Any new developments?" He said, gesturing his toast toward my phone.

The answer, sadly, was no.

I still hadn't received my second payment from Jocelyn. I was still broke.

Yet, there was another query I sensed in his question – had Christopher texted or called?

The answer, again, was no.

I was two for two, and I wasn't particularly keen on the idea of his smug response to the news.

"As expected," he said, and I bristled. "Well, we should work twice as hard now, out of spite."

"Right, because spite work is quality work."

He was halfway out of the room before I'd finished my sentence, gesturing for me to follow. After that unfortunate afternoon with the digestive system shutdown, we both recovered by the next afternoon. Once all was quiet on the intestinal front, we'd managed to empty out the rest of the bedrooms of all their unfortunate treasures – save for one. The mattress room's door was jammed again, and no amount of combat would make it move.

I didn't comment on how unnerved it made me feel. Of all the rooms to have the door stick over and over – the room where I'd seen the woman in blue. If I was prone to superstition, I'd say those mattresses harbored some fairy curse or some other nonsense.

I didn't want to think about ghosts in such an old house. I could just imagine how many dead people might be crawling through these walls like woodworms.

No, thank you.

I followed Bran up to the third floor and watched him duck into one of the freshly cleared rooms. I rounded the corner after him and stopped in my tracks as a chill in the air betrayed the wide-open balcony doors.

"You've got to be kidding me," I said, my stomach shooting up into my throat.

Bran marched out onto the balcony ahead of me, confidently swinging himself up onto the railing to scale the scaffolding like some circus monkey.

I stepped out after him, making an unfortunate point to look down. I instantly regretted every choice I'd ever made in life that lead to that moment. "No way in hell," I said.

"Come on, woman! Ye said ye had the skills, so make yerself useful!"

"Yes, but I'd much prefer doing ground-type things. You know, the kind of things you do on the ground."

Bran returned to the ledge of the roof and looked down at me with a cocked eyebrow. "I thought ye said ye'd done roof work before."

I glowered at him. "Irrelevant."

I had. Many times, in fact.

"All of those rooves were one story off the ground, not a million," I said, wishing I could have another bout of diarrhea to get me out of this new project Bran had his sights set on.

He scoffed, disappearing again overhead. "It's just four stories. Get your capable ass up here."

I hovered on the edge of the balcony, glancing back into the dusty room behind me. We were on the top floor, and this balcony was attached to a bedroom devoid of furniture now, everything within having fallen prey to the constant leaks overhead or the skip out front. I knew well that from that point down along the east wing, many of the rooms had water damage. The roof on this side of the house was barely there in some spots – and it needed the kind of work that required more than one man.

Or woman, as the case may be.

"I've been feeding ye and letting ye squat in my house, woman. Get up here!"

"Watch it, ass. We both know you're squatting just as much as I am."

"Irrelevant!"

I took a deep breath and grabbed hold of the metal pole of the scaffolding. A moment later, I was teetering forward onto the incline of the roof, my chest tight, and my lady bits tingling with the sudden terror of being so high.

"I'm not squatting in your house. Quit saying that," I said, half under my breath. It was getting old, now more than ever, knowing what I knew.

Bran was lunging into the incline of the roof up ahead, leather pads strapped to his knees and a pair of nails pinned between his lips. He gestured to a pile of shingles, nails, and a pair of extra hammers all settled near the edge of the scaffolding.

This is gonna be a freakin blast, I thought. Apparently, I'm even sarcastic in my head.

I bent down and snatched up a hammer and a massive handful of nails, tucking them into my pocket. Then, I dug the sole of my boot into the fresh shingles beneath my feet and made my way up the incline of the roof to meet Bran.

"There we are, lass. See? It's not so bad."

Whipping out the lass to sell that Scottish accent?

I tried not to think of Christopher. He knew very well how weak in the knees it made me when he called me *lass*.

I glared at Bran, keeping my eyes down as I shimmied past him to start the next line of shingles. I glanced down at the previous line already in place. The lines were straight, the nails flush and evenly spaced across. Bran knew what he was doing.

I dropped onto my knees there, set the slate-colored panel in place, and nailed it into position, grumbling under my breath.

We worked in quiet camaraderie, the sound of our hammers echoed into the distance as Led Zeppelin thrummed from Bran's small speaker on the scaffolding. I'd found a rhythm, shifting along the roof on my knees as I followed Bran's progress. He'd reach the end of that section of the roof and mosey back past me, taking up his position at the start to hammer in the first shingle of yet another row.

"At this rate, we'll be onto the next section by tea time! Nicely done, by the way. It's lined up perfectly."

I shot Bran a sideways look, almost startled by the compliment. "Thank you?" I said.

He eyed me but didn't comment. "So, your Dad taught ye this, then, aye? Bit odd that."

I let the hammer rest against my hip as I took the nail from between my lips. "He's my step-dad, actually. And why is that?"

Bran shrugged. "Dunno. Seems most dads don't teach their daughters construction, I'd think."

"And they're the poorer for it," I said, turning up my nose before returning to work.

Bran chuckled. "Took the words right outta my mouth."

I paused. It sounded like the sincerest thing he'd said since I met him. It was almost endearing.

He settled in to start nailing down the next shingle when a shape flitting through the air overhead. I turned to follow it, watching the tiny bird dart around one of the many brick chimneys before taking off for the trees.

I stopped, losing sight of the bird as I took in the view for the first time.

I'd been so wound up in my fear of heights, and not hearing from Chris, that I'd almost forgotten where I was – and how amazing a view it harbored.

Cavendish was the only house for miles in every direction, and the trees spliced down the hillside, leaving a long trail of open, green field to show the full expanse of the grounds. There were gardens for a hundred yards or more, it seemed, and in the distance, statues lined the forest edge where that perfect green carved through it.

My breath stopped as I took in the view, the tiny speck of a church steeple peeking through the trees. I smiled. I knew exactly what church it was.

The tiny bird returned suddenly, diving toward me before rounding the same chimney with an agitated flit of its wings.

"What are you?" I said in a sing-song voice.

"A tit."

"What?!" I said, turning on my companion.

"That's what she is. A tit. Been giving me one hell of a talkin to since I've been up here. I imagine her nest is in one of these chimneys."

I smiled, rising to my feet to take in the full expanse of that view. "A tit? Is that the actual type of bird or are you just being -"

I felt a sickening list in the wood beneath my feet, coupled by a splintering sound. I froze, my fingers splayed at my sides like there was an invisible railing to grab onto.

"No, it is actually a tit, in every manner of the word."

The roof gave way, and I dropped, instantly, my stomach shooting up into my throat. My left leg crashed through the waterlogged wood under me, and I screamed, lashing out my hands for something to grab onto.

Bran straightened. "Oh, shite! Ye alright? Here, grab my -"

"Don't move!" I said, hissing at him like a rabid cat. Inside my mind was screaming – *you smoldering fuck! Back off! I'm gonna die!*

Bran was already on his feet crouching as he moved closer to me, as though he was ducking under something to avoid hitting his damn head.

"It's alright, just hurry -"

I felt the world disappear beneath my feet as the rest of the rotted panel gave way. My other leg dropped through the widening hole, dragging my torso down with it. I scrambled for purchase, anything to grab onto and stop me from sliding down through the roof. My fingernails snapped against the shingles, and the rough surface tore up the top layers of skin on my palms. Still, scraped knuckles were better than broken legs. I clawed my fingers beneath one of the new shingles and held on for my damn life.

My legs were dangling free in the space below.

Bran lunged across the roof, diving onto his belly beside me as he snatched at my hands to stop me from slipping.

My chest pressed up into my chin, catching me as I slid through the roof. I silently praised the boob gods, as my tits created a strange ledge to hold me in place.

Tatas were going to save me? Really? The Turner women's blessing of huge knockers was all that came between me and broken ankles?

That's just fucking great. Thanks, Mom. Turns out you were good for something.

I took the moment to hook the fingers of my other hand on a second shingle.

"Don't hold onto them, hold onto me."

I couldn't look at him, I was too panicked to take my eyes off the shingles that kept me from falling. I shook my head, fighting to steady my panicked breathing. My legs were cold, dangling in the near frigid air of the room below. I could see light in the space between me and gravity, the room below quite bright for one of the long-forgotten servants' bedrooms on the third floor. I fought to bend my elbows and hoist myself upward, but the rotted wood simply sagged in response. I was suddenly sure I was going to fall. I screamed then with complete abandon, caring little what Bran might think of me.

"Is this how I die?" I whispered, trying to make light of the moment despite my growing panic.

Bran shimmied closer, his hands gripping my sleeves. "Ye're no gonna die, drama queen. Ye're gonna be fine."

His words were teasing, infuriatingly so, but beneath them was a tone that terrified me. However joking he might want to seem, he was scared, too.

Oh god. My poor Dad is going to fall apart when he hears the news that I broke myself on this job.

"I need ye to let go of the shingles and let me get my hands under your arms," Bran said, his voice strained with effort.

"No! I'm too heavy! Oh, god. I'm too heavy," I said, twisting my head just enough to glance down at the opening by my shoulder. The golden light cast from the world below shot my heart into my throat.

I shot a look at the chimneys nearby and had a terrifying realization.

Suddenly, I knew where I was.

Oh god, I knew exactly where I was.

Tears stung my eyes, but I didn't make a sound. No amount of screaming could express my protest.

I wasn't dangling over a bedroom on the third floor. I was hanging three stories in the air over the ancient wooden floor of the Great Fucking Hall.

This wouldn't be broken ankles. This would be a death drop.

If it didn't kill me, I'd break every bone in my body. I'd very likely never walk again.

"Oh god! Please!" I screamed, letting sound draw out as I protested to whatever higher power might be listening at that moment – in the middle of nowhere Scotland. It sounded ludicrous, but I didn't care. Perhaps some heroic brigade of Highland Scotsmen was at the ready nearby, always waiting some damsel to cry in distress.

Well, I was in fucking distress, and the only Scotsman for five miles was this asshole before me. At least I could be soothed over to the land beyond by the Lord's Prayer recited in a Highland Brogue.

As far as I was concerned, Bran Douglas was good for fuck all.

"How did I get over the hall? This is going to kill me!"

Bran slid closer still, trying to shimmy his hands under my armpits as he shifted his body toward the decline of the roof. "There'll be no killing today, woman. Ye're gonna let go of the shingles and take hold of me. Come on, Cor. Listen to me. Grab onto me. I'll shimmy down the roof 'til ye can pull your leg up – leverage yerself back up here."

"No, no! No! No!" His hands moved under me and I could feel the sagging wood shift again. I screamed anew. "I can't. I can't, Bran! I can't!"

"Don't be daft! Come on, now. Grab onto me. Do one hand at a time. Come on, now."

I whimpered suddenly as I felt the shingle in my right hand begin to fold. I gripped onto the rough texture, the skin of my knuckles and fingertips scratching and bleeding as I fought with everything I had to hold on.

"I've got ye, Corinne. I swear to ye. I have ye. Ye have to trust me."

"Never," I seethed. To my surprise and disdain, it drew a laugh. Bran's face was just a few inches away now, his fingers pinching the flesh at the sides of my breasts as he fought to get his arms around me. He gave a soft groaning sound as his hand pushed between me and the edge of the hole. The sudden shift in my position caused my fingers to slip on the shingle, and the last of my fingernails snapped with it, the broken shingle tearing free from my hand. I shifted further down through the hole as I lost grip, and I screamed.

Suddenly, I stopped moving. Bran's arm was locked under me, now. "Now, grab onto me, ye stubborn cow," he said, whispering through gritted teeth.

I began to sob openly. "I fucking hate you!" I said. I was helpless there, at the mercy of my left hand holding onto a half-snapped shingle and this asshole, smelling of tea and jam as he breathed just inches from my face. I was going to die in the middle of Podunk nowhere and it was this asshole's fault!

"I'm going to haunt the fuck out of you!" I said, fighting to get a better grip on the shingle that was tearing my hand to pieces. I had no strength to hold myself if Bran were to let go now. I was at the mercy of this man – this near stranger's strength, and I knew better than anyone that I wasn't exactly a featherweight.

My grip faltered again, one of the nails pulling free from the shingle in my hand.

There was no use. I was going to fall. Suddenly, my breathing slowed.

"You're gonna drop me. I'm too heavy," I said, finally meeting Bran's eyes. These tears were no longer panic-stricken – these tears were those of acceptance. I would let go of the second shingle, and Bran would lose his grip. I would plummet three stories to my death with no one in the world who truly cared about me for a thousand miles.

Bran's blue eyes trained on mine with a gentle intensity I'd never seen in any man's face before. He nodded, slowly. "Ye're going to let go, love, and we're both gonna pull ye up. Grab onto me. Come on, now."

His voice was so calm, almost a whisper as he held my gaze. I felt my lips trembling as I fought not to sob, openly.

How could I find the courage to let go? Letting go was going to kill me? He was asking me to accept my death.

The tiny little bird flitted just over my head, drawing my eyes from Bran's, and like I was spring-loaded, I released my hold on the other shingle and flailed toward Bran's shoulders, folding my injured fingers into the fabric of his shirt.

He hooked his other arm under mine and instantly rolled onto his side, pinning his arm between me and the shingled surface of the roof. I felt my body lift just so.

"Come on! Pull yerself up, woman!"

I tugged at the fabric of his shirt, feeling it pull up the length of his back. I cried out as I realized it would soon ride up and leave it too slack to be of any use.

"No! Corinne, kick your leg up!"

I shook my head, terrified that jerking my body in such a way would put too intense a strain on Bran's arms. I continued to weep there, my legs dangling uselessly beneath me.

"If ye don't do as ye're told, we're gonna be here all fuckin day!" Bran growled, his tone teeming with effort and frustration.

The tinge of pain from the shingles digging into my side and the throbbing of my battered fingertips fell to the background as the tiny bird appeared overhead, again, swirling and diving around the chimneys. It found a ledge to settle on and stared down at us both, as though watching some curious beetle in the grass.

"I'm gonna take you with me," I said, a sudden serenity hitting me.

He glared at me in confusion.

I was. I was going to either pull him through, or the water-softened wood of the roof was going to give beneath him as well and we'd both plummet to our deaths with no one coming to check on us for months.

"If we stay like this, you're going to fall, too." I took a deep breath and the tears stopped instantly. "Just let go."

"Ah, fer fuck's sake!"

Bran jerked me upward, lifting me up through the hole in the roof by just a couple more inches. In the instant that I was higher, Bran's hand shot down to the waistband of my jeans and latched onto the belt loop. He then rolled further down the roof, hauling my wide ass upward, inch by inch.

A renewed will to live overwhelmed me, and I finally took the chance of throwing my knee up through the hole. My knee caught the edge, and the jagged pieces of splintered wood and old shingles gouged through the fabric of my jeans, but I ignored it, pushing my weight into it for leverage. Bran pulled again, and soon my hip was at the edge of the hole. Bran rolled us again, dragging me onto my back and snatching me beneath the knee. I curled into myself like a pretzel as he dragged me back onto the roof, the shingles scraping my sides as my shirt drifted up around me.

I felt the solid world beneath me, the assurance of gravity pinning me to the rough shingles, and I fought to breathe.

What if this patch of the roof gave way next?

I didn't feel safe, but I felt alive.

Bran rolled onto his back as we both panted in tandem.

I stared up at the sky, a tiny patch of blue peering through the usual constant gray of the Scottish sky. I took a deep breath, forcing myself to hold it as long as I could. The tiny bird flitted overhead again, tweeting with constant indignation.

I watched it, squinting against the light of the gray sky.

"That bird is a wicked dick," I said.

Bran laughed.

I exhaled. My heart was pounding in my throat, and my stomach was in such furious knots, I feared I might be sick.

After a long moment, Bran suddenly rolled over toward the hole in the roof. I shrieked in fear, reaching toward him to stop him. He turned my way, shooting me a raised eyebrow. "Ye're alright. Just breathe."

I gave a shaky exhale. "Please, don't go so close."

"Don't worry. My weight's well distributed – I'll be fine."

He shimmied over to the hole and looked down into the massive room below. "Holy fuck. That would've been one hell of a fall."

"Please, don't. I don't – I can't breathe."

Bran rolled back toward me, lifting himself up to sit. "Come on, woman. Let's get ye back to solid ground."

I shook my head as Bran took hold of my hands and helped me to a seated position. I fought him. When he tried to convince me to stand, I flat refused, instead opting to scoot down the decline of the roof on my butt.

I might be tearing the ever-loving shit out of these jeans, but I am not standing up.

I stalled at the edge, suddenly frozen in fear at the notion of the drop from the side of the scaffolding. Bran stepped over and climbed down onto the balcony below. Then he turned back, holding his arms up to me as though preparing to catch a child climbing down from the monkey bars on the playground – as though he could catch me out of thin air.

I sat there a long moment, my eyes trained on the garden far below.

"Oi! Turner. Get your head in it. Let's go."

I swallowed and offered my hand to him. He held it tight in his and stepped back for me to climb down, forming a manly wall between me and the four-story drop. I felt the solid stone of the balcony beneath my feet and slumped right down onto my ass there, happy to be shielded by the high stone railings all around.

"Ye melodramatic thing."

"I hate you," I whispered, pressing my hands into the stones beneath me.

Bran squatted down beside me. "That's no way to speak to the man that just saved your life, now is it?"

"You're also the man who coaxed me up onto a roof that was by no means ready to bear my weight."

He took a sharp breath through his nose. "Psh. Details."

I almost laughed at that.

"I suppose I should've double-checked before I set off on it."

My eyes widened. "You didn't check?"

Bran made a grumbling noise. "I know, I know. Was cutting corners because I was in a rush."

I turned on him, meeting his gaze for the first time since he was wrapping his arms around me to pull me to safety, trying his best to calm me down. "You asshole."

I stifled. The word didn't come with half the vitriol I'd intended. Somehow, the memory of those eyes staring into mine, oozing calm and reassurance, made it difficult to maintain a proper amount of rage.

"I almost died. You almost killed me," I said, finally.

He frowned, tilting his head to the side as though conceding. The gesture startled me yet again. I exhaled through pursed lips. I didn't need any more startling.

"Come on, then. Let's go have a look at the roof!"

He grabbed me up, hoisting me to my feet before I could protest, then tugged me into the house. He loosed his hold on my hand and disappeared into the hallway, leaving me alone in the dusty and disheveled space. I stepped lightly and slowly, eyeing each floorboard as though they intended to betray me at a moment's notice.

"Are ye comin?" He called.

I made my way out into the hallway, the skylights and open bedroom doors casting gray light across the floor. I felt the crunch of unswept floors and the give of worn carpet beneath my feet. Just the softness of the rug reminded me of the sickening crack of the world splitting.

I felt the tingling between my legs again, and my stomach shot right up into my throat.

"Aye! That would've been one hell of a drop!"

He was calling from downstairs, his voice muffled by two stories of space. I made my way down the stairs, clinging to the railing as though gravity might suddenly reverse and whisk me up into the sky.

I made it to the bottom step, my hands shaking violently. I was not alright. And I was getting cold.

I moved slowly, following Bran through the grand doorway into the old banquet hall. I found him standing in the middle of the massive room, staring straight up.

I almost didn't want to look. Still, I followed his gaze.

I could see the sky.

There, in the middle of the ancient ceiling, between wooden beams harvested from Viking ships for all I knew, was a three-foot-wide hole.

It was wider than I'd imagined. I should've fallen straight through.

The room spun around me, instantly, and I splayed my hands out to my sides as though there were some invisible thing to hold onto. There wasn't.

Gravity works, ladies and gentlemen.

"Corinne!" Bran called, lunging forward. He appeared at my side just as my knees buckled.

Was I fainting? Was I actually fucking fainting? Could I be any more pathetic?

"I'm fine. Leave me alone."

"Och, ye're freezing, woman. Ye're just grand. Come on, sit down here then," he said, ushering me over to one of the ancient chairs that lined the outer wall of the room. I tried to fight him, something about planting my relatively jiggly ass on the same surface as some proud medieval lady with a considerably leaner ass gave me pause.

Not because of my ass' size, but the chair's age. My ass wasn't an antique.

Still, I leaned back in it, my head falling back against the massive tapestry behind me. It shifted, sending a wave through the heavy fabric that traveled halfway across the room.

Bran squatted down in front of me, his hand on my knee. I stiffened slightly, reaching toward his hand to remove it.

Then I stopped dead at the sight.

His knuckles and the back of his hand were torn to shreds, rivulets of blood pooling and running across the back of his hand. Bruises were already forming across his knuckles. He'd beaten the ever-loving shit out of himself.

Suddenly, I became aware of my own hands, glancing down to see three fingertips stained red from broken fingernails and lines of scratches up both palms. And they were still shaking.

Despite the horror before me, I couldn't feel any pain.

That's not a good sign, is it?

"What did you do to your hands?" I asked, finding it difficult to form words. I cringed, shutting my eyes. Something was off, and I sounded more like a precocious child than the woman I was.

He glanced at his injured hands and shrugged. "Nothin to trouble yerself about. It'll heal."

I swallowed as Bran rose to his feet, eyeing my face for a long moment. I remembered him jamming his fingers into my sides, trying to get them under me when I refused to let go of the shingles. I'd seen his hands before then. They'd been uninjured.

I made the decision to move about two minutes before my body complied, turning to look down at the sides of my shirt.

Suspicion proven.

My shirt was spattered with blood. "Am I bleeding?" I said, my head floating about thirty feet above me.

Bran crouched down again, touching his brutalized hands to my side to lift my tank top up. His touch was so gentle but still confident enough not to wait for permission.

Smart, given it would've taken twelve minutes for me to give it. My head was floating ever further away.

I felt his fingertips graze over sore skin, but as I looked, there were some scratches across my ribs, but nothing drawing blood.

"Doesn't look like it," he said, rising to his feet again.

I stared at the blood on my shirt for a long moment. These stains were from his hands.

I frowned.

Bran had deliberately injured himself to save me. And he'd never let on that he was in pain.

"Fucking Scots," I said.

Bran gave a half-laugh, but it ended quickly as I started sobbing like a child in that antique chair.

"Bloody hell, there's no need for that, love. Ye're safe. Come now, ye're alright."

I leaned forward, covering my face in my hands as the tears just poured out of me. I could no more control this than I could the shaking of my hands. I'd have no better luck controlling the ocean tides.

What the hell is wrong with me?

"Hey, hey. Ye're alright," he said again, the tone shifting to near laughter as he squeezed my knee. This time, I didn't think to push his hand away. "Come on, now. Let's get out of this room, then. I've an idea of what to do with ye."

I carefully took Bran's injured hand and let him lead me back out into the front hallway. He quickly turned me toward the kitchen, bringing me to the massive sink. I let him lead me, like some ugly duckling being tucked up under the swan's wing. He turned the water on and waited for it to reach the perfect temperature before gently setting my hands beneath the stream. I winced with pain, but settled there a moment, letting the warmth travel up the length of my arms.

"There now. Ye're alright, aye?"

I tried to nod, but nothing happened. I just stared at the circles and wisps of red in the water as blood pooled in the sink.

My hands were still shaking, despite the soothing sound of running water, and much to my chagrin, I was still crying. Yet, I didn't feel ashamed of it now.

Bran stood at my side, holding my hands there, his tall frame towering over me as I shrank with each passing moment. The tears were streaming down my face, but I made no sound, watching his own injuries run red under the faucet.

Why wasn't I fighting him? Why wasn't I rejecting this? I could take care of myself! I didn't need him babying me.

Yet, there I stood quietly crying, leaning into the warmth of his chest as his fingers moved over my hurts.

His energy had changed. He was no longer chiding and sarcastic. He'd taken control, doing for me what I wasn't able to do for myself, and somehow – it was ruining me. I'd never let anyone take care of me like this before. I'd flat refused coddling all my life when it was offered.

Perhaps that was the difference. Bran didn't offer. He'd simply taken over, and it had somehow given me permission to fall to pieces.

And I wanted to fall to pieces.

Bran hustled into the nearby bathroom, then returned with a small blue plastic box. He snatched up a kitchen towel and dried off my hands with immaculate patience before leading me back out into the hallway.

"Come on, then. I've got a favorite spot for when I'm not feeling so grand. Follow me."

He carefully took my hand again and led me down a hallway into the downstairs of the east wing. I'd never managed to explore this side of the house. I wasn't exactly in the best head space to go adventuring into the unknown, but I let him lead me down the dark hallway. I caught sight of a grand piano in one of the side rooms as we passed, following along blindly. My head was growing swimmier and swimmier with each passing moment.

The hallway gave way to a brilliantly bright space, leaving me squinting as I stumbled after him.

"Here we are. Go on and have a lie down, here."

I let my eyes adjust to what was a massive conservatory, taking in the stretches of bare branches and old ivy clinging to the glass overhead. The room was glorious; high glass ceilings framed in wrought iron and wood. There were old leaves collected on the glass above, but still, the space was bright as the world outside.

It was unkempt, even in my halfwit state I could see that – old pots and shelves of long-forgotten plant life left to shrivel and dry out.

An appropriate place to bring me, Bran. I'm feeling pretty dried out and shriveled myself.

Despite the dire state of every once green thing, there were details that invited me in. A chaise long, a wrought iron table with a set of matching chairs, and off to one side was an old wooden desk, still covered with notepads and a mug filled with pens.

"I didn't know this room was here," I said.

"Down ye go, feet up," he said, moving me like a stubborn child. I still wasn't protesting.

Why wasn't I protesting?

He quickly took off my shoes and set my feet on the soft arm of the long Queen Anne-style couch. He settled a pillow beneath my head and an instant later, he set a thick quilt over me before pulling up a chair.

I watched him as he set the blue plastic bin on the table, cracking it open.

He snatched up one of my hands and set it in his lap before reaching into his shirt pocket and pulling out a lighter and a hand-rolled cigarette. He lit it before I could protest.

Were I in a better state, I might have pointed out the nerve of his smoking so close to me when I was already such a freaking mess. Then, he held the cigarette out to me as he exhaled.

I mindlessly took the cigarette. Then, the familiar smell hit me.

"Is this pot!?" I whispered like a junior in high school skipping classes with the art kids.

He chuckled. "It is, aye. Your pulse is racing like crazy. Thought it might help calm ye down."

"It is?"

He touched his hand to my wrist, running his thumb over the skin with such a gentle caress, I almost jerked my hand away by reflex. Why did his touch startle me like that?

"Yes, it is a marijuana cigarette. Are ye scandalized?"

I swallowed, staring at the cigarette in my hands. "Pot? I almost died, and your answer is to smoke pot?"

He shrugged, taking up my left hand as he searched the first aid box for an appropriate bandage. "My theory is that it couldn't hurt."

I stared at him in shock, the joint cindering away in my shaking hand. Then, without another complaint, I brought the joint to my lips and inhaled.

The coughing fit that followed only made me more lightheaded.

"There we are. Ye can give it back, then," he said, holding his hand open to me in wait.

I eyed him but handed it back.

He took a long inhale, coughed twice, then handed it back to me.

Despite the absurdity of what was happening, I took another hit. I didn't cough this time. I just stared off into space.

I'd felt like a sad drunk before smoking, but I was fast approaching goofy drunk, now.

I hadn't felt like that in years.

He took the joint from me, quickly took another hit off it, then put it out, stuffing it back into his pocket.

I stared off into space, suddenly noticing the distant sound of Zeppelin still playing from Bran's speaker two floors above. "An abrasive prick and a pothead? I never would've guessed."

He smiled, pressing a cotton ball of hydrogen peroxide to my torn fingers.

I hissed.

"Not quite. My sister gave me a few joints when she heard I was gonna lock myself away up here for a couple of months. Said I'd need something to pass the time in this hole of the Highlands."

"A likely story," I said, letting my head fall back onto the pillow.

I stared at him for a long while, watching his own injured hands work to bandage mine. I fought to keep my hand steady, failing at first, but as the drug began to take effect, my fingers stilled in his, letting him bandage them without any trouble. I even stopped wincing at the sting of his cleaning my wounds.

Cleaning my wounds. He was cleaning my wounds. Wounds. Wooooooounds.

Jesus, I was stoned.

"Why are you being so nice to me?" I asked, suddenly.

He met my gaze, reminding me of that same stern, reassuring look from the rooftop before – when I was dangling forty feet from my death. "Ye did have quite a traumatic experience up there."

"So?"

He smirked. "Ye think me so awful that I'd be unkind after that?"

I swallowed. "No, but still – you're not normally this nice to me."

"I'm not particularly nice to anyone, love," he said, wrapping another band-aid around the tip of one of my broken fingernails.

"Why?"

His eyebrows shot up as he let the first hand loose, taking up the second.

I stretched my arm across my chest, clumsily.

"Let's just say I've known my fair share of bastards. And oftentimes, they want something I'm not willing to give."

The blanket was warming my feet and legs, giving the massive and bright space an almost dreamy feel. I watched dead leaves flit across the panels of glass overhead, the skittering sound echoing through the room.

"What do you mean? They want to make out with you?"

I stiffened.

Where the hell did that come from?

He chuckled. "I wish. No, they imagine I can do them some courtesy. Side effect of having a title. Everyone thinks ye can help them make something of themselves. Which is ironic, given I still haven't made fuck all of my own life."

I watched the leaves overhead again, feeling a smile creep across my face. "That's pretty common among potheads."

He gave my hand a gentle pinch.

I hissed at him, but stopped dead when I saw the mischievous smile. I swallowed hard. "Title? What, like *World's Worst Roofer? Scotland's Most Ornery Toker?*"

He snorted, softly. "Those both sound more appropriate than reality, I assure ye."

I shifted onto my side to face him, watching his face and waiting for him to explain. Unlike any other time in his company, I suddenly didn't mind the silence. I also didn't mind him seeing me stare.

He was a handsome man. He really was.

"If ye must know, I'm the thirteenth Earl of Kinvale."

I laughed, blowing him a raspberry in my disbelief.

He met my gaze, his eyebrows shooting up for an instant before returning his attention to my hands.

He wasn't kidding.

My eyes went wide. "Wait... what?"

He pursed his lips. "Don't act so surprised. Ye'll hurt my feelings."

He wiggled an eyebrow at me and set my hand back on my stomach, now fully bandaged up. He then turned his attention to his own hands, pulling a ring from his pocket – his grandfather's ring, as he informed me – and placing it back on his hand. After giving his hands a quick inspection, he set his elbows onto his knees and leaned forward.

I stared at Bran with new eyes.

An Earl. Bran was an Earl? I'd been holed up in a ruin of an estate with a sarcastic, jaded, grumpy – devastatingly handsome Earl?

"Tell me, how are ye feeling?"

My mind was floating about from notion to notion, at times returning to the memory of dangling from that gaping hole in the ceiling of the great hall, and each time it stirred my thoughts, it caused muscles I didn't even know I had to stiffen – and most of them in the crotch.

I scolded myself and tried to focus on the leaves. "Swimmy. I feel swimmy."

He touched his hand to my arm, giving me a light squeeze. "That's not too bad, then, aye?"

I shot him a sideways glance, inspecting the contours and lines of his face. Despite the assurance that he didn't spend much of his life being friendly, he had tiny lines forming at the corners of his eyes – a sign of easy laughter.

He was funny, too.

"No, not too bad. That was some really good pot."

He chuckled. "Ye sound like a pothead."

I tried to swat at him but barely jerked my hands in his general direction.

I lay there for a long moment, a strange sense of contentment washing over me. I'd almost died just a while before, but as I lay there in that warm quilt, the soothing whisper of the wind through leaves overhead, I felt secure, grounded, and safe. I felt aware and alive. Gratefully so.

And as I suddenly realized, I was starving.

"I think I'm hungry," I said.

Bran began to laugh, rising up to his full height over me. "Well then, I'll have to procure something from the kitchen, for our mistress. Will ye stay here? Please."

I closed my eyes, tugging the quilt up to my chin. "Yes, I would love to."

"Good then," he said. He stood there for a long moment, staring down at me.

I closed my eyes as though I might make myself invisible. A moment later, I listened to the sound of his footsteps shuffling across the tiles of the conservatory. His footsteps stopped by the door for a moment, and a second later, The Psychedelic Furs were playing softly from a speaker on the desk. Then he was gone, leaving me to bask in the warmth of my blanket, the cool of the air, and the sound of New Wave.

Eight

I OPENED MY EYES, unsure how long I'd been dozing there on the settee. Bran's voice drifted through the downstairs. He was singing to himself in the kitchen. I laid my arm across my eyes and listened to the world, pressing my other hand to my heart.

It wasn't racing anymore.

Or if it was, it was racing for a different reason now.

Why did he have to be so nice?

The buzzing in my pocket shot my stomach right back up into my throat. I'd clearly been close to drifting off, again. I scrambled to reach for my phone, half dreading the array of callers I did *not* want to speak to at that moment.

I wasn't exactly in the best headspace to deal with Jocelyn Read, that was for sure.

Christopher calling...

I stared at my phone for several seconds.

"Hello?!" I said, instantly cringing at how shrill and excited I sounded. The notion of hearing his voice – of hearing concern and care after I told him about my day – I wanted that. I wanted to feel that affection.

It's funny how quickly a near-death experience will remind you you're single.

"Hey there, you. How are ye fairing?" He asked.

I responded instantly with, "Fine, fine."

I wasn't fine.

"Sorry I've been so busy the past weeks. Work has been right hell."

"That's ok. I understand."

He began to tell me about his work, the other lab techs and scientists helping with his research, and what massive idiots the lot of them were. I sat there under my quilt listening to the familiar cadence of his voice, the rise and fall of inflection, all in that hypnotic accent of his.

I was so happy to hear his voice.

"Anyway, enough about me. How are ye?"

I took a deep breath. "I've been better, but I suppose it could've been worse," I said. "I actually just had a near-death experience."

"Is that so? What happened?"

I felt my stomach lurch and my lady bits tingle with the memory of it. "I was up working on the roof, and I fell through. Well, almost fell through, given I was pulled back up before falling to my death."

"Pulled? By whom?"

I froze. The tone was almost conspiratorial. Suddenly, I was painfully aware that Christopher was a proud colleague of Jocelyn.

Come on, Cor. He wouldn't run off and tell Jocelyn. He went to school with Jocelyn, but he's seen you have an orgasm. Trust that his loyalty lies with you.

"I mean, I just pulled myself back up. Sorry, I'm a little out of it."

Nicely done, Cor. That was super trusting.

"Well, best not do that again, then, aye?"

I stared across the room, letting the words sink in.

Was that all he had to say?

"Look, I've got to get back to it. Chat soon?" He said.

I sat up on the couch, suddenly distressed. "Wait, will you be around soon? Last time you said you might have some freedom on the weekend?"

He sighed on the other end. "Sadly, no. I haven't had a day in weeks. Gotta finish writing this grant, don't I? I'll leave ye to it. Don't go falling through any more roofs then," he said. Then the line went dead.

I sat there curled into myself as though the weight of my shoulders was too much to support.

Best not do that again.

I replayed his words more than once, interspersed with my own.

I'd nearly died.

I nearly fell to my death. Thousands of miles from home, but only an hour or so from him.

Nearly died.

My stomach was in a new world of knots as I fought against the unfortunate way I felt.

Maybe I didn't let it sound as dire as it was? Maybe he thought I was kidding?

Depeche Mode began to ooze through the speakers on the desk, only amplifying my sudden melancholic thoughts.

"Was that the doctor, then?"

I turned to find Bran standing in the doorway with a tray of tea and a metal stand harboring slices of warm toast. I wondered how much he'd heard, but made no comment. The thought of food was wiping away all other thoughts.

"It was," I said, curtly, praying he wouldn't feel inclined to make comment.

"Will ye be running off to see the lad, then?"

Damn it, Bran. Why can't you just mind your own business?

He set the tray down in front of me, and I snatched a piece of toast. I was slathering butter on it before I found the will to answer his question. "No. He has to work."

Bran sat down across the table from me and poured us both a cup of tea. "Well, then."

And that was all he said.

I wanted to be mad at him. His tone was enough to speak volumes, but I simply didn't have the will to be angry.

I was too sad, too tired, and now too swimmy and hungry and exhausted, and not just from having almost died – though that was more than enough to wear a person out.

Bran passed me my cup of tea, and I took it, holding the warmth in my ravaged hands and letting it soothe the lingering sting of road rash across my palms.

I took a bite of toast and blinked away a sudden desire to cry.

"I don't understand boys," I said, finally.

He chuckled. "It's interesting ye would use that word -"

I didn't want to hear it. "Well, I don't. I'm literally here because of him. He was all excited to have me nearby. Said he'd spirit me away to the Highlands and shag my brains out for weeks, and now I'm here in the Highlands, spirited away, as it were, and he's nowhere to be found. Nowhere to be found and seems to almost get mad at me when I make comment about seeing each other! I just – I just don't understand it."

So much for not wanting to hear Bran's opinion. Damn that devil's lettuce.

Bran watched me snatch up another piece of toast and the butter knife. I was blinking away tears and getting annoyed with myself for it. Why was I on the verge of crying in front of Bran? Because Christopher hadn't regaled me with concern for my wellbeing? Because of all the people in Scotland, he was the one I wanted to soothe this sudden, literary caliber ennui I was feeling?

Soothe away this sense of loneliness. This sense that the only person in the world who really cared about me was a man who made the mistake of marrying my alcoholic mother.

"Would ye like some toast with that butter?"

I startled, looking up to find Bran's eyebrows raised as he watched me buttering my toast. The slice was more butter than bread. I closed my eyes, holding my breath a moment. I didn't need him picking on me right now.

I felt his hand on mine before I could react. A moment later, Bran was scraping off half the butter from my toast onto a second slice. Then he smeared strawberry jam on them both and set them on the plate in front of me.

The kindness only set me off further.

"You must think I'm an idiot."

He shook his head. "No, but I think ye might be ill-equipped for pursuing a shady Scotsman."

I opened my mouth to defend Chris. He wasn't shady – was he?

"Am I allowed to speak on the subject?"

His request startled me. I met Bran's gaze and my expression must've read loud and clear. I was shocked he asked for permission.

He laughed. "I'll admit that we Scots aren't exactly the most expressive lot. I'm certainly not perfect when it comes to expressing interest, romantically. That having been said, if I had a beautiful woman journey all the way across the world to see me, and knew she was just an hour train ride away, I'd drag my testicles through hot coals to go be with her."

I stared at him, my woozy head summoning visuals to go along with this comment. "Well," I said, but the thoughts roiling about in my head wouldn't compute.

He continued. "I will bet this house, right now, that your doctor there has one of two things – either the twat's married or has a girlfriend, or he has a small cock and he's not ready for ye to find out about it."

I coughed on my toast. "That's absurd! If he was married, he wouldn't be able to Facetime with me -"

"- while masturbating, furiously? Aye, I assure ye, he can."

I cringed. The thought that Bran could know – or even speculate that Chris and I had enjoyed randy Facetime sessions made every muscle in my body seize.

"Right, because no married man has ever pleasured himself in his own home while lookin at things his wife wouldn't approve of."

Thinking of myself as *something the wife wouldn't approve of* hurt my heart. I'd been hurt by men before, and whether or not I liked the notion, I knew I'd been the thing a man looked at when his wife wasn't around before.

Not knowingly.

The thought of going through that again made me miserable.

"Fine, if ye're sure he's no with someone, have ye seen his cock?"

"What?!"

"Ye must've. In this modern era of unsolicited dick pics - is it literally the saddest thing ye've ever seen?"

I shook my head, my temper trying to flare, but failing beneath that sense of misery I'd fallen into. Chris had called me up, demanding to see my face, demanding to hear my voice, all while he touched himself and cooed with such pleasure at the thought of having me when I arrived in his neck of the woods. Yet, in all those calls, we'd vowed not to share those intimate visuals until we were in the same room.

Until we could have one another.

It was romantic, wasn't it? It wasn't because he just didn't want me to know how small his cock was. Because who cares? I didn't!

"No, I haven't seen it," I said, finally.

He slumped back into his chair with a smug look. "I'd wager I'm right."

I growled softly but didn't speak. My mind was racing, and with the heavy-headed inebriation, I was overthinking every single conversation I'd ever had with Christopher. And beyond all those sweet nothings he'd said when calling drunk on a late-night, or when he'd had a bad day, I kept replaying one thing over and over.

The way Bran held my hands in his as he tended to me at his kitchen sink.

Coupled with Christopher's words, *"Best not do that again."*

I'd never let anyone take me under their wing like Bran did that day. Not since my mother left me with Kenny Pace at fourteen years old, never to be heard from again.

I'd spent my whole life proving I didn't need anyone. I didn't need any help. Then this abrasive asshole suddenly turns into a pillar of protection and strength and comfort – and suddenly I can't stop thinking about how badly I've wanted that from someone. To let myself be weak in a man's company – in anyone's company.

I had no idea how much I wanted that – what a balm it was to my soul.

I'd secretly hoped to get it from Christopher, and instead, he'd brushed me off.

If you'd just said you needed sympathy. If you'd just told him how upset and scared you were, how you'd thought of him just an hour away, and never getting to see him or feel him touch you the way he'd threatened to so many times. If you'd just told him what you needed –

These thoughts stilled in an instant as Bran's eyebrows slowly raised. He'd noticed me looking at him.

The look reminded me of something I hated to admit.

Unlike Christopher, Bran didn't need to be told that I needed him.

"What makes you an expert on romance?" I said, finally, desperate to change the subject.

He chuckled. "Oh, I'm no such thing, but I do have it on good authority that a person's actions are the only way to judge their merit – in relationships, especially."

"And you know this firsthand?"

"I do," he said, sipping his tea.

I faltered. The sudden notion that Bran might've had a girlfriend or two in his life – that he might have one now, stopped me in my tracks. "I take it you have a girlfriend?"

Oh nice, Cor. Just come right out and ask him his favorite sex position now, too, why don't you?

"Had. Fiancé, actually."

My mouth went dry.

"Good ol' Beth. We're ended now, though."

My next words came out like pulling teeth. "I'm sorry to hear that."

He shook his head. "Och, no. It's for the best. We were on the rocks for three years before I finally stopped taking her back. I might be an imbecile, but I do learn in the end."

I imagined some beautiful Scottish woman, or some fancy London girl with Stella McCartney handbags shopping at Marks & Spencers. "Why did you stop taking her back?"

I froze. I was sure it was rude to pry, but I wanted to hear his answer, nonetheless. I waited for him to reprimand or respond, holding my breath.

He shrugged. "I wanted to be a father, and after two years of trying when I asked if she'd see a doctor with me, she finally admitted she'd been taking birth control the whole time."

My mouth fell open, but I didn't say another word.

"Remind me to tell my sister this shite is fantastic," he said, gesturing toward the joint.

We both settled into the quiet, lost in our own thoughts. The radio began playing *Under the Milky Way* by The Church and my mind delved even deeper. I felt a million miles away.

"Ye alright?" He said, suddenly.

I started at the sound of his voice. I shook my head. "Not exactly, no."

He gave an exaggerated frown and lifted the cover off a plate of cookies. Or biscuits, as he corrected me. My eyes widened. I might be a million miles away, but I wasn't going to say no to chocolate biscuits. I snagged one and took a bite, feeling the crumbs tumble down the front of my shirt. I didn't care.

"Perhaps ye could call your father?"

That was an idea. Still, I shook my head. "Kenny? No. He'd be livid to hear that I went up on a roof without doing my due diligence."

"Blame me," he said.

I chuckled. "Oh, I do. And I will."

He smiled, though there was little mirth to it. "Ye call your father by his given name?"

My eyebrows shot up, surprised by the interest. "No, he's technically my stepfather. He has a new girlfriend - fiancé – that I kinda have to step on eggshells with. Just sorta got used to calling him Kenny when she was around."

"She sounds lovely," he said.

"She's the kind of person you squat in other people's houses to avoid."

Honesty was becoming unavoidable, it seemed.

"Could ye call your mother?"

I tilted my head. "Why? Do you have her number?"

Bran held my gaze for a long moment. "Sounds like there's a story there."

I exhaled and shook my head. Then despite myself, words came. "Yeah. Mum remarries when I'm four. I live in a house with two alcoholics and a dozen broken pieces of furniture until she decides she doesn't want to be a mother anymore after fourteen years and runs off, leaving me with her soon-to-be ex-husband."

Where the hell did that come from, Cor?

"And he kept ye as his own, then?"

I pursed my lips and nodded.

That was some damn good weed.

Bran and I sat in the silence for a long moment. Finally, there was a sharp scratching sound, and I looked up to find Bran relighting that joint and taking a puff. He held it out to me. I waited a moment, then took it from him. Maybe being a little more inebriated would break this dower mood of mine.

I took a drag off the joint and handed it back, blowing the smoke up into the air over our heads, and watching it swirl and dissipate in the bright space.

Bran took another hit and slumped back into his seat, his legs splayed out wide. "Not quite the same, but – Mother moved back to London when I was two, and I was raised by my Nan until she passed. I was six or so. She'd been sick for a little over a year, so we knew it was coming. Then my father inherited the place and locked himself away here, cursing anything to do with her."

"Cursing her?"

"Oh, aye. Of course. He'd tried to gamble away my grandmother's wealth on bad investments. When she realized she was dying, she emptied the family accounts and set up trust funds for her grandchildren without his knowledge. Made sure we'd be taken care of even if Father squandered his own wealth - which he did. Naturally."

I watched his face, inspecting every inch of his stern brow. "Smart lady."

"Oh, simply brilliant. After she was gone, it was just the three of us up here livin in this palatial estate, but without Nan or Mum around it fell apart. Father had always been like this, but Nan somehow managed to fight it over the years. Once she was gone and the staff left, we had to take over – which our father hated us for. Hence the reputation of being *hellions*."

I thought back to the woman at the church and how Bran had bristled at the comment. "What do you mean?"

"Father liked to tell people what trouble we were. He'd tell stories of how difficult we were, of just how much he did for us and the like, and here we were just a constant source of trouble and pain for him after our grandmother's death. What he failed to tell people was that we spent our entire lives with our father locked in his room, never speaking to either of us if he could avoid it. That was all fine when Nan was here – he was a foul prick, to be sure. Still, once she was gone and father wouldn't acknowledge us – wouldn't leave the house – we were stuck up here in this place with no food, no money, and no one to step in and help because no one would believe that the Laird's children were going hungry."

I thought back to the day when I brought a friend home on the school bus only to find my mother had pissed all over the living room couch while passed out from the previous night's drinking. I'd been so humiliated that I never asked any kid to hang out with me ever again, even after she was gone.

"I remember the day Cal stole fifty-pound from Dad's office, and we walked three hours to the shops just to get something to eat. My shoes were too small for me at the time, and my feet were bleeding horrendously by the time we made the trek home."

"My god," I said, barely audible.

"We had to hide the food around the house because if he found it, he'd have killed us – but worse than that, the prick would've eaten it himself. God, I'll never forget how happy we were when he finally sent us to Mum's."

I sat there watching Bran speak, the words flowing from his lips like we'd known each other for a decade or more – like I'd heard these stories many times. I wanted to reach out and touch him, and the urge grew stronger with each passing moment.

He and I shared more in common than I could've guessed.

"It's odd. I've learned the worst part of that sort of abuse – the kind that doesn't come with bruises and the like - is that people look down on ye for it. He could rewrite history if he wanted. Tell it however he liked, and we'd never say anything against it because ye're raised not to betray your parent. If he hits ye, sure. Speak up. But if he simply pretends ye're not there, what right do ye have to complain?"

He ran his thumb over the rim of his teacup, its contents cooling.

"Then if someone denied what we went through, whether it was Father or some silly bint in the village remembering what *troublemakers* we'd been when we were wee – it reopens the wound. It turns ye right back into a child." He stopped, planting his elbows onto his knees. "I wonder how long it takes to get over that sorta thing, really."

I took up my teacup, staring into the swirls of milk within. "I don't think you ever do."

"Nor do I," he said.

We both let silence fill the space between us, Joy Division playing softly on the radio. A small gray shape appeared and trotted over to Bran's leg. Bran smiled as Mr. Darcy rubbed the side of his face on Bran's jeans, purring like a buzzsaw as Bran reached down to rub behind the kitten's ears.

He finally rose to his feet after a few moments, offering to refill the tea and plate of chocolate biscuits. I didn't refuse.

I watched him gathering everything, taking in his every gesture and movement. I didn't even realize I was in rapt attention. The swimmy effects of that joint had further depths than I realized. I closed my eyes, fighting the sudden revelation.

I was growing fond of Branson.

Damn it, I thought.

Then I watched him carry the tray back out of the conservatory, an excited, little gray furball trotting along behind him.

Nine

I WOKE WITH MR. Darcy's butt tucked up under my chin, his nose buried into the crook of my neck. I lay there a long moment, listening to the muffled sound of birds in the distance – birds that sang at all hours of the night.

Despite my previous disdain for the din, the mornings at Cavendish were actually turning out to be almost pleasant. The weeks I'd spent there seemed to be softening me to the place.

I rolled my eyes at myself.

Seriously, Cor? Trapped in an old estate with a handsome earl. You're not Jane Eyre, and Branson isn't Rochester. You're out of here in a few more weeks.

That thought made my chest tighten. I reached up to cuddle Mr. Darcy closer to me. What would I do with him when I had to go my merry way? Where was I going to go?

Not something I wanted to think about yet.

I grabbed my phone. It was 10 am.

I sighed. Bran was certainly going to have a field day giving me a hard time for the late hour. Could he blame me? I went to bed stoned and still shaky.

Yes, he could blame me. If I'd come to know anything about Bran for certain, it was that he would give me a hard time any chance he got.

I smiled. *Dick.*

I rolled away from the kitten, smiling as he rolled onto his back and stretched across the pillow with a big yawn. I felt a tinge of cuteness-rage, instantly, and had to smash my face into his belly while he chewed on my forehead.

I began my lazy morning perusal of my phone.

Two missed calls.

I furrowed my brow like some angry librarian eyeing a book that was three years late. Who the hell was calling me in the middle of the night?

I pulled on my comfy yoga pants, grabbed the now cold cup of tea from the night before, and headed out into the house. I glanced down at my phone as I made my way down the stairs.

Missed Call – Chris.

Missed Call – Chris.

"Oh, did you find the time, you prick?" I said to myself, half mumbling as I shuffled into the kitchen with Mr. Darcy darting between my ankles.

A female voice laughed from the other side of the kitchen. "You must be referring to Bran, aye?"

The laughter caught me completely off guard, and I nearly dropped both teacup and phone.

There was a woman standing by the kitchen sink, her own cup of steaming tea in her hands.

Let me rephrase – there was an Amazon standing by the kitchen sink, long honey blonde hair hanging in soft waves down well past her shoulders.

I felt like a half-peeled potato in her company.

"Kettle's still hot, if you'd like," she said, then offered a startlingly warm grin. I stepped back, fearing that the sheer magnitude of my frumpiness might be contagious.

The woman was impressively tall, wearing gorgeous black heels and a sleek black dress. She had a pair of big black sunglasses on despite the cloud cover outside, and they were now settled atop her head, holding her hair back in the most flattering way.

I swallowed, stumbling over my words. "Hey, uh. I'm – who are you?"

"Cal!? Ye sexy bitch! I'm so glad ye're here!"

Bran came rushing through the kitchen door, lunging around the island to embrace the tall woman. She wore impressive heels and stood at least two inches taller than Bran in them. He wrapped his arms around her, and they held each other there for a long moment, swaying as Bran shook her in his arms.

I stiffened as I watched them. Who the hell was this lady, and why was Bran holding her like that?

"I thought ye said ye'd die before ye came up," he said, finally releasing her.

The woman shot me another smile just as Bran did the same. The resemblance was instantly clear in their identical blue eyes and matching dimples.

"Turner, this is my sister, Cal."

I exhaled, only then realizing I'd been holding my breath as the sick feeling in my stomach dissipated. "Oh my god, yes! Of course," I said, the words coming in an almost shrilly pleasant tone.

What the hell was that, Cor?

"Wait. Cal?" I asked, stepping forward to offer Bran's *sister* a handshake. The graceful woman took it, always smiling with such intense warmth, I feared I'd shrink under her gaze. I'd never met such an imposingly graceful creature.

"Callista," she said, taking my hand. "It's lovely to meet you, finally. Branson tells me you've been an absolute miracle."

My eyebrows shot up and I shot Bran a confused glance. "Wait, what?"

"I wouldn't want to be in your shoes, that's for sure," she said.

"Oh, come now. Ye'd love to roll up those designer sleeves of yours and install a loo in the upstairs, wouldn't ye?"

Callista rolled her eyes at her brother, then reached for me again, her hand open. "Here. Let me take that? I'll pour you a fresh cuppa."

I startled, looking down at the contents of my hands like the appendages had just magically appeared.

Great, now you're acting like a potato. Spectacular.

I handed my stained embarrassment of a teacup over. Callista took a look inside it, then silently set it in the sink and pulled a clean cup from the cupboard. A couple moments later, I was holding a hot cup of steeping Earl Grey with cream and sugar.

"Ye have to come see the place, Cal. Ye won't believe how well it's comin along!"

Bran grabbed his sister's hand and dragged her out of the kitchen, her heels clacking against the ancient stone floor as she went by, her hair flitting through the air as though fairies danced in its tendrils when she slept. She turned to me, offering a pleading look.

I watched them disappear and listened to the boisterous sound of Bran offering his sister a tour of the third floor.

I took my tea back up to my room to relax for a few more minutes. I needed to get some clothes to start work for the day, but I was feeling more than a little asocial. My jeans were freshly washed now, and my work shirt (a tired old Jethro Tull shirt I stole from dad's closet) was only half as dingy as it could be.

I'd be the most glamorous hobo Callista had ever met.

At least I'd worn deodorant the day before. I could get away with another day of stink-free existence.

I slumped into one of the blue satin chairs in the corner of the room and pulled out my journal, flipping open to the first clean page. It wasn't hard. I hadn't done much writing since I arrived.

Almost died yesterday.

Good times.

Then, Chris called last night after I fell asleep.

Twice.

After that 'Better not do that again' comment, I'm thinking I'll hold off on calling him back.

I stopped, staring at the words. Normally when I housesat, I'd spend hours upon hours purging my mind of thoughts until my hand grew tired, but even with everything going on – with the house, Bran, meeting his sister, still not getting paid by Jocelyn – in the midst of all this chaos, I just didn't feel the need to purge any of it.

Save for Chris. Apparently, I was willing purge a little on the subject of Chris.

Given that journal was started when I first arrived in the U.K. months earlier, its pages were almost entirely about Chris.

He'd called.

He hadn't called.

He was texting me all the time.

He wasn't texting me all the time.

I stared at the page, rereading the words and thinking about how much time I'd spent trying to understand the actions of the man who'd asked me to come back to Scotland to see him, only to dissipate like that tinge of jealousy I felt when Bran hugged his sister.

Jealousy?

Had I been jealous? Is that really what I was feeling?

Shit.

I set the pen down on the table and closed the journal. I didn't have anything to say. The sudden activity within the house and the appearance of another heir to the estate were making me feel a little out of place.

She'd called me a miracle – or Bran had. Still, was she currently interrogating her brother about the presence of a professional squatter in her family estate?

What is this random American woman doing mooching off my brother?

I stared at the closed journal for a long moment, then picked up my phone.

Because fuck it.

I'd never been so relieved to get sent to voicemail in my life.

"Hey, Chris. Saw you called. What's up?"

I set the phone down and took that last sip of my cooling tea.

Mr. Darcy was returned to his post, happily curled up on the bed, staring at me with half-closed eyes. I hopped up and began making the bed around him. I stood in the room watching the windows for a long moment, then without thinking, snatched up my perfume from the bedside table and sprayed myself with it.

Because if I was going to live my life as a potato, I was going to be a potato that smelled nice.

I turned back to the house to search for Bran and see if he was ready to start emptying out the next junk-filled room. Or, given his sister was visiting, if he was ready for *me* to start emptying out the next junk-filled room.

I wasn't grumpy, I swear.

I listened in the distance for Bran's excited voice but found the house quiet again. After a moment standing at the top of the stairs, I heard the familiar sound of Bran's table saw whirring in the barn, outside. He was back at work, perhaps accosting his sister with manual labor as he'd so happily accosted me.

Given Callista's perfect manicure, I wasn't sure she'd be as gung-ho to haul junk and install roof shingles.

I set to work on my own, returning to the crock pot room to start dousing the place with a coat of buttercream paint. After one quick coat and still no sign of Bran or his sister's return into the house, I decided to attack the clutter along the hallway, piling up broken headboard pieces and rusting bed slats onto tarps, tossing fallen roof plaster and water-damaged wood planks into the mix, then wrapped it all up like I was planning to hide a body, and dragged the whole shebang down the hall and dumped it into the chute.

When I grew impatient and dumped one too many bed slats onto the chute at once, two of them clattered over the side and to the ground below.

I closed my eyes and exhaled. Going outside wasn't on my agenda.

There was a mist in the air, something bordering close to rain, constantly making it feel as though someone just sneezed in your face. I heaved the last two slats up over the side of the dumpster, brushing the shoulder of my t-shirt across my upper lip to wipe away the dust and rain. I glanced toward the barn, wondering what Bran was working on, or what he and his sister were talking about.

Wonder if they're complaining about you, Cor?

I shook my head, turning back into the house.

If they *were* talking about me, I was going to make it damn hard to think of me as a worthless layabout. I was going to kick ass, take names, paint walls, and chuck shit.

In the dumpster. Chuck shit in the dumpster, not chuck shit like an angry chimpanzee or something – nevermind.

Despite Bran's absence, I managed to put a huge dent in the disarray of the hallway. I organized any boxes and trunks that might harbor things of value within, and even found two more crock pots hidden under chests full of silver and china. I laughed to myself as I picked them up. I could imagine exactly what Bran would have said had he been the one stumbling on such a treasure trove.

After the last run to the chute, I made my way down the now clear hallway to the last room on the left – the buttercream room.

I stood in the middle of the bedroom, the light from the windows glowing over the new paint color. It made the white crown pop in a way the olive-brown couldn't dream of. I imagined a pair of twin beds set against the far wall, a cherry wood chest of drawers and headboard, and a braided rug in the center of the room, pulling in the colors of the curtains and bedclothes to tie the whole place together.

I turned, as though to see Bran's smiling expression when he saw how the room was turning out. Yet, he wasn't there. For the first time in days, he wasn't at my side.

Oh god, I thought. *I miss him.*

I exhaled in exasperation, then turned my full attention back to the second coat of paint.

He's in the fucking barn, Cor. Are you serious? You miss him? Sure, he's fun to work with. And he certainly makes it easier, but – you miss him? Shut up.

I made quick work of painting and gave the hallway a final sweep. I paused for an instant as I caught the slightest whisper of music in the distance – some crooner singing a standard over a sweeping round of horns – not the usual music Bran would play while we worked.

I didn't hate it.

I marched back down the stairs to the front hall, passing Mr. Darcy on the top of the steps as he went sauntering by, clearly hell-bent on a particular location. I glanced back to see him dart down the hallway and into an open door. I spun around to follow.

The jammed door was now open, and Mr. Darcy was happily trotting through it and out of sight.

When I reached the door, he was happily sharpening his claws on the lowest mattress in the pile, the soft tug of his nails creating a rhythmic sound.

The room was the same as I'd last seen it – a pile of water-stained mattresses, a tiny wood stove in the corner, and a fireplace on the opposite side. I lunged into Mr. Darcy's path before he could explore further into the room, pulling him up to my chin to give his head a rub. He purred in my hand, oblivious to the panic he'd caused me.

I could just imagine hearing his pathetic meowing coming from beyond the door, but unlike the night I first found him, in my imagination, the door was jammed again, and he was trapped inside. The thought turned my stomach.

"No, sir. No more sneaking in here, mister. You could get in twouble. Yes, we don't want that."

"He's adorable."

I nearly dropped him, his body squirming in response to my sudden movement. I turned back to shut the door and set him down in the hall.

"Sorry, didn't mean to startle you."

I glanced down over the railing and spotted Callista standing in the downstairs hall. She gave me a sheepish wave.

Callista's version of sheepish still felt like talking to Xena, The Warrior Princess.

"Oh, no. No worries," I said, hurrying to snatch up my broom, again.

Look useful, bitch! Look like you work for your meals!

I gave it a wave, the floor already clear of any dust as I tried not to make eye contact with Bran's sister.

When I finally turned down the stairs, she was gone.

I'd put on a show for no one.

Ridiculous.

I took a moment to glance out the window. The skip was filling up quickly. We'd have to send for a pickup before the month was over at this rate – that is, if I couldn't convince Bran to do something with the crock pots and other still viable items that teemed within the house and now the skip.

I listened to the intermittent whir of Bran's table saw as he worked in the distance.

Probably cutting crown molding or chair rail pieces – or something. I had no idea what Bran did in there, I just knew whatever he did, he was damn good at it. I thought of going in to find him, watching him work, offering him some lunch – anything to be in his company.

You're pathetic, Turner. Completely pathetic.

I smacked my work gloves against my hips and set them down on the steps before heading into the kitchen for a drink. I was breathless and ready for a break – and deep down, Bran's absence was feeling rather detrimental to my motivation.

Part of me was hoping that if I just futzed around long enough, by the time I was ready to head back upstairs, Bran would be back inside.

I hoped.

I shook my head.

If Bran comes back in from working outside, he's going to spend his time with his sister, not elbow deep in dust and debris on the third floor with you.

I poured myself a tall glass of water and cooed to Mr. Darcy as he bounced down the stairs toward the kitchen. "Hey, Mr. Man," I said. "You wanna come sit with me for a minute?"

I made quiet, kissy noises, then headed into the Great Hall, listening to my footsteps echo off the high halls like some ancient tale as I crossed the room. I slumped down onto the wide window seat, turning my back to the room as I watched the drizzle collect on the warped panes of glass.

The music changed, a new song playing somewhere in the distance.

I sat there sipping my water, feeling the immense space behind me like a presence, and set my eyes on the tree line in the distance, the gray sky looming overhead. Despite the streaks of water on the window, I could just barely make out the steeple of the Kinvale church through the trees.

"This was always one of my favorite rooms."

I startled around, fighting not to choke on my water. Callista stood in the middle of the room now, staring up at the genealogy chart over the fireplace.

This woman was trying to kill me.

I stared for a long moment, awestruck by her ability to walk across that floor in those heels without making a sound.

"It really is something special," I said, turning around to sit forward on the window seat. "Almost afraid to sit down in this one, though."

She shook her head. "I'm afraid to sit down anywhere in this house. You're right though, it is something," Callista said, then smiled over at me before turning her eyes back up to the mantle. "I honestly never thought I'd set foot in this house, again."

I swallowed, fighting to find a position that didn't hurt. I couldn't lean back against the lead-paned windows, and both sitting straight and slouching were painful.

Clearly, I wasn't lifting with my legs as much as I should.

"Really? I imagine it will be in pretty good shape soon enough, if Bran has his way with it."

Callista smiled. "No small thanks to you there, so he tells me."

My face grew hot. "Meh, just trying to earn my keep."

The woman grinned at me again, and the resemblance between her and her brother was undeniable. "Well, I hope you're right."

Her accent was undeniably London, but there was a streak of Scottish that peered through every so often.

I stood up, finally unable to tolerate the ache in my back. "Will you move here when the work is done?"

Callista furrowed her brow for an instant in what looked like confusion but shook her head. "No. I don't imagine I'll ever call this home, again."

I forced a chuckle as I tried to break the weight of Callista's tone. "Not a fan of Scotland?"

She shook her head. "Too many ghosts."

The words gave me a chill, though I was sure she wasn't talking about the Lady in Blue.

I walked over to stand near Callista, looking up at the massive parchment over the mantle, the tired old sharpie stain still scribbled over Bran's older brother's name.

Callista sighed, softly. "It's lovely to meet you, by the way. Bran's told me a lot about you."

"Really? I'm sure it's all wine and roses."

Despite my sarcasm, she smiled. "Oh, aye."

There's that Scottish streak.

"Well, he's said only wonderful things about you, as well. Though, I admit, I think half the time he mentioned you, I thought he was talking about his brother."

Callista's eyebrows shot up. "Why is that?"

I gestured up to the chart and shrugged. "He kept calling you Cal, and I saw the names up there when I first got here and just assumed that Cal was short for Callum."

"Oh, it was."

I opened my mouth, but didn't speak, turning to look at Callista's profile. I watched the tall woman's face, waiting for an explanation. Callista turned to look at me out of the corner of her eye and gave a patient smile. "Bran hasn't told you anything about me, has he?"

"I – don't know. He's mentioned his father. Said his father let the house fall into disrepair to - I don't know, destroy his birthright?"

Callista nodded. "Close, I suppose. But he didn't tell you why he wasn't here to stop it? Why our father literally refused to let him set foot inside the house for twenty years?"

I shook my head. "Because he was a dick?"

Callista laughed. "Ah, darling. I like you. And honestly, the fact that you seem to truly have no idea is quite refreshing."

"No idea about what?"

Callista smiled. "I'm Bran's sister, but that's me," she said, gesturing up to the scribbled-over name. "I was born Callum Montgomery Douglas."

My mouth fell open. "What?"

Callista smiled. "Did Branson tell you about our lovely family? About Nan?"

She pointed up to a name on the chart – Helene Lennox.

"Yes?"

Callista nodded. "Well, then I don't imagine he told you that when Nan discovered she was sick, she knew if something happened to her, our father would ravage her fortune as he had with his own. She went and put all her money into trust funds for Bran and I that we would inherit on our twenty-first birthdays. Didn't tell us, didn't tell anyone."

"Our Nan's broker contacted me just before my twenty-first birthday. Was quite possibly the greatest day of my life. I came up from University for the summer, and told father about my good fortune, and more importantly that I would be using some of the money to begin my transition. And he went bloody mad."

I turned to the chart, staring up at the long list of Douglas names, all leading down to Branson and his – sister.

Cal stared up at it with me, quiet for a long moment.

"Our mother knew. She used to let me put on her shoes and dresses when I was very little. I think even father knew. I told him that my name was Callista. Bran always called me Cal, I answered to Cal – I *felt* like a Cal, just not a Callum. Father refused to even acknowledge me and sent me back to London without a word. But poor Bran -"

My stomach turned. I glanced toward the doors of the Great Hall, feeling as though I was betraying Bran to listen to his sister speak of him like this. Still, Callista continued.

"When Bran came home from school for the summer that year, my – our father told Bran that his brother had died."

I held my breath, my chest growing tight.

Callista's voice was smoky and warm, the depths of it changing as Callista began to grow emotional. "He'd let the phone bill lapse, so there was no way to call anyone. Bran was just stuck here in this rubbish dump with our father, grieving alone. I remember Bran telling me about the day our father demanded he take down this tired old thing and cross my name off. God, if he'd known Bran at all – my brother could tell you the exact date that each room in this house was built. Every chair, desk, every banister for christ's sake – he knows exactly how old it is - how precious. This bloody chart is hundreds of years old. Even at fifteen, Bran would never!"

I could see Calista's eyes beginning to glisten as she smiled up at the chart.

"We hire a calligrapher for the job, you see? Whenever it is to be changed, it's done by a professional. Yet, my father asked poor Bran to cross off my name. Like I never existed. Bran said he sobbed the whole time, but the old bastard said he'd do it himself if Bran didn't climb up and get the chart down. So, to appease our father, Bran climbed up there with a marker and scribbled over his dead brother's name, marking the glass instead, always intending to wipe it away one day."

Callista tugged her shawl up around her shoulders as though a chill passed through the air.

Despite the temperature remaining steady, I felt it, too.

"After a Summer stuck up here with our maddening father, mourning me, alone with no one to grieve with and no way to talk to anyone outside the house, Bran was finally allowed to return to London for school. And there he found me – still living with our mother and very much alive, but changed," she said, gesturing to herself. "When Bran realized what our father had done – why he'd done it..."

Callista stopped for a moment, touching her shawl to her cheek as tears spilled over. She dabbed her eyes, being careful not to ruin her perfect eyeliner. Her breath caught in her throat and she forced a smile as she spoke. "He confronted our father and was given a choice. He chose me."

She stopped again, turning her face away, as though searching the room for something. "Father disowned us both."

My throat grew tight. I wanted to throw my arms around this woman and hug her until her bones cracked, but I didn't know Callista. She was no one to me, save for an extension of Bran. And what was Bran to me but some pseudo-employer that I kinda liked to look at, sometimes? I was sure even he wouldn't be all that thrilled either if I were to suddenly hug him until I'd squeezed all the air from his lungs.

Still, I wanted to do just that now, more than ever.

Callista took a deep breath. "Honestly, I really believe he knew. I swear the real crime I committed wasn't that I was a woman, it was that our Nan gave us money he believed was meant to be his. His to spend on endless piles of fuck all to bury us all under until we were all drowning with him."

"I'm sorry you both had to go through that," I finally said, wiping tears from my own eyes. "I'm so sorry."

God, you sound like an idiot.

"Thank you, but it's alright." She turned to face me for the first time and smiled. "I see why Bran likes you so much. You're very expressive. It's very American."

I snorted in a half-laugh, half-cry, my face growing hot in embarrassment. "I think I'm more of a barely tolerated minion, really."

Callista's eyebrows shot up, but she smiled. "Really? How interesting."

The two of us stood there in silence for a long moment. Finally, Callista wiped her eyes again, her voice returned to its former light timber. "I am rather surprised our dear Bran didn't take this down to have it updated as soon as he was allowed back in the house. He is officially the Earl now. I'm sure he's itching to have the title written under his name there."

I turned my head, hiding a grin. "I'm sure it's crossed his mind."

Callista smiled, turning toward the high windows. The light was shifting as darker clouds rolled in. "Poor Bran. Knowing how he felt about this house, finding it in such a state must've nearly destroyed him. Thank god you were here to help," she said, touching her hand to my shoulder.

"Naw. I think I was more of a bunion on the sole of his foot, really. He's tolerating me, at best."

Callista eyed me, curiously. "Corinne. I'm going to tell you something, now please don't repeat it."

I raised my eyebrows, shaking my head to assure her I'd never tell a soul.

"The night Bran arrived here, he called me in a panic."

I frowned and quickly fought to hide my response.

"He was curled up in a ball on the floor of one of the few bedrooms he could even get into, barely able to catch his breath he was so overwhelmed at the state of the place. After our Nan died, that poor man spent his childhood trying to combat this tidal wave before being cast out of the house. But coming home to this? It nearly did him in. Thought I was going to have to hop a train that night. Took me nearly two hours to calm him down."

I blinked, my eyes burning. "I didn't know."

"When I talked to him again two days later, you were here – and he was a completely different man."

I opened my mouth to speak, but no word would come.

"So, don't let him convince you for a minute that he isn't ecstatic to have you here. I imagine if you hadn't come along, he'd have given up by now."

I was frozen for a long moment, Callista content to stare up at the ancient genealogy chart. Finally, I smiled. "I'm trying. It's coming along."

"As he's told me. Now -" Calista started, marching across the hardwood floor. "What on earth happened here," she said, staring directly up at the *Me*-shaped hole in the ceiling.

I approached Bran's sister, stifling a shudder at the memory. "Oh, that's just where I almost died. No big deal. It's cool."

Callista's eyes went wide. "What? Oh, this I have to hear."

Callista took me by the hand and pulled me back toward the front of the house, then led me into the kitchen to have a cup of tea while I relayed the dramatic events of a roofing endeavor gone wrong.

The sound of the saw roared in the distance from outside the kitchen windows, Callista sharing stories of her early childhood at the house, and me relaying only the most pleasant memories of my own.

"God, listen to him out there. Is he always at it?" Callista asked, pouring herself a new cup of tea and giving a wide-eyed look of conspiracy as she added a splash of whiskey. She gestured to me in offering, but I refused. I did intend to get back to work at some point that afternoon.

"He is usually, yes. We're making a lot of progress on the east side. You might not be able to really see it yet because we haven't touched the second floor, but I swear, when we started, there wasn't a single working bathroom in that half of the house."

"Oh, I know all about it."

Callista moved through the kitchen toward the old dining room, continuing to speak as she went. I took that to mean I should follow. Despite Callista's aversion to the home, she seemed to move through it now with a genuine interest, leaning into various doorways and smiling or pointing at various things. I stood outside the billiard room with her, describing the massive pile of instant coffee cans Bran and I hauled out of there when a tiny cry demanded our attention back by the kitchen door.

Meow.

"Oh my goodness! Mr. Gorgeous has come to say hello!?" Calista said, cooing in a high-pitched sing-song. She scooted down the hallway toward Mr. Darcy, crouching down to offer her fingers, inviting the gray fluff to come say hello.

He did.

It was after his breakfast time, and I was sure he was feeling put out to find his dish empty.

"That's Mr. Darcy. I found him my first night here."

"Mr. Darcy?! What a glorious name. Just perfect for this handsome little man."

I smiled. "Thank you. That's what I said. Your brother disagrees with me, of course."

"Of course, he does. Because he's a silly man, isn't he Mr. Darcy?" Callista buried her face into the kitten's fur as he purred in her arms, rubbing his jowls across her nose.

I slipped down the hall past them to start fixing Mr. Darcy his now brunch when Callista snatched hold of my arm.

"Oh, tell me Bran has shown you the library."

My eyebrows shot up, but before I could shake my head in confusion, Callista snatched my hand and led me into the front hallway and down to the lower level of the east wing. I'd only spent a little time on this side of the house with Bran – that afternoon in the conservatory. Still, I felt almost invasive when I ventured to this side without him. It was the side in the most disarray, the side that best exhibited their father's tendencies.

Despite that, Callista careened past the open doors, stopping halfway down the hall, the light of the conservatory glowing in the distance.

"Here we are. Come. Let's see if father sold it, shall we?"

Callista handed Mr. Darcy to me and marched into the dusty old room. The walls were dark mahogany, dozens of bookshelves lining them as high as the tops of the windows. I stood in the doorway as

Calista skimmed across the shelves and glass cupboard doors. All the furniture was covered in white sheets, and the shelves carried a layer of dust so thick, they looked to be painted gray. I took a deep breath, giving the light switch a try.

The room remained dark, lit only by the gray overcast sky outside. *Yet another fixture or bulb to replace.*

"Oh, you're going to love this! Come here, darling. Come look."

I set Mr. Darcy down on the floor to play kill the hemline of the nearest sheet and joined Callista by the far wall. Between the high middle windows, a quartet of bookshelves lay hidden behind a glass door. Calista turned the tiny key in the lock and opened the cabinet, releasing the subtle hint of old moth balls from within.

Callista reached into the cupboard and pulled a red leather book from the middle shelf, cradling it in her hands as though holding a newborn baby.

"It's a first edition. I can't believe father didn't sell it in all this time."

I stood there, holding my hands out to take the treasure. I opened the cover and gasped as I read the front page of the book.

Pride and Prejudice: A novel in Three Volumes

"You're kidding," I said, barely able to force the words out.

"I'm certainly not! It was my grandmother's. My god, it's still in perfect condition. It was quite possibly her most cherished possession"

Callista stooped down to snatch up the kitten and stood there beside me, watching as I fawned over the ancient book.

"This is really it? This is a first edition? This must be worth a fortune!"

Callista nodded. "It would fetch quite a price if Bran were to try to sell it."

"He wouldn't!?" I said, my tone the same as if I'd been asked to feed an infant to a crocodile.

"No, I don't imagine he would, but still. There's a few more in here, if I recall. Oh, yes!"

Bran's voice echoed somewhere in the house; a heated phone discussion seemed to be taking place.

I closed the book and gave it back to Callista as she leaned in to look at the various titles. There were copies of *Frankenstein*, *Ulysses*, and *A*

Connecticut Yankee at King Arthur's Court. I spotted a strange brown satchel on the second shelf but was too preoccupied with the books to ask about it.

Callista slunk back across the room, dragging the white sheet off of a long claw-footed couch before plopping down with Mr. Darcy and throwing her feet up. "Look inside the copy of *Huck Finn.*"

I pulled the worn leather book out of the shelf and carefully opened the front cover. The name Mark Twain was scribbled across the title page, a splash of ink splatter just under it.

I instantly moved to touch the ink blotch, my fingertips stopping just centimeters from the mark. It was like being in a museum, but they'd removed the *Do Not Touch* signs just for me.

"My grandmother was a bit of a reader, and she loved the idea of having first editions of things. She never touched them once she bought them. Just tucked them away to keep them safe."

"This is signed," I said, finally. I was clearly having trouble with words.

"I know, right? I thought you might enjoy that."

Callista dangled a piece of string she'd pulled from the hem of the sheet in front of the kitten and he proceeded to go batshit on the couch beside her. Callista giggled, poking her finger across the satin surface of the couch to tease the kitten into hunting her. I scanned down the spines of the books, my eyes going wide with every new discovery.

"Are they all first editions?"

Callista didn't look up from the kitten. "No, not all, but a good number of them. Some are just signed copies."

"A signed Mark Twain?" I thought aloud. "This is absurd. How do you – how does somebody just live around something this amazing and -"

"And turn the place into a fucking cesspool?"

I startled around at her salty language.

She just smiled. "I believe the inspiration was spite, my dear. Spite, perhaps some illness, and a crippling need for control."

I turned back to the book, running my fingers lightly over Mark Twain's name, feeling an excited shiver of breaking the rules and getting away with it, all in the hopes of feeling an indentation from the stroke of his pen. I smiled.

My phone buzzed in my pocket. I set the book back into its slot on the shelf and pulled it out to find Chris was calling.

Again.

Again? I thought.

Mr.   I-don't-have-time-to-do-much-of anything-but-complain-about-how-busy-I-am-let-alone-come-see-you was suddenly very adamant he get in touch with me.

"Excuse me," I said, slipping out of the library and into the hall. "Hello?"

"Hey! There ye are," Chris said.

"Yes. Here I am," I said, letting the words carry an impatient tone.

"What are ye up to? Still slaving away for that posh prick?"

I pursed my lips. "He's not a posh prick, and I'm not slaving away. Just working. And it's coming along really nicely, actually."

"Oh, fair point. Yeah, hey. I've had another huge load of work dumped on my plate, so I won't be able to meet up at all this month?"

I felt my stomach shoot up into my throat. "Uh, this month?"

"Aye. Just discovered all the samples from the last round of tests are fucking useless because I'm surrounded by idiots who can't seem to remember that when using a laser microscope, it bloody helps to turn the fucking laser on. Bell ends."

"Didn't they do that last time?"

There was a pause. "Aye, now that you say that, this *isn't* the first fucking time. Christ on a bike."

I took a deep breath. "Chris, I came a really long way to see you."

He made an indecipherable sound, cutting me off. "Look, I've had a lot on my plate, and you of all people know that."

"I do -"

"I really don't appreciate ye playing that card, right now."

My face contorted, but I fought to keep the anger out of my voice. "I'm not playing a card. It's the truth. The whole reason I'm here was because you asked me to come see you, and last time I heard from you, you'd spent the evening at the pub with friends -"

"Oh, how dare I take a minute for myself to relax and watch the Scotland match when I've worked for literally fifty hours, and the week isn't even over yet?"

I straightened, feeling my throat grow tight as I fought to stay calm. "It's been a month, Chris. I've been here for over a month. If that posh prick you refer to hadn't been kind enough to let me stay, I would have been stranded here, all because you told me to come -"

"Look, I literally just called as a courtesy. I'm going back to work. Good night."

"- if I'd known you would... Hello? Hello? Are you fucking serious?" I looked at the screen of my phone and my nose crinkled as I fought not to cry. The frustration of dealing with him was growing to a point that I simply couldn't take it anymore. When I didn't hear from him, anger and resentment took hold and settled in. Then he calls, I hear his voice, and all the memories of sweetness and endearment take hold all over again.

I stood there, clutching my phone tight. The sadness began to shift, and instead of wanting to cry, I wanted to punch something. I was no longer asking myself what I'd done to make him change like this – other than do exactly as he'd asked? Instead, I was thinking of what I would give to have a man like Branson talk to me the way Chris used to – when he was drunk after a night at the pub.

Stupid. I'm just fucking stupid.

"Posh prick, aye?"

I startled, turning to find Bran standing just outside the library doorway. I blew air out through pursed lips and opened my eyes wide to stop them from spilling over. "Yeah, I didn't call you that," I said.

Bran smiled, his head half down in a shrug. "No worries. It's not entirely untrue."

"No, it's not, is it, Mr. Darcy?" Callista said in her high-pitched kitten speak as Bran stood aside to let me enter the room. Cal glanced up at us a moment. "Sounds like you should both avoid answering the phone for the rest of the day."

I turned back to the books to avoid eye contact.

She turned to Bran. "Was that who I think it was?"

Bran sighed. "I'll tell ye later."

Callista shook her head. "Should just stop answering the phone when she calls, Branny. Mad cow."

I swallowed, trying to look preoccupied. I was sure they were talking about Bran's ex-fiancé, Beth, but I didn't dare pry.

"What are the two of ye doing in here, then?" He asked, changing the subject as he crossed the room to the glass-doored cupboard. "Just layin about?"

"I was showing her Nan's books. Given this handsome feline friend, I thought she might like to see them. I'm surprised you didn't show her yourself."

Bran's eyebrows shot up. "I hadn't even thought of it. I imagined father would have sold them off out of spite."

Callista continued to direct her comments to the cat, smiling all the while as she spewed a loving sing-song of vitriol. "That's right, because he was a right knob, wasn't he, darling? Yes, he was."

Bran leaned into the cupboard, taking a moment to admire the collection himself.

"Did ye tell her about Nan at all?" Callista asked.

Bran shook his head, but before he could speak, Callista growled her disapproval. "Oh, how could you? She was wonderful, Nan."

Bran pulled out the copy of *Frankenstein* to open the cover, startling me as I spotted the scribble of what looked like an autograph on the front page before he slipped it back onto the shelf.

"Now that was the time to see Cavendish. Och, when we were just wee. That's when the house was truly in its prime."

Bran nodded. "It really was," he said, reaching for the brown wallet on the second shelf. He pulled it out, his eyebrows shooting up as he turned it over in his hand.

"Every room was pristine, every wall was covered in paintings, every room coordinated to Nan's preferred color palette. Do you remember those parties? God! She used to put on these balls."

"Oh god," Bran said, exhaling in a snort.

I moved closer to him to inspect the object. The brown leather was worn and shiny at its fold.

"She would hold these huge fancy dress balls, invite everyone you can imagine. And she so loved history, she'd require a dress code. You couldn't just come as any old tart or vicar, oh no."

Bran shot me a sideways glance and smiled. "Of course not."

Very Mr. Darcy. The ladies all wore these *gorgeous* dresses. Just gorgeous. I was *so* jealous." Callista was becoming more animated with every word, Mr. Darcy purring away in her arms. "Oh, has she seen the portrait, Branny, love?"

"No," he said, and it was the sternest he'd ever sounded.

I couldn't help but laugh. Bran shot me an exasperated look, then handed me the wallet to inspect.

Callista ignored the tone completely. "There is this glorious portrait of our wee Branson in his little tailcoat and cravat. It was painted in his costume when he was – were you five?"

"I was. Nan died right after I turned six."

"She did, didn't she?" With that, Callista's tone turned almost wistful as she headed out the library door. "Of course, I'm in the painting as well, but I try to pretend I'm not. Blech. Where is it, darling brother? We must show her."

"It's not in a pleasant part of the house."

Callista spun around, flitting a hand in his general direction. "My dear brother, no part of this house is pleasant as far as I'm concerned. Lead the way."

Bran rolled his eyes and sighed, holding his hand out to take the wallet.

"What is it," I asked, sensing its pricelessness to him.

He gave me a mischievous look. "Ye're no gonna like it."

I knit my brow, waiting for an explanation.

He turned the wallet over in his hands. "This belonged to my Nan. Was passed down from her grandmother, I believe. It's made out of human skin."

I recoiled, rubbing my hands on my jeans as though I could rid myself of the memory of its smooth feel. "Who keeps a wallet of human skin?!"

He grinned. "My great-grandfather was an attending surgeon at the dissection of William Burke – ye know the Edinburgh Body Snatchers?"

My eyes went wide, despite myself. "You're kidding."

He shook his head. "I'm not. He had this made and gave it to his wife as a gift."

"How romantic," I said, sarcastically.

Bran met my gaze and grinned. "Isn't it, though?"

"Are ye coming!?"

Callista's Scottish tinge was thickening in her impatience, and Bran quickly returned the wallet to the shelf before closing the cupboard and turning the key to lock it up. He then rushed around the couch to recover it with the white sheet. I watched him, seeing his behavior in a new light. Callista describing the love he'd had for the house, even as a boy – watching the way he fretted and fought to restore every piece that he could – it made sense now.

He'd seen it in its glory. His earliest memories were of that house in the care of a doting grandmother.

All this work was Bran's way of trying to shake off the ghosts – to let the real spirit back in.

"It's down in the ballroom," he said, twisting his body to sidestep me as he went through the doorway. Callista took my arm and marched along the corridor behind her brother, her heels muffled on the runner. We strolled through the foyer, past the Great Hall, bypassing rooms I'd never ventured into.

"Wait, there's a ballroom?" I said, gesturing back toward the great hall. "I mean, another one?"

"No, silly girl. That's not big enough for a ball."

Bran didn't speak but stopped at a set of double doors on the right side of the hall. He opened them with the regal flourish they deserved, their movement causing a draft within that made the white sheets flit atop their chairs and tables.

I let Callista lead me into the room, staring up at the plaster filigree of the ceiling. "Jesus, how much of the house have I still not seen?"

The room was easily twice the size of the Great Hall, the far wall of the ballroom jutting out further than the rest of the house. And just as Calista described, there were paintings along every inch of the wall, some covered with sheets, some not, and they'd grown dingy with layers of dust.

The windows stretched from floor to ceiling and a massive chandelier hung at the center of the room. It was in desperate need of a dusting, as well.

"You grew up going to balls, here?" I said, shooting a glance at Bran. He turned and met my gaze. The look surprised me.

He just nodded as his sister began to regale me with tales of the house's former glory – turkey dinners served across the hall or Burns Night with the full presentation of the Haggis.

"It was awful," Bran said, trying to hide a wide smile as Callista swatted at him.

"You loved every second of it! It broke your heart when father shut down this side of the house," Calista said, scurrying around the perimeter of the room, peeking under the dropcloths that covered each painting.

Bran turned his eyes to the floor, giving a half shrug of concession.

"And here it is! Oh, good grief. Just look at that poor, sad little baby."

Callista stood on her tiptoes and tossed the white sheet aside, letting it fall to the floor. There beneath it was an antique-looking portrait of two young boys, the older resting his elbow on the shoulder of the younger.

"Let's see, can I still do that?" She said, lifting her elbow up. She could indeed, and she rested her elbow on her 6'1" baby brother with a satisfied smile. It was cumbersome, but it could be done.

"Cheeky bitch," he said.

Callista laughed.

I let their banter fade into the background as I moved to stand beside them, staring up at the painting. It looked like something one would find in a museum – that its subjects were born of a completely different time. Yet, there in the still expression of the younger boy, there was an undeniable resemblance.

I'd recognize those eyes - and those curls - anywhere.

"Thank god for cameras. Bran would never sit still for something of this caliber back then," Callista said, finally releasing a squirming Mr. Darcy to explore the room. "She did do a wonderful job. Looks no different than any of the other portraits. Save for perhaps for fewer cracks."

Bran groaned. "Aye, well. The two of ye go right on ahead with your art appreciation, I need to get back at it. Sure, I can't convince ye to get your hands dirty, Cal?"

Callista glared at her brother as he sauntered back across the ballroom. He stopped for a moment, leaning in the doorway to wait for her answer.

"Darling, I would rather die."

He chuckled in the doorway, shot me a quick smile, then disappeared down the hall.

I turned back to the painting, my face feeling hot.

"Now that we're alone, sweetie, tell me about your bloke."

I stiffened, keeping my eyes averted from Callista's. "He's – I'm not – I wouldn't exactly call him my bloke."

"No? But you did come all this way for him, aye? Did I hear that correctly?"

Hearing Callista say it like that made me feel awful.

"Yeah," I said.

I had.

Pathetic.

And he'd done nothing to remind me why.

I wondered how much of the conversation she – and Bran - heard.

"I did. Well, he knew I wanted to move to Scotland, and we were getting very close so – two birds one stone. At least that was the plan, but he's been too busy to make it up here, yet."

"Too busy?"

I paused. "Yeah."

"Hmm," Callista said, moving along the wall to uncover the next painting. The face beneath caused Callista to smile to herself before she moved on to the next. I moved closer to the painting, reading the tiny plaque at the bottom of the frame.

Miread Tobin Douglas.

Bran and Calista's mother.

"Well, darling. I wish you luck with that. I hope he was worth the trip."

I swallowed. "Thank you," I said. It was the least sincere thing I'd ever said.

"Though, I will be a nosy busy body and say – when it comes to men, trust their actions, not their words."

There was no question Bran and Callista were cut of the same cloth.

I touched my hand to the shape of my phone in my jeans pocket, remembering the way he'd hung up on me. It had taken Bran's unkind words about Chris to build up the nerve to say my peace and be honest about his behavior, but hearing him respond as he did – with that seemingly unaffected tone. It hurt my heart.

"And, since I'm being a busy body, I'd also mention that you might find my brother receptive were you to tell him how you felt about him."

I literally took a step back. "What?!"

Her eyebrows shot up as she looked me up and down. "Don't be upset. He's completely oblivious – as so many men are."

She gave me a wink.

I shook my head, fighting to find words to defend against this accusation, but the words wouldn't come. I was stammering and floundering with an Amazon looking down at me, a look of almost patient sympathy on her face. And a sarcastic smirk.

"I don't know what you're talking about," I said, finally.

She watched me for a long moment as though waiting for me to go on. When I didn't, she made a soft humming noise deep in her throat. "I see. My mistake."

I stared back at her then, staring into blue eyes that resembled Bran's so perfectly, it was almost unnerving, and I felt my resolve evaporate.

I'd crossed an ocean for a man, yet when Chris hung up on me, it didn't hurt because I still harbored a desperate need to be with him, it hurt because I wasn't surprised anymore.

I'd wanted him to speak to me the way he used to, back before his aloofness felt cruel. Back before he was a simple train ride away. I wanted him to stir me the way he used to, but even in a moment of seething anger, he didn't.

I shot a sideways glance back to the painting of the two boys.

Perhaps, Callista was right. Perhaps I wanted someone else to speak to me in fond words.

I shook my head, pushing that thought away before it could settle.

Meow.

Both of us turned toward the ballroom doors to find Mr. Darcy rubbing back and forth against the doorjamb, impatiently.

"Someone's hungry," I said, glancing at Callista before hustling across the room.

"He's not the only one, darling. Come. Let's find all of us something to nibble, shall we?"

Callista blew past me into the hallway, the tassels of her lace shawl flitting across my arm as she went.

Ten

DESPITE BRAN'S EFFORTS TO convince her otherwise, Callista refused to stay overnight in the house.

"Call me when there's no sign of father in the house, and I will happily stay the night. Until then, this place can fuck right off."

I was sad to see her go as she drove off in her pristine little roadster, her scarf flitting out the open window as she waved goodbye. Bran seemed almost energized by her presence, and we'd managed to career through the last of the downstairs rooms.

There'd only been two left that needed real clearing out.

Well, three, but the door to the mattress room was jammed again when we went to open it.

I wasn't the least bit surprised. Whatever was in the house clearly didn't want us meddling in that room's affairs.

I didn't mention the ghost to Bran when we found the door jammed. I wasn't in the mood to have him roll his eyes at me again.

I woke up the next morning with a whole new drive. We'd managed to completely empty the contents of two floors, just the two of us. We'd toiled and sweated our way through hundreds of trips up and down the stairs, or back and forth along the third-story hall.

Though Bran had wanted to leave the second floor for last, it had half the number of rooms.

We were on a roll.

We were kicking ass!

We were going to be done in no time!

"Hmm," Bran said when I greeted him in the kitchen. It sounded more like the grunt of an antisocial Neanderthal than a proper greeting, but I didn't say anything, slipping past him to steal a bit of hot water from the kettle.

"So, you ready to dig in today?"

He took a sip of his tea but didn't speak.

"I was thinking we could start by relocating the chute from the third story? Maybe attach it to one of the bedroom windows upstairs like you did before?"

He made a disinterested humming sound somewhere deep in his chest, again. It wasn't an answer, but I ignored it.

Clearly, he wasn't as bright-eyed and bushy-tailed as I was feeling that morning.

"Did you eat, yet?" I asked, trying to spur on conversation despite his demeanor.

He shook his head, keeping his eyes to the kitchen window. It was raining again, the water pouring down the panes of glass outside in a constant torrent.

I threw together a round of eggs and toast, setting a plate beside Bran on the kitchen counter as I dug into my own breakfast. By the time I was finished eating, he still hadn't touched his plate.

"Alright, I'm gonna go upstairs and throw on a sweatshirt. Gonna be a wet one, looks like."

He didn't speak, holding his cooling mug of tea close to his chest.

I stopped in the doorway to the kitchen and turned back, watching him. Had I done something to upset him? Was he sad that Callista was gone? Was he simply tired of my presence, finally?

Still, I stood there silent, watching his shoulders, framed as they often were in the morning by the thick cream sweater he wore around the house, the collar higher on one side than the other. His hair was still tussled from sleep, and curls were sticking out just over his left ear.

I turned for the stairs, but stopped.

I was going to regret this, wasn't I?

"Are you alright, Bran?"

He startled, his upper body jerking as though he'd only just realized I was present. "What? Oh, aye. Aye, sorry. Right as rain. Just a bit preoccupied."

I stood there watching him as he turned back to the kitchen window.

"Your breakfast is going to get cold," I said, trying to sound as unaffected as I could. "There's nothing worse than buttering cold toast."

He exhaled in a forced laugh. "I can think of worse things, actually."

With that, he set his mug down and picked up a piece of toast. I took the gesture as a good sign and headed up to my room.

Bran took another half an hour to come upstairs. I took it upon myself to head up to the third floor and begin detaching his makeshift chute from the third-story window. The rain was pouring down outside, and each droplet broke and splattered as it hit the smooth surface of the chute, spraying my face as I leaned out the window. I tied cords to the end of it and lowered them out the window until they were level with the second-story windowsills. All we'd need to do was lean out the window of a bedroom and snag it. Might get a little wet, but nothing compared to marching back and forth to the skip.

I was coming down the third story steps when we met on the second story landing.

"I've got the chute lined up. If you'd come help me," I said, turning down toward the east side of the house. "I was able to detach the doodad alone, but I don't know if I can reattach -"

"Corinne."

"- it alone. I think it was lined up with the windows in -"

"Corinne! Wait!"

"- this room?" I opened the first of the many closed doors along this hallway and was met with a wall of darkness. I stopped dead, standing there in confusion as the sound of movement stirred in nearly every direction. The doorway was completely filled, a pile of stuff so high it blocked all light from the windows inside the room.

And the pile was moving – toward me.

I threw my hands out to catch the brunt of it just as arms wrapped around my waist and yanked me back toward the stairs. The roar of movement grew louder, coupled by the hollow thud of heavy objects slamming into the wall, floor, and doors across the hall. The pile of boxes toppled down, opening a path for crumpled paper, picture frames, old newspapers, lamps, books, and more boxes to follow along behind, a waterfall of stuff pouring from the recesses of this long-forgotten bedroom. When the rain of junk finally stopped, the hallway was completely blocked off, a four-foot-deep pile spreading out in either direction.

We stood there in silence until the last piece of paper flitted down the side of Junk Mountain to rest on the carpet at our feet. It was only then that I realized Bran was still holding me.

I touched my hand to his in a gentle gesture to let him know I was ok. He released me, straightening up, as though he too had been oblivious to the embrace.

"Wow," I said, trying to break the weight of the moment. "That's impressive."

It was meant to be a joke, but I failed horribly. I was too shocked to be funny. Though I might've survived that sea of junk toppling onto my head, I definitely would've been buried, and I would be bruised.

"I'm beginning to think your house wants me dead."

Bran touched his hand to my back, then took a step past me toward the mess. "Ye wouldn't be the first."

He stood over it for a long moment, his hand up to his mouth as he glanced from the pile into the recesses of the room. Though four feet deep had poured out, the junk within was still equally tall and solid. Bran reached up to grab an empty bottle of scotch before it could fall to the floor. The bottle's relocation started a new deluge of file folders and papers pouring down to his feet.

I fought the urge to crawl in a hole and die.

He'd tried to stop me, because as I suddenly realized – watching him stare into the expanse of the room with a look of sad resignation – he'd known. He'd known exactly what we were in for today. He knew exactly what was behind these closed doors.

He'd lived in it.

No wonder he'd gone after the third floor first. It was work, but it was nothing compared to this.

Had I a bulldozer, a tiny tractor to barrel up and down the halls with, a steamroller – something, anything! – we might be able to put a dent in this mess with time, but there was no getting to the window to attach the chute and without that ease of access to the skip, every armful of papers, empty bottles, broken lampshades or old unopened mail would mean a trip down the stairs and out into the rain.

If every closed door on the second floor harbored something even close to this, there was – there was just no hope to finish by the end of the month.

Bran's dower mood made all the sense in the world, suddenly.

You're an idiot, Turner. You're a fucking idiot.

The silence began to feel like a third person, standing there between us, glancing at us both in wait of something.

I didn't like the company.

"Oh! Here! I have an idea," I said, taking off back down the hall toward the first open doorway. I ducked inside to check the state of the place – a dusty bedroom, but dust we could manage. The bed was stripped of bedclothes, and the curtains were gone, but there was a fireplace, and that was all I needed. I ducked back out into the hallway with a smile plastered to my face.

Look unaffected, Cor. Don't let him see you crack!

"We start a fire in the fireplace and just blow through as much of this paper as we can. It looks like that takes up a pretty decent amount of the space, so – let's pyro this shit, yeah?"

Bran was still standing in the same spot, now buried to his ankles in old file folders and envelopes. He pursed his lips, finally letting his hand fall away from his face.

He nodded. "That's not a bad idea, actually. Maybe even a little cathartic."

I exhaled, a burning tension in my ribcage melting away. "Yes! See! I'm not completely useless!"

Bran's brow furrowed as he bent down to gather up a massive armful of paper. He turned back toward me, passing me to enter the dusty but empty bedroom. "I've never thought ye useless," he said, so quietly that I almost didn't make it out.

I didn't respond. Instead, I returned to the massive pile of junk now blocking off the rest of the east wing and filled my arms to the point of clumsy. I joined Bran at the fireplace, dumping the contents onto the floor. He was standing there over the fireplace, his arm resting on the mantle as he stared into the empty hearth. When he didn't move, I dropped down to the ground to start crumpling up pieces of paper and throwing them onto the ashes within.

"Do you want to sit here? Maybe just hang out while I bring you fuel for the fire?" I asked.

He shook his head. "No, no. I'll do the lifting. I imagine ye'd like to burn things, given it tried to kill ye a moment ago."

I forced a smile. The tone wasn't his usual sarcastic manner. He seemed dulled somehow, the way a knife loses its edge with wear and time.

The notion of it hurt my heart.

"Whatever you need. I'd love to sit on my ass burning shit."

He chuckled and nodded. "It's settled. Here," he said, handing me the lighter from his pocket, then he left the room without another word.

I dropped onto my backside, flicked the flint of the lighter, and stared into the fireplace as the mass of dusty old paper took light.

We settled into that system for the better part of an hour, the pile beside me growing to a size that rivaled the mountain in the hallway. I was tempted to go see how Bran was progressing, but something told me to leave him to it. He didn't seem to want company.

I was getting hot by the end of the hour and opened one of the massive windows to let the cool air in. The rain was still pouring down, and the sound of it coupled with the crackle of the fire was almost intoxicating.

Or maybe that was the fumes coming off the old carbon paper.

I listened to Bran come and go, feeling his presence each time he returned like a hand being held out to me that I couldn't take. I wanted him to sit with me – to listen to the rain and watch the fire. I wanted a lot more than that, I was realizing.

"My brother would be receptive," Callista had said.

Receptive to what?

Hey, I liked it when you took your shirt off, could you do that more often?

Hey, you really call me a miracle when I'm not around to hear it? Wanna make out?

I closed my eyes and sighed.

Stop it, Cor. Haven't you had enough of pining for aloof Scottish guys?

I thought of my last conversation with Christopher and frowned.

No more of that, I thought.

A few folders slipped from Bran's arms in the doorway, and he groaned in frustration as he came in.

I waved at him. "Don't worry about that, I'll get 'em."

He shook his head and crouched down, collecting them up and delivering them to me.

I stared up at him, waiting for him to meet my gaze and – I don't know – read my mind?

He didn't look at me but instead headed back out into the hallway.

The fire had grown, giving me more freedom to pile on the flammables. I grabbed up a bundle of file folders and simply threw them into the hearth to watch what happened. The fireball was as satisfying as I'd expected and the air within the fireplace suddenly roared with heat. I threw another handful, then another, gleefully watching the pile at my hip shrink with each new fireball I created. I fought the urge to giggle mischievously as I grabbed two full handfuls of paper and tossed them into the hearth while the previous fireball was still going strong. The roar was impressive, and the heat blasted up into my face with such force, I had to lean back for fear of losing an eyebrow. I watched helplessly as a tiny piece of blackened paper flitted up and out past the metal screen. I snatched up a couple folders and caught the interloper out of midair.

"Well, don't do that again, jackass," I said to myself, glancing toward the door to make sure I was alone and not giving Bran more fuel to mock me.

I was alone – and the pile beside me was half the size it had been the last time Bran brought another round of paper.

He wasn't bringing fodder at his usual rate. He hadn't brought anything at all for a while it seemed.

I sat for a moment, letting the fire fade down to almost nothing as I listened for a sign of Bran in the hallway outside.

There was nothing.

I hopped up to my feet and made my way to the bedroom door, glancing out into the hallway for him. There was no sign of him, save for the state of the hallway – the pile of junk that had nearly killed me and blocked the corridor after careening toward my face with murderous intent – the pile was now gone, only a few not so flammable bits and things now collected along the wall, organized there for later dealing.

"Bran?" I called softly, as though I didn't want to be heard. I was nervous. Bran's demeanor was strange, worrisome, and now his absence was doubly so. I glanced down toward the steps, then moved closer to the open bedroom door.

The hoard within had shifted, a hint of a pathway gouging into the solid mass of stuff. Bran had broken through what was a five-foot-deep wall of paper and trash and junk. He was now standing in the middle of the room atop a foot-deep layer of unopened mail at the center of the room.

His back was to me. I couldn't know how long he'd been standing there like this, but I was afraid to speak for fear of disturbing whatever fugue state he might be in.

Still, I felt I needed to be with him. Something was wrong.

I took a step into the room, careful not to bump into the walls of paper on either side of the path he'd created. I reached the plateau at the center of the room and stepped up into the open space.

"Bran?" I said, reaching out to touch his shoulder, my balance shifting from the uneven ground underfoot.

He glanced over his shoulder but didn't look at me. Instead, he kicked his foot into the layer of debris beneath us, flipping over old envelopes and newspapers. "I remember the last time I saw this room. He'd started tucking things away in here, but I would come in when he wasn't looking and relocate the stash to other parts of the house."

He spoke with such softness, it was almost a whisper.

I searched for something to say, as though the silence drawing out between us was the fuse of some bomb burning down. "Is that why the third floor was the way it was – you were tucking stuff there from the rest of the house?"

Bran shook his head. "No, no. I had nothing to do with the third floor. That started before - when I was still in nappies. Before Nan died."

I scanned the room, idly trying to alleviate some of the tension in the space. The piles were highest in the corners and along the walls, some of it looking to have been tossed in from the doorway long after entering the room became impossible.

"My Nan tried so hard to combat this," he said, kicking the envelopes that settled on the toe of his shoe. "Used to yell at him to take his rubbish upstairs whenever he brought something else home, and when he did leave something in the hallway or one of the downstairs rooms, she'd just snatch it up without a word and walk it over to the bin. Caused a good number of arguments between them, but as a result, Cal and I didn't truly know what our father was like until Nan died."

I didn't speak, waiting for Bran to continue. The air felt electric with every word, like he'd opened a live wire before me to let me watch the sparks.

"This was her room, ye ken."

And the air left the room.

This was his grandmother's bedroom? This landfill of forgotten trash and broken things – this was where the woman that raised him slept when he was a child?

I gasped, then held my breath as though I might be able to take the gesture back.

"This room was pristine when my grandmother was alive – one of the few rooms in the house that was. I remember it was *the week* after she died, my Dad brought home some god-awful collection of vases he'd found at the local church shop, brought the box in the front door, and marched it directly up here to tuck it away in her room. Like she'd never been here. Like there was nothing sacred about the space anymore, and like a dog that searches for the cleanest patch of snow before it'll take a piss, he went straight for it. I snuck in after he went to bed and moved the boxes upstairs. Still, every year when I came home from school, this room was worse."

He paused, his eyes finding the dingy windows, offering only half-light as their lower halves were completely shielded by the hoard. If it weren't for the overgrown ivy and lilacs along the outside of the house, I might've seen this mess from the outside. The green leaves of the lilacs were just visible through the glass, their tips peeking in over the five-foot-deep pile of trash.

"I imagine we'll find several more rooms like this on this floor, but this one? There's no question in my mind that every inch of this refuse pile was fueled by spite."

My hand twitched. I wanted to touch him again, but I was terrified to feel him recoil from me.

I looked around and imagined having to clear this room and three more like it. Just the notion exhausted me. "You think there are more like this?"

Bran shrugged. "Oh, there's worse."

I felt my stomach drop to my feet at this revelation.

"Still, this was the one I was least looking forward to. Because this is the one part of the house where I know for a fact there are pieces of my Nan hidden in here – drowning under all this shite," he said, and his voice cracked with the last word.

My eyes burned. I tried to blink it away.

This was my fault. "Oh, Bran. I'm so sorry. I didn't mean to -"

"Ye needn't apologize. Ye've done nothing wrong."

"But if I'd just – If I'd only waited for you to direct me instead of flinging open the nearest door like a sugared-up toddler playing hide and seek -" My own voice was wavering now. I was furious with myself.

"Stop, Corinne. Nothing about this is your doing."

He still didn't look at me as he said this, and I didn't respond. I was afraid my voice would betray me. That he'd hear the anguish I felt, not just because I was upset with myself, but because I was upset to hear him in pain. Every other room, every other conversation we'd had – I knew Branson Douglas knew struggle in this house, but he'd never faltered in the telling of it. His sarcasm and his jokes were always there to soften the blow of any revelation, but now, in this room, there seemed to be no buffer between Bran's words and the pain that inspired them.

I wanted to drag him out of that place, lock the door, and pretend this ring of hell had never been breached. Yet, it was too late, and we were standing on the bones of a tomb his father made.

I swallowed. "Well, let me help you, then. Here," I said, moving back toward the bedroom door to wrangle up another armful from the wall of papers and truck them back down the hall before my eyes welled up with tears. I marched into the second bedroom, feeling the cool, damp air from the open windows as I dumped the contents of my arms onto the floor. I dropped to my knees and made quick work of throwing papers onto the still cindering embers of an hour's worth of burning.

"And the fire's still going!" I called, blinking my eyes and opening them as wide as I could to hide my state. I didn't want Bran to see when he followed me in.

I heard him coming down the hallway and kept my eyes on the fire, but instead of coming inside, he blew right past the door.

I started, turning to watch the open doorway as his hurried footsteps went down the stairs. A moment later, the front door of the house slammed shut, the sound of it echoing off every surface. I jumped up from the floor and went to the window, pressing my forehead to the glass to see below.

Bran appeared in the driveway below, his feet stomping through puddles as he marched away from the house in the pouring rain. I watched breathlessly as Bran clenched his fists and screamed a string of expletives at the top of his lungs. Then he slumped into the muddy grass, burying his face in his hands.

My chest seized up as though the oxygen was ripped from my lungs. *Oh god, Cor. What have you fucking done?*

I took off down the hallway, running down the steps to the front door. I didn't pause to worry whether he'd welcome my company, but instead barreled across the drive, coming to his side in mid-run, my shoes skidding in the mud as I reached him. I dropped to my knees before him, reaching for one of his hands.

Just as I'd feared, Bran was quite literally falling apart.

He shook his head, still hiding his face from me as rain collected on the curls of hair between his fingers and dropped onto the sleeves of his sweater. "I can't do it," he whispered, his breath catching at the end of the word. "I knew it would be terrible. I knew it would, but I – it's too much. I feel like I'm drowning in there."

I tried to pull one of his hands from his face, but he pressed his palms into his eyes and bared his teeth. If he wasn't weeping, he was close to it.

Pain seared through my chest at the sight.

I watched him, helpless and heartbroken, aching to fix it – but the feeling was more than that. If I could, I'd fix the whole of the world just to ease this man's pain. I'd do absolutely anything.

It was one of the strongest things I'd ever felt – and it was for Branson Douglas.

Shit.

I sat there before him watching as he fought to steady his breathing, and I fought not to cry. I knew there was no magical fix for a lifetime of pain – pain that was now manifested in the form of every saved piece of broken cutlery and trash that his father had ever touched, all smothering whatever happy memories Bran might've had in that house.

Yet, if that magic did exist, I'd travel to the far corners of the world to find it – for him.

He took a ragged breath, finally, wiping his eyes. "I thought I could. Ye know, chin up, lad and all that – I don't think I can go back in there."

He shook his head and buried his face in his hands again.

I wriggled closer to him, feeling the mud slurp beneath me as it seeped through my jeans. I grabbed hold of his hands, feeling the bone of his wrist under my fingers as I pulled his hand into mine and made him look at me.

"Then you don't have to."

His brow furrowed and he frowned, shaking his head.

I didn't let him respond. "I'll do it for you."

He blinked, and a tear escaped down the curve of his jaw. He moved quickly to try to cover it. "No, Corinne."

"Yes. It's not up for discussion."

Bran coughed, steadying himself as he turned to me. "I can't ask ye to do that. It's not your responsibility."

"You didn't ask me. Nor did I ask you."

Bran met my gaze for the first time since I'd joined him in the rain, and his blue eyes burned into me, now red and heavy. I fought to let my eyes speak for me – to proclaim whatever regal ferocity I might possess – a glare I learned from the man I called Dad. A glare that said I would not, under any circumstances, be swayed.

"It's too much to ask," he said, shaking his head and shifting his weight to get up from the sopping wet ground. I leaned back to let him up, rising to stand before him with my back as straight as I could manage, as though I might make myself taller by sheer will.

He averted his eyes now, turning back toward the house.

I lunged past him, grabbing his arm as I blocked his path. "Branson Tennyson Douglas. You are going to get in your car and drive somewhere far, far away from here. Go visit your sister for a day or two, or find yourself a hotel – I don't care, but you are going to get the fuck out of here and let me do what I was hired to do, do you understand me?"

His face contorted in a strange expression of frustration, protest, and somewhere amid these conflicting thoughts, relief.

"Corinne," he said, but he paused.

He was relenting. I could see clearly in his sad eyes that he wanted desperately to relent.

I felt invigorated by it, like some knight roaming the world in search of a worthy cause to fight for. "Go, Bran. I insist. Give yourself a couple days. When you come home, that room at least will be done."

He furrowed his brow, unable to meet my gaze. I took his muddied hand in mine and squeezed. His face contorted, and he had to turn away from me.

It took every ounce of my will not to throw my arms around him and collect him like the pieces of some broken thing.

A long moment passed there, the rain coming down in a constant sheet of misery. Bran's sweater was sopping now, hanging heavy at his shoulders. Finally, he nodded, turning to face me. He opened his mouth to speak.

I moved fast, running into the house before Bran could say a word, and grabbed his car keys from the table in the front hall and his jacket from the coat rack. I stepped back out into the rain, hunching my shoulders against the renewed cold. He took them without a word, looking at his car keys as though they were some foreign and strange thing.

I marched across the drive and opened the driver's side door of his car and waited. He shot me one last look, as though pleading for me to stop him.

I shook my head. "Your sister is still in Edinburgh, yes?"

He nodded.

"There you go. I don't want to see you back here for two days. You hear me?"

He swallowed, stepping into the car to climb in. I steeled myself, fighting to keep up the stern guise.

A moment later, I watched his car lights disappear around the far corner of the drive, heading toward the village and the main roads.

I stood there in the rain, feeling it collect and roll down my back beneath the fabric of my shirt. I don't know how long I stood there before I finally made my way back into the house.

I entered the front hall, feeling the expanse of the place around me as I shut the door.

For the first time since my first night there, I was truly alone, and like some physical thing, I could feel Bran's distance growing with each passing second.

How can you miss him already, you idiot?

Quite easily, as it turned out.

I turned the lock of the door, smelling the smoky warmth from the fireplace upstairs, and as I headed up the stairs to work, I let myself cry.

Eleven

I WORKED ALL DAY.

I fought with aching shoulders and arms to haul massive piles of endless junk mail, newspapers, and forgotten bills into the neighboring room, keeping a constant pyre burning like some eternal flame for Junketha, patron goddess of trash fires.

I managed to clear away the trash around one of the windows and finally attach Bran's chute to the sill. From there I was marching across the teetering mess from window to hallway at a constant clip for hours, burning and tossing armfuls of endless shit into the skip.

During my marathon, I slipped on an old copy of the Daily Mail and went ass over tea kettle into a pile of wire hangers, I rolled my ankle twice as I stepped from the foot-thick layer of trash to the level ground of the hallway, and even dislodged the wrong lampshade from a corner pile, only to have seven feet of trash come pouring down over me in an avalanche of paper cuts and dust.

By dinner time, I looked like I'd been on the ass-end of a wrestling match with a wet badger. Still, I was working. I was moving and fighting to make a dent. I hadn't eaten since breakfast, and truth be told, I wasn't hungry.

The only thing to alert me to the time was the light from the windows fading and a tiny mewing sound coming from the hallway.

I glanced over just as Mr. Darcy tapped his paw to a loose corner of the paper nearest the door. Even he seemed to know better than to venture into this room.

"Don't rub it in, furball," I said, running my hands over my forearms to brush off the newest layer of dust.

I grabbed up an armful of paper, the smell of mothballs and must flooding my nostrils as I brought it all close to the chest, then I made my way out into the hallway, watching Mr. Darcy scamper off ahead to the stairs. He darted out of sight just as I slipped into the second bedroom. The bundle of paper was barely hitting the floor before Mr. Darcy reappeared at my ankle, mewing his protests.

"I'm coming, doofus. Give me a second," I said, grabbing up a few handfuls to toss into the fireplace. They caught in seconds, and I threw in another six of seven handfuls before I was ready to walk away. Mr. Darcy was throwing daggers with his eyes by the time I picked up my phone from the mantle and made my way to the stairs.

The gray blur shot down the stairs ahead of me as I glanced at my phone for the first time in hours.

I'd been working full tilt since Bran left. I was dusty and worn out, but I was motivated by a near panic-driven need to be done before Bran returned – and what assurance did I have that he wasn't already on his way back like the stubborn pain in the ass that he was?

"Alright, you spoiled brat. Don't say I never did anything for you," I said, marching across the kitchen to procure a tin of supper for the mini-dictator. Mr. Darcy marched back and forth in front of his bowl, meowing excitedly when he heard the can open. I stood over him a moment, spooning half the contents into his dish as he wove figure eights around my ankles.

I wanted nothing more than to curl up next to a fireplace with a book and a cup of tea and this little fascist in my lap. Yet, there would be no time for that tonight. There would be no time for that in the foreseeable future.

I left Darcy purring into his food and headed back upstairs to the work.

I rounded the corner into the atrocity that was Bran's grandmother's bedroom and instantly held my breath.

It looked no different than the first time I'd seen it.

Hours. Hours upon hours of work and yet every few inches I'd managed to clear would instantly be filled in with refuse from the massive piles along the walls and corners of the room. Like the sand inside an hourglass, for every grain to drain out, another dozen will fall to take its place. I sighed and headed up to the third floor to grab Bran's wireless speaker. A few moments later, the second-floor hallway was echoing the sounds of Pink Floyd throughout the house.

Not the cheeriest music, but it was Bran's favorite station. I could've changed it to 80's music. I could've switched it over to Classical, but instead, I was busy *riding the gravy train*, surrounded by a lifetime of dust – and I was alone.

At least if I played Bran's favorite station I might not feel his absence like a poisonous gas in the air.

Or perhaps hearing his music would make it worse.

I didn't care. I'd spent all day trudging rubbish into the next bedroom to burn, and it had done me no good. I'd have to find another option.

I growled, softly, letting a few choice expletives fly.

I heard someone chuckle in response.

I didn't move. I took a deep breath and slumped down onto the floor by the open window, the frigid air drifting in at my shoulder. I kept my eyes averted from the bedroom door. I hadn't seen the woman in blue for weeks, but no matter how desperately I wanted to explain the laughter, I knew there was no one else in the house with me. Had it been a man's laugh, I might've gone looking for Branson.

But it wasn't a man's laugh.

I'd fought the notion that being alone in the house might stir the ghost up somehow, and I'd find her in the hallway watching me out of the corner of my eye. Yet, fighting the idea didn't protect me from her company.

She was close by and I knew it.

Every inch of the world around me was haunted, it was only fitting to have *Don't Fear the Reaper* come on the radio as I hauled up handful after handful of musty, yellowed paper and tossed it out onto the chute. I waited, listening for the familiar whooshing sound of objects careening down the length of the plastic contraption and into the skip.

Yet, the familiar sound didn't come. I lifted myself up onto my knees and craned to see outside.

The paper was collected about five feet down the chute, clinging to the wet plastic surface as rain splattered down atop it.

"Great. Fuck. That's just fucking great."

I sighed and rolled my ass over onto all fours to stand up, teetering on the junk beneath me.

I shot a wary look toward the hallway. The door was clear. No undead creatures eyeballing me from the great beyond.

Kind of them.

I grabbed an armful and went back to hauling it to the fireplace, throwing in a few handfuls each time before I headed back to the mess for another trip. I was on my sixth trip when the layers of rubbish by the door shifted beneath me again and sent me stumbling across the room. I caught myself by leaning into one of the higher piles, only to have the papers shift and whoosh – an avalanche of paper flowed downward, encircling my legs in another two feet of rubbish where I stood.

I closed my eyes, listening to the sound of everything around me shifting and moving with the pull of gravity and what I could only assume was the malice of some unpaid karmic debt I must be carrying. When the seismic event was finally over, I opened my eyes to find myself buried up to my knees in a whole new fresh hell.

I grumbled to myself, fighting to pull one of my feet up and out. Instead, I lost my balance and fell onto my ass, my left foot now pinned under my weight and two feet of recyclable hate.

I stared at the ceiling for a moment, noticing the tin filigree around the chandelier just above my head. I spotted movement out of the corner of my eye, and my stomach shot into my throat.

Mr. Darcy appeared in the bedroom doorway and was now contentedly licking his paws.

"You smug bastard," I said, smiling at him despite my unfortunate predicament. I shifted my body weight, trying to lift myself off the piles of papers that held my foot beneath me. No use.

I shifted again, turning myself completely on the pile, but nothing worked. I'd have to dig myself.

I slumped back onto the pile. Dear god, I was exhausted.

"Good thing Bran is only gone a couple days, huh? Otherwise, they might find me here weeks from now, half-eaten by a hungry kitten."

I paused, waiting. No laughter came.

It was only then that I realized who it was that I was talking to.

If I was going to be accosted with her company, I might as well make small talk with the ghost, right?

Mr. Darcy glanced up at me for an instant, then turned his attention back to his paws.

I jumped as the rubbish vibrated beneath me. Then, I pulled my phone out of my pocket.

I've arrived safe in Edinburgh, but I can come back at any point. Please just let me know. Xxxxx

I lay atop the mountain of refuse and stared at the text. Bran was safely in the company of his sister. He'd done as I asked.

He'd trusted me enough to walk away, even if only for a few days.

I felt my face flush, and I smiled, tears gathering at the corners of my eyes. I was happy to know he was ok, but as I lay there in the wake of a day's worth of work with little to nothing to show for it, my heart hurt. I'd promised him I'd fix this. I'd promised it would all be done before he got back.

I took a deep breath and opened the text to respond.

I said two days, and I meant two days. Get some rest and try not to think about it.

I refrained from adding *I miss you* to the end of the text, no matter how true it was.

Then I set the phone on the carpet of rubbish beside me and turned my attention to freeing myself. If I was going to get this job done, it was going to take working through the night.

I was ready for the task.

Twelve

I WOKE UP SIX hours later, my foot still trapped in the garbage heap. I know how to get a job done, ladies and gentlemen!

"Oh honey," I said as I found Mr. Darcy curled into the crook of my armpit, looking sleepy eyed and inconvenienced as I tried to sit up beside him.

My foot was completely numb, and it took another fifteen minutes to dig myself out from the pile. Once free, I was left with a useless slab of lamb shank for a limb and I almost killed myself three times trying to walk across the refuse with a completely dead foot.

Three times. I swear I looked like an angry horse stomping his hooves as I kicked my foot out in front of me with each step.

I found the fire in the second bedroom now stone cold and the house quieter than I'd ever heard it. I also found a simple **Thank you so much, Corrine** text from Bran.

I didn't reply. I didn't exactly feel deserving of his gratitude, at the moment.

And after six more panicked work hours, I still didn't feel deserving.

The room was my Everest, and I had no Tenzing Norgay. Every handful of papers or chute full of broken baskets, trinkets, and junk seemed to only unearth the real project. Sure, the piles around the perimeter of the room were lower now, but there was still no bare floor to speak of.

Mr. Darcy cooed up at me in the mid-afternoon, announcing his displeasure at having still not been fed.

"Sorry, foofball. If it makes you feel any better, I haven't eaten either."

He touched his paw to the refuse pile before hopping atop it to come join me by the window. I was fighting with an old cabinet door, the piece of furniture it was once attached to nowhere to be found in the mess. I angled it through the open window, fighting to get it through. It jammed, the corner of the door thumping into my chest with enough force to leave a bruise.

My temper flared instantly. I had bruises and bumps to contend with as it was, but at that moment, every delay, every fucking snag was making me want to set the place on fire and walk. I slammed my palm into the corner of the door as though I might punish the thing for leaving a bruise. It budged forward, sliding out the window just as the chute dislodged from the sill and went crashing to the ground out of sight, and before I could catch myself, the now unhindered cupboard door went sailing out the open window and careening toward the overgrown bushes below.

I lost my footing and fell, slamming my shoulder into the sill.

I was lucky my chin didn't slam into the sill instead.

I roared, a primal scream of pain and frustration. Had I something glass to throw, I'd have thrown it. I was ready to kill something – anything.

A soft meow called from my hip, and I looked down to find Mr. Darcy watching me, a look of hunger rather than concern for my well-being. I rolled onto my back and sighed.

I wasn't going to finish this job before Bran returned home. Even if I worked without break for food or sleep, I wouldn't even come close.

I'd been fighting tooth and nail with this realization, pretending I didn't know full well when I fell asleep half-buried the night before, or when I woke up still entombed. I'd bitten off so much more than I could chew.

I watched Mr. Darcy pace back and forth beside me, rubbing his face against my leg with each pass. "I'm just disappointing everyone today, aren't I?"

Darcy burbled at me with excitement at being acknowledged. With that, I rolled over on the trash heap and stood up, teetering my way out of the room.

Mr. Darcy rushed ahead of me, glancing back every few feet to make sure I was following.

I made quick work of feeding the creature, all while setting the kettle on the stove for tea. I stood by the sink, losing my thoughts as I stared out the window.

The day was as drech as before, drizzling rain and gray. Despite the stove beside me, I felt the cold like a presence, hovering over my shoulder to watch and judge me as I failed at yet another thing I'd set my mind to. It wouldn't be the first time I disappointed someone – I was pretty sure that was the whole extent of my relationship with Kenny – yet this one felt different. This one made me want to curl up in some hole forged in the piles of the forgotten hoard and die.

The kettle began to hum softly just as a low, harmonic sound carried through the air. I moved the kettle quickly to listen.

Church bells.

The stone church in Kinvale was chiming away, the sound of its song carrying across the hills to Cavendish House. I exhaled. I was startled by how beautiful – how soothing the sound was.

I shut off the stove, hurried across the kitchen for my coat, and headed out the front door into the rain.

The church steps were dry when I arrived, shielded from the rain by tall trees overhead. I approached the massive wooden doors and swallowed.

Would it be open? Were churches in Scotland prone to locking their doors or would this place offer sanctuary?

I pressed my thumb down onto the latch and it clicked. The door groaned as I opened it, offering a dry, dark expanse within.

The echo of it closing carried high into the rafters overhead.

This church was easily as old as Cavendish House, its pillars and floors made of long warped stone. The pews were freshly stained, but their wooden surfaces betrayed years of use, divots to show hundreds of years of praying backsides sitting atop them. At the front of the sanctuary was a simple altar, carved by someone long dead.

My throat grew tight just from the smell of the air. It felt timeless.

I moved across the quiet space with care as even my breathing seemed to echo, and settled into a pew at the center of the room. I leaned back in the seat, turned my eyes up to the stained-glass windows high above, and fought the urge to cry.

"Fancy meeting ye here," a voice called from the front of the room, the lilt of her voice bouncing off every surface. I straightened in my pew to find a familiar face watching me, eyebrows raised in idle curiosity.

Bran and my least favorite person from the church social – Hilda.

I swallowed. Of all people, why did she have to be here?

"Sorry, I just – I can go," I said, pulling my coat around me to make my exit.

Hilda was walking down the center of the church, speaking as though I hadn't said a word. "It does do wonders on the soul, this place. Ye wouldn't be the first to spend a drech afternoon here."

I shot a desperate look to the door. It was twenty feet away. I could make a run for it before she got to me if I bolted now.

Yet, I didn't move. Hilda sauntered up to my pew and stood there, waiting for me to make room. I slid down to give her space and she settled her considerable backside on the pew beside me. We then sat there for a long moment, watching the altar in silence.

When Hilda didn't speak, the silence began to bite at the back of my throat, demanding I fill it. I physically shook my head like a lunatic.

Great. I'm a crazy church lady, now.

"Tell me," she said, finally. "Was it the bells that brought ye in, or something else?"

I stifled a laugh – a laugh that hurt my throat and tightened in my chest. A laugh that wanted to bring tears and sobs with it. I held my breath, staving off the sting in my eyes.

Damn it, Cor! What is wrong with you? Don't cry around Hilda! She'll tell everyone in Scotland about the crazy sobbing woman in church and your legend will carry through the centuries.

I closed my eyes, blowing air out through pursed lips as I tried to settle. "Something else. Both. I don't know."

Hilda nodded. She felt somber now, unlike the last time I'd seen her. Hilda was wearing black slacks and a black shirt, the sleeves gauzy and soft as they brushed against my arm. "I'm told I can be a fair listener from time to time, if ye need a blather."

My face contorted in a forced smile. "I'm not sure I could put it in words."

I stopped, staring at my hands in my lap. When Hilda didn't press, I shot her a sideways glance. She was sitting in an almost serene repose, watching the altar up ahead.

She wouldn't press. If I shared my worries, it would be entirely my choice.

Who was this lady and what had she done with church social Hilda?

"I don't know. I think – I'm feeling a little lost, at the moment."

Hilda made a soft humming sound deep in her throat, but offered no comment, waiting for me to go on.

"When I started doing this – this traveling thing, I did it to escape home. To stop feeling like a burden to my family. And it was going well enough, but since I got here, I've felt different."

She nodded. "Different how?"

"I – I guess I've felt useful. I felt like I was in the right place for once, rather than just – taking up space, somewhere."

"That's a good thing, no?"

I ran my hand over my face, fighting the knot in my chest. "I thought so. Someone needed me for once in my life. And I've worked my ass off – we've worked our asses off. Sorry. Pardon my language."

"Quite alright," she said, smiling. "Ye've worked your asses off and?"

I took a deep breath. "It isn't enough. We've worked nonstop for weeks, and I truly thought we were winning. Little did I know, we'd barely even started. Every time I think we have the upper hand, the house throws some new fresh hell at us, and it's finally just too much. That house is going to win. No matter how hard I try, no matter how little I sleep, or how many bruises I end up with, that house is going to win. And I will have to watch someone I care about lose everything. He's suffered enough, already, why does he have to go through this, too?"

The tears welled up at the corners of my eyes and spilled over.

"I'm so angry and – there's nothing I can do about it. I feel helpless."

Hilda turned to look at me and watched my face in silence. A long moment passed between us, the strange aura of the church humming and creaking all around us. Finally, she reached for me, patting her hand on mine as she turned her eyes back to the front of the church. "Is it as bad as they say?"

I swallowed, startled by the question.

I stared at the side of her face for a moment, and I exhaled. "No. It's worse."

Hilda took a deep breath and shook her head. "That's a shame."

I frowned and let the silence creep in again.

"I was new to this parish when the Douglas boys were young," she said, finally, a thoughtful smile pulling at the corners of her mouth. "Pair of troublemakers, I was told, but I remember the two of them coming into the parish hall on my first church supper. It was the two of them, myself and my family, then the usual crowd of older parishioners or the lower-income families and their children. They were always sweet boys when they were here, but always alone. I'd often thought they looked rather rough around the edges, but they caused not a stitch of trouble."

I turned away, thinking of a little Bran making the trek to this place as a boy in the hopes of supper they couldn't get at home because Dad refused to leave the house, let alone go to the shops for food. My heart broke.

"I'm sad to say I've had some notion of how fallen Arthur let the old house get. My grandson is precocious. Broke into the house with the lads a few years ago. Came home with tales to tell, despite knowing he'd be in trouble for it. Said he fell onto a mountain of old coffee cans when he climbed through the window. Then before he could explore further, he was chased right back out the same window by the old bastard."

I nodded. "That mountain was still there. And it was far from the worst of it."

"There aren't jars of old pish or the like, are there?"

"What?!" I said, appalled.

"Jars of urine? Feces? I know that famous film producer lad kept jars of his own waste about the place."

"No, no! Nothing like that," I said, but I paused. There was a whole wing of the house still buried under trash. Who was I to say for certain one way or the other? "At least, I don't think so."

Hilda leaned against the edge of the pew, staring off as though in deep thought. "There are rumors the Douglas boys are going to lose the house."

I shut my eyes tight as I almost burst into tears. "End of the month. They're coming to -" I had to take a moment to breathe. "There are people coming to inspect the place at the end of the month. There's so much junk everywhere, you can't even see what might need to be fixed."

"And if it doesn't pass, the boys lose it?"

I turned my face away as my face contorted, nodding my response.

"Hmm," she said, again. Then she tapped her ring on the back of the pew for a moment. "Well, we can't have that, now can we?"

Hilda gave the pew a couple more taps, then the whole seat lurched as she stood up. Hilda set off down the aisle toward the front of the church. I watched her go, letting the grief hit me as she disappeared.

I was alone now; I could cry. Tears streamed down my face as I remembered Bran curled up, ass in the mud, his chest heaving softly as he fought what I was sure was a panic attack - what I knew now was a lifetime of harbored pain. He knew enough pain to fill every room of that house twice over. And I couldn't save him from it. I couldn't protect him from the inspectors or Jocelyn. I couldn't undo the lifetime of spite his father left for him.

I was going to fail, and for the first time in my life, I cared.

"I'm glad I caught ye, dear."

Hilda had reappeared at the front of the church, her dark silhouette framed against the golden light of the altar behind her like some dark angel. She moved quickly, her cell phone pressed to her ear as she came closer.

She stopped at the edge of my pew and gestured to the phone, lifting her head up as she put on that familiar, friendly tone from the church social. A flash of white at her throat caught my eye, startling me.

A white collar.

Hilda was the vicar.

My mouth fell open in shock as Hilda spoke into her cell phone.

"Mary, love. That's just grand, but we've more pressing matters. It's time to summon the cavalry."

Thirteen

"A RE YE SURE WE can take these?"

I turned to find Malcolm Seamonds with three crockpots in his arms.

I smiled. "Yes, anything that was in the skip is free to take."

"Ye ken they're still in perfect working order, aye?"

I nodded. "I'm not in the least bit surprised."

Before he could speak further, a woman named Pepe went bustling past me toward the stairs. She was in her early sixties and clad in a perm, thick, black-rimmed glasses, and a Sitka, Alaska t-shirt. "Where is that grandson of mine? Jameson! The lorry isn't gonnae load itself, ye layabout! Sorry, love. I swear he's a good lad. It's since his mates arrived this morning that he's been such a numpty."

"No worries, Pepe," I said, fighting the smile her name gave me. "I can't begin to express my gratitude for everything you've done."

"What, Mom!?" Jameson called from the landing above. "I'm tending the fireplace up here with Greg!"

"Oh, is that all ye're doin? If I find the two of ye smoking that marijuana again, I swear to the Virgin Mary -"

Pepe was up the stairs and gone before she could finish her scolding. I made my way back out to the driveway.

The sky was still overcast and gray, but the rain was staving off for the morning. I was grateful for it.

I was grateful for a lot of things.

My phone buzzed in my pocket and I jumped.

Shit, please don't be coming home yet, I thought.

I rushed for the front doors, glancing at my phone.

Christopher calling.

I stopped dead just inside the door and stared at my phone.

Wait, what?

"Hello?" I said, making my way out onto the front steps.

"Hey you," Chris said, and the tone was one I'd nearly forgotten. "Had a few moments today and thought I'd ring ye up to see how ye're fairing up there."

A white box truck sat alongside the skip and three men were making quick work of rifling through its contents for anything that might be salvageable or saleable. Given Bran's 'fuck it all' approach to the house, they were having quite a bit of luck, filling the truck to ship everything down to the local charity shop. The truck driver waved at me as I passed. This would be his third trip.

I shot him a half-assed wave, still thrown by the sudden phone call.

"I'm doing well, actually."

"Really?" He said. Clearly, my tone made him curious.

I stopped at the far end of the drive and turned to take in the house.

"Corinne, love! Where've they got that chute of yours?"

I looked around for the source of the voice.

I was sure Cavendish House hadn't seen this many people in decades. Hilda's parishioners came in droves to see the inside of the ancient house and help clear out the years of neglect and abuse.

Mary's professor husband, Bruce, was among them. He'd passed me in giddy delight on his way to other far corners of the house, each time regaling me with exact dates, creators, artists, and details of various paintings or pieces of furniture. He'd been a lifesaver, offering to dictate what should and shouldn't be tossed from any given room.

Even Bran couldn't perform such a duty, and not simply because he didn't care to.

I found Bruce now, half hanging out a second-story window trying to crane his head to search for the chute.

"They brought it down to the last room," I called back, waving toward the end of the house as another pile of junk went whooshing down the yellow tube into the skip.

Bruce gave a wave and a thank you, then he was gone.

I smiled as best I could. I was a tightly wound thing. Despite the joy I felt to see each new room cleared, I was scared shitless of Bran's return. This wasn't my home to invite the townsfolk into. This wasn't my family laundry to have aired for all to see. Still, when Hilda refused to hear my protests and barreled us both down the road to Cavendish House in her jeep, I didn't have the will to stop her. And when one after another of her parishioners pulled into the drive, I wasn't stubborn enough to turn them away, especially when salvation showed up with casserole dishes and scrub brushes in hand.

"Who are ye talking to?" Chris asked, just as my phone buzzed again.

I stiffened. I'd nearly forgotten I was on the phone.

There was no forgetting the phone now.

Heading into town now. Be home soon. The text said.

Branson was on his way.

Branson Douglas was careening down country roads toward home.

Branson was almost here.

Fuck.

"Chris, I can't talk right now. Bran's gonna be home any second and I still need to get the -"

I stopped, catching myself a second too late.

"Wait, who's gonna be home?" He said.

"I have to go, Chris. I'll talk to you later."

I hung up and let my hands fall to my sides, the phone slapping against my thigh.

Fuck, again.

I stood there with my eyes closed, listening to all manner of sounds coming from the estate – hammers, hollers, stomping feet, slamming doors, laughing teenagers and grownups alike.

This is what Bran would arrive home to any minute - his house teeming with members of every family in his village, all of them rummaging and running through his house, doing god knows what in his absence.

Now, I was standing in the drive staring up at the manor, trying to settle my racing heart and forget that call from Christopher.

Still, I might be calling him back sooner than later, given I was sure Bran would be kicking me halfway across Scotland in a few moments.

Please don't hate me when you get home, Bran? I thought.

I wanted to catch him when he pulled up. If he was going to hate me for this, I wanted him to hate me and me alone, not the old ladies kneeling on gardening pads as they chopped away at decades of briar and thistle that overtook the front garden of the house.

I stood there for a long moment, watching the house like a child watching an ant farm.

"Hey, what're ye doin, lazybones?" Hilda called from one of the windows. Before I could respond, the glint of daylight on a car hood froze me in my tracks.

A car was coming down the long drive.

Well, it was nice knowing you, world.

Just as the navy-blue roadster pulled up alongside the skip, Mr. Seamonds appeared from within, handing down another armful of crockpots to his waiting daughter, Nicola. He shot me a look.

"Yes, I'm sure!" I called back to him before he could ask again, the words dying halfway out of my mouth as Bran opened the driver's side door. He stood up, slamming the door behind him as he took the first few steps toward the front door. Then he stopped, staring up at the house, its façade now cleared of decades worth of ivy. Bran's hands flew up as he turned, scanning the scene before him, a new jolt of shock at the sight of each person.

I took a step toward him, his arms up, and his fingers curled into his mess of hair. He looked like a man about to be arrested by the SWAT team.

"Bran?" I said, my voice coming in barely a whisper.

He spun around, his eyes wide, nostrils flared. I was about to have my head torn clean off.

"Oh my god, Branny."

Branson was marching toward me as his sister climbed out of the passenger seat of the car, her boots grinding into the gravel drive.

"What in the bloody hell is this?" He said, coming to stand just before me, his tall shape blocking all view of the house.

"I'm sorry. I'm so sorry. I didn't know how to say no -"

"Floyd, dear! So nice of ye to come help with our little endeavor."

Bran spun around as Hilda sauntered across the driveway, wiping her hands on her apron as she approached. She held out one of her hands for Bran to shake. He fumbled a moment in shock, then took her hand.

Before he could speak, Hilda turned her attention to Callista, an expression of surprised appreciation as she looked up at the Amazon that stood before her.

Hilda offered a wide smile.

Callista shook her hand.

"And who is this lovely thing?" Hilda said. Then her expression froze as she took the full brunt of Callista's smile. There was a moment of electrified silence between Callista and the gray-haired vicar.

"It's Callista now," she said, still holding Hilda's hand. The handshake continued for a long moment.

Then, Hilda's expression softened as she placed her other hand over Callista's and squeezed. "A lovely name for a lovely lady. I do hope ye've a change of clothes, love. Wouldn't want to ruin that dress when we put ye to work."

"Oh, no. I didn't come to work -" Callista started, but Hilda pulled her across the drive, quickly introducing her to Mary.

"Oh, nonsense. Here ye are, Mare. Take her inside and give her a pair of gloves and a rag."

With Hilda walking away, I took my chance.

"Please don't be mad at me. I didn't mean to -"

"Are ye fucking mad? The whole bloody village is here!" He hissed, turning to meet my gaze. "Do ye have any idea how fuckin humiliating this is?" His jaw tensed as he glared at me, leaning in to keep our exchange quiet.

I felt tiny there before him. "I know, I know! I didn't – she wouldn't take no for an answer!"

A smiling face appeared beside us, framed in tussled gray hair.

We straightened, our heated whispers stilled by Hilda's sudden return.

"Floyd, was it?" She said, grinning up at Bran.

He sighed. "No."

"No, I didn't think so," Hilda said, interrupting him. She turned around, standing at Bran's shoulder as she looked up at the house and crossed her arms. She gave a contented sigh and smiled, waiting for him to look with her. "We're almost done. Just a bit of tidying up left to be done."

Branson swallowed, audibly. "Wait, ye can't be serious."

"Was quite the undertaking to be sure. Many of us have been working since last night, but we managed, didn't we, love?"

She shot me a sideways glance past Bran. I turned away.

Damn it, vicar. You're going to get me in trouble.

Branson stared up at the house for a long moment, Hilda silently hovering at his shoulder. I joined them in silent inspection. Seven separate chimneys belched black smoke as groups of younger people tended to the fires within, each of them dragging laundry baskets filled with old papers and trash to be burned in one of the many roaring fireplaces. Piles of brush and trimmings from the overgrown garden burned across the drive, and the skip was now filled to near bursting, despite several box trucks worth of goods being fished out of it.

"I remember when you lads – you bairns," Hilda said, catching herself. Her consideration for Callista endeared me to her for life. "I remember you wee ones coming down to the church for tea. I'd been led to believe ye were just bored hooligans. I regret not trying harder to counsel ye both."

Bran stiffened.

Hilda reached for him, giving his arm a squeeze. "I had no idea how bad it was. Must've been hard growing up in this house, not being able to tell anyone what it was like."

Branson's face contorted and he turned, walking across the grass and away from us both.

Hilda pursed her lips and gave herself a nod. "Well, the sooner we're back to work, the sooner we'll be out of your hair. Quit dilly-dallying, you," she said, jutting her forehead at me before marching back across the driveway toward the front door, the back of her black slacks now peppered with white dust.

I waited until she was gone, then turned to watch Bran. He stood just a few yards from me, staring off toward the grounds, the steeple of the very church he'd snuck off to as a child just visible above the trees in the distance. Though we stood silent, the house was teeming with sound just behind us. I knew how changed the place was. I'd seen the now cleared rooms and empty spaces where once decades of junk collected.

If he was going to be angry with me, so be it.

I still wanted to show him.

"Bran?" I said, coming to stand beside him. He didn't look at me. I reached for his hand, taking it in mine.

He let me.

"Come on. Come inside."

I gave a gentle pull, and he ran his hand over his eyes before following me across the drive and into the house.

Figures darted in and out of the kitchen or up and down the stairs as we entered, the smell of wood smoke and food filling the air. Several of the local ladies took the opportunity to treat this project like a potluck, and the kitchen island was covered in various dishes. Thankfully, there was no unfortunate potato salad.

We were greeted by the sound of running footsteps as two of the youngest helpers went darting through, their laughter echoing in the halls behind them.

Clearly, there was little left for them to do but play.

Were I not terrified at that moment, I might've thought it a lovely sound.

The house was toasty warm now from all the fires burning within. Professor Bruce darted down the stairs past us, giving Bran's shoulder a quick pat as he blurted out, "What a wonder this place is. Thanks so much for letting us see it all. Just amazing stuff."

Then he was gone down the stairs, letting me lead Bran to the upstairs hallway.

Bran stopped on the landing as I tried to pull him down the hall. I was sure he knew where I was taking him – the very room that had beaten him just two days before.

"It's alright. Come see."

He met my gaze, his blue eyes burning into me as trepidation read clear on his face.

I gave another tug on his hand, and he relented, passing the first bedroom and the gathered crowd of young people all hovering around the fireplace as they burned the last few piles of papers and trash within.

I reached his grandmother's bedroom door, now closed to signify the job having been completed within.

I let go of Bran's hand and opened the door. The light from within flooded out into the hallway.

His breath caught as he took in the sight.

The high white walls were pristine now, dusted and wiped down, and every piece of antique furniture had been shined. There were two club chairs by the window, a pair of dressers, small nightstands, and a four-poster bed, its linens and bedding freshly washed.

Bran walked across the Persian rug, his footsteps nearly silent as he approached the side table by the windows.

"I made sure this room was done first. I wanted it to be perfect for when you got home."

He didn't speak, setting his hand on the small collection of ornate silver trinkets on the table. There were two crystal bowls with silver covers, a lace hook, a brush, and a hand mirror, all engraved with the same initials – HLD.

Helene Lennox Douglas.

I moved to stand beside him, watching as his fingers grazed over the cursive lettering on the handle of the mirror.

"I know you're mad at me," I said, the words tight in my throat. The sound of my voice startled me in the newly open space. "I don't blame you. I would be, too, but – I just couldn't do it alone."

I watched him, waiting for a response. Bran stood there, his fingers still touching the handle of his grandmother's silver hair brush.

"I tried so hard when you left. I worked myself to exhaustion, but it – it didn't even make a dent. I don't know why I went down to the church -"

That was true. Drawn by the soothing sound of the bells? By divine providence? By a quiet longing for mediocre potato salad?

"- and when Hilda suddenly threatened to bring an army of helpers, I could hear your voice screaming in my head not to let them in, but – I just…"

I stopped, fighting back tears as I remembered him broken down in the mud as he confessed that hidden sea of pain. I wanted to protect him from that riptide, at all costs – even at the cost of his friendship, of his trust.

I would do anything to spare him that anguish.

"I understand if you want me to go and never speak to me again. My stuff is packed. I'm sure I could get someone to take me to the train station, but I just – I couldn't leave you buried under all this. I wouldn't do it."

Bran straightened, turning toward me.

Panic surged in my chest. He was going to let me have it.

I didn't blame him. I had it coming.

His hand moved faster than I could respond, and in an instant, he gripped the fabric of the front of my shirt and pulled me toward him. His fingers grazed up my jaw into my hair and curled against me.

Then, Branson Tennyson Douglas kissed me.

I hummed in startled protest, but the warmth of him, the softness of his lips melted through me like a warm bath on a cold day. I leaned into him, letting him hold my weight as he kissed me again, his arm sliding around my waist.

He wasn't angry. He wasn't going to spurn me and send me away. Still, nothing could've prepared me for this.

Nor for how wonderful it felt.

I grabbed hold of his shirt and pulled at him, kissing him back as I lifted onto my toes. He slid his fingers deeper into my hair, smiling against my lips.

"Branny, this is amazing. You have to come see the – well fuck me!"

Bran and I parted, stepping back from each other as we fought to look innocent.

Callista stood in the doorway with a scandalized look on her face. She pressed her hand to her chest and fought to stifle a laugh as she milked a proper London accent. "Well, pardon me. When you're quite finished, do come find me in the conservatory."

Before Bran could protest, she was gone, laughing heartily as she went.

Bran and I turned to one another, but I could barely meet his gaze. My face was burning.

He reached for my hand, squeezing it in his as he moved toward the bedroom door.

He smiled. "To be continued?"

I gave a nervous laugh, speechless, and watched him stride backward toward the door, a mischievous look on his handsome face. Then he was gone, and I was left with the fire burning just under my skin.

Fourteen

D USK SETTLED IN OVER the grounds as one by one, the helpers piled into their cars and made their way back down the drive toward their own quiet Highland lives.

I stood on the doorstep waving, or smiling when Pepe carried her sleeping granddaughter out to the car, hissing her displeasure at Jameson when he asked to go home with Hilda's grandson, Dermot.

The house felt like the bustling epicenter of some town after a celebration. No one would know by the mood that they'd all spent the better part of a day knee-deep in junk and decade-old dust.

I watched the last car pull away, its tail lights disappearing through the trees, and felt my stomach shoot into my throat. I was alone, and Bran would be home from dropping Cal at the train station, soon.

I swallowed.

He'd kissed me.

Instead of turn on me in a fit of rage, he'd kissed me.

What would the air between us feel like now?

I felt a chill creep down my arms and turned back into the house, shutting the doors against the cool evening air.

The house felt massive and endless in a whole new way. There was an echo in the world now – the echo of empty space. There were crannies and nooks to explore that until that day hadn't seen the air in years. Even the basement was cleared, leaving Branson and Bruce to discover one hell of a Scotch and wine collection tucked away behind old baby furniture that Bran assured everyone hadn't belonged to him or his sister.

I moved quietly now, as though afraid to disturb the empty space, and hustled back upstairs to my bedroom. I could hear the feline protests before I even reached the door.

"Hello, little man," I said, greeting the excited Mr. Darcy. He'd been tucked away up here much of the day, only making an appearance to meet Pepe's youngest grandchild and her friends. He'd received a good amount of love and treats in their company.

I crouched down to give him a good scratch, only to have him rub his face against my knee a little too hard and knock me off balance. I was on my ass on the oriental runner when he decided to go trotting down the hallway, purring with every step.

"Mr. Darcy, where are you going, silly?" I called, making kissy noises and flitting my fingers at him.

He seemed to have something far more pressing on his mind.

I hopped up and followed him, half expecting him to head down to the kitchen and demand more supper, but instead, he bounded past the stairs and down the hall.

"I know," I said. "Gotta explore all the new places, don't we?"

I reached the landing and stopped.

The door – the door I knew very well now, that every single person had tried and failed to open that day – was open. And Mr. Darcy was heading straight for it.

"No, no, no, kitty. Come on, fuzz bucket," I said, crouching down to attempt luring him away. I wasn't sure what startled me so – the door being inexplicably open somehow and what might be inside were I to look, or the notion of Mr. Darcy getting stuck inside.

Mr. Darcy trotted into the room fearlessly, meowing as though he greeted some old friend. I approached the door slowly, stopping just outside.

"This is getting really old," I said.

I imagined a voice responding to me from within.

I recoiled as a gray shape went whizzing past my ankles, heading back for the stairs. I slumped against the hallway wall, my hand pressed to my chest as I fought to quell the panic he'd caused me.

"For Christ's sake, Darcy. Don't do that to me."

I stood there for a long moment, the door ajar just a few inches away. I considered closing it again, as though the notion of freeing what was inside was worse than the mound of dusty mattresses trapped within. We had the skip for another day or two. Bran and I could make quick work of this last offense, if we wanted to.

I sighed.

I didn't want to.

I couldn't begin to imagine what being in Bran's company would be like now, let alone trying to haul dirty mattresses in the dark with him, pretending I wasn't constantly daydreaming about his lips.

I searched the foyer below for a sign of the gray furball, but he'd disappeared. Surely, he was in the kitchen begging for treats.

I glanced back at the door one more time, half expecting it to be closed again. Or more aptly, half expecting some gruesome figure to be floating in the open doorway.

Because your life is a horror movie, it's true. I thought.

I started my way down the stairs, fighting the urge to look back up when a soft melodic sound stopped me in my tracks.

It was quiet and harmonic, with a tinge of sour to every sound. The kind of sour that comes from singing when your throat is too dry.

I clutched the railing in my fists, my palms growing slick as I tried to convince myself that this sound had an explanation.

Someone was playing the piano, downstairs.

I fought the urge to go hauling out the front door and screaming into the Scottish night.

Suddenly, Mr. Darcy appeared in the kitchen doorway, skittering across the front hall toward points unknown. The sound clearly didn't frighten the kitten.

I reached downstairs and turned toward the east wing. If I wasn't mistaken, the sound was coming from the long-forgotten music room.

I stepped down the hallway, weighing each step with the same trepidation I'd felt upstairs.

This time, the gruesome floating figure I saw in my head was jamming hard on some Chopin. Killer.

I watched helplessly as Mr. Darcy trotted into the open door of the music room. The music didn't falter, each string of notes peppered with the sour melody of long out of tune keys. It somehow added to the song's beauty – and its foreboding nature.

If the ghost could tickle the ivories, it could probably do me harm.

I wasn't keen on that idea.

I listened, intently, my heart shooting into my throat. I stepped up to the open door and looked inside.

The once hidden music room was now empty of all its former burden, leaving the long-buried instruments to take up the space with the majesty of aging kings. There was a cello, devoid of its strings, leaning up against the far window seat, an aged teal settee and two gray satin chairs arranged around a worn oriental carpet of gold and burgundy at the center of the room, and beyond all of that, an ancient grand piano sat in front of the dark windows – Branson Douglas seated at the keys. I watched him for a long moment, his face aglow from the light of three candles burning atop the piano.

As I stepped into the room, I noted there was no music on the piano. He was playing from memory.

I stood there in the alive space, listening to this long neglected instrument hum and sing with such fervor, it was as though the instrument was thanking him for giving it a voice, again.

I wanted to thank him, too.

The song stopped, suddenly, and before he looked at me, Bran leaned down to his ankles and scooped up a tiny gray shape. "Careful kitty. You'll catch your tail," he said, setting Mr. Darcy atop the piano. He then turned his eyes to me and smiled.

I just about stopped breathing.

A second later, the music returned, a soft, melodic ebb and flow of sound that made me want to close my eyes and be lost.

"I didn't know you played," I said.

He shot me a glance, his hands moving over one another as the notes moved from high to low and back. "Mother insisted," he said, winking.

I smiled. I stood there in the open space, unable to move closer, unable to turn and leave. I felt like the ballerina in a music box, trapped in place, her only choice of movement being to spin.

Bran tilted his head toward the cello. "That's Cal's. I almost convinced her to play with me today until we realized the extra strings were rusted solid. The first one snapped in her hands when she touched it."

I glanced toward the cello; its wood finish in desperate need of a shine, but otherwise, still solid. I imagined the Douglas children in this room when they were young, practicing the hours away until Bran could play Chopin from memory.

"You won't believe it, but -" I said, nearly cringing at how absurd my voice sounded against his playing.

Bran smiled at me again, nodding to the bench beside him without breaking from the song.

I instantly forgot what I was going to say.

"What?" He said, his grin only growing wider as my face flushed. He chuckled, stopping to give Mr. Darcy a good rub. "Come sit."

I shook my head. "I don't want to get in your way. I like listening to you."

"I can play with ye beside me, love."

I could feel the color leave my face.

His eyebrows shot up as he swayed across the keys. "What's wrong? Don't like me anymore?"

Good lord, how wrong he was.

I met his gaze and saw the daring look in his eyes.

"I don't think I can move."

His eyebrows shot up. "Why's that?"

"I'm nervous?" I said, deciding to tell the truth.

This made him smile even more brightly if that's possible. He turned on the piano bench to face me.

"No need to be nervous," he said, just as I finally willed my feet to move. I came to stand beside the piano, pretending to inspect the bottle and two glasses that were set atop it. Darcy found his way to the edge of the piano, pawing the air in my direction. I scooped him up and let him loose on the rug. He proceeded to do a barrel roll across it, displaying his belly for a quick rub.

I obliged. Anything to slow my progress toward Branson. However much I wanted to relent, I was terrified to be near him again.

I stood up and began watching him like some coiled snake that might strike in my direction at any second.

I'm not saying I didn't want him to. Still, I was so nervous.

I'd spent a month and a half in his constant company – heard his jokes, his burps, his fits of rage and frustration, his cooing voice when he spoke to the cat.

None of it deterred the strange electricity I now felt humming all around me when he was near.

Clearly, he was a good kisser.

He rose to his full height and stood before me, smiling. "Are ye hungry?"

I shook my head.

He nodded toward the glasses on the piano top. "Thirsty? I was waiting for ye to break into the good stuff, here."

I shot a glance at the bottle again. It was Scotch from the basement. Forty-year-old whisky.

"You're just going to drink it? I think that bottle is worth more than I make in a year."

He shrugged. "There are a dozen or more down there."

He shot me a wide-eyed look of conspiracy, before peeling off the wax and pouring me a glass, then he turned back to the piano.

"We could always partake in another form of refreshment."

Ok, he wasn't going to make out with my face again.

I was wracked with disappointment.

"Oh yeah? What's that?"

Branson leaned towards me, reaching into his back pocket. A moment later, he dropped a plastic baggy onto the top of the piano, two massive hand-rolled cigarettes waiting within the cellophane prison.

I caught a whiff of the familiar scent.

Shockingly, this wasn't tobacco.

I laughed. "I thought you said you weren't a pothead?"

He grinned. "I swear I'm not. Our good old Jameson gave them to me today when I caught him smoking in the garden."

"Pepe clearly had his number. She was calling him a pothead all day."

Bran picked up his tumbler. "That he is."

I thought of the circumstances of the last time I smoked such a thing – and how ridiculous it made me.

I moved closer to the piano, ready to take my glass. He sat down and slid aside on the bench, making it clear he expected me to sit with him.

I did.

He snatched up his glass and held it out to me. I took a moment, fumbling with my very thoughts as his arm brushed against mine. Finally, I lifted my own glass.

He clinked them together. "Slainte mhath," he said.

"Slantcha Va," I said in return, the Gallic sounding strange in my mouth. I brought the tumbler up to my lips and took a sip. It was the smoothest Scotch I'd ever tasted, barely burning as it moved down my throat and began to warm me from the belly out. "Wow," I said.

He grinned. "That's what I said."

He set his glass back atop the piano and slid his fingers across the keys. "Any requests?"

I took another sip of scotch and felt an involuntary smile creep across my face.

This was good fucking scotch.

"Um, do you know any Mozart?"

He chuckled, softly. "Aye, I know Mozart. Any preference?"

I took a deep breath, feeling my body sway as I sat there beside him. "Something soft."

His eyebrows went up for a second, then he nodded. "I think I know the one. Sonata No. 11."

"Hm?" I said, nearly spitting my scotch as I tried to respond mid-sip. Before I could recover, he began to play.

I knew the song, instantly. It started with the simplest three notes, played on both hands in a sing-song lilt that made me want to curl into him and close my eyes.

I wanted to curl into him, anyway. He was close to me again. Close for the first time since he'd kissed me, and I could smell the conditioner in his hair, the subtle warmth of his laundry detergent, and beneath that the musty undertone of the house and those once dusty keys. I watched his hands move as the song picked up, his arm moving down the length of the piano toward me. I set my glass on the top of the piano, letting him have my full attention.

Why god? Why does this guy have to be talented, as well?

The speed of his fingers tripled. His arm brushed into me, pressing against my breast as he reached past me to the far keys. A moment later, he'd moved back to the middle. I waited for his arm to come my way again. I found the touch invigorating, wanting to believe he did it on purpose – that he wanted to touch me, too.

"I'm glad you don't hate me," I said. The words startled me.

Where the hell did that come from? I thought.

"Why on earth would I hate ye?"

I swayed, giving a raised eyebrow as my eyes closed. "Because of all those people and -"

He didn't stop playing. "I admit when Cal and I rode down the drive, I was livid. But then I saw ye."

I swallowed, watching his face as his eyes darted across the keys, his hands moving to follow in an instant. "You saw me?"

"I did. And I saw the look on your face."

"What look?"

He kept his eyes to the keys, the music speeding up with each second. "The look of panic. Ye looked so scared. Broke my heart a bit."

I inhaled, sharply. "It did?"

The music slowed and he glanced at me. "It did."

"Why?"

"Because I care about ye."

I felt every muscle in my body tense.

He continued to play, the music slowing again as it came to the end. I knew this song. There would be a big finish. I wanted to hear him play it.

"I was upset at first, but only because ye'd done the thing I couldn't do."

I watched his hands, wanting to touch them, feel his fingers entwined with mine. "What was that?"

His hands moved along the keys in a long flourish, his arms grazing against me again. He touched the keys in a subtle flick of two high notes, then soft chords.

Then he was off again, the song began to pick up, and he gave his full focus to the keys, arpeggios, and scales, his thigh muscles firing as he pressed on the pedals. Finally, he played the final chords with the purpose of a concert pianist, their tones echoing across the room and out into the empty house.

I listened to the house for a long moment, watching him.

"Ye asked for help," he said, finally. "I've always struggled with that. Most of my life, in fact."

I exhaled, only then realizing I'd been holding my breath.

I watched his profile as he reached for his tumbler and took another sip. The space felt thick with memory in the newfound silence. Part of me wanted him to play more. The greater part of me wanted to keep his attention as long as I could.

When the silence carried on too long, I looked around the room, as though some newly bare corner might start up a conversation for me.

"Have you had a chance to explore the house?" I asked.

He took a sip from his tumbler, gesturing to my still full glass. "Nay, I haven't. Was a bit overwhelmed by the thought, actually."

I stared at him in bewilderment. "Really? Well, come on. Give me a proper tour, will ya?"

I hopped up from the bench, feeling reluctant to put distance between us, but happy to break the tension that lingered there.

He grinned, gave a sarcastic eye roll, then downed the last of his Scotch and grabbed the candelabra from the top of the piano. I watched him trot toward the doors and out into the hallway.

"Come on, then! At that pace, it'll take all night."

I groaned at him. "You do realize I've been working for almost forty-eight hours straight?"

He turned, walking backward down the hall as he gestured for me to follow. The grin on his face was glowing gold in the light of the candles. It was reminiscent of those mischievous grins I'd gotten for weeks now, but unlike before, there was no weight hiding behind his eyes. He wasn't dreading the sights that lay before him.

He genuinely looked excited.

"Here we are," he said, ducking into the billiard room. The hardwood was stained in the corner where the refuse pile had been, but nothing a sander and some polish couldn't solve. The walls were a rich burgundy stain of wood, and the panels went floor to ceiling. Now, with the junk cleared out, I could see the carvings that lined the ceiling and cabinet doors. There were shelves filled with games, and who knew what else was tucked out of sight.

The musty stench of its former state lingered, but a day's worth of open windows and lemon furniture polish was working hard to counter it. He practically skipped across the room to a corner of the wood paneling and set the candleabra on the cupboard.

"Ye ready?"

I smiled and nodded. My nod stopped dead as Bran pulled a section of the paneling away from the window sill, stepping aside to open what was easily a six-foot-tall hinged panel.

"Come look," he said.

Despite his company, the house was growing eerie as the light faded outside. There were still a number of lightbulbs missing across the expanse of the place. This room was no different, and the few lightbulbs still working along the wall gave little more light than the candelabra he carried.

I was almost too afraid to join him as he snagged the candelabra and disappeared behind the massive panel, leaving me in the near dark.

"Will you wait?" I shrieked, rushing to follow him.

I was struck the instant I rounded the panel doorway and found a stone staircase leading down into blackness. Bran stood on the third step, the candles casting a flickering shadow of him on the stone wall as he held a hand out to me, waiting to help me down the uneven steps.

"Holy shit? Are you kidding me?"

He beamed. "This isn't the only one in the house."

"Only what?"

"Secret," he said, wrapping his fingers around mine with a firm, but soft grip.

I tread carefully down the steps. This secret place was clearly older than the floor above, a remnant of the original fortress that once stood there.

We reached the bottom of the steps, Bran heaving his shoulder into the wooden door, kicking up dust and debris as it fought to stay put.

Finally, it gave an angry grating sound as it pushed across the stone floor within. I followed Bran into the musty cellar of the house.

The ceilings were surprisingly high, and old metal fixtures stuck out of the ceiling and walls over my head. I strained to take in the details around me – the worn divots in the walls just two feet above the floor, a small square hole that was now boarded up in the corner. I caught a glimpse of a chain hanging from a ring over the door behind me and furrowed my brow in confusion.

"This used to be a dungeon, once upon a time," he said, stepping further into the room to give it more light. "That there's what they call an *Oubliette*. Place they throw people to forget about them."

The hair on every inch of my body stood on end. The room smelled of rust and age. I instantly wondered how much blood had spilled across those stones.

"My grandad told Cal and I that they pulled well over a dozen skeletons out of that fucker when he was a wee lad."

"Oh god," I said, convulsing as though a spider had just crawled down the back of my shirt. The place felt little more than musty and dank. In other parts of the house, the air was alive with a presence. Hell, I'd seen the blue woman traipsing around the top floor more than once, yet it was here that my inner voice was screaming, *"Haunted, haunted, haunted! So freakin haunted!"*

"Ye alright, love?"

"Yep!" I said with a little too much gusto. "Nope! Nope, nope, nope."

He laughed, shutting the heavy door behind us. It was only then that I noticed the interior of the door was fashioned to look like a stone wall face. This was the secret entrance for some foul sadist to come down and torment people, wasn't it?

Haunted, haunted, haunted!

Bran then turned to me, offering his arm. I took it, and he led me deeper into the cellar, leaving the high ceilings of the dungeon behind. The next section of the cellar was lined with heavy shelves, each of them holding what I assumed were barrels of whisky.

Branson led me down a serpentine path of shelves and racks of things, only to stop at one dusty barrel tucked deep into a corner. He released my arm, handing me the candelabra.

"Are these barrels all full?"

He grabbed the barrel, tugging it to the edge of the shelf. Then he scanned around for something, finally returning with a rusty screwdriver. He jimmied it into the barrel cover. I braced myself for a sudden deluge of alcohol.

"Nay. A good lot of them have evaporated by now. The few that have anything left are probably worth quite a bit."

"Really?"

"Aye, these barrels are fifty years old, at the very least. Fifty-year Scotch is not bloody cheap."

With that, the barrel top popped off and the dark recesses came into view. No liquid came pouring out, but a good cloud of dust blustered out into our faces, I turned my face into the crook of my arm as Bran ignored it, giving a chuckle as he leaned into the barrel.

"Still here!" He said, grinning. "My god."

I wiped the dust off my face and moved closer to see. Inside the barrel, there was a small collection of foodstuffs – cans of baked beans, a box of ancient biscuits, an old Boost bar that lay beside two empty Boost bar wrappers. Before I could identify anything else, Bran pulled out one of the cans of baked beans, fighting to read the label by candlelight.

He laughed. "Nineteen-ninety-five," he said. "Think it's still good?"

I shook my head, handing the candelabra back to him. "What is this?"

"This is one of the spots where Cal and I hid our food so Dad wouldn't steal it. I can't believe it's still here."

I frowned before I could stop myself.

Bran gave my elbow a squeeze. "Ah, lighten up. It's not so bad. I'm clearly well-fed, now, ain't I?"

I gave the same half-laugh, glancing at him in the golden light.

He looked beautiful.

There was a creaking sound somewhere among the shelves, and Bran stiffened.

Haunted!

"Come, now. There's another good one upstairs," he said.

I raised an eyebrow, glancing back toward the sound. "Why? Something bothering you?"

He didn't look at me, leaving the screwdriver there as he led me through the rest of the cellar to the stairs. These were not secret stairs. He was in a hurry to get back to the first floor.

Something had spooked him.

I stayed on his tail, trying to ignore the same thoughts I'd had in the dungeon.

Haunted, haunted, super haunted!

I wondered how many more secrets might be tucked away in just the massive cellar, but I wasn't prepared to meet anything in the dark while I explored.

We reached the foyer and Bran shut the cellar door tight behind us. Then, he set the candelabra on one of the sideboards in the front hall before grabbing my hand and leading me up the stairs. I followed close behind, trying to keep pace with him as he darted excitedly upward, taking two steps at a time. He careened around the corner to ascend the second flight of steps to the third floor.

I glanced down the hallway, spotting a familiar sight.

The mattress room door was closed – again.

I didn't have a chance to comment as Bran pulled me down the hallway toward my bedroom.

I admit right now, I had a moment of hope.

"Here we are," he said, turning into one of the empty rooms. It was similar to my own room, but without any furniture to speak of, save for an old rocking horse and an artist's easel. Though it was dark throughout the house, the lights in the hallway and this bedroom were in working order.

"Now, this one might be a bother if ye don't like small spaces."

I crinkled my nose. "This doesn't sound good."

He smiled. "Oh, it is."

Bran moved to the closet door in the corner, opened it, then disappeared inside.

I sighed. If he kept leaving me in creepy corners of the house, I was going to start taking offense.

Suddenly, he peeked his head back out to smile at me. "Are ye coming?"

I fidgeted a second, embarrassed. When I reached the closet door, the back of the usually small space was now wide open, leading into the closet of the next room. I stepped across the threshold toward the adjacent room.

A hand reached out from the wall, grabbing my arm. I jumped with such terror, I nearly slammed my head into the doorjamb.

I turned toward the offending hand, staring into the dark recesses that lay hidden between the walls. It took a moment to focus my eyes, but before I could make out the figure within, a bulb burst to life over Bran's head. He was standing in a tiny secret room between the walls, the hanging bulb still swinging.

Between the two closets, there was a skinny crawl space, barely wide enough for anyone of girth to traverse. Still, Bran gestured for me to check it out.

I sucked in my belly and my chest, shimmying my way through the crevice. Two feet in, the space opened to a small chamber. There was an old stool, some comic books, a set of drawing pencils, and a tired old blanket settled in the corner.

"This is one of the hidden rooms they used to hide Jacobites."

I felt a sudden swell of wonder.

The space took on a whole new life as I inspected the collection of things from Bran and Cal's childhood. The two Douglas children came here to tuck themselves away from the world, but who else had done just such a thing over the centuries? For the first time, I wondered if the Stuart Prince had spent time in Cavendish House. It seemed entirely plausible.

A notion suddenly struck me. "One of the hidden rooms?"

He nodded. "Aye. Not sure how many are up here. Cal and I never really went lookin for more as most of these rooms were filled with rubbish. Luckily, we were content to share this one until Cal moved away."

"You spent a lot of time here?" I asked, letting myself look at him. The space offered little room, and we were pressed close, just a few inches between us. It was spacious enough for a man to lie down on the floor, and certainly enough for a child to sprawl out and color as it seemed they'd done. Still, it left us tucked in close proximity, the only way out a narrow lane.

"When I was in secondary, I had a girlfriend for all of a minute. She kept asking to come and see the house. Wouldn't kiss me until she did, she said."

Bran looked down at the old comic books, crouching down to pick one up.

"I'd been embarrassed, but she assured me she didn't mind, and I was an excitable lad, so I relented. When she came to the house, I brought her up here – to impress her, like and to take her to one of the few places my Dad hadn't ruined."

I ran my fingers over a set of carved letters on the wall – *Callum is a bawbag*. I snorted, quietly. "Did she kiss you?"

He pursed his lips and nodded. "Aye, she did. She then told everyone in school the next day that I lived in absolute squalor."

My chest tightened.

"Chucked me without sayin a word to me, laughed at me in the hall. Told everyone I needed to be deloused."

I fought to search for words, despite my true desire being to fist fight a thirteen-year-old girl.

"That's when I finally asked to go to school in London and live with Mum. If nothing else, he did that right. He pulled strings and had me transferred within a month."

"I'm glad," I said, unable to find anything better.

He shrugged. "God, I haven't been back here in decades. I can't believe this is all still here."

"Did your dad know about this spot?"

"I didn't believe so. Though, that might explain why this was one of the first rooms he blocked off with junk. Deny us this little haven in the hell this house was."

"Would he really do that?"

Bran gave me a sad look, and I knew the answer. "There was little he wouldn't do to maintain control over everyone and everything in this house."

We stood there for a long moment. The thought that the last time he'd been kissed in this room was by a girl who betrayed him made me feel compelled.

I wanted to kiss him. In this room, of all the places in the house, I wanted to let him know that he mattered, that someone could want him without ulterior motive. That someone could want to kiss him, just to reclaim a place that once made him feel safe.

I didn't, of course. Because that would've been brave, and apparently, I'm a chicken shit.

I found the tight quarters to be too much and moved to shimmy my way back out into the open space of the bedroom. Branson clicked the bulb off and followed me, shutting the secret door between the closets as he did.

"Do you think there are other closet rooms like this?"

He nodded, heading back out into the hallway. "As far as I know."

I followed him, spotting Mr. Darcy trotting towards us from the stairs. I smiled at him, and he mewed up at me, his eyes dark from fully dilated pupils.

It was overwhelmingly adorable.

Before I could bend down to snatch him up and smash my face in his fur, he turned around, his ears pointing forward as he watched the hallway ahead. I followed his gaze, knowing exactly what had drawn his attention.

Despite the kitty's sudden interest, the mattress room door was still shut tight.

"Oh wow. Did you ever try the closets on the opposite of that room?"

I pointed down the hallway.

Bran knew exactly which room I was talking about. "No, could never get to any of the closets down there. Even when I was wee."

Before he'd finished his sentence, he was marching down the hallway toward the offending door.

"I swear one of these days you're going to see her," I said, moving to keep up.

He gave me a side-eye then scoffed. "That would be impossible, love, given she's a figment of your wild imagination."

Bran tried the doorknob. Just as expected, it didn't budge. "And ye claim it was open earlier?"

"It was!" I said, feigning anger. "You can pretend you don't believe me, but I know you've felt it, too."

"I've felt a good number of things, none of them involved ghosts."

He gave the door a good hit with his shoulder, but it remained unmoved. I turned for the adjacent room, marching across the now clear space to the closet that was situated adjacent to the closet in the mattress room. I flung open the door, getting a blast of mothball air as I did. The closet was empty save for an old hat box and a bundle of fabric swatches.

I turned to set them aside, laying them atop one another on the otherwise empty floor.

"Christ, wouldn't that just be the way," he said, stepping past me to look inside the closet. I stood aside, watching past his shoulder as he ran his hand along the wooden planks of the closet interior. "I dunno. I don't see anything to hint at a -"

"Look!" I said, pointing to the floor at his feet. There was light cast at the place where the wall and floor meet – blue light, like that from a moonlit window in the space behind it.

The wall wasn't solid.

"Well, fuck me," he said, rapping his knuckles against each board, searching for a change in sound. I stood aside, growing antsy.

Bran dropped to his knees, running his fingers along the lower edge of the wood. He touched his hand to the side and made a soft humming sound. "Aye, there's a door hinge down here.

With him on his knees now, I scanned the wall for a way in. Without the light at the base of the wall, the closet looked like any other; old metal hooks and a crossbar to hang clothes from. Each looked older than the last, save for one, its sheen giving a glint in the little amount of light. I looked closer. Unlike the other hooks, this one had been rubbed smooth along the top, and beneath it, the wall stain was chipped, like someone had been dragging something across it.

I reached out, taking hold of the hook. "Here."

The hook slid downward in my hand. Somewhere in the closet, there was a soft click of a latch.

"Holy fuck," Bran said as the back of the closet shifted inward. The secret door opened four or five inches, then bounced back, a sign of it hitting the pile of mattresses within. "You cheeky thing."

I shot a glance at him and started, realizing he was speaking to me. "What, I didn't do anything!"

"Aye, ye didn't do anything, but somehow, here we are."

"This one's different," I said, trying to change the subject so I wouldn't have to maintain his eye contact.

Stop being beautiful, Bran. And charming. Just cut it right out. Or take me. Your choice.

The previous secret doorway had been two false backs to two separate closets with a crawl space in between. This one was just a thin wooden door closing off the two rooms from one another. The closet door in the mattress room was no longer attached to its hinges. If the mattresses were clear, the secret door would open fully out into the room. If I remembered correctly, there was a fireplace just inside, set into the wall to the right. No wonder there wasn't a hidden room here. There would be a brick chimney going up through the walls.

I nodded. "Yeah, If we just take this off the hinges, we could have easy access. The door's a little shorter, but I imagine we could sneak the bastards through."

It was as though my father was speaking through me.

I gave the door another quick push, feeling the soft bounce on the opposite side. I sighed at the notion of there still being more to do. Still, one room out of dozens and dozens was nothing to complain about.

"Corinne."

I startled, turning to find Bran standing behind me, watching me. I swallowed. "Yeah?"

"Ye've done enough, love."

I exhaled. There was such a weight to what he said, as though I'd fought as his champion against an undefeatable beast.

It wasn't untrue, I realized, but still – it was hard to hear that kind of intensity in his voice.

I tried to shake my head, searching for words to protest this declaration, but none came. I knew to him what had happened in that house was a miracle. I knew it in the lightness of his steps, in the carefree tone of his voice. In a matter of hours, I'd seen Branson Douglas go from a shadow of himself to a Prince surveying his kingdom with pride.

However many caravans of church parishioners it took to get it done, I'd been the catalyst, and he looked at me as though I could walk on water.

I turned away, unable to maintain eye contact with him. He took hold of my hand, running his thumb over my fingers. My face burned.

"Ye know I'm grateful, don't ye?"

I snorted. "Yes, I did get that impression."

"Ye did?" He asked, his eyebrows shooting up.

"Well, yeah. I mean, you did kiss me and all."

My stomach shot into my throat.

Damn it, Corinne, why'd you bring that up?

"Aye, I did."

I met his gaze, giving an awkward shrug as he held my fingers in his hand. I felt a gentle pull as he tried to bring me closer to him.

Oh god, I thought. *Is he going to do it again? Please, let him do it again.*

Despite my nerves, when he gave my hand another gentle tug, I let him pull me toward him. He was towering over me now, taking in every inch of my face with a sleepy look. His free hand moved up to the side of my face, brushing my hair aside.

He sighed in frustration. "Why do ye have to be taken, Corinne Turner?"

My eyes went wide under a furrowed brow. I stared up at him in confusion. "Taken?"

"Aye, taken. Your lad there in Perth, is it?"

"Christopher?" I said, and his name came out like I was spitting out a fishbone mid-bite.

"Aye, Christopher."

"He's not – we're not -," I said, stumbling for words.

We'd never been, Chris and I. Not really. I'd done that thing I'd always done – jumped through one hoop after another after another, trying to make a man see me with the same affection I felt.

If I just make him laugh enough. If I just give him enough space. If I was just near him, we'd be together. He'd see how wonderful I am, and we'd be happy.

"We were never technically together."

His eyebrows rode upward. "Is that so?"

"He told me to come to Scotland to see. If I was nearby, that maybe we could see if we wanted to date – or something."

I felt absolutely ludicrous admitting this out loud – that I'd traveled across an ocean for a guy who thought he *might* like to date me.

God, I'm an idiot.

"Ye've seen his cock on Skype, he invited ye all the way here, but he's not sure he wants to date ye?"

I closed my eyes. Pathetic. "I didn't see his cock, I told you that."

"Well, I can tell ye right now, that Christopher is a fucking bell end."

I snorted, loudly, turning away from his fingers as he tried to brush my hair aside again. "So -" he said, and the word felt like a bomb. "Does that mean I can kiss ye, again?"

I inhaled sharply but didn't speak. I could hardly turn my face up to him, my stomach was in such merciless knots. I fought to catch my breath.

His lips drew close to mine, and I recoiled in nervous panic, my face flushing hot. I turned my face away, feeling his lips graze against my temple. My whole body was wound tight.

I opened my eyes as his arm found its way around my waist, watching the open closet door as I willed myself fearless.

A shadow passed across the light along the closet floor. We both lunged back, Bran and I separating as I moved away from the closet. I shot him a sideways glance.

He was watching the closet floor, too.

I grabbed his arm and pulled him toward the hallway. He followed without a word, running out onto the stairs as we bounded downward and away from the eerie sight.

We reached the front hall and I spun on him, swatting his arm. "You saw it!" I hissed. "You saw it, too! I fucking told you."

He groaned, but the conviction in his voice was gone. "I didn't see anything."

"Yes, you did! Yes, you did. So there! She's *not* my imagination."

"Ye're mad."

I lunged toward him, pointing at him with a strange mix of exasperation and affection. I knew he'd seen it, and I knew it unnerved him, but he simply couldn't admit that he had – and as a smile cracked across his face, I knew why.

Because he liked seeing me flabbergasted.

I growled as his grin grew with each passing second, and before I could weigh the repercussions of my actions, I grabbed Bran's shirt and kissed him.

It was the only suitable response to what I was feeling. My body tensed as I realized what I'd done, and I felt him tense in surprise. I made to pull away, but Bran's arms wrapped around my waist. Then he kissed me back, and we both melted into each there in the middle of the front hall, the echoing expanse of the room like a third person, watching with mischievous relish.

Finally, I thought.

I made a soft sound deep in my throat and moved my hands toward him, searching his body for safe places to hold onto him.

His kiss was warm and smoky, and I could taste the honey of scotch on his lips. I let my lips linger open between each kiss, wordlessly inviting him. I inhaled sharply, as though I might pull him into me with my breath.

He suddenly broke from the kiss and grabbed my hand, pulling me down the hallway.

I heard a soft mew from the steps, glancing back to find Mr. Darcy trotting along behind us.

Oh, you might want to go find something else to do, little man, I thought.

Bran dragged me back to the music room, spinning me around to walk me backward across the grand space. He backed me up to the sofa, and I fell onto it with a thud and a poof of dust that vibrated through the floor. He knelt there on the settee beside me, his lips finding mine as though they were the only source of oxygen in the room.

I'd never been kissed like this before.

He leaned over me, a wicked smile on his face as he held his lips close to mine. "I've wanted to do this for weeks," he said.

A cacophony of sound echoed through the room as the piano suddenly burst to life.

We both jumped, turning toward the piano in time to see a tiny, gray furball hop up onto the keys. I laughed, but it was stifled as Bran turned my face back to his, his teeth grazing my lips as he smiled.

My belly grew warmer than any scotch could manage, and I pulled him into me, wanting to taste his lips again. He obliged, this time letting his tongue slide into my mouth. I squirmed in response to the sensation, wanting to feel him against every inch of me.

He seemed to understand, as he nudged his knees between mine and lowered himself onto me, pressing his weight between my legs.

I gasped, but his mouth quickly stilled my breath, kissing me deeper still. I could feel his body, the hardness of him.

My mind stopped.

I opened my legs wider, wrapping them around him, and he groaned, relinquishing my lips long enough to kiss down over my jaw to my throat as his hands moved up my sides.

I squealed, the sudden purpose of his touch drawing panicked laughter, similar to being tickled. I wasn't ticklish, but his fingers felt electric.

I ran my hand up over his stomach to his chest. He grabbed it, and I watched in giddy excitement as Bran pulled his Bauhaus T-shirt up over his head, baring his pale, broad chest to me. He was on top of me before I could speak, pinning my legs apart as he settled there, grinding his body into mine.

I finally found my voice. "I can't believe this is happening," I said, the words coming in breathless gasps.

He smiled down at me. "Oh, it hasn't even started, love."

With that, he pressed his lips to my collar, moving down over the skin there as his hands moved up my sides to my breasts. He took hold of me through my clothes, and I shrieked, the sound quickly disintegrating into a laugh. He smiled up at me before kissing my skin again, the fervor of our movements sending a thumping vibration through the settee that seemed to resonate across the house.

"You like that, do ye?" He said, hooking his fingers under the cup of my bra. He slowly pulled at the fabric, making my whole-body freeze as I whined in feigned protest. Whatever intimacy a kiss carried, he was about to barrel past that with purpose.

"Goodness. If this is how you get after being spooked, I hope that ghost comes around more often."

He raised an eyebrow. "I didn't see any bloody ghost."

I growled as he fought to hide his wide grin.

I curled my fingers into his mass of wavy hair, feeling the same thumping vibration travel through the hardwood floor and up into the sofa.

We both stopped, Bran lifting himself up to look toward the door of the music room.

I felt my stomach turn. "I was kidding," I said, speaking to the house around us. Of all the things I wanted to see at that moment – Bran naked, for example - the ghost wasn't one of them.

The reverberation returned, a rhythm of bangs that seemed to shake the house.

Was this the woman in blue again? Was she about to go on some Christmas Carol-type tear to deter our lustful embrace?

I looked around the room, clutching Branson to me as we listened.

Even Mr. Darcy's ears were pinned back when he came skittering toward us to escape the sound.

Boom. Boom. Boom.

It was someone banging on the front door.

"Who the fuck is that?" Bran said, rising to his feet and hustling out into the hallway.

I sat there for a moment frozen in indecision.

Should I go with him and meet the visitors? Perhaps someone forgot a belonging while they worked in the house that day?

I wasn't sure I wanted someone from the village giving me the side-eye when I appeared in the hallway with a shirtless Branson.

Still, I sat up on the sofa, listening intently.

"Who is it?" I heard Branson call.

The following words startled me to my feet. I stood there, palms out, twisting and turning about the room, as though clearing an invisible table in my panic.

"This is the Polis," had been the response.

What the hell are the Polis doing here?

"Is there anyone else in the house?" I heard, this time the voice was clearer. Bran had opened the door.

"What right have ye to come barging into my house?"

Footsteps came stomping through the foyer, a pair of them quickly closing in on my location. I stood there, straightening my shirt as I awaited my impending meeting with the law officers of Scotland.

Shadows on the hall floor hinted at their approach and a sudden realization struck me.

I lunged across the breadth of the music room to the piano, snatched up the plastic baggy with the two joints inside, and stuffed it into my pocket.

"What d'ye have there, miss?" The voice said from the door.

"What? Nothing. I don't have anything," I said, fighting to sound as calm as possible.

I turned to find two police officers and Branson entering as Mr. Darcy darted off down the hall. Before I could argue, the officer stepped over to me, giving me a raised eyebrow as he glanced down at my jeans pocket.

This officer was taller than me by several inches, ginger eyebrows that were fine despite a pronounced brow, and lips so thin, they were barely visible.

I met his gaze, shaking my head. I could hear the sound of other footsteps stomping through the house, but couldn't be sure how many officers were there.

I couldn't help but wonder where in the world they managed to wrangle this many officers in the middle of East Overshoes Nowhere Scotland.

"I don't have anything," I said.

"Is that so? Well, ye can empty yer pockets now, miss, or we can do it by force at the station. Yer choice."

I swallowed, shooting a glance to Bran.

He stared at me, a look of confusion and worry on his handsome face. "Damn ye, ye've no right coming in my home at this hour -"

"We had a report of trespassing, sir. Now, empty your pockets, miss."

"Trespassing? By who?" We both said, our words jumbling together.

The officer glared at me, taking a step closer.

I felt the air leave my lungs as I realized I couldn't fight this man. I reached into my pocket, felt the cellophane crinkle under my fingers, and pulled the tiny bag of pot out to hand to the officer.

Branson gave an exasperated, but worried growl. "Corinne!"

"What do we have here," the officer said in a sing-song voice.

"That's mine," Branson said, trying to step forward and take it from his hand.

The second officer pressed his hand to Bran's chest, warning him.

"I'm sorry," I said, unable to find anything better to say as the officer took the drugs from my hand.

"Ye've not to be sorry for. That's fucking mine."

"Well, then why was it in her pocket, lad?" The officer said, taking hold of my arm. "Looks as though you're both under arrest."

"Fer fuck's sake!" Branson said, yanking his arm out of the officer's grasp. "Ye've no right!"

The ginger officer glowered at Bran, giving the other officer; a shorter, stockier fellow with pronounced ears and a bald head, a nod to take my arm as well. "Well, I'd say we have every right, given the owner called into the station to report a break-in on the premises. And look what we find when we arrive."

"Owner? *I'm* the bloody owner!"

"I imagine Jocelyn Read would disagree, lad. Come along, now."

The officer pulled me toward the doors and I felt my legs go wobbly. *Arrested in Scotland for drugs. Good lord, what is my dad gonna say?* I saw a flash of Diane in my mind and cringed, fighting to push the image of Kenny's fiancé away. I walked along with the officer, as obedient and polite as a person could be.

Bran was happily being the complete opposite.

The other officers met us in the front hall, the door to the house waiting wide open. I saw the open door and a sudden revelation struck me.

"Wait! My cat!"

The officer tightened his grip. "Don't make a fuss, miss."

"Wait!" I said again, but I didn't fight this time. I scanned the floor of the front hall, praying that Mr. Darcy was hidden away somewhere from the ruckus and hadn't slipped out into the dark world outside. "Did you see a cat? A little gray kitten?"

One of the new officers shook his head, but I was still in a panic, my eyes darting back across the front hall.

How long would I be gone? How long until I could come home and feed him or replace his water?

Come home? I thought, and the words stilled in my mind.

"I'm so sorry, Branson," I said as he was led past me toward a separate car.

"Ye've nothing to apologize for. We'll figure this out. I promise."

An instant later, Branson was in the back of a police car, the lights flickering overhead, blinding me to any sight of him.

I let the ginger officer and his stocky friend help me into the back of their car, and winced as the car door was shut after me. Then I turned and watched out the back window as we rolled down the drive, Cavendish House disappearing behind the trees.

Fifteen

"**T**HIRTY-TWO DAYS?" THE OFFICER asked, repeating what I'd just said.

They'd separated Bran and I upon arriving at the station. They were booking Bran for trespassing on his own property, and they booked me for possession.

I wanted to pretend this interrogation was more pleasant than the hour spent waiting for it to happen, but it wasn't. Every time the ginger cop – a man I now knew as Officer Blake - glared at me from under that prominent brow of his, I felt sure I'd be in the stocks if they had such a thing.

"Yeah," I said.

Thirty-two days was how long I had left on my grace period after overstaying my Visitors' Visa. Thirty-two days before I'd be expected to leave not only Scotland but the U.K.

Normally, I didn't have a problem with moving on from a place, but now?

Let's just say Mr. Darcy wasn't the only thing I didn't want to leave behind.

"And you say you travel around the world, stayin in other peoples' houses?"

I hated that response. "I'm a housesitter. It's a perfectly reasonable job."

He glared at me, and I thought better of taking a tone with my interrogating officer. "Do you have another job lined up after this?"

"No," I said. I didn't add the fact that I hadn't even been looking. I'd come to Scotland with blind hope that I'd never leave again. That hadn't gone quite to plan, and I was now being offered a lenient response to possession charges if I simply promised to get the fuck out of their country.

"Do you even have a departure ticket?" he asked.

I swallowed. "No, sir."

"Did you enter the U.K. with the intention of staying here, indefinitely?"

I shook my head.

I was lying.

He stared down at his forms as my ass began to go numb against the hard metal seat.

After what seemed like ages, he exhaled. "I need to inform ye that possession of a Class B substance is punishable with up to five years prison sentence and an unlimited fine."

"Oh god," I said, closing my eyes as I fought against the images of living in a Scottish prison with hundreds of Scottish women, all of whom could more than likely kick my ass in their sleep.

"Now, I'm gonna let ye off with a warning."

My eyes burst open, and I lunged at the officer. He tensed, his hand moving toward his baton, but I was hugging him before he could whip it out to beat me with it.

"Thank you so much! Thank you! I'm sorry! It won't happen again."

"Aye, it won't, because within the next thirty-two days, you will be leaving the United Kingdom. You've already overstayed by thirty-eight days. If you don't leave voluntarily, you will be deported. Is that understood?"

I nodded, vehemently. "Yes, sir. Of course. I'm as good as gone."

He nodded. "Good then. Now, I believe your mate's here to take ye out of my sight."

"My mate?" I said, but the words were barely past my lips when the officer stood up from his desk and marched off, determined to ignore me from there on.

I shot a glance to the second officer as he stood aside, holding an arm out as though to lead me to the next prize viewing on The Price is Right.

I stood up and scanned the station, searching for any sign of Branson. There was no one save for the two officers and a quiet gentleman manning the reception area of the station – and then there was the man standing behind the reception counter, smiling at me.

Christopher Menzies looked shaggy, his dark hair having grown down to his shoulders now, and his smile was still the same cheeky, almost roguish kind of charming that had rendered me all those times he'd sent me selfies or popped up on my computer screen for a late-night Skype session.

I stood there frozen to the spot.

"Come on, then. It's getting late. We've other things we'd like to get done, thank ye very much."

I startled, turning to acknowledge the officer beside me as he stood waiting with his arm still extended. I scurried toward the doors. "Sorry."

I rounded the counter and came to stand before Christopher, a man I hadn't seen in six months. A man who'd heard me orgasm more times than I could count.

Here he was.

I thought I remembered him being taller.

"Ye look gobsmacked. Are ye alright?" He said, leaning in to kiss my temple.

It took every ounce of will not to recoil.

"How did you know I was arrested?"

He gave a sigh. "Symptom of being friends with Jocelyn. She was in a right state when she heard what the lot of ye were up to. I don't believe she expected ye to be arrested with that shifty bastard, though. Who knew ye were such a hardened criminal?" He said, giving me a smirk. "Shall we, then?"

I tensed at the words *shifty bastard*, but I didn't say anything.

He draped his arm across my shoulders. I slipped out from under the weight as politely as I could and let him lead me out the doors. I was stricken by his sudden appearance.

"It's a bit of a drive back to Perth. Do ye need anything at the shops before we start off?"

I stood at the passenger door of his car and shook my head, as though coming to from after a long trance. "Wait, I can't leave Bran here. Do you know how much his bail is?"

Chris smiled. "Ah, ye really are a sweetheart. He's sorted. His Missus came and picked him up."

I stopped still. "His missus?"

Chris nodded, unlocking the driver's side door. "Aye. Missus, fiancé, whatever ye call such a person back in the good ol' U.S. of A."

Chris ducked down into the driver's seat and leaned across the car to open the door for me.

I thought of what woman Branson might've called to bail him out of a jam like this.

"You don't mean his sister, do you?"

I felt a twinge of pain at the thought of Cal coming down to the station to save her brother and neither of them taking the time to consider me. Still, that thought was better than Bran still having a fiancé.

Christopher gave an odd chuckle. "Ah, no. I mean his partner, Beth."

I stood there in the crisp air, my skin prickling as I stood in little more than a t-shirt and jeans.

"Beth? But they're not together anymore," I said, the words coming in spurts of panic.

"I imagine she'd be shocked to hear this news. Come on, love. Ye'll catch a cold out there."

I didn't move.

Little more than an hour before, I'd been in the arms of Branson Douglas. He'd kissed me and touched me the way I'd longed for Christopher to touch me once – hell, for anyone to touch me. I could still feel the lingering sensation of having been aroused by a man's touch, and now the man who'd inspired my even being in Scotland was here, no longer inspiring my rampant lust and affection, but instead a pain that broadsided me like being hit by a bus.

"Corinne," he said, but I didn't respond.

This was the man who'd disappeared the second I hit the same country as him. The man who'd ignored my texts and stopped calling.

I can't wait to see you.

I dream about holding you.

Why can't ye be here, right now?

All nonsense when he as good as shipped me off to the middle of nowhere to live in a dilapidated estate like a character in a Bronte novel when it was time to put his money where his mouth was.

No, no. Don't come stay with me. Go live in a Gothic nightmare.

I had every reason to recoil at his arrival.

Still, he had come to my rescue. And the man who was now settled comfortably into every nook and cranny of my thoughts was off with his more *On* than *Off* again girlfriend?

The former fiancé, he'd called her.

Not so former. He'd lied to me?

I remembered Cal asking if she was the one calling days before.

Oh god, I thought. *Was I the other woman?*

Was I really this foolish? Was every man in Scotland out to break my heart?

"Are ye comin, love?" Chris said from inside the car.

I stood there in the quiet air, staring off at the endless dark across the way, and searched for a place to flee to. There was nowhere in the world for me to go.

I took a deep breath, swallowing the knot in my throat that threatened to turn into tears, and climbed into Christopher's car.

Sixteen

"**A**RE YE ALRIGHT?"

Despite the reasonable speed Christopher kept when he drove, I was feeling nauseous and miserable. I nodded, staring out the window as we made our way to Perth, an hour and a half drive away.

"I'm fine. I'm just not feeling well."

"I'm sorry about the kitten. If I could, I would say grab the bloody thing and bring it along, but I'm just -"

"No, no. It's fine."

We'd been about fifteen minutes out of Kinvale when I remembered Mr. Darcy back at Cavendish House. I asked Chris to take me back so I could grab him.

It was partially out of spite – wanting to take Mr. Darcy away from that place and all the memories of Bran and Bran himself.

Yet, a stronger pull of Cavendish was the idea of unloading on Branson Douglas. I was sure he'd go back to the house before anything else. I wanted to scream at him, letting his fiancé hear every damn word of what I had to say.

Where had she been this whole time? While he was slaving away in the middle of nowhere, trying to rebuild his birthright, why wasn't she at his side? Why hadn't she been there to support him?

For the same reason she'd lied to him for two years about being on birth control – because despite never meeting her, I'd decided she was awful. Yet, she was still the fiancé. Not former, current.

His Missus.

For the love of god, why were they still together?

And why had he lied to me?

I pressed a knuckle under my eye, trying to wipe away tears without Chris seeing.

These were the thoughts of a desperate woman, and I knew it. I felt hurt and lost, and despite how many hours Chris and I spent on the phone those past six months, he'd been too busy recently to even respond to a text.

He was as good as a stranger to me, now.

I glanced back at my duffle bag in the backseat.

Chris had managed to grab my things from an enraged Jocelyn Read, who was busy stomping around Cavendish House when Chris arrived in Kinvale to save me. He'd gone to procure my things first, a wise effort, he'd said, given the tirade Jocelyn was on.

"Whatever work ye managed on the place, she was two seconds from destroying it when I got there. I can only imagine what Bran has in store if he tries to go back. Oh, I almost forgot."

Chris reached into his pocket and tossed me my phone. "I grabbed the cord, as well. She said if there was anything left behind, she'd mail it."

"Did she say it that nicely?"

Chris chortled. "No. Not at all."

I glanced down at the blank screen, my stomach suddenly in my throat. I pressed the button to bring it to life.

Nothing. The battery was dead. What a surprise.

With no charger in the car, I settled back to my work of staring out the window and trying not to weep.

Chris was kind enough not to expect much of me. He drove in silence, rolling along the winding roads in the pitch black. I could imagine the vistas of green out there in the dark, but unlike any other moment in my life, I didn't long to get lost in them. I felt nearly betrayed by the place.

I'd come in the hopes of a man who promised lust and affection but never showed up, and instead gave my heart to a liar.

Scotland can suck a dick, I thought.

"Oh, aye. Here we are."

Chris suddenly pulled the car off to the side of the road and shut off the engine. We sat there in the near dark, a golden glow of light peeking from over a small hill.

"Come on, then. I've something that might cheer ye up."

I closed my eyes tight, hoping the tell-tale signs of tears would be gone before he could see my face. "Where are we?"

"It's just something I think ye could appreciate."

I sighed, set my phone on the center console, and climbed out of the car. The air was still crisp, but not as biting as it had been in Kinvale. Chris offered me his hand as he led me up the uneven terrain, a very gentlemanly gesture for a man who doesn't respond to texts.

I followed to the crest of the hill. As the golden glow came into view, I gasped.

A beautiful stone bridge was there, glowing in the golden street lamps as its reflection flitted and danced in the dark water beneath. It was the most picturesque thing I'd ever seen.

"This is the River Tay. Flows right through the middle of Perth."

"It's beautiful."

"Aye, it is. I think you'll find Perth to be very lovely."

I took a few more steps down to the sidewalk, coming to stand at the stone wall that protected the river from whatever was above. I stood there for a long moment in silence, watching the ripples on the water.

"Perth is like a thistle, ye see. Lovely to look at, but full of pricks."

I forced a laugh. "Yeah, is that why you live here?"

He gave me a smile, but his eyes showed contrition.

I turned down the sidewalk, heading for the bridge. Despite my exhaustion and hurting heart, I felt compelled to stand on that bridge – to be a part of something that picturesque – that perfect.

Chris walked along behind me, letting me have space. I made my way onto the bridge, a single car rolling over it as I turned the corner. I reached its center, now able to see the buildings and lights of the center of Perth. I leaned against the railing, feeling the cool air blowing across the water.

"I'm sorry, Corinne."

I startled, turning to find Chris leaning on the railing beside me, his dark eyes cast down to the water.

He took a deep breath. "I haven't been the man ye deserve. It was all well and good when ye were across the country, but once ye were here – and so close?" He paused, turning to look at me. "It made me realize what a mess I am."

I swallowed. This apology had been the thing I'd wanted for months now. For him to explain himself, for him to explain away the way I felt. Yet, he'd never mentioned the change. When he did call, it was always excuses and brush-offs, until even idealistic and naïve me couldn't pretend anymore.

"I was out of work, was still living with my ex -"

Ha! Bran was right.

My heart sank at the thought of Branson.

"- and I just didn't think I had much to offer ye. And ye come on a bit strong, ye know?"

My eyebrows shot up. "Oh, of course. Because inviting me to come stay with you and *shag to death* wasn't?"

His face contorted, and he nodded. "Aye, ye're right. I guess shagging didn't seem so intense. It was just that – ye were clearly having feelings and the like."

"Well, congratulations. You successfully quelled that."

The words flew out of my mouth before I knew what I was saying. His expression made me almost regret it.

"I deserve that," he said, moving toward me until he could take my hand in his. "I know ye could go anywhere in the world, right now, but - will ye stay a while? Will ye let me try to make it up to ye?"

I swallowed, then licked my lips as though I was suddenly dying of thirst. I'd spent so many days longing for his company when I knew he was little more than a train ride away. Yet, here he was beside me, and it did little to comfort my heart now.

Someone had sidestepped him, and the affection I'd harbored for him was all but a distant memory in the wake of Branson Douglas.

A man who'd won my heart while his belonged to someone else.

I wanted to rail against Branson. I wanted to beat my fists into his chest and make him hear me, make him know what pain he'd caused me. Had my phone been charged, I'd have unleashed a fury upon him in text.

I knew beneath that, I wanted him to wrap his arms around me and make it better.

Yet, the same realization I'd had about Chris when Chris disappeared came back to mind. The one that stopped me from unleashing that same hurt on Christopher just weeks before.

If a man can hurt you so much you feel sick, he's not going to be the cure. There will be no relief in seeking comfort from a man whose actions say he doesn't care.

I knew this. It wasn't the first time I'd had my heart broken.

I turned to face Christopher, contemplating his offer.

What choice did I have? I had nowhere else to go.

I took a deep breath. "I don't know what I have to offer you, now," I said.

He shook his head. "Ye needn't offer me anything but your time? Company? Spend a few days. If after that, ye can't stand me, then I'll drive ye to the airport myself."

I met his gaze, those dark eyes framed beneath stern, thick brows. He looked rakish and charming, and his smile stopped me in my tracks, just as it always had.

I'd forgotten how beautiful his smile was.

"Alright," I said. "But don't even try to put the moves on me."

He chuckled. "Duly noted. I'll sleep on the couch, then."

He offered me his arm, and I took it, letting him walk me back to the car and take me to his place.

Seventeen

T HE TEXT CAME IN on a Sunday morning, nine weeks later. It gutted me all over again.

The house is mine. Officially. Thank you, Corinne. I couldn't have done it without you. Xxxxx

It gutted me more than the first round of texts I received my first night at Chris' flat. It gutted me more than the worried texts that followed, which then turned to hurt texts before shifting dangerously close to angry texts.

I had ignored them all.

I didn't know what else to do. I knew responding would only hurt more – having to explain how I couldn't bear to see him again, knowing he'd been with someone else all along. And I knew I'd spill my heart at him if I opened my mouth – tell him I'd fallen for him - that to me it wasn't just hooking up, and that I was now heartbroken.

I'd learned long ago that such a conversation wouldn't bring me any comfort.

I didn't want to give him the power of knowing he'd hurt me.

The last text he sent was a month and a half before.

You didn't even say goodbye.

Somehow, this newest one gutted me even more than that one.

That was saying something.

I turned away from Christopher, coming to sit on the edge of the bed.

"Are ye really gonna leave it like that?" Chris said, lying back on his pillow, his arms up behind his head, chest bared.

I stared out the window to the beautiful streets of Perth. The days were getting shorter, leaving the light canceling curtains as more of a decoration than a necessity. The town center was bustling by this hour with Saturday shoppers and every other manner of local getting ready for the Christmas season.

I'd grown accustomed to walking these beautiful cobblestone streets. They were the only friend I had in Scotland, now.

"Come on, babe."

Christopher's fingers grazed down my bare shoulder, and his voice came in a familiar lilt. It was morning, and as per usual, Christopher was in the mood for sex.

Or a blow job, in particular. A near-constant request whenever I was on my period.

It wouldn't be the first time he'd cajoled me into such acts in the early morning, but I simply wasn't in the mood. I also wasn't too keen on getting another crick in the neck from holding myself just so as to let him hump at me until he was done.

"Cut it out," I said, shrugging his hand away. "You're going to be late."

He groaned but relented. I wasn't wrong.

Sex was one thing. Finishing quickly was Christopher's forte during sex, but a blow job? He took all the time in the world to finish when it was a blow job.

I walked into the kitchen and filled the kettle, then turned my attention to the cabinet to grab a couple egg cups. A few moments later, Chris was finishing up his shower, and I was sitting at his small dining table, my eggs and toast already polished off.

Life in Perth with Christopher was growing on me. Despite his distance when I'd first arrived in Scotland, he'd become quite doting since whisking me away from the police station in the Highlands. He smelled wonderful, a side effect of the Scotsman's love of cologne, and he did the washing up without a word of complaint. He took me around his small city, on day trips to Edinburgh or Aberdeen. He even let me drive his car through Glencoe on a weekend camping trip.

And in our day-to-day life in Perth, we walked through the park, watching hot air balloons take off on a sunny Sunday afternoon. We hiked to the top of Kinnoull Hill, catching glimpses of does as they darted through the trees along our path. We even kissed on that same bridge over the River Tay the night I finally let him touch me.

Even the sex was pretty good.

It was almost exactly as I'd dreamed it would be when he first told me to come to Scotland.

I sat back, listening to the sounds of the street outside, my heels resting on one of Christopher's low windowsills.

"Oh, I nearly forgot. This came for ye yesterday."

I turned to find Chris standing in the kitchen doorway in a towel, his dark hair shorn short now, slicked back by water. He handed me a manila envelope, the familiar logos of American postage across its surface.

I snatched it from him, trying to hide my unmitigated joy, and tore my butter knife across the tape.

A moment later, I was holding my brand new passport in my hands.

"I'm sorry ye had to get a new one," he said for the umpteenth time. He'd gathered my things from Jocelyn the night of my arrest, but despite my hopes, it wasn't in my bag.

It was yet another thing swallowed up by Cavendish.

Still, it didn't take long to get the new one squared away back home, Dad running back and forth to the post office for me once it finally arrived.

I ran my fingers over the pristine blue booklet, feeling the stiff cardboard beneath. I held my freedom in my hands.

Finally.

Chris sat at the kitchen table, the towel falling open across his thigh. I averted my eyes.

"I still don't understand why ye didn't just go back to the house to have a look around. Jocelyn was angry, but I'm sure she'd have let ye look."

I took the last sip of my tea, shaking my head. "This was just as well."

"It's the cat, isn't it?"

I frowned.

In part, I thought.

"Jocelyn says he's been well-tended."

He shot me a sideways look. I think he knew as well as I did why I wouldn't go back. I'd done my best to hide my crying fits when I first came to stay with him. Or when I'd received frantic texts from Bran wondering where I was and if I was ok.

Those had hurt beyond measure – the feigned concern. He'd gone from despising my presence to desperate to know I was alright in the two months we spent together. The only problem was the damning little secret he'd kept throughout.

He had someone else to worry about far more than he should be worrying about me.

I often wondered if she was nearby when he was texting me.

I was strong, though. The texts continued for days, then weeks, only slowing finally when he heard from Jocelyn that I was staying in Perth with Christopher.

I felt as though I could read his disdain through the polite regard.

I hope she finally paid you for your time, he'd said.

God, I cried for an hour that day.

Still, I never responded.

And that was the hardest part of all of it.

I wanted to text him back. When I finally tasted Irn Bru, I wanted to tell him it tasted like the devil's buttcrack dipped in cotton candy. When I finally got behind the wheel of a car and drove down a country road, I wanted to tell him it was a miracle no one died. When I discovered that his theories on Christopher's penis size were correct, my heart hurt. That wasn't the kind of thing you tell a man you want to be with – especially about the man whose company you actually keep.

I wanted all of these things, and all the while, Christopher was the one who'd finally come through. When it mattered, he gave me a roof over my head and time to get my shit together. He fed me and kept me, took me out to the club with the sticky floors, or the pub that smelled like its septic tank backed up one too many times over the past fifty years.

"It's a local treasure. Ye'll grow to like it," he'd said.

He was right. Perth was one of the most beautiful places I'd ever been.

So why was I so ready to leave?

Christopher got up and dressed, crunching on his toast as he hurried around the apartment. I pulled his laptop out of its case, setting it up on the kitchen table to 'diddle away the hours,' as he called it.

I waited until he was pulling on his jacket, then I opened the familiar website.

I had five messages - all for potential housesitting jobs.

The closest one was in Norway.

"Oh, by the way."

I startled, nearly slamming the laptop shut as I turned to face Chris. He stood in the kitchen doorway, his grin and dark brown eyes looking as dashing and pirate-like as ever.

"Yes?"

"Been invited to a big party this weekend. Some posh prick. Thought ye might like to go."

I fought the urge to openly cringe. "I don't know. Not sure I'm feeling up to posh prick parties."

"Ah, come on. Ye barely leave the flat unless I drag ye out. It'll be good for ye. Spend time with more than just me."

I stared at him a moment, shooting a sideways glance at the laptop. *The Norway job started this weekend. I guess that one's right out.*

Still, the villa in Florence doesn't need me until the end of the month. As long as I don't cross paths with any immigration officers between now and then, I should be fine. Right?

"Can I think about it?"

He grinned, and I knew the look well. That smile said he'd won. "Of course. I'll text when I'm on break," he said, rushing across the kitchen to give me a kiss. I let him, puckering just enough not to let on that I wasn't in the mood for kissing.

He was gone a moment later and I was alone.

I stared at the laptop screen. This wasn't the first string of housesitting jobs I'd turned down. A couple in London had asked me to watch their two cats for a month, a family in a Chateau in the south of France was looking for someone to take care of their guest house for the winter. There'd even been an older couple in Key West, Florida who needed someone while they sailed around the world on a cruise ship.

I had to turn them all down because I still hadn't gotten up the courage to go back to Kinvale and search for my damn passport. Or my hair straightener, my makeup, half my underwear - for Christ's sake.

I just couldn't bring myself to see him, even if it was only for a few minutes. Even if Chris was at my side. I didn't want him to see the pain in my eyes when I saw his face.

I didn't want him to know how much I still cared.

And above all of that – I didn't want to meet his fiancé.

I stared at the new housesitting offers, struggling with a very different thought. Instead of steeling myself to let potential clients down, I was steeling myself to let Chris down.

How would he take it when I finally picked one of these new jobs and armed with my new passport, I leave?

Because I was going to leave. And not just because my Visa was run out and I gave every police car and officer on the street the side-eye for fear that they could smell the criminal element on me.

I was leaving because I didn't love Chris.

I loved Branson, and I needed to get as far away from him as was humanly possible.

I considered that posh party he was so excited about and opened the message from the couple in Norway.

If nothing else, I could give him another week, couldn't I?

I quickly shot off an email declining the lovely offer and asked them to keep me in mind when they needed someone again. Then, I opened the message from the man in Florence. My fingers hovered over the keys, ready to write the same email once more.

End of the month. Just a couple more weeks of pretending you're alright, pretending the accent of every man on the street doesn't break your heart, or that the smell of smoke and licorice on the air doesn't make you homesick for the country and a tired old estate that you brought back to life with your own hands.

I stared at the message for another long moment, then I shut down the website without responding, clearing the browser history for good measure.

I grabbed a ten-pound note from my purse and a moment later headed down to my favorite kebab shop to eat my troubles.

Eighteen

"Hurry up, will ye?"

I glared at Christopher as I darted around to the passenger side door of the car. I had my new makeup bag in hand and my hair still in pins as I climbed into the car.

"What? We're gonna be late," he said, chiding me when I glared at him.

I was more than mildly irritated. Despite knowing the party was that night, he'd decided to spring our departure on me ten minutes before we needed to leave.

I could've throttled him.

"Ye look lovely. Don't fret."

"I'm not fretting," I said, a snarl in my voice as I pulled down the visor to finish my makeup.

I was done soon enough, curling into my seat to watch the world go by outside. Chris drove us into the country, the familiar smell of licorice and smoke creeping through my cracked window. Though it was bittersweet, I let myself bask in the smell for a long while, Christopher playing some god-awful band on the radio.

We drove on for a long while, the daylight fading quickly. When Chris' playlist restarted on his phone, I reached over and searched for something new to listen to, choosing a greatest hits list of Led Zeppelin.

"If we could make a pit stop, soon, I need to use the restroom," I said.

I then set the phone down and turned back to the window, closing my eyes as the cool air blew my hair away from my face.

I heard the familiar hush of my window rolling up and opened my eyes just as it closed, leaving the air in the car stagnant in comparison.

I turned to look at Christopher as he loosed his finger from the window switch.

"Hey," I said, moving to roll my window down again. I pressed the button only to find nothing happened. He'd locked the window from his door.

"Christopher. I need the air or I get carsick."

He shot me a sideways glance. "Sorry, I'm cold. Here, turn on the fan if ye need," he said, turning the knob beside the radio. A second later, he changed the song on the iPhone from Zeppelin to System of a Down.

I stared at him for a long moment, anger bubbling up so quickly that I feared I might start an argument. I turned back to my window, trying the switch again just as a familiar sight flew past the window.

I startled, turning in my seat to be sure of what I'd seen. The picturesque church was unmistakable. "Wait. Are we in -?"

The road curved to the right and the familiar gate came into view. We were in Kinvale.

A second later, we were rolling down the long drive of Cavendish House.

"Christopher!" I cried, a mix of exasperation and terror creeping up my spine. I wanted to scramble away from the approaching house, claw my way through the backseat and out of the car if I had to.

The drive was lined with cars, and as the house came into view through the trees, I could see the warm glow of golden light from the conservatory and all the lower windows.

It looked breathtaking.

And terrifying.

"What the fuck are we doing here?" I yelled, finally letting loose my growing frustration.

"It's a party," he said in a cheerful voice, as though he was discussing fine weather.

"You know I don't want to be here."

"Ah, come now. Ye'll do fine," he said, reaching into the back of the car. "Here. Ye'll have to put this on."

I furrowed my brow, looking down at the garment bag now strewn across my lap. I didn't speak, darting my eyes from the open doors of the house to my companion's smug face.

He gave me a grin. "It's fancy dress." And with that, he gave me an eyebrow waggle.

I wanted to slap his face.

"I don't want to be here, Christopher. You know that. Why didn't you discuss this with me before you just dragged me out here -?"

"I didn't drag ye, and I didn't discuss it with ye because I knew ye'd just be stubborn about it. So here we are. Now, put on the dress, there. I got ye a size or two bigger than ye take. Thought it'd be better to make sure it fits."

I made a sound between an exasperated gasp and a war cry. "I'm not going in there!"

"Ye can't be serious? Even Jocelyn is inside," he said, as though this would be the deciding factor. When I didn't move, he rolled his eyes. "Fine. Then sit in the car, if ye like. I'm rather looking forward to seeing the place all fixed up, finally."

Then, he climbed out, stripped off his jacket, and tossed it inside the car before marching across the drive in a perfect tailcoated suit.

If I didn't hate him at that moment, I might've said he looked dashing.

I sat there in the car, the sound of old-fashioned music carrying across the still Highland air. I curled my fingers into the garment bag, forming fists until my knuckles were white. I wanted to punch something, but more than that, I wanted to flee. I wanted to get as far away as I could from this place – and more aptly, the people inside. I had no doubt that if this event was as big as it looked – as big as Callista and Bran's grandmother's time-honored parties – Branson's soon-to-be bride, Beth, would certainly be inside.

And she'd more than likely have picked her own dress for the evening – and it would fit.

I wanted nothing more than to take off into the night, but I desperately needed to use the bathroom, and I knew full well the nearest shops were miles and miles away. I sat there staring at the front doors of the house and cried.

The knock startled me nearly out of my skin. I turned my face up, trying to wipe the tears from my eyes as discreetly as I could.

Mary looked down at me with a gentle smile. "You alright, sweetheart?"

I nodded, quickly, forcing a smile as I opened the car door. "Oh, yes. I'm fine."

Mary opened her arms to give me a hug, the sequins and lace of her dress scratching at the fabric of my sweater. I felt like a dowdy matron in comparison.

Mary held her gloved hand away from me, a lit cigarette smoking between her fingers. She shot me a stern look. "Don't tell Bruce. I'm supposed to be done with this nasty habit. He thinks I'm in the loo."

I nodded. "Of course not," I said, wiping my eyes one final time as I collected the garment bag from the front seat.

"Oh, is this your dress? I can't wait to see it," Mary said, taking a drag on her cigarette. "What a nifty shindig, huh? I've never been to a party like this before. Someone said they used to do medieval feasts here when they were young. I mean, how cool?"

Her New England accent almost soothed my otherwise frantic heart. Still, no amount of missing R's could soften the blow of meeting the soon-to-be Beth Douglas.

I swallowed, folding the garment bag over my arm. There was no escaping this. It was only a matter of time before someone else noticed the sad weirdo crying in their car. It was time to suck it up and be brave.

It was time to let go.

Mary stubbed out her cigarette and offered her arm to me with a grand flourish. I took it and let her lead me up the steps of Cavendish House.

Nineteen

T HE HOUSE WAS ALIVE – like some roiling, writhing thing. There were couples in their fancy-dress walking through the front room, men and women in pressed black slacks and white shirts carrying trays of hors d'uerves and champagne flutes.

It was exactly as I'd imagined it when Bran and Callista told me about their grandmother's parties.

A part of me wanted to relish in every minute detail of it – from the music and the décor to the clothing, but the far greater part of me wanted to hide and never come out.

I could hear the party in full swing in the ballroom down the hall and ducked into the bathroom off the kitchen hallway to change. The dress was a sequined burlap sack of beaded black and silver.

I looked like a fancy hot dog bun and I wanted to die.

I sat in the bathroom for a long while, willing the party over so I could run outside into the Scottish night, but it was early, and by the sound of it, people were having a damn fine time.

This party wouldn't be over for hours.

I folded my clothes up and tucked them under the sink before heading out into the quiet hallway. However long I'd been away, I knew every part of this house. If I wanted to, I could hide for the duration. Still, that wasn't the classy broad thing to do.

I made it as far as the kitchen, feeling the massive dress swish and roll around me as I stepped, the shoulders slipping down on one side, then the other when I deigned to fix the first.

I took a deep breath as I stood in front of the massive kitchen fireplace and closed my eyes. "Florence," I said. "End of the month."

The decision was made. I was getting the fuck out of Scotland.

"Corinne? Oh, I'm so glad you could make it!"

I opened my eyes, darting backward as though the word were an attack. I met the gaze of Callista Douglas as she set an empty hors d'eurves tray onto the kitchen counter. She was an absolute vision – a Greek Goddess in navy blue, her hair in pin curls on either cheek, a headband and feather in her hair.

"Christ, what are ye wearing?" She said.

And like the woman made of coffin nails I thought I was - I burst into tears.

Her arms were around me in an instant. "Ah, no need for that, love," she said. "Come on, then. Let's do away with this frock, shall we?"

She took my hand and led me out into the hallway and up the stairs, rounding the landing to come to a familiar room - her grandmother's old bedroom. Though I remembered it better than almost any other room in the house, it had changed.

It was clear Callista had been staying here for some time.

The thought of Callista coming home to Cavendish and not fleeing in terror made me almost smile.

Almost.

I was a blubbering mess – blubbering messes don't smile.

"Alright, I'm sure I have something for you. Ah, yes. Here we are. Try this on for me, will ye?"

Callista pulled a white and gold gown out of her closet, laying it across the bed like a wedding gown.

"What size shoe do ye wear?"

I swallowed, looking down at myself as though I'd never seen my feet before. "Oh, uh. Nine?"

She nodded, ducking her head back into the closet. "Aye, here we are. That'll do," she said, setting a pair of white t-strap heels onto the floor by the bed. "I'll leave ye to it. When you're decent, we can fix that makeup of yours. You've got a set of raccoon eyes like ye wouldn't believe."

I stifled a laugh that wanted desperately to be a cry.

Callista's Scottish accent was thicker now, a sign of time spent north. She crossed the room, coming to tower over me, and her presence made me feel tiny. "It's alright, love. There's nothing a night of looking gorgeous can't fix."

With that, she ran her hand over my arm, then left me alone to change.

The dress was soft, silk-lined, and heavy with beadwork, but it fit – loosely, but in a flattering way. I called after Callista to let her know I was decent just as I slipped my foot into the first shoe.

The shoe was a little snug, but not uncomfortable.

As Cal entered, I considered the idea of one of Cal's shoes being almost too small for me – Cal, who was inches over six feet even when she wasn't wearing heels. I took a quick glance at her feet, then at my own.

She marched up behind me, moving me over toward the vanity like a doting matron. She was laughing. "They were my Nan's shoes, love. The dress as well."

I took a sharp inhale, feeling almost criminal to be wearing Bran's grandmother's things – especially with him affianced to another woman. "Oh, god. I can't wear this. I couldn't -"

"Hush, now. Ye look bloody stunning. Ye'll wear em, and you're welcome."

The tone was a feigned stern, but she was smiling at me in the mirror as she pulled my hair up behind my head.

"There's makeup remover in the tin there. Why don't you wipe those eyes of yours, while I pin this mass, here?"

I nodded, feeling her fingers tug at my hair. A second later, she was running a soft brush over my hair. I closed my eyes, letting the sensation slow my pounding heart.

It was a sensation I hadn't felt in decades.

She pulled, and I swayed with each movement of her hands, letting the sound of the music drifting up through the floor take me to another world. When she finally released me, I didn't want to open my eyes.

"There, now. What d'ye think?"

I straightened up and looked at myself in the mirror.

I didn't breathe.

I stared into the mirror at my face, the curls all smoothed out and pinned atop my head, cascading down the nape of my neck in perfect spirals. She'd tucked a crystal band into my hair as well, and I spotted the tiny gems glinting in the light as I turned from side to side. I could see myself there, but I was changed. I'd traveled through time, somehow, and I now stared into the face of another life.

Suddenly, I wasn't so afraid to meet Bran's fiancé, however painful that might be.

I took a deep breath, tapping my knuckle to my eyes to keep them from welling over and running my eyeliner down my cheek again.

"Come on, then, Cinderella."

Cal stepped back, holding the back of my chair in wait. I stood up, shimmying the dress down over my hips before taking Cal's arm and letting her lead me out into the hallway. I glanced up the stairs to the third floor as we stepped out onto the landing, but my attention was quickly stolen by the people milling in the hallway.

"What visions!" Hilda crooned as she handed her coat to one of the hired waiters and barreled to the foot of the stairs. She'd dolled up in a beautiful black silk dress with a long sheer coat over the top. She looked more like a mother of the bride than a flapper or a Gatsby-era girl, but it suited her nonetheless.

"We've missed ye, dear Corinne. What have ye been up to these past weeks?"

Before I could answer, Callista gestured for Hilda to move with us toward the ballroom.

Hilda snatched up my free arm the second she saw a chance. "My grandson is here, as well. The whole family, I do believe. I came on my own. Had to close up the chapel, of course."

"Of course," I said, happy to have someone I could hang onto as we made our way down the hall.

The music was growing louder with each step, and I soon realized this music wasn't playing over some speaker system – there was a live band. I folded my fingers over Hilda's, clutching her hand on my arm as I stepped through the double doors into the ballroom.

She shot a sideways glance at my hand, then my face. Apparently, I wasn't hiding my nerves all that well.

The ballroom was teeming with people, and the spell was undeniable. Every face, familiar and otherwise, was dressed in the Gatsby era – flapper dresses, lace and beads, headbands and feathers. The gentlemen were in their rented, tailored suits, tailcoats, and tuxes, their hair slicked back or perfectly parted to the side.

The spell of the mirror upstairs overwhelmed me, yet again, and I found myself lost in time, holding onto Hilda for dear life.

Hilda wasted no time snatching a glass of champagne from one of the passing servers. She took two, trying to offer me the second glass. When I refused it, she shrugged, giving me a mischievous grin as she happily downed the first glass and set the empty flute right back on the tray.

The server laughed and walked away.

"So, where is our dear Branson, then? He must've been over the moon when it was made official, aye?"

I scanned the faces, both searching for and dreading a familiar face.

When my eyes passed over the ballroom doors, a familiar figure appeared, turning her face back toward the doors as though she were arguing with someone just out of sight. Before I could relocate, Jocelyn Reed turned haughtily away from the door and marched directly toward me. I braced for impact.

"Oh! Oh, Corinne. Hello," she said, just before bumping into me. "I'm sorry, I didn't see you."

I shook my head. "That's fine. You're fine."

She turned to the passing server, grabbing another two glasses of champagne. Unlike Hilda, Jocelyn had no intention of offering one to me.

She stood at my shoulder, close enough to make me feel like she wanted to talk to me, but she stood silent, sipping at her champagne as she glared around the room. Hilda was now carousing around the room, mingling with parishioners and strangers alike. She was a spectacular social butterfly.

"Are you having a good time?" I instantly cringed at my question. No one in their right mind would think Jocelyn was having a good time.

She sighed. "I was, actually."

"Really? What changed -"

"Are you living with Chris?"

Her question startled me, leaving me dumb for a moment. "Um, I guess. It's temporary, though."

"Is it?"

I furrowed my brow, turning to look up at her, though she did not return my gaze. "Yeah."

She nodded. "Good."

She set her first champagne flute down on the nearby table, then turned to look me square in the eyes. "I know what you must think of me."

My mouth fell open, but she didn't give me a chance to respond.

"Everyone thinks the same thing. The second you saw the place, I'm sure you thought, *what the hell is wrong with her for marrying him?*"

Jocelyn was clearly under the influence of more than just one glass of champagne. I stood fast, letting her pour whatever her heart needed to get out.

"I was young, and I was trapped where I was. If you'd had the home life I did, you might make some questionable decisions to escape it, too."

I stared at her.

Like traveling across the world to live in other people's houses?

She brought the second champagne flute to her lips and knocked it back in two swallows.

"Hey, how many have you had?" I asked, but she ignored me.

"I never slept with him, if that's what you think."

"I think that's none of anyone's business."

Jocelyn turned to me, holding my gaze as though seeing me for the first time. I felt as though I was seeing her for the first time, too.

"You're a good person, you know that?" Oh, yeah. Jocelyn was steaming drunk. "And you know what? You deserve to be happy!"

These words stung, somehow, but I fought not to let it show on my face. "Thank you," I said. "So do you."

She gave me a sad smile – the kind of sad smile a drunk person gives right before they're going to tell you they love you and start ugly crying into their shoes.

"Christopher fucking Menzies," she said, swaying slightly as she spoke. "You deserve better, darling."

I frowned, but before I could press her for an explanation, Callista appeared, scooping an arm around Jocelyn's shoulders. "Hey, mum. Why don't ye let me take ye for a lie-down, aye?"

Jocelyn glared up at Cal, her furrowed brow almost comically exaggerated. "You think you're funny callin me mum. It's not funny. I don't find it funny."

Callista gestured to me. "You alright, love? I'm gonna take her upstairs. Why don't you go – Ah! There he is," Cal said just at my shoulder. "Bran!"

Before I could protest, I saw the head spin around in response. Bran was smiling wide, his beautiful eyes crinkling at the corners as he met his sister's gaze. Then he followed her gesture to Jocelyn – then to me.

We locked eyes, and his expression changed, instantly.

His mouth fell open, and his hand moved to his chest. I was frozen to the spot, watching as this man I'd fallen helpless for laid eyes on me – and despite my nerves and trepidation, I knew with unwavering certainty that Branson Tennyson Douglas thought I looked beautiful.

I had a fleeting memory of the atrocity of a dress I'd been in when I arrived and felt a shudder down my spine.

Thank you, Callista, I thought.

Because Bran looked breathtaking, too.

Hilda made herself known at my side again, trying to move me through the crowd as the band began to play a new song. "I'll leave ye to it, then. I'm dying to hit that buffet," she said, then she was gone, weaving through the crowd to peruse the offerings along the sideboard.

There were couples dancing across the newly waxed floors, as well as several sitting in club chairs or on settees at the corners of the room, drinking their cocktails and conversing.

Despite the burning flush in my cheeks as he approached, I couldn't take my eyes off Bran.

Damn it, I knew this would happen, I thought. *That's the fucker who broke your heart, Cor. That's the guy who let you fall for him, all while he was neglecting his betrothed. And neglecting to tell you about her.*

He made his way through the last of the crowd and came to stand before me. We stood there for a long moment, the newest song hitting a crescendo as the happy couples danced in rhythm.

I felt movement at my shoulder and quickly realized Cal was gone, leading the drunk Ms. Reed out of the ballroom.

Neither Bran nor I spoke for a long moment. I wanted to yell at him, tell him what a bastard he was, but when my lips moved, those weren't the words that nearly flew out of my mouth.

What I almost said was, "I miss you."

Well, that would've totally blown my cover, I thought.

"Ye look -" He started, his arms opening to gesture at all of me. "Ye are – captivating."

Well, if that isn't the most magical thing to be called by a man, I don't know what is.

Bastard.

"Thank you," I said. Even at my worst, I have good manners. I bit down on the return compliment and instead gestured to the room. "This is amazing."

He grinned. "Ye think so? Cal wanted to go with Nan's old favorite -"

"A medieval feast?"

He smiled, shaking his head. "No, she was like you. Loved Austen. But I said I wanted something different. Breathe some new life into the place."

He turned, taking in the room. I followed his gaze. Every face had a smile or a champagne flute. There wasn't a dowdy expression to be found now that the poor morose Ms. Reed was on her way to bed.

"You invited Jocelyn?" I asked, finally, hoping to fill the heavy silence between us. It seemed like a better question than, *"Where's your fiancé? I've never wanted to meet anyone less in my life."*

He shrugged. "I did. Felt like the right thing to do given the outcome. Bygones and all. She didn't seem to be having a good time, aye?"

"Or too good a time."

"Aye," he said, forcing a laugh.

I found myself at a loss for words. All the grit I'd possessed through all those weeks of ignoring his texts despite heartache and pain – it was all but evaporated now that he was close again. I couldn't summon anything beyond sadness. The desire to be close to him was just as powerful as ever.

The crowd on the dance floor gave a whoop as the horns came back. I smiled, watching Mary and Bruce cutting the proverbial rug as they went careening by on the dance floor.

"Would ye care to dance?"

My heart stilled, and I looked up into Bran's cool blue eyes. I shot a look around the room, inspecting every female face, wondering which among them was his soon-to-be wife. Yet, when he held his hand out to me, no force on earth could stop me from taking it.

Bran led me across the ballroom, coming to stand at the edge of the dance floor. He wrapped an arm around my waist, and I gasped, my cheeks instantly turning red from embarrassment as his other hand took mine.

He took a step, leading me out into the droves of dancing figures. I clung to him, suddenly timid, as though being led into heavy traffic. Yet, he held me close to him, his hips and arms showing me where to go before his feet could move. Just as I found my stride, the lively song ended, and the horns quickly shifted from the upbeat tempo to the slow, moody horns of a slow dance.

Bran pulled just a hair closer.

I held my breath.

He pulled my hand to his chest, our bodies swaying as the horns lilted higher. Then, the singers came forward, their harmonies low and hypnotic. I turned my face, letting my body lean into him as I hid my eyes. The dancing figures moved in around us and the rest of the room disappeared.

I know. Oh yes, I know,

that you and I will never meet again.

For you – for you were meant for someone else.

I held my breath, fighting to make my feet move as the song knocked the wind clear out of me.

Do you remember that night?

Oh, yes, that night - that night when first we met?

I fell in love with you and now I simply can't forget.

"Corinne?"

I let my body sway to the horns as though Branson and I were two halves of some solid thing. I couldn't respond to him. I'd been punched in the chest so hard I could barely stand.

"Why did ye disappear like that? Was it something I did?"

I exhaled in an exasperated laugh that instantly turned to tears. I turned my face further from him, damning him for every second I'd spent with him.

Oh darling, believe me.

If we never meet again beneath those moonlit skies,

I know that my love will follow you

As the years go passing by.

Oh darling, I know.

"If I could go back in time, I'd do anything to stop ye from getting in trouble. I can't begin to apologize for that, I know -"

"For what?" I said, exasperated.

"For ye getting arrested. I should've fought harder."

I pulled back just so, looking up to meet his gaze. "I don't care about that!"

His brow furrowed. "Ye don't? Then why – why wouldn't ye talk to me? I tried for fucking weeks -"

"May I cut in?"

Both of us were startled at the sudden intrusion, and we turned to find Christopher standing beside us, that same smile chiseled across his handsome face. Yet, unlike any moment before now, that smile wasn't the charming stunner I remembered – it was smarmy.

Bran stiffened, looking from him to me and back again. Then he frowned, and my heart broke all over again. "Of course. Have at it," he said, releasing my hand.

Then he was gone, weaving through the crowd until the black fabric of his suit was absorbed by the crowd.

For you were meant for somebody else –
Somebody else, not me.

The song ended, flowing into a second slow song, though this one was of far lighter fare. Chris took hold of me with one arm around my waist and swayed somewhat clumsily as his second hand was occupied with what looked like a brownie.

I fought like mad not to roll my eyes.

"Two of ye seem to have made up, then."

It was almost a question, but I didn't acknowledge it with a response.

He watched my face for a moment, then shrugged. "Ye want a bite?"

He brought the brownie closer to my face, and I pulled away. It looked decadent and rich and moist – just like the last time I'd eaten a brownie at the Church Supper. "No, thank you. I doubt I'll be partaking in brownies for a long while."

"Really? They're spectacular. This is my third one."

"Mmhm," I said, trying to further the conversation. "As I recall, Branson was rather fond of them, too."

Chris raised an eyebrow as he looked down at me, then he popped the last bite of brownie into his mouth, and without wiping his hands, placed his open palm flat on my ass.

I cringed, pulling from him, inadvertently.

"Ye alright?" He asked.

I nodded. "Just feeling a little hungry, maybe?"

"Ah, well there's plenty to eat if that's the case."

He didn't let me go, continuing to sway off rhythm. I turned my eyes to the other couples in the crowd, watching the way they flowed together, happily lost in the song and each other.

I took a deep breath, searching for conversation. "Did you get a chance to say hello to Jocelyn?"

Chris rolled his eyes. "Oh, aye. If that wasn't a bloody mess?"

"She did have a lot to drink tonight. I'm guessing she's upset about the house."

"The house? No, she never cared about the house. She wanted the money. No, she's pissed because ye're staying with me and she thinks she should just be able to move back in when whatever scheme she's up to falls through."

I looked up at him, confused. "Move *back* in with you?"

"Aye," he said, as though he'd simply mentioned rain coming.

"You used to live with Jocelyn?"

We stopped dancing at this point as I stepped back to watch his expression.

He gave me a sarcastic look. "Ye knew that."

"No. No, I didn't. When did you guys live together?"

He gave an exaggerated blink, as though he was astounded by my imbecilic questions. "For the past two, maybe three years?"

A sudden rush of connection flooded my mind – the sporadic facetime sessions, the sudden distance when I arrived, the magical *friend* with a housesitting job. I thought of Jocelyn earlier that night, arguing with someone just out of my view. Where was Chris during that scene?

"Jocelyn is your ex-girlfriend," I said, and it wasn't a question.

"Aye? Ye say this like it's news."

I swallowed, staring at his smug face as the happy couples danced around us. I stood there in a confused state.

"You were still living with her when I got to Scotland, weren't you?"

At this, he frowned. "Aye. We weren't together anymore, just living together until she could find her own flat. She was dragging her feet given what with this nonsense and all."

The dancers swirled around us as the next song started – another upbeat dance number.

The two of us stood there, still.

"I came all the way to Scotland for you, and you were still living with your girlfriend – who you then had me work for. Did she know?"

He scoffed, shaking his head. "Of course not. Life was difficult enough, I didn't need any more drama."

I turned and stormed off through the crowd. I felt his hand at my wrist, pulling me back.

"Come on, now. Don't cause a scene. It's not like I was cheating on ye. We weren't together. I wasn't with either of ye."

I shook my head, fighting to make my words sound as classy and pompous as I possibly could. "I don't feel that I can discuss this, right now."

I turned and walked away, heading toward the ballroom doors.

"Corinne, ye're being ridiculous."

I spun around to face him, my capacity for old-fashioned British manners having disappeared. "Are all Scottish men complete assholes?!" I yelled.

The whole room lulled for a moment, turning to look at me.

"Right?" A voice called from the buffet. Everyone turned to find Jocelyn standing there, two sheets to the wind, holding up yet another champagne flute.

An instant later, Callista was at her side. Clearly, Jocelyn wasn't supposed to be back at the party. Cal shot me a confused look, then she led Jocelyn back out into the house.

I felt my cheeks flush with embarrassment. "Just – just leave me alone for a bit. Please," I said, then I turned and made my quick exit from the ballroom, hauling down into the front hall to get away from prying eyes.

Sadly, the party wasn't confined to the ballroom, and people were milling about the front hall all the way down the corridor to the conservatory. I shot a glance up the stairs to see Cal leading a weepy Jocelyn off to one of the guest rooms. Despite having avoided the house for almost two months, I darted up the stairs after them, moving quietly across the landing.

Out of habit as much as expectation, I turned up to the third-story landing. I'd always looked up, every night as I went to bed, always half expecting to see a woman standing there, watching me.

She never was, but I looked nonetheless.

There was no one there, and the familiar door – the mattress apocalypse room was still shut tight.

I wondered if it continued to give them trouble once they emptied it of its contents.

I could hear Cal cajoling Jocelyn into bed somewhere in one of the side rooms and took the opportunity to sneak up the stairs to the third floor. Though I shot a wary eye toward Mattress Mountain, I turned down the hall, slinking into the dark as the beaded tassels of my dress flitted around my knees. The few cracked or beat-up doors had been replaced, and every light sconce had a new bulb. It was surreal to see this hallway in such a pristine state.

I reached the far end of the hall, glancing out the window at the gardens outside, the now-dormant plants lit up in a patchwork of golden squares from the light pouring through the high windows below.

I found my former bedroom door shut, giving a soft knock before opening the door a crack.

"Anyone in here?" I said. When no response came, I slipped into the familiar quiet of my old bedroom.

It was exactly as I'd left it – bright cream and buttercup walls with white trim and coordinating window treatments to match the made bed. I took a step inside, heading for the bedside table in the hopes of finding the book I'd left behind – a book the Acton Library would like to have back at some point, I was sure.

Meow.

I spun toward the bed just as a dark shape stretched from its nook between the pillows. They'd tucked Mr. Darcy away in my room for the night.

I'd been too scared to ask about the kitten, fearing they'd sent him off to live elsewhere. Yet, here he was, slinking across the bedspread with his buzz saw purr on full blast, waiting for me to pet him. I dropped to my knees by the bed, the beaded hem digging into my kneecaps, as I reached for him with two hands and began scratching his head.

He barrel-rolled toward my face, slamming his nose into mine before displaying his belly.

If I could freeze any moment in my life to simply live in, this might be it.

"Hey, my handsome boy. Look how big you are," I said, talking in that same sing-song voice that Bran often mocked me for. Still, of all the heartbreak and disappointment I'd felt since I arrived in Scotland, this little creature had been true to me from the moment we met, and despite the time I'd been away, it was clear he remembered me.

It was clear he forgave me for leaving him behind.

My face contorted as I pressed my chin into the mattress, tears welling up now beyond anything I could control, and I cried. Mr. Darcy responded by licking my nose and shimmying across the mattress to be closer to me. I thought about having to leave him again, tonight, and the sobs came with triple their force.

This was the one truly good thing about Scotland – this little creature – and I couldn't take him with me. I had nowhere to take him to.

"Corinne? You alright?"

Mr. Darcy rolled up onto his chest, his ears back for a second as he appraised the newcomer. I made quick work of wiping my eyes and settling myself, not wanting Callista to see me in such a state.

I stood up to face her, the dents in my knees beginning to sting as the beads pulled away from the skin.

"I don't mean to interrupt, love, but have ye seen Branson?"

My eyebrows shot up. There was a tone of worry I didn't expect, but I fought to hide my own concern. "Have you asked Beth? Maybe he's with her?"

Cal pushed the door open a bit more and leaned into the doorjamb. "Beth?"

I nodded, fighting not to sniffle.

"Beth, the ex-fiancé?"

"Yes?" I said, but Cal's tone made my answer feel silly. "Ex-fiance?"

Cal made an exasperated sound, like the mere mention of the woman drew bile into the back of her throat. "Darling, if Beth were on the premises, she'd be dead and buried in the garden by yours truly."

I swallowed, unable to find words.

"Why would ye think Beth was here, let alone that Bran would be anywhere near her if she was?"

I shook my head, trying to find the right way to confess my foolishness. "I thought they were -"

"Is that why ye up and vanished on him? Because ye thought he and Beth were still together? Who in bloody hell told ye that? Did somebody tell ye that?"

Cal had crossed the room to me, an urgency to her movement.

I splayed my palms before me as though I could push away her frustration. She stopped a couple steps from me as Mr. Darcy began to pace on the bed, trying to draw one of us in for further rubs.

"Did Jocelyn tell ye that? To make ye leave?"

I shook my head. "No, no. Tonight's the first time we spoke since -"

The urge to sob came flooding back with such fury.

"Well, it's no matter now. I can't bloody find the prick. Tell him I'm lookin for him if ye find him, will ye?"

I nodded, but couldn't bring myself to speak as Cal marched back out of the room, her head held just a little higher than before. She was not pleased with me.

Meow.

I turned to the furry beast, giving him another round of chin rubs as Cal's footsteps clacked down the steps in the distance. I scanned the room for a moment, finding Mr. Darcy's food and water bowl near the bathroom door. They'd given him everything he'd need for the night, tucked away from the crowds and the open front doors.

I bent to give him a kiss on the top of his head before heading to the bedroom door, glancing back to find him sitting on the bed watching.

If a cat could have a worried expression, Mr. Darcy nailed it.

"I'll be back, buddy. Ok?"

His ears perked forward, but he didn't move. I shut the bedroom door behind me, coming to stand in the dimly lit corridor, my palm pressed to the door as though I could send love through solid objects to the animal within.

However much I didn't want to leave the cat, Callista seemed concerned for her brother, and I couldn't just sit in some corner pining for something that was gone.

I snuck into the room across the hall, checking the closet to see if Branson was hiding in his childhood hideaway. The tiny room was empty.

I headed back into the hallway just as a draft drew goosebumps on my bare arms.

I heard Cal asking another guest if they'd seen Branson down below, and I stopped at the railing to make my way down.

Yet before I could take another step, something seemed amiss out of the corner of my eye. I turned and found the familiar door open now. Not just open a crack as per usual, but wide open. I glanced down toward the front hall far below and turned, sneaking closer to the doorway, as though making a sound might betray my presence and inspire the door to slam shut, leaving me locked out again.

I reached the door and took a deep breath, the cold air sinking bone-deep now as I drew the courage to look inside.

I pressed a hand to the doorjamb and peeked within.

The room was exactly as I remembered – dark, gray, and dingy, with peeling wallpaper and a mound of ancient mattresses. The ceiling was still stained brown and black with water damage and the tiny wood stove peeked out from behind the mess. Clearly, they hadn't yet been able to clear this single holdout of a house formerly in shambles.

I pushed the door wide open, kicking a small box up against it to hold it open.

"Ha!" I said, letting my inner wiseass out.

As if this ghost couldn't move a box.

I turned back to the stairs but was quickly rewarded for the slight with a shock, as movement startled me from the open doorway.

The initial shock was nothing compared to what followed. I turned toward the darkened hallway and watched as the silhouette of a woman marched out of the open doorway and down the hallway before me, her skirts swishing around her in absolute silence. I stood frozen as she walked away from me, the window at the end of the hall giving enough light to silhouette her shape – as well as shine right through her.

She reached a door in the middle of the hall and turned, disappearing as her skirts hit the threshold of the room.

I stood there for a long moment, the sounds of the party below drifting up through the floor. Should I call for someone? Should I run to tell someone what I'd seen – find company that was solid and alive to help quell this sense of otherworldliness that seemed to be seeping through my skin?

I took one glance toward the stairs behind me, then summoned every ounce of courage I had and followed her.

I knew the room she'd turned into. Bran and I had worked on it that first week as it offered the easiest access to the roof above. I moved slowly, the heel of my shoe beginning to grind into my skin with each step. I reached the open door, and without giving myself time to consider what I'd find, lunged into the doorway with a sidestep.

God, you're an idiot, Cor. What do you think you're gonna do? Scare a ghost?

The room was empty – no blue lady standing in the doorway glaring at me or gazing longingly out the French doors to the balcony beyond. It was as well put together as any other room now – fresh paint and wallpaper, new window treatments, and a matching bedspread on a previously missing bed.

Everything about the room seemed untouched and perfect, save for the wide-open French doors.

Damn it, I thought. *If that's not a ghostly invitation to my death, I don't know what is.*

I stepped into the room, making my way across the room. I was halfway across the room when a sound startled me so badly, I nearly dropped to the floor as though prepping for the Blitz.

"Fer fuck's sake," a voice said somewhere close by, followed by the same sound again – a bottle shattering in the bedroom fireplace, dropped there from the chimney above.

My gait tripled now as I made my way out onto the balcony. I leaned back onto the railing to look at the roof above.

Branson was marching across the roof, snatching up another bottle of beer about ten yards away.

"Bran? What are you doing?" I said.

He slumped down onto the slanted tiles, cracking the bottle top with the ring on his finger – his grandfather's ring. He didn't seem to hear me.

I stood there for a moment, wondering whether I should run to find Callista and get her up there to pry her brother from his perch, but I didn't want to leave him. From the sound of his grumbling voice, he was in quite a state, and that wasn't his first - or second - beer.

I shot a wary glance to the drop beyond the railing and began kicking off my heels. The stone was cold beneath my feet, and I had to shimmy my fitted gown practically up to my hips to get any use of my legs, but after a moment's struggle, I was on the railing and climbing up onto the roof.

He seemed completely oblivious to me still, a pair of chimneys blocking me from his view. I made my way up the slant of the roof, watching the edge to gauge how far from the balcony I ventured.

"Bran," I said, coming around the second chimney, holding the hem of my dress high enough to have full range of motion in my legs.

He startled, dropping his bottle of beer. It didn't shatter, but instead rolled down the slant of the roof as Bran helplessly took a step toward it and watched it disappear over the edge. A second later, we heard it hit the bushes below.

I took another step toward him, every step as wary as the first. I couldn't say my fear of heights was any less intense since my last trip to the roof of Cavendish House. "Bran, why don't you sit down?"

The view from the back of the house was empty, with nothing to see for miles.

He stared off into the darkness that swept across the horizon there. "Don't patronize me."

Despite clearly favoring booze, these words were startlingly sober.

"I'm not patronizing you. Your sister is looking for you – she's worried about you."

"She should be."

My chest tightened. "I'm worried about you."

"Ye are?" He said, sarcastically, glancing at me over his shoulder. "Go back inside, Corinne."

"I'm not going anywhere without you."

He snorted and marched across the roof to an object just under one of the chimneys – a six pack of beer with two bottles left. "Well, then ye'll be up here a while," he said.

The music from the ballroom far below was drifting through the quiet Highland air, giving the rooftop an eerie feeling. Even so, the rooftop with Bran was far more appealing to me than what I'd just seen in the hallway below.

I watched him a moment. He wasn't at his best, and the three-story drop wasn't something I wanted to leave him alone with.

"Come on. You saw everyone downstairs. These people want to celebrate with you."

"Celebrate? None of these wankers want to celebrate with me. They're here out of idle curiosity. As evidenced by your lad, Christopher, down there."

I felt my nostrils flare against the cold air. "He's not my lad."

"And they're not my well-wishers."

We both stood there in silence as Bran cracked the cap off his bottle with his ring, again.

"You worked so hard for this. You should get to relish it."

"Relish it," he said, purring on the words as though he'd never heard them before. Then he exhaled in a sad laugh and shook his head. "Ye know, this night – these people and this party – this was all I ever wanted. Just to save this piece of my history, do right by my ancestors, many of whom I have it on good authority were a bunch of massive cunts."

I took a step closer as he took a long swig of his beer.

"It's all bullocks. I wanted to restore Cavendish to its former glory, to take it back from my father and make a home here -"

I opened my mouth to speak, but he looked at me out of the corner of his eye, and it froze me to the spot.

"This isn't home. The only thing that ever made this place feel like home was having you in it."

Had my chest been made of paper, my heart would have burst from it.

"Branson -"

"Now, every room just feels haunted by ye. I can't spend a moment in any part of it without remembering your laughter there."

The tears I'd fought so hard to hide downstairs returned now with a fervor. I couldn't begin to combat it.

"I'd give anything to change what happened – say no to ye when ye offered to help me. I should've never put ye in that position, but instead, I get ye fuckin arrested!"

"It was my choice," I said, but he wasn't listening.

"But I was so desperate to reclaim what I thought was mine – to be this man who might make my Nan proud – keep this useless family line going."

I could feel the pain in his voice and wanted to go to him, to hold him and warm him until the pain melted away.

"And now here I am at some god-awful party, and I don't know how to be this man anymore."

He turned to me, and I was sure he could see right through me.

"I don't know how not to love ye," he said, and it felt as though the earth moved beneath us.

I took a step toward him, my throat growing tight as I realized I was going to pour all those dark corners of my heart out – all those moments I'd ached to be near him.

I reached for him just as his eyes went wide, his expression shifting to one of sudden fear, then his face dropped before me as the roof gave way beneath his feet.

I dove for him, the beads of the dress and the surface of the roof tiles scraping across my chest as his weight dragged me closer to the newly formed chasm. Bran reached for me, his hands holding my arms, the cold metal of his grandfather's ring grazing my bare skin as yet another ill-fated beer bottle rolled down the slant of the roof and dropped three stories down. This time, it shattered.

"Ye gotta be fucking kiddin me," he said, his voice straining as he moved his hands to grab hold of the roof tiles.

"No, just hold onto me. I have you," I said, then turned my face out toward the expanse of nothing that lay beyond the house. "Help! Anybody! We're on the roof!"

Bran shook his head and he growled, trying to hoist himself back up through the hole in the roof. We both heard his jacket tearing as it caught on some jagged edge of wood and nail.

"For fuck's sake!"

"Can anyone hear me!?" I screamed. I took a breath, ready to wail again, but Bran's grip on the roof slipped and he shifted downward. I shrieked, shimmying closer to anchor my elbows against the rough roof surface. I was already bleeding; I could feel it. "Help!"

"They can't hear ye. The band'll be too loud."

His words were unnervingly calm.

My heart was pounding so fiercely, I could feel my pulse – in my chest, my ears, the injured skin of my elbows and knees – everywhere. I was beginning to panic. Unlike Bran, I wasn't strong enough to haul him back up through the roof like he did me. I wouldn't be able to pull him to safety alone.

"I'm sorry," I said, fighting not to burst into tears. "Please! Someone help us!"

He met my eyes. "It's ok, Corinne. It's my own fault. All of it."

I knew he referred to more than our current predicament, but I didn't want to hear it. That tone of resignation frightened me. I grit my teeth and began to shift myself around. If I could hook my legs on the edge of the roof, maybe I could pull him up – or he could use me to climb back through.

My ankle slammed into something hard, and the pain shot up through my leg like electricity. "Ah, shit!"

"What? What's wrong?" He said, his fingers already curled into my arms.

My eyes were closed tight as I fought to ignore the pain, but the sheer frustration was enough to make me want to fight an inanimate object. I turned just enough to see what I'd hit, then kicked it with my better foot.

The metal spire hummed with the vibration, but that was all. My eyes widened as I recognized what it was. I shot a look to the nearby chimney and exhaled.

Bran groaned. "Christ, I always knew this house was gonna fucking kill me."

"You can let go."

Bran's arms tightened on me. "Hold on! Fuck no! Ye're not resigning me to the hereafter, woman. Are ye mad?"

"No, look where we are."

273

Bran met my gaze, his blue eyes searing into mine. Then he shot a glance over his shoulder, gripping me tighter as he was rewarded for the effort with the loss of another inch.

"You can let go. The rafters aren't that high over the ceiling, and the ceiling is rotted. You should go straight through."

His brows knitted together as he searched my face for an explanation. I gave a head tilt toward the tiny woodstove chimney at my feet.

He looked over, and his expression softened. "Ah, Christ. This is gonna suck."

I gave a sad smile and nodded. "You ready?"

He blew out through pursed lips. "Aye. Here we go."

I loosened my hold on him as he did me, and in an instant, he dropped through the roof. I lunged forward as the house shuddered beneath me. I peered through the hole in the roof and found Branson lying prone atop a massive pile of mattresses a story and a half below me, the shattered remnants of the rotted ceiling scattered across him.

Twenty

"A RE YOU ALRIGHT?" I called.

He groaned in response.

There was a ruckus in the house below. The sound of a grown man falling through the ceiling was enough to rouse party-goers' curiosity.

I heard a familiar voice. "Branson?!"

Clearly, the pesky door was still open as the light from the hallway shifted below me. People were milling into the room. I fought to right myself, shimmying away from the softened roof to scurry back down to the balcony and into the upstairs bedroom.

I felt a sudden dread as I stepped into the dark room, remembering the phantom from earlier that evening. Still, I needed to see that Bran was alright, so I turned my eyes to the floor, refusing to look around the room as I darted through and down the hall.

"What happened, ye bell end?"

I reached the open doorway, excusing myself through the curious onlookers. "He was sitting on the roof and it gave way," I said.

Callista shot me a scathing look, though it was clear her frustration wasn't directed at me. "What was he doin on the roof?"

"Getting hammered," I said, my voice low enough not to inform the curious folk nearby.

"Getting pished on the roof?"

"I'm not pished! Alright, I'm a wee bit pished," Bran said, groaning.

"Of course. Because that's a responsible idea. Jaysus, is everyone aff their heid, tonight? Here, help me get him to bed," she said, and the accent was so Scottish, I almost didn't recognize it.

I stood aside as Cal hoisted her brother onto his feet, then I stepped in, taking one of his arms over my shoulder.

"Ye don't need to bloody carry me! I'm fine," he said, shaking Cal off.

He didn't try to shake me off, and the gesture wasn't lost on me.

Not one bit.

I let him lean on me as we made our way past the gathered company, and I followed his lead to the stairs, my bare feet padding across the old hallway runner. We reached the downstairs landing and he turned down the hall as Cal rounded past us, opening his bedroom door for us to enter.

Bran slumped down onto his made bed, his arms splayed out around him as Cal made quick work of stripping him of his shoes and socks.

"And here I thought I'd never have children," she said, shooting me a cheeky grin.

"Shut it, ye trollop!" Bran said.

I stifled a laugh, as did Callista. "Don't mind him. He says a lot of nonsense when he's inebriated."

My insides twisted at those words. I instantly heard my cousin Patti's voice asking me, *"Was he sober when he said it?"*

"Who doesnae?" Bran said. It seemed the Douglas children's accents were amplified by both temper and drink.

Cal hoisted his legs up and threw them onto the bed. Then she tossed his shoes to the floor in front of the closet. I watched them, catching a glimpse of a pair of cat dishes on the floor.

Bran let Mr. Darcy sleep in his room with him.

The notion made my heart swell and break in the same instant.

I followed Cal out into the hallway. I was sure Bran was sound asleep before she shut the door to his room.

The onlookers had dispersed by now, many of them milling in the front hall just below.

"Ah, love. Ye're a mess!" Cal said, rushing over to me. She took my arm by the wrist and lifted it up, letting me see the extent of the blood on my arms; it was running from elbow to wrist. "Come on, then. Let him sleep it off and let's get ye sorted."

Soon enough, she had me in her en suite bathroom, washing my wounds and bandaging me up before helping me get out of the dress. As beautiful as it was, in a single night I'd put it through some serious paces.

"I'm so sorry," I said, pulling my sweater back on over my head.

Cal smiled. "It's fine. Nothing that can't be fixed. There's no blood, thank god."

I sighed with relief.

Just as I buttoned my jeans, a figure appeared in the doorway. "There ye are! I've been lookin all over for ye. Are ye alright?" Christopher said, marching into Callista's bedroom without request.

"Me? Yes, I'm fine. Why?"

"They're sayin someone fell through the roof?"

He shot a look from me to Cal, then quickly back to me.

I shrugged. "That would be Branson, but he's alright. I just got a bit scratched up."

"Ye weren't on the roof with him, were ye? What on earth were ye thinking?"

I shot a quick glance to Callista, hoping my eyes could convey my thanks as I led Chris out of her bedroom. "His sister was looking for him, so I helped her search -"

"*His sister* needed your help? Aye, that's grand. Look, are ye ready to go. I'm not feeling so well."

I fought not to look down the hallway to Bran's room. Bran who'd moments ago called me *home*. Bran who'd declared his love. Bran who was sound asleep in a drunken stupor.

I turned back to Chris who stood waiting for a response, his brown eyes wide in near exasperation. I remembered all the times Christopher called me up after a few pints, suddenly teeming with affection and lust, murmuring sweet nothings to me into the wee hours of the night.

Yet, every time he sobered up, those sweet nothings turned to something else - just nothing.

Because he'd still been living with his ex-girlfriend, Jocelyn Reed? Or because he simply didn't mean them.

The flood of thoughts overwhelmed me, but I knew there was nothing to be done tonight. Bran was asleep, and even if I woke him, he was drunk. Nothing we said to one another would be as worthwhile as what might be said when he had his wits about him, and if I was going to tell him how I felt – if I was going to find out that he, like Christopher – only truly adored me when he was smashed, I wanted him to remember that fact when he woke the next day.

I took a deep breath and forced a smile.

Whatever happened from here, there was one fact I couldn't escape.

All of my belongings were at Christopher's house.

If I was going to have my heart broken and then have to flee the country, I was going to need a change of clothes.

"Ok," I said.

We made our way downstairs, Christopher rushing off to grab his coat while I headed down to the ballroom. There was someone I wanted to say a proper goodbye to.

Yet, as I approached my dear Hilda, she spun around with a look of exasperation.

"Please, tell me ye didn't eat any of those bloody brownies."

I knit my brow in confusion. "I didn't. Why? What's wrong with them?"

She sighed, snatching a beautifully moist square from someone's plate as we passed.

Though the woman made to protest, Hilda shot her a dismissive look over her shoulder. "Believe me, you'll thank me later," she said, turning to me to speak in a hushed whisper. "My bloody grandson thought he'd be a dear and bake his famous brownies for tonight. The last time he baked them, I had half my parish come down with the trots."

I gasped. "Oh my god. It was the brownies?"

"So ye did have one!"

I nodded. "Bran and I both were in trouble after the church supper."

"Aye, you and every other person there. Apparently, he thought it would be good for a laugh to put laxatives in the bloody things. I only just realized when I caught him and his idiot friends giggling in the corner every time someone picked up a brownie. Och, I could throttle the lot of 'em."

"God, I hope everyone is alright."

She exhaled, her nostrils flaring. "When I tossed them in the bin, the plate was still pretty full. I imagine there are a few poor souls here that'll be in a bit of discomfort soon enough. That lad's gonna be cleaning the church lavatory for a year, the little shite."

I couldn't help but laugh to hear Hilda swear.

A man gestured wildly in the ballroom door, and I caught sight of Christopher waving to me. He was ready to go.

"Hey, Hilda. I have to leave, but I wanted to make sure I got the chance to say thank you, again. It was so wonderful meeting you."

She opened her arms, pulling me in for a swaying hug before running a hand over my tussled hair. I fought not to wince when she held my arms, giving them a squeeze.

"Ye've been such a dear. If ever ye're back in Kinvale, I demand ye come to the parish to say hello."

I smiled, fighting the sadness that was creeping in. "I will."

With that, I turned and made my way for the door. I followed Christopher out to the car, leaving the party still in full swing, within.

I stopped by the passenger side door, turning to look back up at Cavendish House. Its glowing windows gave an appearance of many eyes looking back at me, wide with expectation – as though the house itself was asking me not to leave.

I felt a pain deep in my chest. I knew I would return the next day – I had to. I had to know for sure whether Bran meant what he said. Yet, even with the plan to return once more, I'd resigned myself to leaving this place behind. If Bran's drunken words were little more than just that, I'd be heading off into the world without destination, armed with little more than a passport and a map to Florence, or France, or Key West for all I knew.

I didn't want his words to be the result of drink, but I'd been fooled by more than one man before now. Fooled too many times to count.

I glanced at Christopher.

All I knew was that my time at Cavendish was more than likely ending – truly ending. And unlike before, this time I had a moment to say good-bye.

I remembered little Mr. Darcy and felt the urge to run back inside.

You'll see him tomorrow, I thought. *If nothing else.*

"Hello?"

I snapped back to reality and found Christopher holding his keys out to me. "Could ye drive? I'm not feeling so good."

I looked at the keys as though they might bite me, but I took them, rounding to the driver's side and climbing in.

I felt overwhelmed with distrust. I was sitting beside the man who'd given me a place to stay for two months now, but he wasn't the man I'd grown comfortable with. He wasn't even the man I was planning to leave at the end of the month.

He was something new, and despite my resolution to bow out with grace, something was chewing at the corners of my mind.

We were rolling past the little church when I couldn't stand the silence anymore. "Why did you tell me Bran was still engaged?"

Chris exhaled through pursed lips. "Phew, pardon?"

"Branson. You said he and Beth were together."

I'd planned to wait until we were home for this conversation. Or perhaps I'd planned not to have it at all. If I was honest, I'd been entirely ready to pack up and leave before Branson's declarations, but now it felt almost imperative that I hear Christopher declare just what sort of man he was.

"Well, I dunno. I was just relaying what Jocelyn told me."

"Jocelyn, your ex-girlfriend."

"Oh, ye can't be serious -"

"When?"

"When what?" He said, throwing his hands up as he turned to glare at me.

"When did Jocelyn tell you they were together."

Chris squirmed in his seat as I picked up speed around a curve. "Christ on a bike, Corinne. Does it matter? I don't know, some time ago."

"So not recently?"

He rolled his eyes. "Recently enough? We don't exactly sit around the fire chatting about your dear Branson, now do we?"

"I don't know. Do you?"

"Enough! Ye want to talk about Branson Douglas, then let's. As I recall, ye told me nothin happened between ye."

"Nothing did," I said, the words catching in my throat. Not for lack of wanting, and not for lack of trying, but whatever we'd shared before I left Cavendish had been soured in my memory the minute Christopher got ahold of it.

"Right. Ye're a terrible liar."

I laughed, a strange haughty sound that I had no control over. "Well, that's fine. You're skilled enough for both of us."

He turned toward the passenger door, ignoring me.

"Why did you tell me Beth picked him up from the police station?"

He sighed. "She did, didn't she?"

"No," I said, waiting in the heavy silence. "His sister did."

He chuckled, shaking his head. "Ye mean the He-She?"

And there it was – every time he'd laughed when I mentioned Callista, every time he'd taken that tone when he called her *his sister* - I'd known and wished to God I was wrong, but the truth was in the open now, and he'd clearly been itching to let it out the second he had the chance.

Everything Bran ever said of Christopher was true, but the most important piece had waited until now to wholly reveal itself - Christopher truly was an asshole.

I slammed on the brakes, and given Christopher hadn't buckled his seat belt, he went careening into the dashboard of the car.

"For fuck's sake! Learn to drive, will ye?"

"You know Jocelyn told me I deserved better than you, tonight."

He rolled his eyes, but he was beginning to squirm in discomfort. "Course she did. Let me guess, the two of ye are besties now, aye? That would explain why she was so wary of calling the polis on the two of ye."

I straightened, my head cocking to the side like a curious bird. "Jocelyn called the cops? How the hell did she know he was even there?"

Chris opened his mouth but didn't speak, instead giving a forced sigh of exasperation.

I gasped. "It was you! You told her to – you heard me say he was there!"

The revelation hit me with such force, I took the keys out of the ignition and threw them at him.

He curled into himself, groaning. "Come off it! Ye're overreacting! He wasn't supposed to be there!"

"You know what? I think I'll walk."

"What?! Are ye insane?"

I reached into the backseat, searching for my purse. At least I had my essentials with me – passport, license, phone. I snatched it, pulling it over my shoulder, ignoring the sting as the strap slid over my scratched arms. "Drive safe."

"Corinne!" Chris said, putting on the sternest tone he could. "I'm literally going to shit myself in a second here."

"Don't worry. There's a gas station about twenty minutes further down the road. Though, if I remember correctly, you're going to be glued to the toilet for the next four hours. Enjoy it."

With that, I turned back down the road and started the long trek back to Cavendish House. I knew I was burning a bridge – knew damn well Christopher would more than likely burn my things before he'd let me come pick them up, but I didn't care. I couldn't be in the car with him for one more second.

And what was five miles down dark country roads in the middle of nowhere Scotland? That or three miles through pitch-black woods and fields.

I'm a brave girl. I can handle a little darkness, I thought.

I reached into my purse and pulled out my phone. If nothing else, I had a flashlight on –

God damn it!

My phone battery was dead.

Again.

"Corinne!" Christopher called after me, followed by a groan of pain as I'm sure his insides clenched.

I remembered the sensation well.

He deserved it.

"Call Jocelyn to come and save you, why don't you?" I called behind me. I could hear him growling in pain and anger, but I didn't bother looking back.

I was going back to Branson. I was going to be there when he woke, and I was going to tell him exactly how much he meant to me and let the chips fall as they may.

Let's see if he thinks I 'come on a bit too strong,' I thought.

My shadow shifted on the ground before me as a new set of headlights approached, and I glanced back toward the incoming car, giving a second's thought to hitchhiking my way back to Cavendish House. The temptation of being out of earshot of Christopher's gastrointestinal nightmare was almost too much to resist, but I kept my eyes forward, not wanting the headlights to burn into my retinas in the dark.

The car slowed down as it rolled alongside me. I turned, a moment's tinge of hope that perhaps this was someone from the village I knew.

It was.

"Oh fuck," I said.

"Are ye in need of assistance?" Officer Blake said, climbing out of the passenger side door.

I swallowed. "No, sir."

"Aye!" Christopher yelled.

The officer shot a look back to the car. Apparently, he hadn't seen Christopher crawling out of the passenger's seat.

Then he turned his attention back to me. "Ye're jokin."

I looked up, meeting the stern gaze under Blake's pronounced brow. He was smirking.

He recognized me.

I closed my eyes, cursing every god that might be able to hear me. "Please, I'm just trying to get back to -"

He whistled, softly, signaling me to stop right there. He didn't want to hear anything I might have to say. He held his hand out to me and waited.

I knew exactly what he was waiting for.

I was screwed.

I scrambled to pull my passport out of my purse, then handed it to him, my stomach lodged in my throat.

He shined his flashlight on it, flipping through the pages. There was no new stamp.

There were no stamps at all, actually.

Christopher let out a yelp and darted off the road into the tall grass, disappearing from view as the malevolent brownies won.

Officer Blake raised an eyebrow, shining the flashlight in my face. "Am I correct in assuming ye've no other visa paperwork since last we spoke?"

I exhaled and every ounce of fight I had in me evaporated on the cool air. I shook my head.

Without another word, Officer Blake took a step back and opened the back-seat door of the police cruiser.

And for the second time in my life, I was arrested - in Scotland.

Twenty-One

A ND DEPORTED.
"You're kidding!?" I said when Blake shared the news.

Ok, technically he was, but the outcome was the same. I was to vacate the U.K.

Immediately.

When I tried to argue my case, ask to retrieve my belongings from Christopher's flat, or at the very least, charge my phone and make a call, Officer Blake had simply smiled and informed me that I was lucky he didn't clap me in irons for the possessions charge as well as overstaying my visa. I attempted to argue, but it did little good.

"It's a blessing I'm not ringing immigration, right now," he said.

Instead, they let me use the station computer to book my plane ticket, then I spent the night in jail.

It'll be a great story to tell your kids someday, you say?

In the immortal words of every Scotsman I've ever known – "Get to fuck."

When morning came and a plainclothes Officer Blake swung his keys in my general direction, I shouldn't have been surprised.

He was taking his day off to drive me to the airport himself.

"Wouldn't want ye getting lost on the way," he said as he held the passenger door open for me. "Besides, been promising my sister I'd stop in for a visit for weeks now."

Still a good story for the kids?

Blake climbed into the driver's seat, buckled in, and fidgeted with his phone and the radio for a moment. "There we are," he said, just as The Song Remains the Same by Led Zeppelin began to play.

More Zeppelin? You've got to be kidding, universe, I thought.

I shot a sideways glance as he plugged his phone into the charger. Not an iPhone. My phone would remain dead for the foreseeable future.

We were a half-hour into the trip when Officer Blake – Duncan as it turned out – stopped for petrol.

"Might I run in and buy a charger for my phone, maybe?"

He shot me a look, eyebrows raised as though I'd asked to pet a rabid badger, but he nodded, standing by the car as I hustled inside.

There was all manner of plugs and trinkets by the cashier. I snagged a cheap green cord and handed the lady behind the counter my last ten-pound note.

Before she could ring up my purchase, I tossed a Boost bar onto the counter, as well.

Duncan Blake was climbing into the driver's seat just as I unwrapped my cord.

"Tryin to ring home, then? Let 'em know ye're on your way?" He asked, pulling onto the highway.

I shook my head. "No. Just – didn't really get a chance to say goodbye to someone."

"Is this that bloke what was shitting himself on the moor, last night?"

I couldn't help but chuckle. "No, definitely not him. I imagine he'll be burning my clothes in effigy by now."

Officer Blake, as I couldn't bring myself to call him Duncan, made a soft humming sound deep in his throat. "The trespasser, then?"

I didn't answer, plugging one end of the cord into my phone. I shrugged.

"Ye've got quite a few suitors, here. I can see why ye weren't in a hurry to go."

"I wouldn't say I have suitors."

"No?"

I shook my head.

"Well, that trespassing lad – he was rather fond of ye."

"Why would you say that?"

Officer Blake shrugged. "Well, when we were booking him, he kept asking about ye. Wanted to know whether we were charging ye or no. Didn't seem to care one way or another about his own predicament."

My insides began to dance, remembering the night I'd left him in the station.

"Now, who was this bloke with the trots, then?"

I sighed. "Long story."

Blake clicked the indicator to switch lanes, then leaned back in his seat. "Well, we've got an hour or so."

"Ah shit," I said, my head falling back against the headrest. I ran my hand to the opposite end of my new cord and discovered I'd purchased a wall plug set rather than a car charge set.

I really was just shit out of luck, ladies and gentlemen.

Before I knew what was happening, I'd turned my face to the window of Blake's car, tears streaming down my cheeks.

All I wanted in the world was to hear Bran's voice. I wanted to say what was tearing at its chain in my chest, to let him know that however drunk he may have been the night before, I returned his affection, and I didn't need alcohol to say so.

It hurt enough knowing I wouldn't get to say it to his face, but now – somehow, the thought of ringing him up from the airport felt trite. I mean, who wouldn't be won over by, "Hey, I'm basically being deported, have no job lined up, and am pretty much homeless if you don't count living in my childhood bedroom for the next few weeks, but – any chance you could spare a smile for one of Interpol's most wanted?"

God, what would I even say, if he answered?

"Ye alright over there?"

I straightened, realizing Officer Blake was eyeing me, concerned.

I wiped my eyes, nodding.

His eyebrows went up in wait, an expression of friendly concern and curiosity. I sighed and despite my better judgment, told Officer Blake everything. Chris, Bran, the house, my dad's girlfriend, nearly dying on the roof – everything.

"And now, I'm in a police officer's car being escorted out of the country, and I can't so much as text him where I am, let alone how I feel."

The last word hung in the air for a moment, Officer Blake drumming his fingers on the steering wheel.

I took a bite of my Boost bar as Officer Blake took the exit that would lead us to Edinburgh Airport, and I tried not to cry.

"So, ye come all the way to Scotland for a bloke, who turned out to be a chancer. Ye end up in the Highlands at his behest, where ye meet an Earl?"

"Yes," I said.

"Ye end up fond of the Earl, but then ye're arrested, and the chancer tells ye the *Earl* is the real chancer, so ye go *home* with him -"

"It wasn't like that -"

He wasn't listening to me at this point. "-only to find out the Earl might really love ye, and the chancer's a prick, which we all knew. So, now ye've spent nine months in Scotland with fuck all to show for it, and ye're a bloody criminal."

"Well, when you say it like that -"

"Ah well. Could be a lot worse," he said.

"What?"

He turned the car through a roundabout and pulled into the parking lot for the airport just as it began to drizzle. I felt my throat growing tight as he parked along the drop-off curb.

"Here's what ye're gonna do. Ye're gonna get on a plane, leave the country, go home, or anywhere else in the bloody world, and like a fucking adult, ye're gonna stay there for as long as it takes to get a proper visa. Then, if this bloke really is as lovely as ye say, ye can come back and shag yourselves senseless."

I opened my mouth, partially offended, but no words came. I suddenly felt like I was talking to my father.

"Or, better yet, lass. Don't. Don't cross an ocean for some chancer prick. Why don't ye let a bloke come to you?"

This suggestion made my heart hurt.

"Or do ye think yerself not worth it?"

I sat there for a long moment, my purse straps wrapped around my fingers. "I don't know."

"Aye, perhaps there's yer problem," he said, and I felt like the air left my lungs. Officer Blake leaned in, watching me for a moment. "You and my sister are just alike, ye know that? Brilliant women, but absolute rubbish when it comes to the lads."

I fought not to let my expression betray surprise. If there was one thing I never expected Officer Blake to call me, it was brilliant. "I don't know about -"

"So here. I'm gonna give ye the advice I'd give my sister, whom I love dearly. Ye ready?"

"Yes?"

He pointed his forehead at me, eyebrows raised. "Never – and I mean never - cross an ocean for a lad ye're not absolutely certain would cross an ocean for you? Understood?"

I swallowed. "Understood."

"Good. Now, get the fuck outta my country."

I couldn't help but laugh as Officer Blake leaned across the car and opened the passenger side door for me.

"Yes, sir," I said, then I hopped out, coming to stand on the sidewalk as he sat in the driver's seat, waiting for me to go inside.

Clearly, he wasn't leaving until he was sure I was heading toward my flight.

I rolled my eyes and ducked out into the rain, running across the crosswalk and into Edinburgh airport.

Despite modern technology, I couldn't offer up my phone for a quick check-in, leaving me to wait in line for fifteen minutes to get my boarding pass. I checked the clock – I had an hour.

Boarding pass in hand, I made my way to security and found myself behind a massive gaggle of Scottish secondary students on their way to Japan for a school trip. The ruckus from their chaperones trying to wrangle them was almost worse that the kids, themselves. After finally snatching my purse up from the conveyor on the other side, I glanced at the nearest clock again – I had forty minutes.

It's fine Corinne. You have plenty of time, I thought, bustling through the terminals toward my gate. I could plug in there, get enough of a charge to call Bran, have a solid twenty minutes to talk, if need be, then still have ten minutes before boarding started.

Doable. Absolutely doable.

Suddenly, the sing-song voice of an airport announcement came over the speakers.

Now boarding Flight 1330 to Boston at Gate 20.

"What the hell!?" I said, drawing the attention of an older couple nearby.

Oh shit! Shit! Shit! Shit!

I ran past the World Duty-Free shop and down the corridor toward the higher gates, glancing down at my boarding pass and passport as I hustled.

It read 11:15.

Why the hell were they already boarding at 10:15? Because the universe hates you, Corinne. How is that not obvious by now?

The metal clasps of my purse and its contents were jingling violently as I ran down past the other gates, scanning the seating areas for signs of plugs and outlets.

I slowed my pace as I reached Gate 15, reaching into my purse for the phone charger. Twenty yards ahead, there was a large crowd gathered around Gate 20, all of them milling forward at an infuriating speed.

I hurried along the aisles, searching for open outlets. Each one I passed was already in use by some other traveler.

After what felt like an eternity, and another announcement for my flight, I finally stopped at the nearest plug, and followed the cord to its source.

A twenty-something man in a tracksuit sat there swiping his thumb across the screen of his phone. He looked fully ensconced, but I reached out to touch his hand and prayed.

"Oi, darling," he said. He wasn't Scottish.

"Hey, I'm sorry to bother you, but my phone is completely dead and they're boarding my flight as we speak. Is there any chance I might be able to steal this from you for a minute or two?"

"Sure thing, love," he said, unplugging his cord.

I swooped in with my own, double-checking the screen to be sure it was charging.

"Are you on that Boston flight, there?"

I nodded.

"Boston, huh? Bet ya sound like that movie there – wha' is it? Good Will Hunting?"

I forced a laugh and shrugged. "Probably."

He offered me the seat beside him, but I politely declined, standing there with my phone clutched in my hands as the line to board my flight withered and thinned with each passing second.

Flight 1330 to Boston. All remaining passengers should board at this time.

"Come on, come on," I said, squeezing my phone in my hands as though I was throttling someone's throat. I held it close to my chest.

"What'd ya say your name was?"

I felt a hand graze my leg and nearly swung out. I turned to find Mr. Tracksuit had been speaking to me.

I fumbled for words. "Corinne. My name is Corinne."

"Ya sure ya don't wanna have a sit-down?"

"No, I'm fine."

I watched the last person in line - a tall man in a tweed jacket - fumbling with his carry-on at the gate desk. I willed him to drop his bag or search for his passport – anything to slow him down.

Yet, like any modern gentlemen with a smartphone does these days, he displayed the screen of his phone to the gate attendant, and in two seconds, he was on his way down the gateway.

God damn it!

Final boarding for Flight 1330 to Boston at Gate 20. All remaining passengers please board at this time. The Gate is closing in five minutes.

"Wouldn't ya rather sit -"

I looked down at my phone, exasperated to find it still blank, yet just as I bent down to pull the plug, the familiar bitten apple symbol lit up the screen.

"Finally!"

Mr. Tracksuit reached for me, planting his hand over mine. "Before ya go, maybe I could ring ya sometime?"

"Seriously, no!" I said, loud enough for everyone around us to hear. A couple guys chuckled, glancing over their shoulders as Mr. Tracksuit glared at me.

"Well, alright. Don't have to be such a -"

I leaned into him, my finger extended just inches from his face. I knew the exact word he was about to utter and I was ready to smack it right out of his mouth.

Today was not the day to piss me off.

"Say it. Go on, say it. I fucking dare you."

He splayed his palms and leaned back. "Alright, calm down. Jesus."

I glared at him for a second longer, reading true fear in his expression. Then I summoned the only quote I could think of from Good Will Hunting as my parting glance. "How 'bout them apples?"

A woman nearby began openly laughing as the two gentlemen gave me a slow clap. I turned from them all, hustling across the terminal to my gate as I fought to pull up Bran's number.

The gate attendant glared at me. "Boarding pass?"

I handed her my passport. She continued to glare. It was only then that I realized the paper pass was no longer wedged between the pages. I scrambled for my purse, ramming my hand into each pocket. No crinkling occurred. It was gone, probably lost to the general vicinity of Mr. Tracksuit.

I've never been so sure in my life that God hates me.

I made quick work of bringing up the flight app on my phone, pulled up my electronic boarding pass, and showed it to her. It was scanned and settled within seconds.

I hurried down the gateway and discovered my phone was at one percent charge.

Somebody give me something to stab!!

The rest of the passengers were already on board as I reached the plane. I quickly made my way down the aisle to my seat, fighting with my saved texts to find the last one I received from Bran. I waited for my seatmates to clear a path for me, distractedly stepping on the middle woman's foot when she couldn't be bothered to get up.

I shot her an apology, all while fantasizing about headbutting her.

I slumped down into my seat, breathless, just as I found the text.

The house is mine. Officially. Thank you, Corinne. I couldn't have done it without you. Xxxxx

I pulled up the phone number as quickly as I could, and despite the thumping in my chest, pressed send.

"Madam. There's no cell phone use during take-off."

I turned to face the flight attendant. It was clear my eyes conveyed the full extent of my rage. "I'll be done in a second."

The flight attendant didn't move, hovering in the aisle.

Jesus, I'm going to end up beaten by an Air Marshall if this lady doesn't leave me alone.

"Ye've reached my voicemail. Ye know well enough what to do," the voice message said.

He didn't answer. I exhaled. Just the recording of his voice left my hands shaking.

"Madam."

"Please! For the love of god, could you just be the first person today to cut me some fucking slack!?"

The flight attendant's eyes went wide as my two seatmates gave me a startled, British look of 'Well I never!' I didn't care, the voicemail beeped in my ear.

"Branson. I'm sorry, I wanted to do this in person, but – I'm – they put me on a plane home."

"Is there a problem, here?" A male voice said, another flight attendant joining the first for backup. I ignored them both.

"I don't know how much of last night you'll remember when you get this, and I might never see you again, but I just wanted – I needed you to hear me say it before I left."

"Madam?"

"I love you, too."

"Madam," the voice grew sterner now, and I turned to meet their gazes, waving my phone in the air to show them I'd finished my call. They both gave me a pursed-lip stare, then moved on to harass some other poor traveler. I turned the phone upright to end the call and my breath stilled.

The screen was black.

My phone had died, again, and I had no idea how much of the message made it through.

I slumped back into my seat as the captain came on over the speakers, pressed the phone to my forehead as I fought the urge to punch a hole through my window and chuck the technological nightmare out onto the tarmac, and then nothing.

I was so tired, I couldn't even cry.

I tucked my phone into my purse, buckled my seatbelt, and leaned back, watching as we pulled away from the gate.

Twenty-Two

"T HIS IS A NICE surprise! I didn't expect to see you home so soon," Kenny said, rounding the corner of his SUV to greet me outside Logan Airport.

I offered a grin and closed my eyes tight, trying not to burst into tears as he wrapped his arms around me. Despite my efforts to stay away, the familiarity of his goofy grin and Boston accent always made me feel like I was home.

Except now. Even his exaggerated "Wheyah's all yah stuff?" couldn't lighten the weight I carried.

"It's a long story," I said, climbing into the passenger side of the car.

"Yeah? Anything you can tell me? We got an hour's ride easy with traffic this time 'a day."

I didn't immediately respond, pulling my phone out of my purse to check it again.

It had a charge. I'd plugged it in upon landing in Boston and checked for a response from Bran.

My call had been thirty-three seconds long. Long enough for the whole message to get through.

He hadn't responded.

And I'd had three hours sitting on the floor of an airport terminal to think about it as I waited for Kenny to get my call and rush into Boston to pick me up.

I slumped back into my chair and closed my eyes again.

"Come on, cricket. You alright?"

I gave him a sad smile.

"Did the Scotsman turn out to be a douche bag?"

I exhaled through my nose in a half-laugh, and let my head fall back. "One of 'em sure did. Hence my not having my stuff."

I caught Kenny making a familiar face out of the corner of my eye, eyebrows raised and nostrils flared. "I'll kill 'im."

I reached over and patted Kenny's hand. I didn't speak, closing my eyes as he pulled away from the curb. Thankfully, he didn't press. Instead, he turned on the radio and we listened to Dire Straits for the whole ride back to Acton.

The house had changed again since I was last home. The shutters were now a deep forest green instead of the burgundy color they'd been when I was a kid. It looked nice enough against the pink of the house, but still – it was strange.

My childhood home always felt strange now that Diane lived there.

"Hey, honey! Look who's here," Kenny called to the figure on the porch. Diane was sitting in one of the rocking chairs smoking a cigarette, her hair freshly bleached blonde.

"And what're you doing smoking that nasty shit?" Kenny said, hopping up onto the porch to give Diane a kiss on the cheek.

She held eye contact with me as she spoke. "Stress."

"Ah, don't worry. Work nonsense always passes," he said. Then he turned back to me. "Come on, kiddo! You gotta see the basement. Worked on it all Summer."

I nodded, bending down to give a dutiful kiss on the cheek to my stepfather's girlfriend. "It's nice to see you."

"You too, honey," she said, exhaling smoke at me just as I pulled away. I fought not to recoil.

I followed Kenny inside, regaling him as he took me through the newly finished basement. He'd finally created his man cave, something he'd only felt inclined to do since Diane moved in and took over his living room and office. Now, the basement harbored a pool table, a wide screen TV, and a second guest bedroom with an en suite bathroom.

He'd done the work entirely alone, his usual sidekick being on the other side of the world for the duration. I let him know just how impressed I was, trying out the new leather couch as he snuck behind a Guinness bar to grab himself a beer out of a tucked-away mini-fridge.

Kenny took a swig on his Sam Adams before suddenly lunging around the bar toward me. "Oh, and check this out!"

He snatched up a small remote control from the coffee table in front of me, and in two clicks, *Never Going Back Again* by Fleetwood Mac lilted from every corner of the room.

"How's that sound system, huh? Got the whole Bose setup in here. Doesn't even need a subwoofer anymore – it's all hidden away."

I forced a smile, pulling myself up from the exorbitantly comfy couch. "You went all out, huh?"

"Hey, if you're gonna do something, gotta do it right, right?"

"Damn straight."

"Oh, that reminds me. You got any pics of that old house you were working on?"

He came toward me, leaning his shoulder to mine to look down at my phone in my hand as though I'd already brought up some before and after shots. Instead, the phone screen was blank.

No photos of the house.

No missed calls.

No texts.

Nothing.

"I might have a few, but I'm actually feeling kinda lagged out. Do you mind if I head upstairs and take a nap before supper?"

He turned his eyes away, a gesture that felt beyond strange. Apparently, Kenny had something he didn't want to say.

"What's wrong?"

He gave a half shrug. "See, I was thinking ya might like sleeping down here, maybe?"

I knit my brow, glancing back to the new guest room. "Well, I wouldn't want to invade your new man cave."

He gave an exaggerated pout and shook his head. "Oh, you don't need to worry about that. It's no different than having you off the living room in your old bedroom."

I paused, watching him take another swig off his beer. "My *old* bedroom?"

Not my current bedroom. Not the room I left ten months earlier with every intention of crashing therein when I needed to stop back home.

"What happened to my room?"

Kenny sighed. "Diane sorta started working in there – said it was easier than trucking up and down the stairs for her artsy stuff."

"Artsy stuff?"

"Yeah, you know she does all that quilting. She put her machine and desk in your room, and one thing led to another – and well there's no bed in there anymore."

"I don't have a bedroom?"

I fought so hard to hide the emotion in my voice, but it cracked.

"No! No, cricket. You have a bedroom. Here, come look. It's really nice down here. Can't even tell it's a basement."

U2's *Where the Streets Have No Name* started playing, and I snatched up the remote to quiet the stereo. However much I might enjoy the Edge's guitar riffs, I simply couldn't stand the cacophony of Bono and Kenny's voices at once.

I walked into the bedroom, and though I had to contend that it was as luxurious as any space I'd ever slept in, the slapdash pile of my things dwelling in the corner felt like a metaphor for the entirety of my life.

Still, the massive queen size bed had no less than seven pillows atop it, and I wanted nothing more than to bury myself in them, forgetting the world.

"At least down here you have some privacy," he said, opening the bathroom door to let me see the steam shower and bath. It was beautiful. "This way, maybe if you find a fella who actually deserves ya, you can have him over without having to worry about grouchy old Dad hovering around."

"Ew, Dad. Stop. Not happening."

He gave me a sad smile and shrugged. "Hey, don't say that. It's a matter of time before some guy sweeps ya off your feet. Just you wait. Oh!"

Kenny dodged out of *my* new room and down the hall past his TV room. Before I'd even reached the hall, the space flooded with light as he opened the door to the outside.

My eyebrows shot up.

"Installed this bad boy, as well. You can come in at all hours, no one'll be the wiser."

"Sweet. That'll really help when I start my career hooking down by the White Hen."

He chuckled, shutting the door as he came back my way. He gave me a gentle punch in the arm as he passed. "Come on, now. Don't say that. Besides, the White Hen's not there anymore."

"Seriously? Is nothing sacred?"

He laughed. "Yep. It's a Seven-Eleven now. Anyway, I'll leave you to get cozy. There's food in the fridge if ya get hungry."

Then Kenny was gone, hustling back up the stairs to the ground floor where he was greeted by Diane's voice. I couldn't make out their conversation. I was grateful for it.

I didn't even bother to close my bedroom door, but instead set my still silent phone on the bedside table and slumped into the mass of pillows.

I slept for six hours, waking to the sound of the upstairs TV playing an episode of some Crime Drama Kenny enjoyed. Diane must've gone out. She didn't like my Dad's crime shows.

I remained there for a long moment, staring up at the ceiling as the daylight faded outside. There was a sudden burst of noise upstairs as someone came into the house. An instant later, the TV went silent.

Diane must be home.

Well, that was a short reprieve, I thought.

I closed my eyes, listening to muttered voices for a moment. The sound was familiar, but I didn't feel like visitors, no matter what family member or cousin might've come by for supper. Instead, I ignored the knot in my stomach and rolled over to the bedside table to check my phone.

Still nothing.

I sighed, slumping back down and pulling a pillow up over my head.

"And who's asking?" Kenny said.

I pulled the pillow aside. The voices upstairs were raised enough for some choice phrases to get through the floor.

"Might I speak with her?"

I sat bolt upright.

"I don't know what you did to my girl, but if you think I'm just gonna let you in here. You're lucky I don't put your lights out, right now!"

"I'm sorry, sir. I didn't mean to disturb ye."

I gasped, bolting up from the bed toward the dark TV room. I slammed my thigh into the back of the couch. I winced, stopping for a split second to regain my composure.

That's gonna leave a bruise.

"I'm not sure I want to get Corinne for you. I don't know if you're going to upset her further – I mean, what kind of man -"

"Dad! That's not him!" I hollered, trying to run up the stairs and failing. I reached the basement door and stopped, staring at the man in the doorway of my father's house.

"There ye are," Bran said. "Ye're a difficult one to hunt down."

The air left the whole of the world.

"How did you -?"

I couldn't finish the sentence. Kenny was standing between Bran and I, an inch or two shorter than Bran, but he filled the doorway like a golem, daring Bran to step out of line. Yet, when I spoke, Kenny shot me a sideways glance.

Apparently, something about my expression spoke volumes, because Kenny stepped away from the door, letting Bran come in.

"I rang up our dear Jocelyn. Even your Christopher, there. Discovered ye'd been deported?"

"What?!" Kenny said, his eyes going wide.

I held my palms out, trying to find the gumption to defend myself, but I was weak. For the first time, Bran's presence made me feel weak.

"I wasn't deported. I'm not deported, Dad. I just overstayed my visa, so when I got arrested that second time, they -"

"The second time? Ya'h kiddin. Jesus, I need a beeyuh. You want one -?"

Kenny leaned in toward Bran, waiting with a deliberate expression.

I straightened, realizing my bad manners. "Oh, god! I'm sorry, Dad. This is Bran. Branson. He's the man I was helping fix up his house."

Kenny's eyebrows went up with an appraising look as he eyed Branson. Then he extended his hand. "So, not the one who refused to let her collect her things before she was shipped home?"

Branson's eyes went wide. "He didn't? What a bell end!"

The corner of my mouth curled in an *Aw Shucks* expression. I shrugged. "I don't think I can blame him. I did leave him shitting himself on the moor."

Branson fought a smile. He'd barely looked away from me since he walked into the house. "Somehow, I don't doubt it for a second."

I felt his nearness like an electric current, and I wanted nothing more than to touch him.

He wasn't a world away, he was here, breathing the same air, filling the space.

I wanted to throw my arms around him and crash to the floor.

Kenny gave him a nudge. "Well, you didn't answer my question. Beeyuh?"

Beer, in a full-blown, almost overzealous Boston accent.

Bran smiled. "No, but thank ye. I might take ye up on that later, though."

"You got a deal if you show me some pics from that house of yours. God, what I wouldn't give to get my hands on a place like that."

His volume faded as he disappeared into the kitchen.

For a moment, I thought Bran and I were alone, but with a quick glance around the room, I realized Diane was watching us from her seat in the living room.

I felt her eyes like pinpricks on the back of my neck.

"Do you want to go for a walk?" I said, finally.

I couldn't bring myself to take him downstairs – not with Diane watching.

He grinned. "I'd like that very much."

I felt my stomach shoot into my throat. We would be alone, and from that smile, that was exactly what he wanted.

My heart nearly stopped.

What, Cor? What did you think he was going to say? 'No, I only came here to spit at your feet! A curse on your house, wench!' Of course, he wants to be alone with you.

I fought to hide my frantic thoughts from playing across my face and grabbed one of my dad's jackets from the coat hook. A moment later, we were walking down the long driveway toward the road.

"Ye alright, then?" He asked, finally.

I hadn't said a word since we left the house, afraid I might blurt something out or suddenly take on the habit of speaking in tongues. I nodded, hiding my eyes from him.

"Wait, no! I can't believe you're here!" I said, unable to keep the thoughts to myself anymore.

He turned to me, smiling down at me as the light faded across the world. "Well, of course I am. This is where *you* are."

I knit my brow, trying to find a crack in that smile, something to betray his ulterior motives - the same motives I'd found in every other man's smile. Every other man I'd let myself care for.

I opened my mouth to speak. What did I want to say?

There must be some mistake. How could anyone just up and hop a flight across the Atlantic -?

For me. He'd crossed an ocean for me.

I turned away, making a grand gesture of looking both ways on a road that saw more squirrels in a day than it did cars. Then I crossed the quiet road to the field across the way, sliding around the old farm fence posts that lined the conservation land across from my father's house.

This was the path into the woods where I'd skip school as a kid, or where I'd sneak off to read books in the grass when I was home. All to avoid my step-mother – I mean, Kenny's girlfriend.

I pulled the coat tight around my chin, pretending I was chillier than I was. The night was crisp, but the bite of winter wasn't so sharp yet, the dried leaves still flitting on their branches with each breeze. When I shoved my hands back into my pockets, I felt pressure at my elbow. A second later, Bran hooked his arm in mine, matching my step as he pulled me closer.

"So, where does this path go?" He asked, his tone chiding. He could tell I was nervous.

The bastard.

"It does a long loop through the woods. There's a field on the other side – an old landfill that they covered over. I used to go there to watch the stars."

"That sounds lovely. Let's go there."

"You sure?" I said, my breath turning to vapor as I spoke. "It's a bit chilly, don't you think?"

He shot me a sideways look, gently pulling my arm as he walked. "Naw. Nice night for it. I'm sure we can find a way to keep warm."

Had he not been marching us along, my feet would've frozen to the spot. Soon, we were under the shade of tree cover, the leaves overhead blocking out what little light remained.

Dried pine cones and leaves crunched underfoot with each step. I clung to his arm now, not out of a need for warmth or comfort, but simply because I still couldn't believe he was here. I felt that if I released my hold on him he might float away like a dream.

"Aye, this must be it?"

The trees parted, opening to the massive clearing and the hill known to the neighborhood kids as Makeout Mound. I didn't inform Branson of its informal nickname.

"Come on, then," he said, taking my hand as he marched up the hillside toward the peak. My breathing grew labored, but I fought to keep up with my taller companion. Soon enough we were atop the mound, and the stars were appearing overhead.

Bran slumped down onto his haunches, then sprawled his legs out before him. "This looks like a good enough spot."

I stood there for a moment, staring off into the world. I knew this view well – nothing but treetops and chimney smoke rising in the distance. For an instant, it reminded me of the Cavendish grounds and the sea of green that surrounded it. I felt a soft squeeze at my fingertips and looked down to find Branson waiting for me to join him, his smile wide and beautiful even in the dark.

I dropped down onto the grass beside him, curling my legs up under me. We sat in silence for a long moment.

"I bet the view doesn't compare to Scotland."

"I dunno. It has its appeal," he said, flashing me a wicked grin. Then, he leaned back onto the grass.

I held my breath a moment, trying to decide if I should join him. Finally, I made a soft groaning sound as I rolled down onto my back. "I never got the chance to look while I was there -"

"So, I see what ye mean about your Dad's Missus, there."

I exhaled, feeling the tension in my chest release. "God, you felt it, too?"

"Hard not to. I believe she was tryin to scour a hole through me with her eyes."

I laughed. "I've no doubt she was."

Branson rolled onto his side, suddenly, propping himself up on his elbow as he looked down at me. "Are ye no happy to see me, Corinne?"

My eyes went wide and I rolled up to meet him. "What? No! I mean, yes! I am happy. I'm *so* happy -" I stopped, the last words straining through as my throat tightened.

"I wasn't so sure. Ye seemed more startled than excited," he said, giving me a sarcastic look. Still, I could see he was worried.

"I guess I was startled. And embarrassed, honestly."

I averted my eyes. I wasn't prepared to be so honest.

"Why would ye be embarrassed?"

I shrugged. "Well, you came and found me at my dad's house, where I'm now confined to a basement guest room, and I've nowhere else in the world to take you. As you once said, I'm a professional squatter, and I don't even have another house lined up to squat in. I'm just -"

He brushed a strand of hair behind my ear. "Why do ye need to take me somewhere? I didn't come for the scenery, I came for you."

"You say that, but -" I fought the sudden wave, but it overtook me so quickly, a tear rolled down my cheek before I could catch myself. "You wouldn't be the first man to change his mind."

Branson's fingers drove into my hair, and he pulled me toward him, planting his soft lips on mine. I gasped against the kiss, but as he waited for my response, I softened to him. He kissed me again, letting his lips linger for a long moment before releasing me.

"I'm not changing my mind. Ye found me in a dilapidated hovel," he said, and I couldn't help but give a sad laugh. "And when ye found me, I was the most broken thing in the place. I'm not anymore, and that's because of you. I'd come find ye no matter where ye were."

I wanted to let those words sink in, let them permeate my bones and live there, but as I looked up to meet Branson's steely blue gaze, he pressed his forehead to mine, then kissed me.

I shuddered as his hands moved across my hip, pulling me closer to him. I wrapped my arms around him, a clumsy endeavor with our coats still around us. Still, he pulled me into him and I locked into place, my head resting on his arm as he kissed me again. Suddenly, I couldn't feel the cold. All I could feel was the racing of my heart and the solid warmth of Bran's body against mine. Bran shifted over me, letting me bear half his weight.

Bran's hand moved down the front of my coat, prying open the buttons before sliding his hand under the bulky fabric to feel my skin. I gasped at the cold touch of his fingers, but the surprise was quickly replaced as Bran's tongue slipped into my mouth.

I groaned softly, unable to hide my need of him. I hooked my leg around his, and he responded by driving his thigh between my legs, letting his weight press between them. I shrieked, but the sound came in barely a whimper as he kissed me deeper still.

It seemed he wanted to pick up right where we left off that night in the music room.

I clutched him to me as his body moved against mine. I wanted him, just as desperately as I had the last time we'd touched each other like this.

I gasped, pulling away from him. "Stop. Stop, this is torture."

He pulled away, looking down at me with a furrowed brow. He smirked. "That's the point."

He buried his face in my neck, kissing my ear and my collar.

"Yes, but I don't have anywhere to take you. This isn't fair."

He stopped kissing me and made a face. "Take me?"

"I guess there's a hotel in Westford. It's down the road a ways, but _"

He chuckled. "Woman. I'm having ye on this hillside, and that's final."

"What?!" I shrieked, just as he rose to his knees and shrugged out of his coat. Before I could protest, he opened my coat and tore up my shirt, baring my belly to the cold air. He grabbed the fabric of my bra, threatening to pull it aside.

I squealed, reaching for his hands to stop him.

He let me, giving me one of those heart-rendering smiles of his. "Madam?"

He spoke in a mix of bedroomy voice and snooty valet, and I couldn't help but laugh. I held my hands over his, searching for the courage to let myself be seen. I could feel the open air on my skin, feel the world, immense and endless around me, yet somehow, the thought of being with Branson there didn't scare me.

Being caught was far less horrifying than not getting to have him.

"I'll stop if ye like, but the last time I had ye like this, the Polis came and ruined everything, and I've been dreaming about it ever since."

I held his hands, watching his face. He wasn't alone in the dreaming. Just the way Christopher kissed me – sloppy and tiresome – was enough to make me long for Bran. Even when I thought Branson was with someone else, my heart ached to think the best kiss I'd ever received would be nothing more than a memory. Now, I was weak to that same kiss and could only imagine how much better everything else might be with him as well.

"Well, then. We can wait," he said, shifting away from me.

I grabbed him by the shirt, yanking him down onto me. In the instant it took to bring his lips to mine, I caught a flash of that smile.

He pressed his weight over me, his hip grinding between my legs as he kissed me. I tried to stay quiet, but the sensation was so surprising and so good, I grabbed at the belt loops of his jeans and pulled him down onto me. His tongue explored my mouth in teasing bursts, pulling away to kiss me as I caught my breath. I curled my fingers into the mass of curls behind his ears and kissed him back, harder. I wasn't ready to say what I wanted, but I hoped he would hear me, nonetheless.

Yes. Please, don't stop. Please keep going.

Suddenly, he lifted himself up onto his elbow, glancing off across the hillside. I followed his gaze, startled.

Then, he looked back at me, giving me a quick eyebrow raise as he lifted my shirt up again. "I do believe we are alone."

He'd put on his best Vincent Price impression, and I couldn't help but laugh as his fingers grazed over my belly. I curled into myself in protest of the sensation, but my laughter was the stronger force, and Bran's fingers found their way to my breasts, squeezing them through my bra. The sensation stopped my laughter, instantly.

He kissed me then, tugging my bra aside as he did. My nipple was hard against the cold air, and I gasped as he bent to my breast, taking my nipple in the warmth of his mouth.

My mouth fell open, but I didn't make a sound, watching the flicker of stars high above me.

His tongue played at me, then he pulled away, blowing gently on my breast. The cold air pricked at the moisture he'd left from his tongue, and I felt goosebumps rising across my skin.

I shuddered, reaching to cover myself, but he caught my hand, pulling it aside. "Oh no. None of that."

He rose to his knees, his hands sliding down my belly to the button of my jeans. There was an instant of fear – fear of being caught, fear of being seen.

Yet, my eyes went from his hands to his face and I remembered who it was there on the hillside with me. I didn't fight as he unzipped my jeans. Instead, I reached past his hands, pulling the buttons of his jeans open, as well.

He groaned his approval but didn't let me finish. Instead, he grabbed the waistband of my pants and yanked them down, underwear and all. I squealed at this, my ass frozen against the cold ground beneath me. Without having to be told, Bran threw his jacket down on the ground beside me, then yanked me upward, pulling me against him until my weight was supported by his thighs. He turned just so, and rolled me right back down, this time the fabric of his jacket beneath me.

He moved with purpose, stripping my jeans down the length of my legs, tugging my shoes off in a clumsy fervor that left me laughing on the ground.

"I do so love it when a half-naked woman laughs at me."

I grinned, my face burning despite the cold air. "Yeah? Does this happen often?"

His eyebrows shot up as he tossed my jeans aside and lowered himself over me. "No, but if ye'd like to make it a regular occurrence, I could be convinced."

I gasped as he pressed himself onto me. The air was growing colder, and my breath came in thick bursts of vapor.

"Are ye warm enough?" He asked, as though he'd read my mind.

I nodded, curling my fingers into the fabric of his shirt. I couldn't feel the cold with him this close. The whole of the world was a mirage to me there. I reached for him, struggling to get close enough.

His hands moved up my belly, squeezing my breasts. He pressed himself against me, rolling over me again and again. I could feel the stiff shape beneath his jeans, and I whined softly as I grabbed the belt loops again.

He bared his teeth, biting my shoulder gently as one of his hands drifted down my side. Before I could find words to protest, his hand moved across my thigh, sliding up between my legs.

I gasped, my head falling back as his hand grazed over my sex, teasing me.

"Ye're so warm," he said, his voice rumbling deep in his chest.

I held my breath, waiting to feel what he would do next.

He pushed himself up, then, kneeling before me as he ran his hands down the inside of my thighs. I squirmed against it, turning away so he wouldn't see my face. His thumbs teased at me, pressing against me as I held my breath. When his thumbs began to move, I gasped, and my hips rose toward him. I couldn't look at him, I was too shy to meet his gaze, but I couldn't fight the need to feel him.

He took his hands away, leaving me open to the cold air.

I felt a brush of warmth along my thigh and startled, curling into myself just in time to meet his gaze as Branson's smile disappeared between my legs.

The warmth of his mouth hit me with such force, I cried out, my voice echoing across the hillside.

"Branson! Please," I said, searching for words to protest, but he parted me with his tongue, his hands wrapping around my thighs for purchase. I curled my fingers into the grass, fighting not to scream out into the dark. Still, even as I fought to be quiet, my hips began to move again, rising to meet his mouth.

Dear god, what Branson Douglas was doing to me should be illegal.

My head fell back and I sighed, whispering a string of expletives as he picked up speed. I reached down, feeling the tendrils of his hair between my fingers. His tongue slid against me and he glanced up, watching me for a response.

I folded my fingers with his at my hips, my stomach tightening as I watched him. Suddenly, he lifted his head, kissing my thigh while his fingers slipped across my thigh, and without warning, plunged inside me.

"Oh god," I said, the words catching in my throat.

Branson played me there, the stars peering down at us, brighter with each passing moment, but my eyesight was growing blurred. I arched my back, my ass rocking on the ground as I moved with him, aching to find release.

I'd wanted to feel this for so long – longed for it when Christopher shot me his flirty smile from across the airwaves, longed for it when he asked for blow job after blow job, never returning the favor.

I longed for a man to want to please me as desperately as I wanted to please them, and here I was helpless beneath the stars – and I was pleased.

"Fuck," I whispered, feeling the muscles in my legs seize. Yet, I didn't climax. I felt every sensation and my body wanted to, but somehow it didn't happen.

I slumped back onto the ground, frustrated, not wanting to ask Branson for further effort. He'd already done more than any man before him.

"I'm sorry," I said, closing my eyes.

He chuckled, kissing the inside of my thigh. "Oh, love. If I'd wanted ye to come, ye would've."

Then he rose to his knees, tugging his jeans down. I watched him, watched his cock spring from beneath the fabric.

I bit my lip.

By his rule, Branson Douglas wouldn't be afraid to send dick pics.

He lowered himself over me, positioning himself between my legs. I watched his face as he reached down, pressing himself against me with intention.

Bran met my gaze, pausing there for a moment as the head of his cock slipped against me. He smiled.

"Are ye ready for me?" He asked.

I held my breath, staring up at him, his beautiful face surrounded by the stars. I'd never seen anything so beautiful in my life. I wanted to capture that moment and savor it forever.

Yet, more importantly, I wanted him to shag my brains out.

"Yes!" I whispered.

He bent to kiss me, his tongue sliding into my mouth for an instant, then he slipped inside me, my body taking him wholly as he sank over me.

I gasped, my fingers curling in the fabric of his shirt as he pressed as far into me as my body could allow.

He closed his eyes, mouth open in barely a sound. "Christ."

I reached down to his bare backside, pulling him into me and against me, urging him onward.

He opened his eyes and smirked down at me, then he did as I begged him to, his hips retreating just so. Then he plunged home again, filling me completely. I lifted my legs around him, giving him all control.

He took it, gladly. Suddenly, Branson was holding me there, his body rocking over me, his hips grinding against me as he plunged inside me over and over, the sensation stilling any sound I might make. I was breathless and helpless there, clutching him as he made love to me. I sank my teeth into his shoulder, stifling a cry as he doubled his pace.

"What have ye done to me?" He said, whispering in my ear as he thrust harder, letting me take all of him in feverish rhythm. I cried out, my fingers digging into his shoulder as I curled into him. The same sensation rose again, a heat searing through my sex, teased with each thrust ever closer to release. I clung to him like ivy as he growled over me, rocking us both with the force.

I held my breath, my head falling back as he held me against him, and I shuddered all over, my body convulsing beneath him in waves.

He didn't stop, his breathing growing labored and hoarse in my ear as I held onto him, my body melting into the hillside. I let my fingers curl into his hair as I watched the stars overhead, each one brighter than the next. For an instant, he and I were the only living things in the world, floating among the stars.

He thrust deeper still, drawing a cry with the sudden sting of him, then he trembled, his hips jerking in slow rhythm as he collapsed over me.

I held him in my arms, breathing in the smell of him on the cold air.

He kissed my jaw and my throat before he lifted himself up to look at me. When he found me smiling, watching the stars, he rolled to lie beside me. Branson gazed upward, the clouds from our breath joining each other before dissipating in the dark.

"Remind me to shag ye on the roof when we get back home."

I laughed, softly. "And kill us both?"

He gave my thigh a pinch. "After it's sorted, of course."

His fingers searched across my belly until he found my hand, then he entwined his fingers with mine.

"When *we* get home?"

Branson squeezed my hand. "Aye. Ye're stuck with me, love. Whether ye like it or no."

I caught sight of a shooting star out of the corner of my eye and smiled.

Twenty-Three

I WOKE TO THE smell of coffee and the sound of classic rock from the kitchen radio upstairs – Kenny was getting ready for work. I stretched in my bed, sighing into my pillow at the familiarity of it. I might've deflated at the sound of Diane's voice joining Kenny's upstairs, but before the sleep could wholly leave my eyes, I felt a hand move over my hip and across my belly. Branson pulled me into him in his sleep, humming softly in my ear as he settled beside me. I wriggled my ass into him, pulling him close.

Bran mumbled some unintelligible thing, then lifted his head, blinking a moment as he read the environment.

I watched his sleepy expression, the tussled bedhead flattened on one side and robustly spherical on the other.

He was beautiful and goofy as hell.

He smiled at me, wrapping his strong arms around me as he inhaled, his face buried in my hair. "Good morning. God, ye smell good."

"Why thank you. Feel like waking up?"

He groaned. "I dunno. Will ye shag me again if I do?"

I laughed, swatting his hand as he groped my ass. "No. Not in my dad's basement, thank you very much."

He sighed. "Rubbish excuse."

"Alright, let me rephrase. Not in Diane's basement. How about that?"

Diane's voice spiked in volume upstairs – another of their little disagreements. I leaned off the bed, grabbing my old laptop from my pile of stuff.

Bran's eyes were only half-open by the time I was perusing the housesitting site for jobs or new messages.

The Florence couple had changed their dates – a month later.

Key West was still open, but I didn't bother responding to that one. Margaritaville just wasn't calling to me.

I took a moment to check the newest jobs listed; a small villa in northern Spain, a flat in London – can't do that again. Not yet, anyway.

Then I spotted a new listing that piqued my interest.

Globetrotting couple needs a reliable house-sitter for their vacation home in Costa Rica. Gorgeous views, in-ground pool, and walking distance from shops and sandy beaches. Required stay - three weeks.

"Costa Rica, huh?"

I startled, looking down to find Branson awake, watching the screen as I scrolled through.

"Yeah, it's beautiful but doesn't exactly get me closer to Scotland. There's one in Spain, too. Maybe I could find something in Ireland?"

"Why exactly are ye tryin to get closer to Scotland?"

I paused, fighting the urge to look at him. "Well, I can't stay here. I'll go insane. And I thought it might be easier to see each other if I'm close. At least until I can actually return to the U.K."

He groaned in a morning stretch, rolling onto his back. "To fuck with that, I'm goin wherever ye're goin."

He said it with the tone of a man asking for ketchup on his burger.

I stared at him a long moment. "Really?"

I looked down at him, watching his sleepy eyes as he scanned the computer screen.

He didn't say anything but instead reached for the laptop screen, tapping his finger on the picture of Costa Rica. "There. Says single or couples welcome. That one."

I turned on the bed, my belly in my throat with an excitement I'd never considered. "But what about the house? Don't you have to get back?"

"Nay. The trust pays for upkeep. Already hired grounds and housekeeper. And Cal is spending a bit more time, as well. She might like to bring her lad up. Shag in all corners for a few weeks."

I turned from the screen to Bran's face. I knew that I had the rating and reputation to get the job, sight unseen. If I applied, there was almost zero chance they wouldn't pick me. Still, the thought that this man – a man who once called me a professional squatter – now wanted to travel the world with me *squatting* in other people's houses?

"Are you real?" I said.

He reached for me under the covers, his fingers playing at my inner thigh. "Oh, I'll show ye how real I am."

I giggled and swatted at him, but didn't fight.

Maybe if we're really quiet, I thought.

"Hey, you love birds up yet? Got a pot of coffee on if you're interested."

We parted instantly, watching the door as though someone was about to bust in with a video camera.

Kenny was calling from the basement steps. The distance of his voice was strange now. Before, he'd give a quick knock at my door and call from the hall. Now, it was like hearing Gondor calling for aid.

"Sounds good," I called back, cringing as Branson chuckled beside me.

I quickly clicked the *Message Now* link and typed up my usual introduction.

Very reliable and experienced house-sitters, here. Traveling as a couple and available to take care of your place while you're off gallivanting. You can find references and ratings on my profile, but please feel free to ask me anything. I'd be happy to answer any questions you might have. Hope to hear from you soon.

I pressed send and rolled out of the bed, grabbing my ratty old bathrobe from the pile of relocated stuff. Branson groaned and stretched, the early morning sunlight peeking in from the basement window. It cast a column of light down the length of him as he tried to discreetly reposition himself under his boxers.

I looked up to his face to find he'd seen me watching. He gave me a smarmy eyebrow raise.

I rolled my eyes, trying to hide the blush. "I imagine that's the look given by one of those weird dudes in trench coats who goes around flashing people their junk."

"Well, I have been practicing."

I laughed, turning for the basement stairs. "Do you want some tea?"

He naturally did, and I headed upstairs to start the hot water. I stopped in the basement doorway, regretting the decision to ever leave the basement again.

Diane was sitting at the kitchen table, alone, already fully dressed for the day.

"Morning," I said, fighting to make it sound as cheery as possible.

She made no similar attempt, sounding like a prison guard as she said, "Good morning."

I went to pour myself a cup of coffee and discovered a massive Keurig machine where the old coffee pot once was. Its presence surprised me. Kenny was a staunch environmentalist and prided himself on making every house he built or remodeled as eco-friendly as possible.

Christ, there was a composting pile five feet deep in the backyard when I left, yet there was now a spinning display of K-cups where his decades-old coffee pot had been.

I shrugged, pouring myself a cup from the still steaming carafe.

"Did you two sleep well?"

I froze for an instant, the half & half nearly splashing across the counter as I did. "We did, yeah. Really nice bed down there."

"Yes, that was the point."

I turned around to face Diane, leaning against the counter as though I actually wanted to engage her in conversation. "How's the quilting coming? Dad says you are sewing a lot these days?"

She chuckled to herself, turning a page of the paper as though I hadn't spoken. "How long are you planning to stay this time?"

I took a slow breath. "I'm not sure. I was looking at a few other sitting jobs before I had to come home."

She pursed her lips and made a quick humming sound. "You know, this really does have to stop."

"What does?"

315

I felt my heart shoot into my throat. I knew this tone. I'd recognized it in just her greeting – she was going to pick me apart. Still, even with the warning, nothing could stop my stomach from tying itself in knots. I saw movement out of the corner of my eye. Branson was at the basement door.

Great. Now I get to be humiliated in front of the most handsome man alive. God, I love coming home.

"I don't know how we can be clearer. You're a grown woman."

"I know that."

"Yes, well you need to start acting like it. Kenny doesn't need to be dropping everything at a moment's notice to pick you up from the airport because you're in between couch-surfing trips."

"I'm not couch-surfing. I get paid to do what I do."

"But not enough to have your own place to go to. Kenny says you were deported this time?"

I rolled my eyes, my grip tightening on the mug in my hand. "I wasn't deported. I'm literally only here because I had nowhere else to go. I'll be gone in a matter of weeks. Days if I can help it."

"Yet, it never dawned on you that it might be inappropriate to bring a man home with you, this time."

I shot Branson a look, deliberately avoiding eye contact. "I didn't know I would have company. Did Dad say something? Was he upset?"

Diane slammed the paper down on the table. "And you need to just stop with that."

I watched her, my brow furrowed. "With what?"

"Calling Kenny *Dad*. For God's sake, Corinne. He's suffered enough for marrying your mother, but why he feels he has to keep paying for that mistake, I will never understand."

My throat grew tight. I hated Diane's criticism, but this was new. This was not something I expected to hear. Had Kenny said something to her? Was he tired of having me around?

"I can't stop calling him *Dad*," I said. "He's my Dad."

Tears were welling up in my eyes, and I turned away from her, pretending to refill my coffee mug.

"No, Corinne. He isn't, and he never was. I understand him taking you in when your mother took off, but once you were eighteen, you should've done the adult thing and moved on. Now, you're bringing guys home, getting deported from other countries. You have no business still expecting him to drop everything to be a father to you. You need to gather your things from downstairs and find somewhere else to go. Both of you."

"I've been her father since she was two years old, Diane."

I dropped my mug, and it shattered, pieces of it skittering across the kitchen floor and coming to a stop at Kenny's feet. He stood there in his work boots, a tired green flannel with holes at the sleeves that I'd bought him for Christmas seven years earlier.

He stood in the kitchen doorway, his keys dangling from his fingertips.

"She's lived here longer than you have. This is her house. She doesn't have to go anywhere. Neither of them do."

The air instantly left the room.

"Of course, while they figure out their next move." Diane's tone was excruciatingly saccharine. "What are you doing home, honey?"

He glared at her. "Forgot my phone. They don't need to go anywhere," he said, glaring at me as he said it, as though he might burn the words into my forehead, permanently. "May I have a word with you, please, Diane?"

"Of course," she said, glancing at me to let me know I should leave the room.

I bent down to snatch up the bits of coffee mug, but before I could reach the sink, Kenny stepped between me and the kitchen door.

"Outside, please."

There was a silence in the house that gave me the shivers, but Diane made a couple more attempts to speak sweetly – to me, Kenny, or even Branson as she passed, then she went out onto the porch with Kenny.

Branson hurried across the room, coming to stand beside me as I burst into tears. Branson took my face in his hands and kissed my forehead.

Before Branson could say a word, Diane's shrill voice cut through the silent house. "What?! You can't be serious!"

My eyes went wide and I looked up into Branson's face. I frowned, trying not to weep there in front of him – like a chided teenager.

He smiled at me. "Hey, ye're alright. Your Dad's clearly handling it."

I shook my head. "I feel awful. I hate thinking I'm causing fights just by being here. And you having to see it?"

"Love, you didn't cause that fight. She brought that on her fucking self. And I'm glad I was here. Shh."

Diane's high-pitched voice continued to flit through the walls, but I did my best not to listen.

Bran wrapped his arms around me, giving me a tight squeeze.

I wiped my eyes.

"I can see why ye weren't so keen on comin home."

I exhaled, a half-laugh that wanted desperately to be a sob. Bran just squeezed tighter.

"Maybe we should sneak back downstairs, try to dodge this."

I made quick work of sweeping up the kitchen floor, then grabbed Bran's hand to lead him back to the guest room.

My timing was off because our path was quickly blocked by the blur of Diane marching into the house and down the hall toward my old bedroom.

A moment later, Kenny walked into the kitchen, calmly picking his phone up from the kitchen counter where he'd forgotten it. "Did you get to have some, at least?" He asked, gesturing to the coffee pot.

Before I could respond, Diane came charging back through, grabbing her purse and her keys before heading out the front door with a slew of god knows what under her breath.

Then she was gone.

Kenny's eyebrow touched his hairline and he pursed his lips. "Well, you two have a nice afternoon. You should have the house to yourself for the day. Pick something good for supper tonight, my treat. Not every day you get to take a *Laird* to dinner, is it?"

"Da -" I caught myself, nearly choking on not being able to say the word. "Kenny. I'm so sorry -"

He turned on me, stepping in with his finger pointed. I braced for a scolding, just as I would have when I was thirteen years old. "It's Dad. Do you understand me?"

"Yes, sir," I said, meekly. I knew his tone wasn't angry at me, but his face was red now, and whether or not I was the cause, he was ready to set fire to something he was so mad.

"Has she always talked to you like that?"

I froze. I didn't want to answer this question. Kenny and Diane had been together for five years and lived together for three. I'd stopped working with him and started housesitting all over the world just two months after she moved in – to escape her talking to me exactly like that.

Kenny frowned. Apparently, my thoughts played on my face. He had his answer. He straightened.

"This is your house, cricket. You come and go whenever you need to," he said, then he turned to Branson. "Both of you - if she decides to keep you around."

Kenny gave Bran a wink, then turned for the kitchen door. "See ya for suppah! Pick something good," he said, heading outside. "Knew I should've taken the day off."

And with that, my father was gone, marching across the dirt driveway with his keys spinning around his index finger.

Bran stepped up behind me, letting me lean against his chest as I wiped my eyes. "Your Dad is a fucking legend. And that accent is pure brilliant."

The weight of the air evaporated.

I smiled, brushing away the tears that still lingered in the corners of my eyes. "Yeah? I can talk like that, too, if you like."

"Can ye now? Well, he did say we have the house to ourselves all day, hmmm?"

He wrapped his arms around me, making a point to squeeze and pinch me in the right places. I squirmed against him, doing my best to collect the box of cheap Salada tea from the cabinet with him attached to me like a barnacle, refusing to release his hold until I was running back down the basement steps with him to bed.

Twenty-Four

I T TOOK US THREE months.

The couple in Costa Rica confirmed within hours, and we were buying our plane tickets before Diane returned to pick up some of her things. She no longer lived there by the time Kenny brought us to the airport two weeks later.

I wish I could say I regret being the catalyst for that relationship's end, but I can't.

From a poolside, three-week stay in Costa Rica, we traveled to California to watch a family's beloved Golden Retriever for two weeks, and I finally got to see the Great Redwood Forest. Bran and *Doug the dog* were pretty pleased with that, as well.

After a quick stop back with Kenny for Christmas, we flew to Stockholm and weathered a Swedish winter in the center of the city for a month. Bran learned to swear in Swedish, and I learned the abomination of Kalles Kavier, a smoked, creamed roe that was a favorite of his new local friends. He'd eat it in the morning, then threaten to kiss me.

That didn't go well for him.

I received notification that my Extended Stay visa paperwork was accepted while we were rolling out of bed in Heidelberg, Germany one morning.

The stay in Heidelberg ended, and we were on a flight to Edinburgh within hours.

It was official.

I was going home.

"Ye awake, love?" Bran said, squeezing my thigh.

I blinked, taking in the views outside the car. I knew those fields and houses – Kinvale.

We were close.

I watched the familiar church go by, my stomach shooting into my throat as we rounded the corner onto the drive of Cavendish House.

The trees that once blocked the view of the manor were now leafless in the cold months, and the massive house loomed up ahead with a new life. There was a tower of scaffolding on the backside of the house, but otherwise, it looked brand new.

Bran pulled the car up to the steps and I exhaled.

God knows how long I'd been holding my breath.

I stared up at the steps as though looking through a portal in time. The steps were no longer cracked, the flower pots brand new and full of ornamental branches that wouldn't wilt in the cold. The door had a fresh coat of paint, and the massive knocker gleamed as though buffed fresh just that morning.

For all I knew, it was.

"Ye ready?"

Bran squeezed my thigh, but there was no urgency to his tone. He didn't seem surprised by my response to the house. I imagine he'd had that reaction once or twice in his life, too.

"I can't believe I live here," I said, softly.

Bran chuckled. "Ye have to go inside to live here, love."

The spell broke and I turned back to face him.

A burst of movement from the doorway startled me, and I turned to find a familiar figure bounding down the steps toward my door, a wide smile framed by his salt and pepper beard.

"What?!" I screamed.

Kenny pulled the passenger door open and dove in to give me a hug and a kiss. He practically pulled me out of the car, he was so excited – not to see me, but just in general.

"How're things?" Bran said from the driver's side.

"You weren't kidding! That was some of the shoddiest roof work I've ever seen."

"I never claimed otherwise," Bran said, laughing as he pulled our bags from the trunk – or boot, as he called it.

"Young lady, you should've never let this guy up on that roof. Wasn't a shingle up there that wasn't jerry-rigged."

I stumbled for words, still so shocked to find Kenny there. "Hey, I wasn't involved in the roof, thank you very much. I'll probably never do roof work again after this place. What are you doing here?"

Kenny smiled. "Well, Bran knew how much I wanted to get my hands on the place, and he needed a contractor, so - here I am."

"What about your crew? You didn't bring Larry or -"

"No, no. Hired a couple local guys for the bigger jobs. Everything else I'm doing with you two."

Bran groaned, carting our bags up the front steps and through the open doorway. "Don't remind me."

I stood there frozen a moment, unable to follow him, but Kenny was oblivious to my trepidation, throwing an arm around my shoulder and hauling me forward into the house.

The front hall was alive. The nearby kitchen was teaming with sound and movement, someone cooking tea for the evening. The banisters and wood sideboard were gleaming with a fresh polish, and somewhere in the distance, someone was playing what sounded like a cello.

"Well, hello there!" A voice said from the kitchen door. I turned to find Bruce's familiar face. Kenny took his leave, following Branson up the stairs to regale him with details about the roof and other upcoming projects.

I reached out a hand to shake Bruce's, but he ignored it, leaning in to give me a hug. He was dressed in work clothes, and his blue coveralls were dusty.

"Not a bad way to spend retirement, aye?" He said, giving a twirl so I could see the whole of his dusty outfit.

I smiled. "What is?"

He waggled his eyebrows at me. "I'm your new groundskeeper. Couldn't think of a better way to spend my time."

"Welcome home, dear."

I turned to find Bruce's wife, Mary, standing in the kitchen doorway, wiping her hands on her apron. I stepped in to greet my fellow New Englander. She smelled like Christmas Dinner.

"Tea will be ready in an hour or so. Why don't you go settle in for a bit? Callista is in the music room, as well."

Mary and Bruce – Housekeeper and Groundskeeper.

I stood there a moment, dumbfounded as Bruce gave me a quick squeeze before heading back out to work and Mary returned to the kitchen. I turned toward the stairs, as though I could see through walls, and smiled at Branson, wherever he was.

I made my way down the hall to the music room and leaned into the doorway, not wanting to disturb her playing. The sound of her cello hummed and vibrated throughout the room, like a chorus of monks chanting until the air itself was alive. She didn't notice me at first, and I watched her for a long moment, waiting.

Callista's bow moved across the strings in a long slow pass as she played the last note of the piece. I stood there for a long while before she looked up and smiled.

"Took ye long enough," she said, setting the massive instrument aside to rise and greet me. She padded across the hardwood in bare feet, a wool shawl draped across her shoulders as always and threw her arms open to me.

I accepted the hug with such joy, I almost teared up.

She squeezed me in a way only a six-foot-plus woman can, and we swayed. "Ye've been missed," she said, finally.

I squeezed her back just as my father's New England accent bellowed from somewhere on the roof, "Coldah than a witch's teat out heeyah!"

We both shook in each other's arms with laughter.

When Cal released me, she was smiling wide. "I'm rather fond of yer father. He's quite a character."

"How long has he been here?" I asked, suddenly realizing that Cal and my Dad had been roommates.

"Just a few days. It's been nice. Almost like having *you* around – if ye had a beard and ate like a bear."

"Who says I don't?"

Cal laughed, heading out into the hall. I followed.

"I'm not sure where he is at the moment, but I imagine there's a feline that would love to see ye."

My eyes went wide and I made a high-pitched sound. "My kitty man!" I said, then headed off down the hall.

"I'll have a look down here," Cal called, but I was already bounding up the stairs to the third floor. I scurried down the hall toward my old bedroom and peeked inside, making kissy noises to call the furry thing to me. The bed was made in a white knitted blanket, and there was a divot just below the pillows – Mr. Darcy had been here.

I turned back down the hall, and out of habit glanced at that familiar door.

The door to the room that once housed a mountain of mattresses was now open, letting cool light shine into the hallway from its windows. I took a step toward the door, the familiar sense of trepidation rearing its ugly head. Even though I'd come to believe she was a good spirit, the thought of seeing her again unnerved me. I stepped into the doorway and looked inside.

The space within was transformed - a quiet reading room where there'd once been an atrocity. There was no figure standing by the window, nor any foreboding sense of being unwanted. It was just a cozy, quiet space, as inviting as any other room in the house.

"Found him!" Cal called from downstairs.

I turned for the stairs and hurried down, waving to Mary as she ducked her head out to see what was going on. I went toward Cal's voice and stopped in the double doors of the ballroom.

Cal was sitting on one of the antique settees, Mr. Darcy curled into a ball beside her. He was happily napping the afternoon away.

"Mr. Darcy," I said, trying to keep my frantic affection to a calm whisper.

The cat, now twice as big as I remembered him, shifted in response to my voice, his ears perking forward as he turned toward me.

He mewed, closing his eyes in a contented blink as he jutted his chin out at me. I lunged down to the floor beside the couch and proceeded to give his chin a two-handed scratch. He burst into a couch rattling purr.

And for the third time that day, I almost cried.

"What're ye two doing in here?" Bran said, appearing in the doorway.

I shot him a quick smile but refused to relinquish attention from my cat.

My cat. My little Mr. Darcy. Who was sitting on a settee – in my home.

My hands froze for a moment as this notion sank into my bones.

I kissed the top of his head and sat down beside him, smiling up at Bran as he approached.

He crossed the room toward me with a broad smile. I tilted my head up to meet him, and he kissed me.

Yet, I didn't kiss him back.

Something on the wall behind him caught my eye, startling me in such a way that I could barely think, let alone kiss.

"What's wrong?" He said.

I stood up from the settee and walked across the ballroom toward the wall. The last two times I'd been there, the paintings on the walls were either covered with white sheets or hidden behind a mass of people.

Now, there was nothing to block my view of this image – of a dark-haired woman in a long navy-blue dress.

I came as close to the painting as my courage would allow and stared into a familiar face.

She stared back at me with a strange, serene smile – as though she knew far more than I ever would.

"Who – who is this painting of?"

I stood there alone, waiting for Bran to respond. Yet, it was Cal who answered my question.

"That's our Nan. Helene Lennox."

I muttered the name to myself – *Helene Lennox*.

"So, you have a name," I said to myself.

"What's that?" Cal asked.

I turned, finding her still petting Mr. Darcy, oblivious to the revelation I was having. "I've seen her."

Cal looked up at me, eyebrows raised. "Ye have? When?"

"Since I first moved in. She's the one who kept that door on the third floor locked."

I waited for Cal to give me a sarcastic look, the same look her brother always gave me. Instead, she glanced at her brother, eyes widened. "Third floor, aye? Sounds right. Ye didn't tell me that," she said. "Bran and I haven't seen her since we were wee."

I stood there for a long moment. "Wait, you know about the ghost?"

I glanced at Bran. It was only then that I realized he'd been inching away from us both, moving toward the far corner of the ballroom.

Cal answered, not realizing the weight my question carried for her brother. "Aye, I've seen her many times. With how haunted this place is, she's far from the worst. There's a headless man that haunts the cellar. Bran and I spotted him once. Once was enough for me. I still won't go down there. And there's the carriage that ye hear drive up to the door from time to time. That's not so bad."

My mouth fell open, but I didn't speak at first. Too many memories and revelations were flooding to the fore of my mind – the sound of horses and gravel at my window, the strange look on Bran's face when something shifted in the cellar. I clenched my fists, my fingernails digging into my palms. I glared at Bran. I love him with my whole heart, but I was still prepared to murder him. "Wait. You've seen her?"

"Has he seen her? Christ, he slept with the light on 'til he was fifteen because he was all terrified Nan would come to tuck him in at night."

"I'm going to kill you," I said.

Bran threw his hands up. "Oh, come on!"

"You told me I was crazy and you knew damn well I wasn't? I swear to god, you're never getting laid again."

His face cracked in a huge smile, but there was contrition there. "What do ye expect? Ghosts bloody terrify me. I didn't want her to be back, so I -"

"So, you called me crazy?"

"I didn't call ye crazy. I said ye were -"

"Daft."

He fought to stifle a laugh. "Alright, I'm sorry," he said, rushing across the ballroom to me. "Will ye forgive me? I can assure ye, lying about a ghost is far from the worst thing I've ever done."

I turned away from him, swatting at his hands when he tried to hold me. He wouldn't be deterred. "Come on, I love ye. Don't be cross."

I stared up at the eerily familiar face, dressed in a gown from a time long before her own - a portrait like the one of the two Douglas children in their Regency costumes. A portrait that was commissioned before she passed.

I'd seen this woman hovering around that god-awful room for weeks, Bran denying her existence at every turn, yet here she was – proof. Proof that not only did she exist, but Bran knew and loved her.

Very well.

And she knew and loved him, too.

"Oh my god," I said, suddenly.

"What?" Bran and Cal asked in unison.

I felt my eyes welling up as everything began to make sense.

"That's why she wouldn't let us in that room."

Bran wrapped his arms around me. I stopped fighting him. I was too moved to refuse his affection.

"What are ye on about?" Bran asked.

"If we'd been able to get in, we would've cleaned out the mattresses."

He chuckled, softly. "Well, of course, we would have."

I stared up into his grandmother's face and felt endless affection for her.

"What would've happened to you if those mattresses weren't there? The night you fell?"

Bran's hold on me loosened, and neither sibling responded to my question.

I turned to face him. "She knew. She knew you were going to fall. If we'd cleared that room out, you'd have broken bones -"

"At the very least," Cal said, rising from the settee to come stand beside us.

"But you walked away from that unharmed."

"What tosh," Bran muttered, but he was staring at his grandmother's portrait intensely.

"It's not tosh. Tell me, has the door jammed since? Since you fell?"

Cal and Bran glanced at each other, then back to the portrait.

Cal shook her head. "Not once."

"I didn't think so," I said. Then I stood there with the two Douglas children, taking a couple steps back as they both simply stood there, taking in their grandmother's portrait.

"Tea's ready."

The three of us jumped. Mary stood in the doorway, watching with a bemused look, then she walked away without a word.

I followed her out. Branson and Callista didn't join me in the dining room for another five minutes.

Dinner was a loud and laughter-filled affair, Kenny and Bruce taking turns regaling everyone with tales from their many exploits in contracting, grounds-keeping, and professing. Mary and Bruce joined us for dinner, something I learned was the standard practice in the new Cavendish House. We feasted on something I was quite familiar with – American Chop Suey with garlic bread and grated cheese. A true Masshole meal if ever there was one. It was phenomenal, and though Bran was rather quiet, he happily helped himself to seconds.

After dinner, Bruce retired to the billiard room with Kenny and Mary, the two of them finished with work for the day. I made to join them, but when I found every member of the household present except the Douglas siblings, I excused myself to find them.

I discovered Callista standing in the ancient hall, staring up at her family tree.

"I'm trying to convince Branny that our next dinner party should be a medieval feast. Mary says she makes a brilliant Lamb Pie."

I smiled, moving to stand beside her and follow her gaze. I scanned the familiar names down the line, smiling when I spotted Helene Lennox. Yet, something had changed about the chart.

Where it once read Callum, scribbled over by ancient sharpie marker on the glass, it now said *Callista* in perfect calligraphy.

I gasped, then cringed, wishing I'd been able to catch myself.

Callista smiled. "Aye, I haven't a clue when he had it done."

We stood there in silence for a moment, and I began to wish there was a fire roaring in that massive fireplace. The thought set my romantic heart alight.

"I'll start pestering Bran for that medieval shindig myself. As far as I'm concerned, it's a moral imperative."

Callista's eyes lit up and she nodded her agreement.

I glanced over to the darkened windows and imagined all the generations of people who'd sat on the bench there, staring out at the world. I still couldn't quite grasp that I would be one of them.

That my child would be one of them.

I touched my hand to my stomach but then thought better of it. Branson and I hadn't told anyone the surprising news – news we'd only just discovered on the same morning my visa paperwork came through. Despite Branson and I being new, I didn't feel a hint of trepidation at the news. And from the sting of tears I saw in his eyes, it was clear Bran didn't either. We were sure.

We were both completely and utterly sure.

Discovering Kenny there that day made the news almost impossible to keep to myself. I wanted to see his face light up when he heard. There was very little in the world I'd ever looked forward to more.

"Did you happen to see where Branson ran off to?" I asked, finally.

Callista lifted a hand, pointing a finger upward, and I took my leave to hunt down the father of my child.

I glanced down the hallway of the second floor but saw no light peeking from any doorways. I glanced upward to the third-story landing, and a shape made my heart shoot into my throat.

After a moment, I recognized the familiar silhouette of Bran's back and made my way up the stairs toward him.

He didn't turn around to look at me when I reached the top of the stairs. He just stood there staring into his grandmother's former sewing room, his shoulder braced against the doorjamb.

"You alright, sweetheart?" I said, announcing my presence so as to not startle him.

He shot me a glance over his shoulder and held his hand out to me. I took it, coming to stand behind him in the doorway, my arms around his waist.

He pulled my hand up to his lips and kissed it. "I am, actually. I'm right as rain."

I looked into the small room, no sign of the grime and despair that once festered there for years. I remembered the last time I stood in this room – Branson lay on the floor, head hung back in drunken discomfort as his sister and I helped him to his feet. I remembered the words he'd said to me on the roof, and just the thought made my heart swell all over again. Then, I remembered the woman who'd led me to him on the roof – the woman I'd seen in this room more than once, who I was certain kept Branson from harm in a way only she could.

I squeezed Bran's hand tight in mine. "I have a thought."

He turned to me, kissing my temple as I leaned into him. "What's that?"

I paused, searching for the right words. "You could tell her first."

I didn't turn to meet his gaze, almost afraid to find a sarcastic or impatient look on his face.

Yet, he turned back to the dark room, stepped forward, and took a deep breath.

"I'm gonna be a dad, Nan."

His voice cracked on her name, and my chest tightened.

We both stood there for a long moment, the sound of laughter and billiard balls being racked drifting up from the foyer below. It sounded soothing in the grand space - like life was as it should be.

Still, the quiet of his grandmother's sewing room felt heavy.

And nothing happened.

When Branson finally turned around, he shrugged at me, his eyes glistening with tears.

I held my hand out to him. "Come on, then. There's socializing going on downstairs you should take part in."

Exactly as he'd always wanted.

He smiled and took my hand, closing the door to that infamous room, as though out of courtesy for the unseen presence within.

A soft thud from inside the room stopped us both in the doorway. I turned back to look into the quiet space.

The room looked unchanged, with high-backed chairs and a table by the window, the tiny woodstove still tucked in the corner. Yet, there was a dark square shape now lying in the middle of the braided rug.

I froze at the sight of it.

Branson stepped in, crouched down in the middle of the room, and picked up my missing passport from the floor.

"Ye've got to be kidding me," he said, turning it over in his hand.

He turned, looking up at me with a confused expression.

I didn't say a word.

From day one, some unseen thing in Cavendish was trying to stop me from leaving.

Perhaps, Branson's accident wasn't the only thing Helene Lennox anticipated.

Bran rose to his full height and crossed the room to me, holding the passport out for me to take.

Bran wiped his eyes, but he was smiling.

"Maybe we could tell everyone now?" I asked. The sound of the laughter drifting through the house made me long to add to that mirth. I stared up at Bran's handsome face, feeling the cardboard shape in my hand, and waited.

He glanced down at me, then back to his grandmother's favorite room.

Then he nodded, and we made our way downstairs, my hand running over a five-hundred-year-old banister as we went.

THE END

Afterword

Phew boy! What can I say about this one?

Well, if you've read any of my previous books (and especially the Afterwords), you'll know firsthand that *something* in this tome is based on the truth. One of my superpowers; turning heinous people, circumstances, and events into comedy or horror, depending on which of my books you're reading. In SHAKE OFF THE GHOSTS' case, the horror and comedy go hand in hand.

Firstly, I apologize to anyone who has loved or known someone who has hoarding tendencies. It's one of the hardest things to be a bystander of, and I found myself triggered repeatedly while writing this story. Let's just say, I'm not a huge fan of the show – you know the one. I end up crying or screaming incoherently at the screen in a rage. And I'm writing this from a dining room table in my cluttered house, where every bit of mess either becomes invisible to my neurodivergent brain or the fixation of my neurodivergent brain at any given moment. I'm grateful not to have inherited the hoarding/collecting tendency, but I inherited some of the baggage that goes with it. Like thinking my worth weighs entirely on how clean my house is whenever someone walks through the door. That's a hard one to break.

But I didn't start writing this bad boy thinking I was going to thrust myself through a few years of therapy in a matter of a few fictional months. I started this bad boy because I love a man in a kilt.

And once upon a time on a trip to my beloved Scotland, I had one of the most amazing experiences a kilt-loving single American woman could have. I narrowly escaped a housesitting job for a couple who wanted to force me to stay on as their live-in maid after they returned. (That was terrifying. I swear, if the husband turned out to be a serial killer, I wouldn't be surprised.) In my desperate escape, I booked into a ski lodge, only to discover an entire 'stag do's' worth of men in kilts staying the night, as well. After finishing WRITING MR RIGHT, I totally thought this night was proof that I control the universe with my mind.

They were rugged, drunk, ornery, some of them hilarious, and one was a dreamboat. By the end of the night, I was hammered, nearly peed my pants, and the soon-to-be groom tried (unsuccessfully) to kiss me. I was riding high on that night for weeks, thereafter. And when that dreamboat hunted me down on Facebook days later, I thought I'd witnessed the beginning of my own romance novel.

But as is so often the case with the tales from these Afterwords of mine, alas I was fucking mistaken.

Dreamboat was a flaming hot disappointment, dear readers.

Let's just say, I was a bit of a douchebag magnet for a good portion of my romantic life! (We could circle back to that hoarding era if we wanted to go deep into why that is, but let's not get carried away! Gotta let my therapist earn her keep.)

What can you do?

I was discussing this with my partner this past week. I've written some of my best romance stories in the aftermath of terrible breakups. Something about resetting my soul after encountering one of those aforementioned douchebags. If I can get lost in a world where men like Bran swoop in to infuriate and invigorate, then I could recover from those who disappoint and destroy. I think many of us have used Romance as a means to escape from douchebags - since the time of Austen, herself.

It was also my declaration to the universe that I'd happily take a fixer-upper mansion to call home, one of these days. Now that I have the handsome man on my arm, it's the next logical step, right?

I hear you can get a French chateau for a song, these days.

Ah shit. Now I want to write *that* book, too.

About the Author

MIRANDA NEWFIELD is the sarcastic, sailor-talking author of Romantic Comedies CATCH MY FALL, SHAKE OFF THE GHOSTS, and WRITING MR RIGHT. Given her love of open-door steamy scenes, as well as repeated threats of moving to Scotland, many of her stories end up peppered with accented f-bombs and laugh out loud inappropriateness. When she isn't writing, she's probably posting on social media about the fact that she should be writing.

Miranda lives in Chelmsford, Massachusetts with her husband, two kiddos, and three jerk cats that are probably ransacking the house, right now.

Also By

For more from *Miranda Newfield,* click here.

CATCH MY FALL

SHAKE OFF THE GHOSTS

A SONG FOR THE SEA

WRITING MR RIGHT

Writing As

For Gothic Romance by *Michaela Wright*

WILLING

HYSTERIA

HEARTLESS

THE LAIRD'S AGREEMENT

And for those who enjoy Bear Shifters and Paranormal Romance, you can find *Michaela Carr* titles, here.

SAVING HER BEAR

BEARLY BURNING

THE UNCHOSEN BRIDE

TRUE NORTH

THE WAY HOME

Keep In Touch

For news on future releases, sales, bonus scenes, and giveaways, sign up for Miranda's newsletter at: https://bit.ly/MWrites
Follow her on Goodreads and FB: @MirandaNewfield or contact Miranda at MirandaNewfield@gmail.com. She always loves to hear from you.

And if you're interested in joining the Miranda Newfield ARC team and receiving free ebook copies of her titles in exchange for an honest review, you can sign up at: https://bit.ly/MWrites-ARCS

Made in United States
North Haven, CT
25 September 2023

41971022R00211